SLAYBOY

SLAYBOY

Copyright © 2024 Cosimo Zitani

DEDICATION

Dedicated to Charles Northcote, for had he not read the first few chapters and inspired me to finish it, this book would not exist.

ABOUT THE AUTHOR

Follow SLAYBOY @SLAYBOY_SLAY on Instagram for more information about the author.

CONTENTS

CHAPTER 1
VIRGINIA AND THE JELLYBEANS

Toronto
Saturday, September 15, 1979, 11:07 a.m.

Mamma enters the living room and positions herself between my line of vision and the television screen. "Virginia's standing on the street corner," she says.

I stare at her blankly.

"Go get her," she adds.

"Why?" I ask, confused.

My sister, Virginia, is six years older than me. She is twenty and perfectly capable of making her way home by herself.

Mamma takes a deep breath, looks to one side, and then back at me. "Something's…wrong. Maria Montana just called me. She saw Virginia on the street. She's not…acting…normal," she says.

I'm not really sure what that means or what I can possibly do. "People will see her…" she adds, "They'll talk."

Mamma stands before me, unwavering. Clearly, she isn't going anywhere until I comply with her demands.

Her voice shoots up an octave and triples in speed and intensity, "You have to get her now!" She demands.

Mamma would usually bribe me to do things with chocolate. She knew I would do anything if candy was the reward at the end of the line. Today, there isn't any kind of incentive dangling in front of me – just a desperate plea and a worried look in her eyes.

Reluctantly, I get up and head out the front door.

As I walk up the street, I have no idea what I am about to encounter.

The Shiny Red Raincoat
Toronto
October 1972

I am in first grade. One morning it is raining so heavily that Mamma forces me to wear Virginia's hand-me-down shiny red raincoat. It is double-breasted, has a pointy collar, and the sleeves are too short for my arms. I am mortified.

Virginia walks me to school, holding a clear umbrella over us to shield us from the wind and rain. I feel protected with her beside me. I am not sure if it is because of the umbrella or the fact that I know she will deflect any unwanted insults anyone hurls at me along the way.

When the school is in sight, my heart starts to race. There is a separate entrance for younger grades, and it is here that I part ways with my sister. I will have to fend for myself. I am dreading the ridicule I will be subjected to as a result of wearing this preposterous garment.

I see a group of boys in my class. They are all wearing identical yellow raincoats and look like an army of rubber ducks splashing in a shiny, wet gaggle. One of them spots me and signals to others. In an instant, they're a glistening mob rushing toward me, puddles of water exploding under their feet. I am on the other side of the chain link fence, but I can already see the malicious glee in their eyes. I brace myself for public humiliation. Virginia looks at me, standing awkwardly in fear.

"Just tell them you're the Head Fireman," she says, and then she is gone.

When I enter the arena, the yellow jackets immediately circle me like vicious sharks in for the kill. I am surrounded. My eyes dart around in panic. I don't know what to do. I am petrified.

"I'm the Head Fireman," I blurt out.

Silence.

The swarm is confused. It does not know how to respond. My eyes light up. They've taken the bait. I state my claim a second time, this time more forcefully. Clearly, my red raincoat has given me authoritarian status. I am different not because I'm a poor kid wearing my sister's ill-fitting, hand-me-down raincoat. I am different because I am a leader.

With my newfound bravado, I wield an imaginary hose and run to the school to save it from burning to the ground. Raindrops strike my face as I scream orders to my subordinates; I cannot believe, for the life of me, that Virginia's idea worked. I would never have been able to come up with anything like this by myself, and I know it.

Toronto
September 15, 1979 11:16 a.m.

As I approach Virginia on the street corner, I become acutely aware of how unprepared I am to handle the task at hand. I see a woman standing in a doorway. She's a ghoulish vision in a black leather dress, thigh-high black boots, and waving a broken umbrella. Her mane of jet-black hair is enormous, and her face is concealed by large, circular black and yellow sunglasses. She looks like she's possessed by a crazed wasp trapped behind a pane of glass. She's frantic. She's buzzing. She opens and closes the defective umbrella. I'm not sure what to do. I am positive even a Head Fireman would have had difficulty handling this situation.

I try to talk to this stranger, but it's like I'm not even there. Virginia is having an intense conversation with someone who is invisible. A stream of incoherent gibberish spews out of her mouth and she continues to maneuver the umbrella like a weapon. I am careful to keep my distance. I try to persuade her to listen to me, but it is like she is in another dimension and can't hear anything I am saying. 'Bringing my sister back home from the corner' was not going to be as easy as it sounded. I resent my mother for sending me on this retrieval mission solo. It is clearly a two-person job…maybe even three.

It is a busy Saturday morning. The streets are full of people. Everyone is staring at the frantic, buzzing woman. Then they glance at me. This would be something that I grew accustomed to: strangers staring at Virginia and then looking at me. At first, the expressions on their faces are difficult to decipher. I am not sure if it's curiosity, shock, horror, or sympathy. I would eventually build up the courage to confront their gaze. Today, I am only able to look at the ground. I feel guilty by association. This mentally unstable person is my sister.

Before my mind can fully comprehend the situation, in an instant, it is as if the pane of glass has shattered, and the crazed wasp is free, flying down the street with lightning speed.

I am helpless, following a few feet behind her, struggling to keep up. She opens and closes the umbrella as she speeds up the street, and this appears to propel her forward even faster, as if she has sprouted a pair of wings. I call out her name, but she ignores me.

Virginia comes to a dead stop in front of a supermarket. It's as if her antenna has detected something. I am not sure why this structure has caught her attention, but it most definitely has. The building is painted yellow and black and, in an odd way, matches the colors of her outfit. It is like she has arrived at the mothership. I wait to see what she does next. Then, as if pulled by a powerful magnetic force, Virginia makes a B-line through the automatic doors. I have no choice but to follow her.

The store is a beehive of activity. Virginia zigzags her way through the aisles. People stop. People stare. Yet without a care in the world, my sister breezes past them and heads to the bulk candy station, where she opens several bins and floats over them like a bee hovering over a bed of flowers. She reaches in with her bare hands, pulls out a chocolate-covered almond, and pops it into her mouth. Then, immediately inhales a strip of red licorice, a sourworm, and a jellybean all at once. She stares at the ceiling while she chews as if she were contemplating astrophysics. I stand there watching, mortified.

Great, I think to myself. She is refuelling.

Virginia grabs a clear plastic bag and fills the bag halfway up with jellybeans. Then, she's on the move again. She flitters up and down the aisles, swinging the bag of jellybeans like she owns the place. She tosses the candy into her mouth as she nimbly maneuvers herself past shocked shoppers and their shopping carts. Occasionally, something will catch her eye. She will stop to pick up and examine a jar of gherkins or a can of crushed tomatoes, eventually losing interest and discarding each item immediately.

I continue to follow her like a reluctant shadow. Virginia makes her way to the express check-out counter. The cashier is a woman in her early twenties with dirty blonde hair pulled back into a ponytail. You can tell by just looking at her that she doesn't tolerate any bullshit. This girl is surely not in the running to be 'employee of the month' anytime soon. We make our way to the front of the line. The cashier eyes Virginia skeptically and then turns to me. I recognize the look. The girl takes the bag of jellybeans and tosses it on a scale.

"Four thirty-four," she announces.

My sister's dress is equipped with hidden pockets, and she starts to pull out change from various places – dimes and nickels from one pocket, pennies from another, and a couple of quarters from somewhere else. She spreads the assortment of coins on the conveyor belt and starts to add up the change. Virginia is counting…and she is counting very slowly; it is as if she is a six-year-old learning addition for the first time. The process is excruciatingly painful. The cashier lets out an exasperated sigh. When Virginia is done, she has $2.83 laid out on the conveyor belt.

"Two dollars and eighty-three cents," my sister announces triumphantly.

"It's $4.34," the woman shoots back.

"That's all I have," Virginia replies.

The woman shifts her gaze to stare at me. I don't have a cent on me. The cashier lets out another frustrated breath and glances back at Virginia.

"It's four dollars and thirty-four cents!" She repeats louder and more forcefully.

Then – and this surprises me more than anything – Virginia calmly responds, "I want $2.83 cents worth then."

Now, my sister was well within her right to make this request, I think to myself, and part of me is hoping the cashier would just let us go…but no…they are clearly at a standoff.

The cashier abruptly walks away from her register, makes her way past the line of people behind us, and disappears down an aisle. She reappears a few minutes later with another plastic bag and begins the laborious process of transferring candy from one bag into another. Her first weigh-in comes in at three sixty-nine.

It was agonizing to watch my sister count her change, but in comparison, this scenario is absolute torture. I can feel the angry eyes of irritated shoppers searing into my back. I do not dare to look over my shoulder. The third weigh-in comes in at $2.78 cents. The cashier throws a couple of jellybeans back into the bag, and we are at $2.83.

Hallelujah!

I turn to see an enormous line of shoppers stretching deep into the cereal aisle. Everyone is staring at us, and I do not have to question the expression on their faces.

As Virginia walks away, the cashier and I make eye contact; I feel compelled to apologize to her. We're responsible for the endless bitter queue that lies in our wake. "Sorry," I say faintly.

Virginia is more than a few feet away from me, but she immediately whips around, charges toward me, and rips off her dark glasses. She unveils her twisted, tormented face for everyone to see. Blood red crimson lipstick is painted around her eyes. She opens her mouth; a piercing wail from the Gates of Hell emanates from the depths of her soul.

"SORRY? SORRY? DON'T YOU DARE BE SORRY FOR ME!" She screams.

There it is. The sting.

Sharp and painful.

The entire store falls silent.

The. Entire. Store.

I stand there frozen.

Petrified.

Virginia turns and strolls away. She is humming to herself, seemingly unaware of what has just happened, swinging her broken umbrella in one hand and the clear plastic bag of jellybeans in the other.

I walk out of the store in a daze. Virginia is nowhere to be found.

I make my way home without her. When I appear empty-handed, my mother sits on the couch with one hand awkwardly covering her mouth.

Virginia

My sister

Walks the earth alone

A fireball of energy

Her white flames

Like powerful wings

Consume her

And she is lost

Roaming in the burnt remains

My hands and face are blackened

As I stand beside and watch in horror.

Virginia

In many ways, the sister I had known died that day in the checkout line of that grocery store. I would not know it then, standing like a stone statue, tears rolling down my face, but I would eventually come to embrace what she had prophetically screamed: I would learn not to be sorry for her.

From that day forward, Virginia will struggle with this fiery demon inside of her. She will disappear for years at a time. We will search the city streets for her. We will show her picture to strangers. Sometimes we find her, sometimes we don't.

When my father died, Mamma told me that now, I was the 'man of the family'. This position came with several undesirable tasks regarding my sister's situation.

One time, I had to bring Virginia to a mental health facility called 'The Clarke Institute of Psychiatry'. They made me sign some papers, and male nurses strapped her down to a stretcher. I was told this was for her own well-being, so she could not harm herself or others. Virginia was livid. She shouted, screamed, and struggled as the nurses overpowered her.

My heart sank as I watched her disappear down a corridor. I stood there and listened while her desperate screams faded away. Virginia was placed in a locked ward, treated for a few weeks, and then released.

The doctors explained that Virginia had rights. She could refuse treatment if she wanted to…and she did. This created a tedious mental health merry-go-round of recurring events. We were told she had schizophrenia. She was also bipolar. She was on her medication. She was off her medication. In the hospital, she was always medicated. Everyone in the ward appeared to be heavily sedated. One is to assume insanity is far more palatable if everyone is sleeping.

I was not sure whether Virginia's behaviour was the result of her mental disorder, the anti-psychotic drugs, side effects from these medications, or mind-altering substances off the street with which she was self-medicating. She was on the streets. She was off the streets. She was in a shelter.

We were told that she was putting out her cigarettes on her mattress. She was a fire hazard. She could not stay at the shelter. She was on the streets again. She disappeared again. The cycle repeated…again.

Virginia had always been a smoker, and I am not sure if this was the reason a thick, dark cloud appeared to have permanently positioned itself over her life. There is a black and white photograph of my family long before I was born. In the picture, my mother and father are sitting on a couch surrounded by their three daughters. The two older girls are holding dolls, but Virginia, just a baby at the time, is on my father's lap, clutching his pack of cigarettes.

When I got my first apartment, I came home one day to discover Virginia lounging on my couch with a lit cigarette, blowing smoke rings into the air. She had broken a back window and let herself in. She was wearing a second-hand fluffy pink jacket, holding a side plate and using it as a makeshift ashtray. The dish was brimming with butts. When I entered the kitchen, the gas burner was still on. It was like I had to be the Head Fireman again, only this time, there was a heavy burden to this role. It was the first time in my life that I told Virginia to leave. When she broke in a second time, I decided that I had to move to a higher floor.

As time progressed, so did Virginia's condition. She was clearly not living in our world. She was in another dimension. I had often wondered where this alternate reality was, but by that point in my life, I had become all too familiar with other planes of consciousness in my own mind-altering adventures. I was all too eager to escape reality - **traveling** on planes where a passport was not required.

Virginia developed savvy survival skills from living on the streets. Once, she told me that she'd been panhandling to make extra money; surprised and yet intrigued, I asked her how much money she could make in a day.

Virginia looked at me with an air of contempt.

"I don't work all day," she scoffed.

Yeah, she said that. But who could blame her? Who wants to work all day? I certainly don't.

As the years progressed, our continued attempts to help our troubled sister wore the family down. Exhaustion took its toll. We remained painfully aware of our powerlessness in this situation; we knew we could not save her. Ever so slowly, we all let go, everyone except for Mamma.

She only did when Alzheimer's finally wrestled the memory of Virginia away from her, but that's another story.

The Second Sting
Toronto
September 13, 1998, 2 p.m.

I am high. I haven't slept. I am on my way to visit Virginia in the hospital. She is at 'The Clarke Institute of Psychiatry'. I have been coming here for years…but as I approach the building, something is different. As I walk by the fresh new signage on the building, I try to ignore it, but I cannot. The letters are seared into my eyes. I try to un-see it, but it is impossible. The name of the institution has changed. It is not called 'The Clarke' anymore.

The new sign reads: 'The Centre for Addiction and Mental Health'.

"Addiction and Mental Health" – These two words together penetrate my core. I never thought there was a connection between these two concepts, yet here they are, side by side and plastered in block letters across the front of a building. It was like another sting.

Like that day when Virginia walked away from me long ago, swinging her clear plastic bag of jellybeans, I could only look at the ground. The sign was a sign – a marriage of two words that, together, would foreshadow what was to come. It would still be one more year until I left the country…when I boarded the kind of plane where a valid passport is required.

Shortly after I visited her, Virginia was released from the hospital, and, like always, she disappeared.

CHAPTER 2
A CLASSIC REDUCTION

Stalled along the road of life, I pause to rest my head

I cannot take another step

My battery is dead

An angel has been with me

She's been here all the way

An angel with jumper cables

Here to save the day

With just one touch, sparks have flown

I am awake; I am alone

The angel has flown home

And I am on my way

Toronto
September 18, 1999, 5:52 a.m.

I look down at the mirror. A white line severs my reflection in half. One quick snort is all it takes to make me feel whole again. I can finally see myself…but from this angle, I can't say I recognize who is staring back at me. It is not just my altered exterior, my bleached blond hair, gaunt face, or green contact lenses. Beyond that, it just doesn't look like me. *I'm Manny Lamondo…but who have I become?*

I look up. Bare walls. Empty apartment. Angie stands silhouetted against floor-to-ceiling windows. Gleaming glass structures shoot up behind her like giant mirrored monoliths. The configuration of the buildings conspires with the rising Sun and delivers an unforgiving beam of light directly into my face. It is 5:52 a.m. My flight is to leave at 8:45. I am cutting it close, but that's how I roll. I am confident we'd be able to zip up the highway at Mach 5 to get to the airport in time.

Angie. I didn't really know how she had come into my life. I mean, I knew how…our paths were destined to cross, given our nocturnal behavioral patterns and mutual love of pharmaceuticals. I am sure our connection appeared to be as shallow as the narrow white line stretched along the reflective surface between us, but on a parallel-universe meta-physical level, it was something far deeper. It sank beyond the powder through the glass, past the thin layer of silver, to a place where an arrow of destiny has the ability to sail across the expansiveness of space and pierce the heart of darkness.

There was no denying that the timing of our worlds colliding was impeccable.

Angie appeared from out of nowhere, just in the nick of time, to help push me into the next chapter of my life at the exact point when I was incapable of getting there myself. Once this task was accomplished, she was gone.

Angie was part of a vast cast of colorful characters, eccentric personalities, and actor-slash-model-slash-waiters who had featured cameos in my life. She was an extra. She didn't have a major role. No one did. Me included. I was barely there myself.

I guess the most remarkable thing about Angie was the fact that she was there. Period. If I were to personify her as a punctuation mark, she would not be an exclamation point (!). She didn't stand out; she was neither **bold** nor *italicized*. She was more of an asterisk (*), a footnote, or a hyphen (–), a literary device that connected two thoughts bound by a common thread. It is possible that she was a sentence that's an integral part of a story if only because it leads to the ending. On second thought, she was more than that. Much more. She deserved to be a chapter, a short but important chapter in a book or a novel.

Angie was intrigued by my carefree, free-fall, laissez-faire attitude. She confessed on numerous occasions that my outlook on life exhibited fearless courage, combined with strong-willed intention, cemented by unshakeable faith. The hard truth of my current emotional make-up consisted of something more like stone-cold desperation, combined with incomprehensible demoralization cemented by recreational drug use. I was already way past the point of no return. This was one last ditch at survival.

My life had been reduced, like a French sauce. It was as if I'd been simmering in a saucepan over relentless heat, and all of my worldly possessions had evaporated around me.

Everything I owned could be compressed into an internationally approved regulation-sized rectangle, a small carry-on with wheels. For someone as materialistic as me, this was torture. I did not want to be reduced. The process of being reduced was not pleasant, let me tell you…and as the steam was intensifying like the fog on a dance floor, this was exactly when Angie appeared: a dancing mirage…with party favors to boot.

It could have been possible that her physical manifestation was just plain luck, and I was in the right place at the right time. Angie was a good person - one of those human beings who actually liked helping people.

One night, a guy in a stalled Jeep flagged her down and asked her for a boost. Angie was all too eager to give him a hand.

Winnipeg Winter-pig weather had seasoned her into an expert mechanic, so when it turned out the guy didn't know what to do with the cables, Angie took charge. With a flick of her arm, she motioned him back into his car, hooked up the vehicles, and told him when to pump the gas. It was with this same bravado that she parachuted into my world, metaphorical cables in hand, and jump-started my battery. I was dead inside. The electric jolt was to prepare me for what was to come.

I did not know it then, but I was about to embark on an adventure that would alter the course of my life and transform my being at its very core, destined for a place where I would finally be able to see myself in the reflection of a mirror. One that hangs vertically on a wall and not horizontally on a table.

"Told ya we'd make it," Angie says as we skid up to the airport departure drop-off.

She gets out, gives me a big hug, and watches me as I grasp my life on wheels and race toward the automatic doors. I am about to wave goodbye one final time, but when I turn around, she is gone. I stand there for a moment and take a deep breath. The magnitude of what I am about to do washes over me like a wave of JPG. I turn and hurry through the doors. I am on my way.

After checking in but before going through US customs, I step into the men's washroom for one last bump. I would not know it then…but it would be the last speed bump at the end of a long, twisted yellow brick, mirror-ball road. When I come out of the men's room, the Sun is up - full up and far too bright. I slip on my shades and walk toward my future.

On the flight, I flirt with an airline attendant. He brings me a little fancy chocolate, an extra blanket, and a fluffy pillow. Later, he motions me to the back galley for a little in-flight entertainment. We duck into the restroom, and I officially join the mile-high club.

Upon my initiation, I noticed his name tag; Gustavo.

CHAPTER 3
LITTLE JUMPING FISH

South Beach
September 18, 1999

My cab pulls up to a two-story lime green apartment complex on Lennox Avenue. I notice a sign in front of the building that says, "Lopotomy Apartments". As I make my way to the front entrance, I can't, for the life of me, stop thinking that the 'p' is really meant to be a 'b,' and while I think I've arrived at my tropical destination, I am really checking in for a mind-altering surgical procedure. On some level, this could not have been a more accurate assessment of what was to transpire. I roll my life on wheels down a green-carpeted hallway. It's the last door on the left at the end of the hall. I take a deep breath and knock.

South Beach
September 27, 1999

My days are spent going to the beach. I am sure it is helping me to focus. I need a break from my life…a vacation from myself. I am sprawled out on my towel like a dead white whale slathered in sunscreen.

My world is small and simple in this sun-drenched paradise. It consists of an eight-block-square radius bordered by Ocean Drive on the south, Alton Rd on the north, Lincoln Rd. on one side, and 12th Street on the other.

Everything is slower here. The air is liquid and thick. There's color everywhere. Beauty is undoubtedly the target. Ocean Drive is propped up like the facade of a pastel movie set. It is pale pink, lush green, and aqua blue. Tourists flock to the Versace Mansion to snap photos of themselves on the infamous steps. Lincoln Road stretches out like a lazy alligator shaded by swaying palms, and 12th Street Beach is the home of muscled gods bronzed to perfection.

Latin music seeps out of open windows. You can smell the café con leche in the air. The streets are packed with art and culture and young slim models clutching black portfolios. There are countless art galleries, and like the effortless stroke of an artist's brush, The South Florida Art Center's window swirls around a corner.

One can watch Russian doll-sized ballerinas pirouette at The Miami Ballet School. Alton Rd is as far north as I will go and is the closest thing to a normal street in any other place.

The most amazing feature of this modern paradise is not the weather, the ocean, the nightlife, or the state-of-the-art design; it is most assuredly the wildlife bursting at the seams. It's everywhere.

One morning, an enormous white crane lands a few feet away, stares at me, and then just flies away. On another day, I am mesmerized by a flock of parrots chirping in a tree. There are the iguanas, too, not native to Florida, but these largish lizards have taken to the tropical environment and are flourishing.

Of all the nature, none is more spectacular than the enormous Tree of Life that sits in the HSBC parking lot at the top of Lincoln at Alton. The tree is dead, but every day, around five in the afternoon, it bursts with life. Starlings by the thousands flock to this spot. It's quite a sight to behold, a tremendous force of nature.

Swarms of black shifting patterns sculpt the sky, and the sound of the songbirds is almost deafening. I can just sit and watch this spectacle for as long as it lasts. It is as breathtaking as a magnificent storm; only these raindrops have wings.

South Beach is perpetually in flux. Everything is impermanent. People are forever coming and going. Planes land. Planes depart. Cruise ships float in. Cruise ships float out. Even though there are thousands of people circulating this art deco dreamland, there seems to be an unconscious, or maybe conscious, will of the city to abolish any trace of them.

Maids sweep into unkempt hotel rooms. Pillows fluffed. Porcelain polished. Floors waxed. Beds made. Everything is tucked tight and crisp, restored to a state of stylish elegance. The aesthetic is white on white on white. Teams of busboys descend on ravaged patio tables. Surfaces wiped clean, reset to perfection. The tone of the beach appears to be set by the ocean waves, forever rolling in and out, relentlessly erasing any evidence of human existence created in the sand. It's as if the Hand of God wields a giant squeegee, and he's pissed off at the mess we're making. I am sure the maids and busboys would agree.

I notice that very late at night or very early in the morning, depending on how you want to look at it, the crack between night and day, the city is restored to a state of grace. My favorite place is to sit at the edge of the ocean, where the earth, water, and air coincide. I am not sure if it is because I like being where all of these elements converge or if I am secretly hoping to have an encounter with God's squeegee.

I am not sure if my rendezvous with such a divine implement will have the desired cleansing effect on me. It's more likely that I will just be flattened to death by its rubber edge.

Nevertheless, I love 'The Beach'. I am astonished that human beings actually make eye contact here. People even say, 'Good Morning'!

I don't know how to respond. I'm from a big city where, at morning rush hour, it is perfectly acceptable to march around like an automated robot, coffee in hand, ignoring the rest of the fleet.

Who am I kidding? I was never up in the mornings, and if I was, it was because I was making my way back home from the night before. I was obviously the defective bot that was moving a little speedier than everybody else. Maybe they were just ignoring me?

At any rate, even though I've only been here for a few days, South Beach feels like home, and I don't really know why.

I am an avid Sun worshipper, and the beach is not too far from the Lopotomy Apartments. I walk through Flamingo Park, past the basketball courts, cross Meridian Ave, and make my way down 12th until I hit Ocean Drive. I tip-toe across the hot sand to 12th Street Beach. It's the place to be.

I wade past steroid-infused, bubbled bodies until I find a spot where my ego is not too self-conscious to expose itself. I flick my towel, and it floats down to the sand. I stretch out under the Sun. The heat is unbearable after only a few minutes. I venture into the ocean to cool off.

For some reason, there are not many people in the water today. I am waist-deep when something catches my eye. I am not quite sure if I am seeing correctly, and so I am still. It happens again. There, right before my eyes, little fish jumping up out of the water. They are like wet, wingless birds, shiny and silver, bursting up through the surface and fluttering through the air. I scan the surface of the water. There they are again! Fish streaming through the air! Are they flying fish? I'm not sure. They are like little glittering dashes of light. They spring up and appear for mere seconds, shimmering in the Sun before disappearing again. I think this is one of the most beautiful things I have ever seen. Fish soaring through the air, the Sun catches tiny droplets of water splashing off of them as they fly. The fish draw me deeper into the ocean. The water is up to my chest, and the silver jumping fish are so close. I hear little soft splashes as they burst in and out of the blue. I drink in the ocean and the sky and the beauty of it all.

I want to reach out and catch a little jumping fish, if only for a moment. A part of me believes if I am able to do so, I will be able to hold on to this moment forever. I will be able to bathe in the glittering light of wonderment for eternity. It is like there is nothing else in the world except for the vast ocean, the magnificent sky, and the magical school of flying fish.

The piercing shrill of a whistle breaks the magic spell. I turn my head. A lifeguard is waving her arms back and forth, motioning me back in. I look towards the ocean and scan the surface for more flying fish, but there are none to be found. They are gone. The whistle-blower has wiped the sea clean of magic. I look back to the lifeguard. I am the only one in the water out this far, and so reluctantly, I make my way back to dry land.

While en route to my towel, someone approaches me and tells me the little fish are jumping because there are larger fish, most likely sharks, down below trying to eat them. The little jumping fish are jumping for their lives. It's not an aquatic show. I am told when I see jumping fish, I am to turn and move in the opposite direction. I stand sopping wet like a sunburned novice. I feel kind of stupid. I did not know why the fish were behaving so abnormally, but now, it makes perfect sense. I'm also somewhat disheartened, not only because I feel for the little fish jumping for their lives but also because from this moment on…I know too much. I'll never be able to bathe in the glittering light of wonderment anymore…let alone for eternity. I also know in my soul that when I am attracted to beauty, it is usually a danger in disguise. I sit for a while, steaming in the Sun, then decide to leave.

I wander down a side street, thinking about the little fish frantically catapulting themselves out of the water to escape the jaws of a predator. I know for a fact that only a desperate attempt for survival would make them instinctively lunge themselves out of their natural environment and into the unknown. It dawns on me that this is exactly why I am in Miami. I have thrust myself into the unknown. I am a little jumping fish, jumping for my life. I notice a great, white vintage automobile following me.

It's been circling the block, passing back and forth. The vessel coasts through the lush green streets as if it is gliding through swampy water, with its rear tail fins cutting through the humid air. The car stops just ahead of me. Its driver is a silver-haired, suave Argentinean with a swarthy accent. He has clear blue eyes, a shark-like nose, and perfect white teeth. He looks like he should be on a ski slope in the Alps somewhere and not in Miami Beach. He motions me over and asks me where I am going. "Nowhere," I say. He asks me what I am doing. "Nothing," I answer.

At the time, I had no idea how apropos my answers were. He motions me to get into the car, and I jump in without hesitation. His name is Santiago.

CHAPTER 4
THE OSTRICH
SITUATION

South Beach
September 28, 1999, 11 a.m.

I'm back at the beach again because I don't know what else to do. I am in the exact same spot as yesterday, but it's like I'm somewhere else entirely. Everything has changed. The water is not as clean or as clear as it was the day before, and the sky is not as blue. It's overcast and gray. Seaweed has washed up on shore and created a messy barrier of green sludge between the sand and the water. The beach is barren, scattered with the occasional tourists, the homeless, and the unemployed. I am not sure which group I belong to, but I snap open my towel and take my rightful place among them.

I look out at the dreary landscape and contemplate my dreary circumstances. My life has collapsed like a house of maxed-out credit cards. I take a deep breath, and even though it's cloudy, I slather Australian gold coconut oil on my already bronzed Italian skin. I've lost everything that defined me.

I am legit lost...for real this time - not like all the other instances when my self-centered angst told me I was when, really, I wasn't. I can feel the dark undercurrent of uncertainty pulling me out to sea, deeper into unsettling, uncharted territory. It is like I am screaming for help on the inside, teetering on the brink of despair, but no one can hear me. I slip my thumb into the waistband of my bathing suit and yank it down an inch. On the bright side, I am developing a killer tan.

Toronto
1987

My film professor stops the flatbed.

He just screened my final film, but instead of giving me a mark, he looks me square in the eye and says, "You're going to make a lot of money."

This was to be true; however, what he didn't tell me was that I was also going to spend a lot of money – far more than I would make. I wish he had given me that little piece of advice, but no, I had to discover that on my own.

Toronto
1990

Almost immediately after film school, my career blasted off like a rocket. I become a commercial film director. The trajectory is quick and meteoric. The ad biz is youth-oriented, and apparently, I fit the demographic. I am a direct link to a coveted target market. I am treated like a rock star. I am signed and put under contract. I am retained.

Retained. This was an unfamiliar concept to me. When I discovered that it meant that I would receive a generous salary but don't have to work every day, it was the best moment of my life. I had hit the jackpot. This financial arrangement helped to foster a distorted attitude regarding the concept of money, and not for the better, let me tell you. It was like they were just giving me loads of cash every month…because I was me.

I quickly discovered that in the temperamental world of advertising, I possessed none of the diplomatic qualities a film director required. This made me…um, how can I put this… 'difficult' to say the least. I was also inexperienced on large film sets, and my naïveté was evident in my interaction with the clients and crew.

Once, when on location, a director of photography used a twelve-by-twelve reflector board to bounce light onto the talent, and I was overheard referring to it as 'The Big Shiny Thing'. Everyone on set was thoroughly amused. I was not sure if I was offended or flattered, but for the remainder of the project, the crew continued to call it that.

Toronto
1996

As the decade progressed, 'it' happened. I worked less and waited more. The combination of a disposable income plus free time created the perfect storm for the natural disaster that was me. I got the distinct feeling that I'd been shelved. This surface was pleasant; it was an expensive shelf like one would find in a high-end retail shop, but it was a shelf nonetheless, and I was placed there like a packaged good gathering dust.

What I did not know at the time but later discovered was that, like anything that sat on a shelf for any given length of time, I had an expiration date.

South Beach
September 28, 1999, 2 p.m.

'Beep' 'Beep' 'Beep'

An obnoxious queen a few towels away answers his cell phone.

As I listen to his pretentious babble, his glaring flaws are begging me to take out a two-barrelled shotgun and assassinate his character, putting him, me, and everyone else in our vicinity out of our collective misery.

I can't take the shot. The gun will backfire. I know it. He reminds me of *me*. The conversation, just a few feet away, is an indication of how far off the shelf I have fallen. I'm not even in the store anymore; I am on the street…in the professional gutter. My bar code's been deactivated. I haven't landed a project in years. No one will work with me. I can't even afford a cell phone anymore. I try to comprehend how this happened and how I got here.

Capturing Freedom
Toronto
March 5, 1996

I rip open the envelope. A script and storyboards fall onto the table. Flip phones have entered the market. They are smaller and more refined. They are mainstream. These new gadgets offer humanity mobility and, with this newfound motion, freedom. The concept features a man who has the ability to walk through walls and transcend time and space with the use of this hand-held device. Surrealism: I am intrigued. I read a few lines. I do a few lines. I soak up the words 'transcend time and space'. This is my kind of project. I like this time and space shit.

The clients are in Vancouver. They are looking for a director to 'bring' something to the concept. When I scan the brief, one of the bullet points under the marketing objectives reads, 'Capture freedom'. It is one of those oxymoronic phrases in the ad world that doesn't any make sense whatsoever… that you can capture something like that, stuff it into a box, and sell it like cornflakes.

The agency has also sent extensive information regarding customer research. I am not sure why they have included this material, but I scan through it. The findings reveal that it is important for consumers to have the ability to get rid of the phone when they want, so it is crystal clear that it isn't controlling them. One doesn't want to be too accessible, especially when a collection agency is trying to track you down. I can relate. I push the script, storyboards, and the brief off to one side.

This is what they want, but it is my job to take this idea and run with it, and I am good at that. I am good at running. I have been doing it my entire life. I am hit with a massive tsunami of ideas. I do not know where they are all coming from, but this concept of capturing freedom has clearly struck a prolific nerve.

My thoughts are like screaming babies, helpless infants begging me to reach out and harness them lest they be lost in a Sea of Oblivion. I do another line. I take out my sketchpad and start to sketch. I pull on a thread of inspiration. The strand unravels before me. I follow the twisted fibers through my mind's eye of a needle, then stitch a yarn until it fabricates a quilt of my own understanding.

Toronto
March 7, 1996

I climb down from my shelf for a two o'clock conference call with the agency. We exchange a few pleasantries, and then it is down to business. I launch head-first into my presentation. This project is mine. I can feel it.

I have walked through my share of walls in this lifetime, not to mention accidentally bursting through the occasional screen door now and then. I wouldn't exactly say "freedom" was the emotion I felt after having catapulted through the aforementioned, ever-elusive sheer barrier at an industry event one evening. One too many martinis may have made their contribution to this unfortunate mishap, but on further investigation, I was convinced the lighting rendered the screen invisible. At any rate, I was noticed at that party…and wasn't that the point? To be noticed.

I am almost done with my pitch. It is time to close the deal. Now, in my experience, taking too much liberty with someone's idea can have disastrous consequences, but if this was truly about capturing freedom, it was one I was willing to take.

"One more thing." I added casually, "He's not holding the phone in the last shot…on the beach…"

"Oh? What's he holding then?" The art director asks.

"A sea shell." I announce with conviction, "He has it up to his ear."

There's silence on the other end of the line. I may have gone too far.

I elaborated my point of view like a seasoned lawyer rationalizing a line of thinking in an attempt to sway a jury. There was a valid reason for totally obliterating the product in the last shot.

"We're trying to capture freedom," I state while looking down at a mirror on the table. "Everyone has a childhood memory of holding a shell up to their ear…listening to the ocean," I continue.

I use my finger to make a swirly symbol with the white powder, then bring my finger up to my tongue and lick off the residue. "We want to recapture that moment. We want to end with him feeling free. The phone's not a phone. It's a shell." I conclude.

Dead silence.

Nothing.

Silence seeps through the speaker and hangs in the air like a revolting stench. I look at the phone. I reach over and tap it gently to make sure it is still working. An eruption of euphoria bursts out of the speaker.

They love it!

The next day, my agent tells me they've booked me for the project. We are to begin pre-production immediately. It is on my business-class flight to Vancouver, after my third glass of wine and just as many motion-sickness tablets when it happens. As I gaze out of the window over an endless seascape of puffy clouds, I have a vision. It is hazy at first and a little out of focus, but then it fully crystallizes. Ostriches…big, beautiful, fluffy ostriches running in slow motion along the expansive stretch of sky. My heart starts to race. I sharpen my gaze.

The giant birds leap effortlessly, bounding over the cotton-like formations. In my mind's eye, I can see their feathers billowing as they stride majestically across the sand, successively in slow motion behind the man with the shell. I get goosebumps, they're ostrich-sized.

I was always told that clients wanted a director 'to bring' something to their project. Well, I am bringing ostriches. It is my job to capture freedom. This is the chef's kiss. It is another risky idea, but risks are what the ad business is all about.

Ostriches would come to symbolize a 'new wave' in commercial advertising. I would be the visionary director credited with ushering in the newly minted animal. Cows were so last year. I would win a Clio. Then, a Gold Lion. I would be launched onto the international scene, whisked away to bigger and brighter things. After all, my career in advertising was only a stepping stone to what I was really meant for, and that, of course, was feature films. I was destined to win an Oscar, all because of 'Ostriches Running on a Beach'.

I nest in my business class seat and have another glass of wine. I stretch out my legs as we soar to the coast.

Vancouver
March 10, 1996

As soon as we land, I need to speak with my agent.

I am excited to share my newfound inspiration, but there is no reception on my cell phone as I wait by the luggage carousel. I hold my arm up and wave the phone above my head in a futile attempt to connect with some invisible entity. I thought that this device was supposed to help humanity transcend time and space, but right now, it is only making me bat-shit crazy. After what feels like an eternity, even though it has only been a few minutes, she answers. I spew out the ostrich vision.

When I am done, there is no response. Dead silence on the other end. I wait for the concept to sink in and brace myself for another wave of euphoria, but when she finally says something, it isn't the reaction I am expecting. She is…reluctant.

Reluctant.

I remain calm, even though I am fuming on the inside. She obviously is not able to see how majestically the ostriches have been racing through my mind, relentlessly over and over, back and forth, so much so that they have left three-toed tread imprints etched on my somatosensory cortex. I am exasperated.

I hang up and decide to take matters into my own hands.

Once again, as a visionary director, I would have to forge ahead, leading the way for the visionless masses.

When I found out that the Production Manager had experience with big-budget American features, I knew she would understand. When I tell her I want ostriches, she doesn't flinch. "How many?" She asks, pen poised on a production clipboard.

"Three," I say.

She nods as if my request is nothing out of the ordinary. I breathe a sigh of relief, and as I watch her walk away, I think to myself, well, that was easier than ordering a cappuccino.

A few hours later, she approached me and told me the ostriches are doable, but they are expensive. They would most likely eat into the company's mark-up. She looks at me inquisitively through her thick glasses and blinks a couple of times. I assume this is a nonverbal cue as to what my next move would be.

"Please proceed," I snap back. "I'll pay for them out of my director's fee if I have to."

"There's an ostrich farm not too far away," she responds, "I have a meeting with the owner later this afternoon."

I could almost taste my Oscar.

Later that day, she told me she had secured two birds, but there was a catch. The breeder only had two ostriches that he would release to us.

"One of the ostriches only has one leg," she says, "the other one is missing an eye and is blind." She stares at me and blinks. Then asks if they would 'work for me'.

Would they work for me?

"No," I respond, "Disfigured ostriches would not 'work for me'."

She tells me she will investigate other options.

Later that day, my agent called.

"The clients love where you're going with the project," she informs me, "but they're not sure about the ostriches. They're…concerned. They don't see how they fit into the overall concept."

"It's about freedom," I respond flatly.

I am fuming inside. She is pressuring me to drop the ostriches. From that point onward, I screen my calls and any from my agent, let roll over to voicemail.

The following day, the Production Manager tells me she has found another ostrich farm, but it is much farther away. It will be even more expensive to ship the ostriches to the location. Furthermore, she has had ongoing detailed discussions with a Park Ranger, and there is a problem with the ostriches roaming freely. They will have to be chained up or put behind a fence, and the Ranger would need to be standing by with a rifle prepared to shoot the birds, with a tranquilizer should any of the ostriches escape and try to make a run for it.

I am livid. I am trying to 'Capture Freedom' for Heaven's sake. 'Capturing Freedom' is not an easy task. The ostriches need legs in order for me to 'Capture Freedom'. They cannot be blind. They can not be fenced in or chained up, and they most definitely cannot be tranquilized! I storm out of the meeting. I could use a shot of whatever that Park Ranger had loaded up in his gun right about now. This is clearly not working out.

Back at my hotel, things only get worse. The front desk clerk hands me a stack of messages from my agent, all of them regarding 'The Ostrich Situation'. The 'Ostriches' have now become a capitalized 'Situation' in quotation marks. I am sure that, by the way, that desk clerk was eyeing me, he thought I either worked for the World Wildlife Fund or was a hitman for the mob.

In my room, I stretch out on the bed, but I feel like I am boxed into a coffin. How can I even attempt to 'Capture Freedom' when I feel so trapped? The ostriches have become a flapping mess, an enormous albatross around my neck. I order room service. Eggs…scrambled. I punch a feather pillow to mold it into shape, but I just can't get comfortable in the king-size bed. The phone rings.

It is that incessant, persistent ringing that insists one can no longer ignore the outside world. Reluctantly, I answer. It is my agent. She tells me to check out of the hotel immediately and get on the next flight back home. The clients have decided to go with another director to help them 'capture freedom'. "You're…" how did she put it, "free to go."

South Beach
September 27, 1999, 11 p.m.

As I sit on the deserted beach, I look at the night sky and think about the ostriches leaping over the clouds. The vision that never came to be.

I have made it a habit to come here at night. I'm hungry, but I've discovered that if I push through the feeling, the hunger disappears. I hear distant laughter coming from Ocean Drive. People are eating on neon-lit patios. They're intoxicated. They're happy. They are on vacation. It becomes evident to me that even though I am in Miami, I am not on vacation. I want to escape. I want to sink my head into the sand. I feel like a one-legged, blind ostrich 'jonesing' for a tranquilizer shot.

I see someone approaching in the distance. He's wearing loose white linen pants and an unbuttoned white shirt that billows in the warm sea air, revealing eight-pack abs. He's holding a pair of sandals in one hand as he wades ankle-deep in the water. He passes by me and sits on an abandoned lifeguard stand. He watches for a moment, then walks away, turns to glance at me, and nods. I follow him to an abandoned area of the beach. It's fast. It's aggressive. My shirt is yanked off. He maneuvers himself behind me. My head is pushed down, deep into the ground. I get a mouthful of sand. A sea shell lodges itself into my ear. Life is good.

Later, while brushing fine specs of granular sand off my face, we exchange pleasantries. He's visiting from New York. His flight leaves tomorrow. His name is Julio.

CHAPTER 5
THE RING OF TRANSFORMATION

South Beach
November 12, 1999

My welcome at the Lopotomy Apartments is wearing thin, and I know it. I have resorted to sleeping on the floor. I use a yard of an Egyptian tapestry as a mattress and a rolled-up towel as a pillow. I am not really sure why the Egyptian tapestry made it into the carry-on, but it did. Maybe, on some level, a part of me knew it would eventually become my bed. I have never slept on the floor before. I tell myself it's not that bad, but it is.

I get up early and leave the unit before my host wakes up. I return in the dead of night, only when I'm sure that said host will be on a second cycle of REM. I am an invisible ghost. I drink a glass of water, rinse the glass, and put it away. I wipe up the watery ring on the counter.

During the day, I can be found at the beach working on my tan and trying to figure out what I am going to do with my life.

At night, I am an apparition wandering the streets. I'm a lost soul. I float by restaurants and shops. I look at the happy people. I'm observing the world through new eyes. This unfamiliar vantage point does not have the most aesthetically pleasing view, but it is different, so I drink in the experience. Everything feels thin and diluted like I've poured water into the empty shampoo bottle of my life. In an effort to stretch out my finances, or lack thereof, I have made a conscious decision to eat less. I am lighter, and it's that much easier to float. I may just float away into the clouds, never to be heard from again.

I am drawn down a side street. I stop at a little gallery. Through a narrow window, I see a court jester staring back at me. It's a portrait, from the shoulders up, a simple line drawing immortalized in an opulent frame. The drawing draws me deeper into its vacant gaze. I stare into his eyes. *The Fool.* I'm not quite sure if this is a painting or a mirror.

I make my way to Ocean Drive. I pass a photographer snapping images of a wafer-thin model. A few feet away, a disheveled homeless man is bathing in a public shower. They're relatively close to one another but light-years away. Miami Beach is a city of extremes, but I guess all cities are if you look closely enough.

I can feel the soft sand sink between my toes as I walk towards the water. It's cool and damp. I have made it a habit to come here every night to sit by the ocean. I dig my hand into the earth and swing my arm around me, as far as it will go, then twist around and do the same on the other side, creating a circle around me: *My Ring of Transformation.*

The circular shape appears to have a magical property. It is able to free my mind from perpetual worry. This ring around my body releases me from my current set of circumstances, this nightmare that has become my life. I sit and listen to the waves. I'm able to breathe. I've lost almost everything in my life that has defined me, but for some reason, while sitting here, just breathing, I feel…OK…Is this possible? I pause for a moment. It's a fact that even if I had all the money in the world, at this moment, it would make no difference; I would still just be here…framed by this circle in the sand, breathing. As I continue to ponder this thought, I think I even feel a little happy. Now, I'm truly perplexed.

My nocturnal excursions to The Ring of Transformation have not only helped to keep me grounded; I'm finding countless things on the ground, too. I am not sure why this is happening. Either people in Miami are extremely careless, or something is intentionally dropping breadcrumbs onto my path. Maybe it's a combination of both. Then again, it's possible I've just been looking down more often.

One night, on my way back from the ocean, I see something glittering in the distance. As I get closer, I discover it is a generous pile of silver coins that's been dumped onto the sidewalk. It's an enormous mound of change that looks like a pirate's treasure from a children's storybook. It's as if a lazy philanthropist wanted to give to the poor but couldn't be bothered to go any further than the sidewalk.

It's a miracle. I drop to my knees. There are tears in my eyes as I pick up every last dime, even though part of me is embarrassed that I am doing so.

I notice the ring on my finger as I pick up a quarter, and I am again reminded of how far I have fallen. My ring…it's one of the few things that I haven't lost. It found its way onto the carry-on, too, so to speak…

I close my eyes to see the light

I cover my ears to hear

I starve myself to taste the fruit

Salvation is near

Montreal
August 21, 1993

Rue Duluth is one of my favorite streets in Montreal, scattered with tiny boutiques and unique artisan shops. A display window in one such shop is filled with medieval-inspired artwork, jewelry, miniature metallic figurines, and full-scale suits of armor. I peer through the glass in the window and notice a ring. It is a big, thick, silver ring about an inch wide, with elongated black diamond-shaped markings sweeping around its circumference. It resembles the kind of ring fit for a king, a fashion accessory worn by an elite ruler in a Gothic fantasy mini-series. I have never been one to covet jewelry, but for some unexplainable reason, this ring is calling out to me. It wants me… or maybe it is the other way around? I hastily reach for the door. It is locked. The store is closed. It goes without saying that I am disappointed. When I want something, I usually want it immediately.

I look at the ring again, cupping my hands around my eyes and pressing my face up against the window to eliminate as many reflections as possible. If the ring is truly meant to be mine, it will be here the next time I am back in this city.

Montreal
August 14, 1994

I turn onto Rue Duluth, and from a distance, I can tell the shop is open. My pace quickens, but as I approach the store window, I get a strange feeling in my gut. I am convinced the ring is gone, and when I look through the glass, I am right. It isn't there anymore. Then, out of the corner of my eye, I spot it.

I enter the store excitedly. A heavy-set man who looks like a blacksmith from Middle Earth with a full hobbit beard approaches me.

"That one," I say as I point to the ring, "the one with the black diamond markings."

The hobbit reaches into the display with his fat fingers, picks it up, and gives it to me. At last, the ring is in my hands, but when I try to slip it onto my finger, I can't. It's three sizes too small. I don't even try to force it. I feel gutted.

The hobbit tells me he can make me an identical ring, one that will fit, but it will take time. He sizes my finger. I leave a deposit and go back home.

A month later, a package arrives. I open it quickly. After what feels like an eternity since I first laid my eyes on it, my ring is finally on my finger.

The ring becomes me. People notice it, and by association, people notice me. The thick jewelry becomes a conversation piece, the cornerstone of my image as a young up-and-coming film director. It is a symbol of my success. It is a king's ring. And I feel like a king.

Over the years, this chunk of jewelry proved true to its form - silver peaks with deep black valleys. I wore it religiously on the ring finger of my left hand as if I was wed to my ego. The ring caught glimpses of light while I grasped at straws, rolled up dollar bills, and spiralled down the dark tunnel of despair to a portal that spat me out onto this spot of sand on South Beach.

South Beach
November 14, 1999

It's a gorgeous night. The light glistens off the surface of the water. I slip the ring off my finger and hold it between my thumb and forefinger. I study it carefully. It is still a thing of beauty. It does look like a king's ring, but as I sit here, one step away from homelessness, I am painfully aware that I am not a King. This piece of jewelry is one of the few things that did not evaporate into thin air during the reduction. It survived, and even though I love it, it is not a reflection of me anymore, and what's worse is that I know it. Material possessions from the past are of no use to me anymore. I decide not to resist the tide. I'll go with the flow…and help usher in the future. I look at this beautiful piece of jewelry one final time, then, in a dramatic film-worthy gesture, throw it as far as I can into the sea. It doesn't make a sound. I do not hear a splash. It just disappears.

I look out at the expansive body of water and then back down to my bare hands. It is as if the ring never existed. I feel like a fool framed in this circle of dirt. I lift myself up, turn my back on the ocean, and fade into the night.

South Beach
November 17, 1999

I'm back in my circle again. My Ring of Transformation. It's been three days since I've cast my ring into the ocean. I've been here every night. When I look out over the water, I know my ring is in there…somewhere. I feel kind of stupid, but I am sure it was the right thing to do. I get up, brush the sand off of me, and head back to the Lopotomy.

I am on the sidewalk adjacent to Flamingo Park. The lamp posts create circular rings of light on the pavement. I move in and out of darkness, in and out of the light. It's eerily silent, dead quiet when I kick something in front of me. What looks like a metal washer from a hardware store rolls along the ground. I can hear its thin rattle on the cement. The sound cuts through the empty air. I follow the arc of its trajectory. The thing wobbles for a moment and comes to rest under a pool of light right in front of me. This object has earned my attention and is now commanding it. It wants me to notice it. I slowly walk toward the light.

It wants me to pick it up.

I reach down.

I do not believe my eyes.

This cannot be possible.

It's not a washer.

It's a ring!

I turn it over in my fingers. It's thin and silver and gold with diagonal black markings. It doesn't look like my ring, but remarkably, it has a similar aesthetic. It's a modest ring, simple, understated…not as flashy as a king's ring or even a prince's ring. It's a man's ring. I slip it onto my finger. It fits perfectly.

I cannot believe what has just happened. The hair on the back of my neck is standing on end. It's unbelievable. Priceless, really. It's like I just performed a magnificent magic trick, but I was the only one to witness it.

I am standing by myself in the middle of the street on a hot summer night. From one moment to the next, my circumstances have not changed, but somehow…they have, and in a somewhat grand and spectacular way. My ring has been returned to me; it has been transformed.

I'm beaming, filled with hope. I can feel it. Is this a sign that I will be transformed? Granted a new life in this tropical world? This magical city that swallows sacrificial objects and spits them out in an altered state of grace?

I gaze at the new ring on my finger in disbelief. I'm too excited to go back to the Lopotomy. I'm floating on air but in a good way this time. Even though I don't have a penny to my name, I feel like a million bucks.

I am gliding along Lincoln Road. All the shops are closing.

The waiters and busboys are breaking down patios and stacking things up. A busboy smiles at me. I walk away a few steps and then turn to look back at him. He has stopped in his tracks while holding a patio chair. I turn to approach him. He sets the chair on the ground. His name is Alejandro.

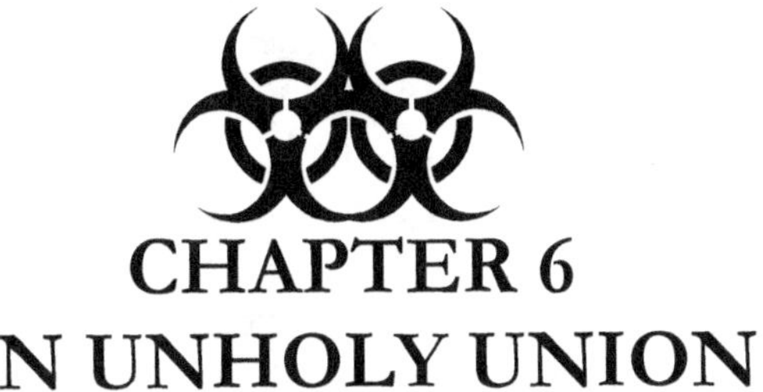

CHAPTER 6
AN UNHOLY UNION

Toronto
September 20, 1966

There was something about sheer blind velocity that always fascinated me. As early as I could remember, the need for speed coursed through my veins. I was told that I could run before I could walk. I would fling my infant self between the furniture in our living room. My tiny feet raced out in front of me as I left the security of one couch…and hurled my little body in an attempt to catch up to the rest of me until I landed face-first onto the sofa on the other side of the room. The extreme nature of this activity and the visuals that accompanied it were too frightening for me to absorb, so naturally, I shut my eyes.

This was risky behavior for a youngster, to be sure, but the configuration of the furniture in the room created the illusion of a safe space. It was like a padded prison cell for toddlers. The large couches created enormous soft barriers that book-ended my father's armchair on one end and the crown jewel of the living room, the television set on the other. Televisions, at the time, were not paper-thin wall-mounted monitors but rather big brown boxy free-standing monstrosities that demanded a sizeable chunk of real estate from any room.

Shortly after that, while blindly bouncing back and forth like a beach ball on a hot summer's day, I veered off course, of course, and collided head-first into the pointed corner of the TV. That was the first time I experienced the painful truth that lack of vision coupled with a desire for terminal velocity was an unholy union destined to end in catastrophe. It was also the exact moment that the powerful visual medium of television first made an impression on me, both literally and figuratively. To this day, I have a patch on my left eyebrow where hair does not grow to prove it.

This early epic fail was not enough to eradicate my love of moving through space as fast as possible, and even though I kept my eyes wide open for future ventures, on many levels, I still was not able to see.

Cheetah Boy
Toronto
October 29, 1976

I am ten years old. My favorite animal is the Cheetah. This big, lean cat is the fastest animal on earth, and in my heart of hearts, I want to be like this svelte feline.

I run up and down the hallway of our home, pounce on the couch, and jump to the floor. I am Cheetah Boy. I sprint around the corner into my parent's bedroom, past a full-length mirror, toward a chest of drawers, and pull out Mamma's leopard print scarf. I wrap it around my head. It isn't the correct animal print, but it is close enough. As I bolt through the house, the material inevitably falls over my eyes. I look blindfolded but can still partially see through the sheer fabric. At night, I race into the kitchen to devour cookies. I eat an entire row. Every night.

When my mother takes me for my annual check-up, the doctor puts me on a scale, and her eyebrows go up...way up. She records a number on her clipboard, then pokes her pen deep into my stomach. Most of it disappears into a roll of flesh. It is like a magic trick. Poof!

The doctor tells Mamma I have put on far too much weight since my last visit. I have to go on a diet. A diet!

I am devastated. Back at home, I stand in front of the full-length mirror. It is like I can see myself for the very first time. The filter is gone, the 'cheetah' filter. I am not a cheetah. I am a walrus. I poke my finger into my stomach just like the doctor did. I had never noticed this before. I thought I was 'FAST', but it turns out I am just 'FAT'. The 'S' was gone. I must have eaten it.

From that point forward, I don't have the will to be Cheetah Boy anymore. I just flop on the couch like a blubbery walrus and shovel in Cheetos instead. On occasion, when Mamma wears the scarf, I just stare at her with my orange-stained fingers and fat walrus eyes.

This brush with obesity is short. The next year, I hit puberty and grew 6 inches. The fat around my midsection stretches out with me, but even to this day, sometimes, deep down inside, I still feel like a sluggish sea cow.

Whoosh!
Toronto 1984

I am falling. Plummeting to the earth at an incredible speed. Eyes shut tight. The powerful rush of wind forces itself down my throat. It is impossible to breathe. Deafening screams reverberate in my ears, but a thunderous roar overpowers them as the car whooshes over the planks. I have always loved roller coasters... the twists and turns, the highs and lows, the dips and the drops. The anticipation as the train creeps up the steep slope.

The rattling hypnotic sound of the chain taunts the rider with the inevitable fact that what goes up must come down.

Clink. Clink. Clink.

I prefer vintage coasters, the older ones that are constructed out of wood. Where you can hear the lumber creaking while being whisked along a curve. I love the kind of coaster where the risk of flying off the rails is an actual possibility.

When I was in high school, a theme park opened just north of the city. It takes a combination of buses, subways, and an eternity to get there, but I tolerate this exhausting endeavour because I am positive it is my destiny. The anticipation I experience on the journey to fill out an application is not unlike creeping up the steep slope of a coaster.

Clink. Clink. Clink.

The HR woman conducting interviews looks like an animated Disney princess. She has a plastic face with big blue plastic eyes, blonde hair, and a perfect, pearly white plasticine smile. She tells me that employees at the park are cast members because 'we're all on stage'. This sounds exciting. I imagine myself backlit, working the platform as the wind blows through my hair.

"Unfortunately," she says, somehow still able to smile while speaking, "We've cast all of the roles on our Attractions."

The only 'role' she can offer me is a server position at the Rib Shack. I'd still be a cast member, though, and as a cast member, I'd still be 'on stage'.

I come crashing down to reality. It is far from the rush I was expecting.

It is a humiliating summer. Most of it is spent standing over a steaming tray of ribs, holding tongs while wearing a mauve medieval costume that includes a floppy purple hat. To add insult to my rib injury, a coaster is in my direct line of vision. I can see and hear it in the distance, through the steam wafting up in my face, past the hungry people lining up for the Rib Shack special.

Toronto
March, 1985

Another plasticized HR Princess sits across from me. She is a different branch of royalty compared to the one from last year.

She has the same plastic features and the same uncanny ability to speak through her smile, but she is the brown-haired model. She flips through some papers. Apparently, I got rave reviews at the Rib Shack.

"I'm done with my 'role' at the Rib Shack," I quickly reply. "I want to work on a coaster."

She shuffles through a few papers, then glances up at me, "I can put you on an attraction," she says, smiling, "but it's not a coaster."

"I'll take it," I answer back, relieved that I am finally free from the Rib Shack's ruthless grip.

Toronto
June, 1985

It is another humiliating summer.

I am placed in the children's section of the park. I am floppy hat-free but required to wear orange pants and a white shirt with thick rainbow suspenders. I work on a ride called Happy Landing, although it is arguable if my landing had been anything but. Giant white swans float around a pond pulled along by dorks on an underwater conveyor belt. The ride is the opposite of a rollercoaster, designed for families with young children, babies, and elderly grandparents.

It isn't that bad on sunny days. The dock faces south, and by the middle of the summer, I have an awesome tan, except for two vertical lines that run down my torso.

On rainy days, it is miserable. Most of the rides close down for safety reasons, but the swans at Happy Landing aren't flustered by a little bit of water. This attraction stays open even though it doesn't attract a thing.

On a particularly stormy day, a group of water-logged cast members at Happy Landing decide to take matters into their own hands.

The water level in the pond has risen significantly, and we discover that if we hit the emergency stop button at the exact moment when a swan is approaching a turn, we can free it from the mechanism below. The giant rogue birds drifting aimlessly are considered a safety hazard, and the attraction has to shut down until the swans are sequestered. We are all in on the conspiracy and take turns smacking the button in an effort to free a swan... and, ultimately, ourselves from the miserable weather conditions.

I am on a break, sitting in my sopping wet orange pants in the cast member lounge when a Park Supervisor gets a loud crackling message on his walkie-talkie, "Rogue Swan at Happy Landing."

I try to suppress a grin.

The supervisor looks at me and exclaims, "That's the fourth one today! Those swans are flying all over the place."

I try not to look guilty as I bite into my wet tuna fish sandwich.

Toronto
1986

This summer, as destiny, plastic princesses, and pure stubborn will would have it, I am finally cast on a coaster! It is an old-style wooden rollercoaster in the medieval section of the park. I am beyond ecstatic. I walk up the wide ramp to my starring role on 'The Wilde Beast'.

The 'role' requires me to check hand stamps and make sure kids are taller than the height restriction. I have to do a safety check on the lap bars and give a thumbs-up when everything is clear. Sometimes, an obese person will try to squeeze into a seat. It is an embarrassing scenario as they twist and shift their bodies in a futile attempt as I try to close the latch. If the bar does not lock around them, they are denied permission to ride. I know all too well the fate of an overweight walrus, and I can't help but empathize with them. They have to waddle their way down the exit ramp to a fried onion ring stand at the bottom of the incline. A bucket of deep-fried battered vegetables is their consolation prize as they watch svelte cheetahs feast on the beast.

One day, my manager tells me I am ready to operate 'The Beast'. I am a little intimidated. I am only in high school, and my overbearing mother has never even let me use the washing machine; operating a rollercoaster seems a little out of my league. When I am escorted up to the control booth, I am surprised to discover the console looks like a preschool toy. It is almost infantile. There are only two buttons: a big green button for 'Go' and a big red button for 'Stop'. I recognize this panel. It is installed in my system, too.

Then they tell me the red button has its limitations. I can use it at any point when the beast is going up the lift, but once it is over the first drop, the coaster is on its own. Gravity is the only thing keeping it moving until it pulls back into the station.

That is me, too. I am the Wilde Beast.

As the operator, it is also my job to make an obligatory safety speech over the PA system to caution riders not to engage in risky behavior. I sit up on my perch and spew out a safety spiel like a parrot over and over, endlessly, throughout the day. I warn 'guests' to keep their arms and legs inside the car. I tell them not to stand up. I instruct them to secure loose items.

The beast gobbles up hats, glasses, wallets, and stuffed animals, and at the end of a shift, we have to venture under the coaster to retrieve them. Sometimes, I just stand in the heart of the contorted construction, motionless as the beast whooshes past. The ground trembles and the earth shakes. I hear the intoxicating mix of screams of terror and delight.

When we are not working, 'cast members' are granted unlimited access to the attractions. I take full advantage of this perk and ride the beast to my heart's content. I prefer the last car. I am convinced the tail of the beast is where I can be whipped to my satisfaction. I certainly do not obey any of the warnings that I have repeated ad nauseam throughout the day. I lift my arms, close my eyes, and shimmy out of my seat until I am almost standing.

Then, one day, something unfathomable happens. My stomach does not even twitch when we drop off the highest point. It feels like I am lounging on a couch eating Cheetos.

And just like that... the thrill is gone.

The Beast isn't wild anymore. It is as tame as a rogue swan drifting aimlessly in a pond at Happy Landing.

Whoosh.

The Energizer Bunny
Toronto
January 1996
Saturday night, 2 a.m.

The cab speeds along the dark, slushy street as I slouch in the back seat in a T-shirt, sporting dark sunglasses. I don't wear a coat in the winter. I don't even own one.

I take taxis everywhere, unhindered by the inconveniences winter weather attire demands, conveniently wrapped in a heated metal shell on wheels that magically disappears when I am done with it.

The car pulls up to a nightclub. It is here where I emerge from the steely epidermis, a restless butterfly breaking free from a protective cocoon. In my peripheral vision, I vaguely notice common people standing in a massive, crowded line. They are huddled together, wrapped in layers, but still look frozen to the core. I glide past them effortlessly, a cheetah in a cheetah's body wearing a tight-fitted cheetah print shirt. I am ushered through velvet ropes and in through the back door.

I am a VIP! a VIP of what I am not exactly sure…but a VIP nonetheless. This means I don't have to stand in line, I don't have to pay to get in, and I am coat-less, so I don't have to wait in a queue for a coat check either. I am able to dive into the shirtless, sweaty crowd as fast as possible because time is precious. I claw my way through the slick bodies and claim my space on the dance floor. I tear off my shirt, even though it has taken me over an hour to decide what to wear. I have resorted to dancing by myself because no one can keep up with me.

Like a werewolf compelled by the lunacy of a full moon, the music transforms me into an Energizer Bunny on steroids. I just keep going and going and going. I have an endless amount of battery power. I am not sure where it is coming from, but apparently, I have discovered a limitless supply. The hypnotic progressive beat penetrates my body. The faster the track, the faster I move, my arms flailing around like an air traffic controller on acid.

I am aggressive on the dance floor. My choreography is assault-worthy. More than one unsuspecting queen has suffered the consequences of my infamous fist-clenched pirouette. Roadkill left in the wake of my quest for ecstasy.

For it is only here, in this surreal environment of light, sound, and motion, that my senses are overloaded to the point where I am granted freedom. Freedom from myself. This elusive level of bliss is challenging to maintain. The euphoria of this nature must be monitored throughout the evening like I have diabetes or something. I have to ensure I am always topped up.

I go out every night of the week because I can. I am still on a retainer, and this arrangement has granted me an all-access, non-stop, limitless pass. Weeknights are for the elite, the true enthusiasts.

Weekends are palatable, but too many rookies truck in from the suburbs; the vibe is just not the same. I don't even attempt to go anywhere until well past 2 a.m. until I am certain the crowd is thinning out. Things don't usually start to get going until 4 a.m., anyway.

The two clubs I frequent the most are called Joy and Fly, and on most nights, I can be found flying joyously between them.

Hardcore clubbing, if executed correctly, unquestionably qualifies as an extreme sport. It is as intense as an Iron Man marathon. Dancing for twenty hours straight without eating is not for lightweights. This workout regime appears to be the only thing that burns the pesky walrus fat off of my cheetah's body. Sweat pours out of me as if I am standing in a shower. My attempt to hydrate myself is futile. The more water I pour into me, the more drains out I feel. I have become some kind of human filtration system. I tell myself the water is purifying my body, but it is just trying to flush out all of the toxins.

After not eating for days, the mere thought of food becomes repulsive. In this fasted state, I have an epiphany;

'chewing' was a colossal waste of time! I became obsessed with finding an easier, more efficient way to nourish my body and discovered the process of juicing carrots is the solution. Those sinewy rabbits know, and so does this Energy Bunny. My diet consists solely of carrot juice... oh and cocaine.

Did I mention the cocaine?

I keep going and going and going.

As time presses on, the beta-carotene is improving my vision. I am sure of it. I buy a top-of-the-line juicer. My fridge is chock full of carrots and nothing else. When the crispy supply is depleted, I throw on my sunglasses and quickly hop like a bunny to get more. I absolutely detest going to the supermarket. I am not sure why. It is possible I'd had a traumatic experience there.

My cart is brimming with carrots and nothing else. I can tell by the way customers are looking at me that they are wondering what I am doing with all of these root vegetables. As their gaze drifts up to meet my shielded eyes, I am not sure if it is because I am looking thin and fabulous or because my skin is starting to turn a shade closer to orange. I don't care. They don't know that I'd discovered the elusive secret to The Fountain of Fat Loss, and with that kind of judgemental attitude, I certainly am not going to tell them.

I focus on the carrots. Their crunchy bodies being individually pulverized as I force them through the spinning blades of the juicer is nothing less than exhilarating. I have the power to transform them into liquid form, and I can transform myself as well. The carrots taunt me... dangling in front of me… hanging from a stick. I grasp at them with all the voracity of a starving beast yearning to reach an ever-elusive, unattainable goal. I must be thinner, faster, and leaner. I must be happy. I have to be able to see my abdominal muscles. I must be perfect.

I fall down a rabbit hole, but unlike Alice, I do not find myself in a magical, wondrous land. No, this is something quite different.

The Palm Springs International Film Festival, Palm Springs
January 11, 1998

It is a blind man's bluff for that, I'm sure

The cloth wrapped firmly around my head

Provides comfort in its darkness

My hands, Bound to my desire

Do not touch my pain

It is a blind man's bluff to think I'm feeling fine

To chart my course by the wind and the chimes.

I am the only sunburned participant at The Palm Springs International Film Festival. Burnt to a crisp. Busted. I haven't been spending my time sitting in a dark theatre watching films, even though that's why I am here. I've been lounging by the pool, soaking in the Sun, misted ever so softly by a continuous spray of fine water droplets. My short film, Blind Man's Bluff, is screening at the festival for its World Premiere. This was a sign. I was destined for bigger and better things.

However, the experience of watching the film in front of an audience was far from what I had imagined it would be. I craved this kind of exposure for as long as I could remember, but sitting in the dark theatre, I just felt exposed. At a reception after the event, my social anxiety kicks into high gear. I stand with my back against the wall by the shrimp dip, looking like an awkward lobster. I am overly self-conscious while speaking with the other attendees. They're all pasty white, pale film-goers; it's like they haven't seen the sun in years.

My attempt to discuss the thematic undertones of the film in an academic context, like a proper intellectual, falls short. When people ask me why I made my film, I have no idea how to respond.

"I'm exploring addiction," I blurt out.

The response is thrust out in front of me like an African warrior shield meant to effectively deflect any further human interaction. It works. The pasty people around me step back, giving me a wide berth. This gives me the opportunity to look around the room and observe the other filmmakers engrossed in animated conversations with their respective entourages.

As I stare at them, I wonder what on earth compelled me to do this; project my innermost thoughts onto a screen for all the world to see.

Was it possible that such a public display of the inner workings of my psyche was really an unconscious cry for help? Why couldn't I just write in a journal like everybody else?

The fact that I had the audacity to believe that I had the capacity to explore the devious territory known as addiction like I was exploring the Serengeti was laughable. That I could drop my compass, pack up my binoculars, jump into my open-air jeep, and leave whenever I wanted to. That I was in control. It doesn't work that way.

I had no idea what I was exploring. I was dancing with the Devil, flirting with disaster, as blissfully unaware as someone double-fisting martinis at a cocktail party, jokingly referring to themselves as an alcoholic while ordering a third.

I had not experienced the true horrors of addiction... yet. I was in the grips of a deadly disease. Denial was a part of it. There was no escape. I was still falling down the rabbit hole... like an out-of-control rollercoaster with no red emergency stop button... about to land in the jaws of a bona fide beast.

The Redundancy of Eating and Sleeping
Toronto
June 1999

I make a new friend on the party circuit. They call her Tina. She is as stunning as a supermodel, with a shock of bleached blonde hair pulled back into a high ponytail that accentuates her flawless face. I am mesmerized by her crystal blue eyes. They radiate like powerful glow sticks that need to be shielded by dark shades, even in the dead of night. She is super sexy and seductive and, somehow, even more energetic than I am. We laugh at the craziest things.

Tina promises to take me to higher heights, and she does. She grasps me firmly by the hand and leads me deeper down the tunnel.

Tina devours my thesis on "The Redundancy of Eating". She adds her initials to each page and co-signs the document. She even has the power to have it notarized. Tina truly understands me. I love her so much. She tells me she will send it to a publisher she knows. Tina has contacts... loads of friends in high places. She agrees with my radical concepts... Food is repulsive! She convinces me that sleep is too.

I see her point. I can save so much time by not eating or sleeping. I can accomplish so much more. I am far more productive at night, in the dark. Sunlight has become an enemy. It is to be avoided at all costs.

I usually sleep all day and wake up when the Sun starts to set, but when I am with Tina, she forces me to push the envelope. She knows I can do it. She calls me at all hours of the day, and when she does, I feel compelled to answer her. When I am in her company, the line between dreams and reality blurs. Light creeping through the cracks of my drawn shades must be abolished immediately. I am sure people are spying on me. Is there a camera in the air vent? I rip up the carpeting to check for a wiretap.

Tina is also infatuated with roller coasters. She loves amusement parks. She likes to be amused, that one. When I am with her, there are moments when I feel so high I feel I can touch the face of God. These moments of enlightenment are followed by sheer death-defying drops to the depths of despair. It is a magnificent plunge back to earth.

I am alone. The bleak, empty nothingness of the harsh morning swallows me whole. Tina is gone, but her malicious cackle echoes like a demonic Harpy in a cavernous void.

One day, something extraordinary happens… Tina, the thrill of her is gone; it vanishes into thin air, just like the Wilde Beast...

Whoosh.

This was the day my battery died.

When I opened my eyes... and I didn't like what I saw.

Furthermore, I couldn't stand to look at another carrot.

The marriage of sheer blind velocity had rooted itself deep in my psyche, and I was starting to realize their codependent tendencies were getting me nowhere fast. I didn't know then, but it would take time to uncouple this Unholy Union... lots of time...

The Crash
Toronto
October 2016

"How did your motorcycle get upside down?" a man's voice, strong and persuasive, trying to wake me from a deep slumber.

I open my eyes. Was I dreaming? I am lying down, but I wasn't in my bed. A silhouette stands before me, pointing ominously over my shoulder. My head feels incredibly heavy as I lift it from my concrete pillow.

I turn my head to look through a narrow window. My peripheral vision is limited, but I can finally see it: an art installation in the middle of the intersection. My motorcycle was perfectly upside down, resting on its handlebars and seat. It is a vile public statement, as unsettling as an inverted crucifix. This isn't a dream; it is a nightmare.

I find myself in the middle of the road, a few feet from the scene. I am not a stuntman, but I somehow had performed this complicated trick. I try to piece together how it happened, but my mind is shrouded in a thick fog.

I attempt to get up. A police officer gently pushes me back down.

"Wait for the ambulance," he says.

Confusion engulfs me as I am strapped to a wooden board and loaded into the vehicle like cargo. I am wheeled into an emergency. Doctors examine me and conclude I am free to go.

It feels like I have been hit by a truck, but to my surprise, the police officer tells me I hit the truck; it did not hit me.

"The good news is that you're walking away from a motorcycle accident," he says, "The bad news is I have to give you a ticket for careless driving."

I feel like I just got bitch-slapped.

"What happened?" he asks.

The last thing I remember is seeing the truck in front of me. I slammed on the brakes... and, like the toddler that I am, shut my eyes and hoped for the best.

My bike is demolished. I am told it can not be repaired. Yellow ticket in hand, all I want to do is go home and forget the whole thing.

The Unholy Union was taking its toll on me.

Toronto
December 2016

Just before Christmas, I received a gift from the motorcycle dealership. Inside the package, there is a mug with the brand name of the bike printed across it.

Triumph.

I sit in silence, holding the cup in my hands, and ponder the message. I have triumphed over something, although of what exactly... I am not sure.

CHAPTER 7
THE CRYSTAL BALL

Miami Beach
November 24, 1999

I'm racing down Ocean Drive on rollerblades when my accelerated stride screeches to a snail's pace. I am appalled by the amount of people on the street. I've only been here for a couple of months, but I already feel like an entitled local, despising the influx of tourists during peak season.

My surly attitude stems from the fact that each week, people from all over the world show up with friends, family, and money to spare. I don't have any of those things anymore. All I have is my Ring of Transformation, but it hasn't transformed anything yet.

That was all about to change.

I zip up 8th Avenue and decide to take Pennsylvania. I am back up to speed when I see a young Latino on the side of the street waving his arms frantically in the air. His hair is jet black and spikes up out of a thick red headband. He's also on blades.

"Stop! Please. Stop! Stop!" he pleads in a thick accent.

There is something likable about this young man; I can't quite put my finger on it. By nature, I am a suspicious urbanite and will usually not stop anyone waving at me, but then again, nothing is normal anymore. I grind to a full stop directly in front of him. He has dark, alert eyes and a sincere smile. He's holding a pen in one hand and a crumpled sheet of paper in the other. He introduces himself as Ricardo.

"Hello!" He says enthusiastically, "I am happy that you stopped."

Little did I know that stopping was about to set in motion a series of events that would alter the course of my life.

"I am helping my friends," Ricardo continues, "They are filming a commercial, and they are looking for people who can rollerblade."

He thrusts a piece of paper and the pen toward me, "Here. Please. Write down your name and number."

I take the pen and paper and jot down my info. "You know, I'm also in the film business." I confess, "I'm a commercial director from Toronto."

Ricardo's black, glassy eyes light up. "I am also a director in Chile," Ricardo continues, "but here in Miami, I do not tell anyone this. I tell everyone that I am a grip...and only a grip. I will do anything to work. This is why I am helping my friend with casting."

I admire his work ethic. I wonder if I would do anything on a film set other than call the shots, but I know myself too well.

"Do you know 'Crystal Ball'?" He asks. My ears perk up.

"Crystal Ball?" I repeat.

"Everyone in Miami knows Crystal Ball." Ricardo continues, "And Crystal Ball knows everybody. Crystal Ball is... art director. He works all the time. If you meet Crystal Ball and he likes you, you will get lots of work here."

Ricardo continues to talk about Crystal Ball, insisting on starting or ending every sentence with his name. In a very short period, this person known as Crystal Ball has garnered a reputation of epic proportions.

I imagine Crystal Ball as the physical incarnation of the ancient divination tool...a rotund bald guru wearing circular glasses with the ability to see into the future like a powerful telephoto lens and grant careers in the film industry with the snap of a clapboard.

It is only after Ricardo has repeated Crystal Ball's name several times that I realize the inflection he has been placing on certain syllables, along with his thick accent, has made me entirely misinterpret the name.

It's not 'Crystal Ball'. He's been saying Cristobal the entire time.

I feel like an idiot, but I have been fascinated by divination for as long as I can remember, so I would be willing to do anything to meet someone named Crystal Ball, even if it's because the name has been mispronounced.

The Supernatural
Toronto
Oct 30, 1989

I was always obsessed with the supernatural. Apparently, the natural was never enough for me.

Spirits, prophetic dreams, fortune-tellers...I was convinced there must be other facets to our dimension. What did the future hold? Was this possible to know?

Could our destiny actually be foretold in a crystal ball? I was so impatient that all I wanted to do was fast forward to the end of my life to see how it all turned out.

The Tarot Deck
New York
Oct 31, 1989

I was wandering around the West Village and was drawn into an occult shop. Inside, I see a deck of Tarot cards and purchase them. It is an impulse buy. When I returned home, I threw the deck in a drawer and forgot about it.

The Window
Toronto
March 16, 1991

I am going through old boxes when I find the deck of cards. I pick them up, shuffle them, and, with the help of a guidebook, make my way through the process of laying out a spread. To my surprise, the cards reflect an accurate representation of my life. I am intrigued.

I begin to consult the Tarot daily. The cards appear to give me a bird's eye view of my life. It is vast and panoramic as if I have discovered a window into a different world that I can gaze into endlessly. This gateway frees me from the mundane boredom of daily existence. I am fascinated. Through repetition and practice... and because I am on a retainer and don't have to work every day, I teach myself to read.

The process is not unlike learning another language, math, or music. There are 78 cards, and each card represents something. When the cards are laid out in a configuration, all one has to do is connect the dots. It is like the cards are sentences, and when they fall into different combinations, they lay out an infinite number of paragraphs. The Tarot comprises The Major Arcana, the Minor Arcana, Kings, Queens, Cups, Wands, Swords, and Pentacles; together, they facilitate a portal into a different dimension. It is a deep well of knowledge that is centuries old, and for some reason, I am granted an all-access pass.

I practice with family and friends. I forge through each spread with the use of the guidebook to prove I am not making things up. It is a slow and laborious process but a necessary one. The person sitting across from me knows that I know exactly what is going on in their lives. The cards accurately reflect what we both knew to be true... and the guidebook legitimizes it. It is right there in black and white. I am in awe that this tool allows me to see into this other dimension... especially considering my lack of vision in this one.

I continue to read everyone I know. I read my friends, and I read for their friends. Reading becomes a party trick, and because of that, I am invited to a lot of parties. I sequester myself in a separate room, and people line up to see me. This setup is extra beneficial, absolving me of the social anxiety I always experience at parties, and it saves me from walking through screen doors. It also saves me from small talk. I am always amazed by the deep, meaningful conversations that materialize with strangers when a few tarot cards are scattered between us.

Although at some all-night coke parties, I am just giving the same reading over and over again. Spreads cut with the sharp edges of Swords, littered with an endless empty stream of Inverted Cups drained of love. The Devil frequently appears on these occasions as if Lucifer himself were the guest of honor, presiding over the evening's festivities.

At one such party, I met a guy called Thor, a bartender at a local bar called The Thirsty Beaver.

After his reading, Thor looks at me and says, "A group of other psychics hang out at my bar on Tuesday nights. You should come. I'll introduce you to them if you'd like."

I have never thought of myself as psychic, but I assume Thor was impressed with his reading, so I don't contest the label.

"Sure," I reply.

Psychic Friends
Toronto
Tuesday, July 22, 1997

I make my way to The Thirsty Beaver, an English-style pub on the main floor of a Victorian house in Cabbagetown. Thor is behind the bar. The place is pretty empty, except for ten people gathered around him.

Thor introduces me to an indigenous man called Eagle Eye. I am intrigued as I have been incorporating

Native American divination practices into my readings. Eagle Eye is heavyset with long black hair pulled back into a ponytail. He has a lazy eye that drifts vacantly over my shoulder.

This man appears to be looking at me and not looking at me, all at the same time, depending on which eye I focus on.

Eagle Eye stares deeply at me with his one eye, "You're one of us. You're a seer," he says, "I can see it."

"I am not sure if I can see anything," I confess, "I just do this for fun."

"He's good," Thor interjects while wiping a glass.

"You can make money at this if you want," Eagle Eye says as he hands me his card, "I'll help you."

"I don't do it for the money," I answer back, "I have a career that pays well enough. I'm a film director."

The Eagle's eyes light up, or at least the one that is looking at me does. He tells me he has made dozens of television and radio appearances. He questions me about my divination process with the cards.

"I just spread out the cards and talk about what I see," I reply, "Nothing really means anything to me, but it seems to make sense to the person sitting across from me."

I am captivated by the piercing stare of his Eagle eye.

"Tarot cards, palm reading, and crystal balls are just a means to the end," he explains, "The real active agent of any divination tool is in the person's ability to read between the lines."

Eagle Eye practices psychometry; he gets visions from holding objects and personal belongings.

"We all have different abilities within the divinatory arts. We're like musicians in an orchestra…all playing music but using different instruments to play the same song," he says.

He motions to an odd assortment of individuals behind him, His psychic friends' network. Dionne Warwick is not among them. I scan the gang of eccentric individuals knocking back drinks. At the rate at which they are guzzling beverages, they look more like a bunch of raging alcoholics than enlightened souls.

Eagle Eye introduces me to each of them individually and gives me a short explanation of their abilities as if they are superheroes in the Marvel Cinematic Universe.

La Contessa is a giant, standing 6'3 in flats. She is a mature woman who looks like a cross between an aging drag queen and Big Bird. She speaks with a British accent and wears heavy blue eye shadow with her dark hair pulled into a tight bun.

"She's clairaudient," Eagle Eye whispers, "She hears things."

La Contessa stares at me down her long bird-like nose and extends her hand.

"I have to wash my hands after each person I read….you know…It's like I just wash them away, and they're gone….down the drain," she says.

La Contessa is talking to an equally tall blonde man in his late thirties with a Swedish accent called Bartholomew Bergamore.

"Bartholomew's a Deep Trance Channeller," Eagle Eye informs me, "He channels an entity called Dr. Copperspoon."

Bartholomew nods.

As we walk away, the Eagle leans into me and says, "Dr. Copperspoon's 83, quite knowledgeable, and very opinionated."

Hillary is an older, disheveled woman with curly hair who looks like a hippie from the 60s. She wears Janis Joplin vintage glasses with red lenses.

"She's an Astrologer at heart, but she uses crystals and tea leaves too," Eagle Eye explains, "She's also an expert in Reiki and Reflexology."

Hillary smiles at me.

"You look like you need a sweep," she says.

I am not really sure what she means when she positions herself behind me, puts her hands on the back of my neck, and sweeps them downward off my shoulders.

"There," she exclaims, "Better?"

Octavio is 50ish, decked out in a deep purple suit with a loud floral print shirt. He is a numerologist, and he tells me he is an 8.

"You're a 9," he announces after I have given him the day, month, and year of my birth, "You came here to learn how to help people," he says.

His wife Anastasia reads eyes and palms and can see auras. A colorful scarf is wrapped around her head like an Egyptian turban, and she is wearing an assortment of eclectic necklaces and jewelry. Anastasia cocks her head to one side as she looks at me, then leans over and whispers, "You have a lot of energy…but it's scattered, yes?"

I smile at her and nod, then turn to Thor to get a drink.

"What do you think?" He asks.

As I look at these people, I see that they have all been polite enough, but something is off about them as a collective. There is a bit of an edge, an attitude, a competitiveness between them. It is a shark tank. They have not completely accepted me into their group. Then again, I am not sure I want to belong to such an oddball assortment of individuals. I don't really fit into this group, and you didn't need to be psychic to see that.

The Five Dollar Question
Toronto
August 1997

Eagle Eye takes me under his wing, so to speak. He's established in psychic circles, so if he has a scheduling conflict, he recommends me for a gig. He 'vouches' for me….and that seems to be enough in the world of psychic CVs. Through his support, I get a lot of opportunities that would not usually come my way. I read at restaurants, private parties, psychic fairs, and corporate events. It is the first time that I'm 'paid' for reading, and something does not sit right with me when a financial transaction is incorporated at the end of it all. Monetizing this feels wrong, like I've sold my soul, and I already feel like a sellout from working in advertising.

What's left? My body? Do I just become a full-fledged, multi-pronged prostitute? Offer a trifecta of serviceable options spanning the scope of the human experience: Is one in the market for spiritual guidance? Advertising expertise? Or maybe you just want a blow job? Perhaps I can provide all three for a discounted rate?

Eagle Eye reads at a restaurant called Slick on Sundays, but he can't do it anymore because of another obligation. He asked me if I would like to take his place.

"It's a great way to practice. Get your name out there," Eagle Eye says while staring intently at my left ear.

I am to charge $5 for a question and $10 for a mini-reading. I am initially excited, but as the week progresses, I start to panic.

Sunday

I sit down at a table in the middle of the restaurant and put out a little sign I made out of topography letters that spell out 'readings'.

People are hanging out with friends, eating, drinking, and laughing. I am the only person sitting alone. I immediately feel self-conscious. I shuffle the deck, fan out the cards, and scoop them back up again. I make eye contact with someone from across the room. They're not quite sure what to make of me. I am not sure what to make of me either.

I start to regret agreeing to do this.

A thin guy wearing a brown leather jacket approaches me. "What's this?" He questions, motioning to the cards.

When I tell him what I do, he doesn't believe me. He's skeptical, but I can tell he is intrigued. He keeps asking me questions as if I am some kind of fraud who is doing this to swindle people out of five dollars. A part of me wants to tell him off, but this is my first day, so I bite my tongue.

He hovers over me like an annoying mosquito, and even though I am delivering several verbal rolled-up magazine swats, he isn't getting the hint.

It dawns on me that the situation I put myself in is like putting an enormous target on my back. I've attracted a shooter, and he's using me for target practice. After bantering back and forth for what feels like an eternity, I realize that he really wants a reading but isn't willing to part with five dollars. I want him to go away. I get an idea that's a win-win for both of us.

I explained to him that if what I say does not immediately connect with him, he doesn't have to pay. He can keep his five bucks…and leave. These terms appear to please him, so he sits down in the chair across from me.

I lay out a spread. The Queen of Wands and Five of Swords are the first cards that appear. I ask him if he has just ended a relationship with a woman with reddish brown hair. His jaw drops. It looks as though his eyes are going to pop out of his head. He reaches into his back pocket, pulls out ten dollars, and hands it to me immediately.

"I'm assuming you want me to continue?" I ask.

"I can't believe you just said that," he replies.

"Teach me how to do this," he demands at the end of the reading.

"I'm not sure if I can teach you." I answer back, "I can tell you what all the cards mean and how to put out a spread, but after that, I'm not even sure what I do. I just read what I see."

He heads to the bar to get a drink, and I see him chatting with a few people standing in a group. I have a line-up of people waiting for me for the rest of the afternoon.

I will quickly come to learn that when people consult a Tarot Card reader...they want immediate proof of your abilities. They want you to pull a rabbit out of a hat. They want proof of the magic. They want you to tell them things that they haven't told anyone. They want to believe you are legit.

The following week, the mosquito comes back. He slams ten dollars on the table and asks me to read him again.

"It won't work." I respond, "It's too soon."

My experience has also taught me when someone, including myself, is too demanding to know the future…the cards don't work. They just don't. They become two-dimensional playing cards. Just cards. A solid shut door.... not a window into another dimension.

There is nothing to see.

Nov 24, 1999
South Beach

Ricardo smiles at me with his big black eyes, "I will give you Crystal Ball's number." he says, "Call him!"

I don't have anything to write the number on, and Ricardo only has one crumpled sheet of paper filled with skaters he has stopped throughout the day, so I have no other option. I extend my arm and tell Ricardo to write the number on it. I ask him for his number, too.

I feel like I have found a friend, and one in the film business, too. We're laughing on the street as Ricardo scrawls the digits on my skin. I have not done anything like this since grade school.

I quickly skate back home, holding my arm out and away from my body, careful not to sweat the digits out of existence. I do not want anything to happen to the information inked onto my flesh. These configurations of numbers are the most important thing in the world to me right now.

When I get home, I call Crystal Ball, confident that if he's as busy as Ricardo says he is, I will just get his voicemail. I am thrown off guard when he answers.

No one answers their phones anymore.

"Crystal Ball?" I say, realizing after it's too late that I've called him Crystal Ball and not Cristobal…then I realize it doesn't make a difference.

"Yes?" He asks.

I launch into an animated explanation of the reason for my call. I put a spin on my current set of circumstances. I do not tell him that I am broke, almost homeless, and at the end of my rope.

"Ricardo passed on your contact information," I explain.

"Ah, Ricardo… good guy," he responds. "Can I take you to lunch tomorrow?"

I have not been invited to a business lunch in ages. "Yes!" I answer back, "I'd love to meet you."

Crystal Ball offers to pick me up at Lennox and Lincoln at 1 p.m.

I hang up. I look at my new ring and twist it around my finger a couple of times.

That night, I go to my place by the ocean, sit in the sand and sculpt a circle around me. I breathe in and out as I listen to the waves. I watch God's squeegee work its magic in the sand.

I tip-toe in the middle of the night and take my place on the floor beside the coffee table. I spread out my Egyptian tapestry and roll up a towel. I have gotten used to the floor. It's actually not that bad.

It takes me a while to fall asleep. I'm excited for tomorrow. A part of me is thrilled that I will be eating a proper lunch and not a can of tuna. I hope Crystal Ball is able to see my future. I know how fickle crystal balls can be.

Masquerade
Toronto
Oct 31, 1998

I am reading at another one of Eagle Eye's cast-off gigs. It's a corporate event, a Halloween party, and everyone's in costume. I know the night is not off to a good start when the first person to sit across from me is a large woman dressed as a clown.

She's wearing a bright orange wig, a red bulbous nose, and a multi-colored polka dot onesie. I introduce myself. Then ask for her name as I usually do with new clients.

"I'm a clown," she responds with an arrogant edge to her voice.

I dislike this surly jester immediately. I feel like a target again. Part of me wants to tell her right there on the spot that I won't be able to read her, but I take a deep breath and politely ask her for her name again.

"I'm a *clown*," she repeats, emphasizing the last word as if I didn't hear her the first time or notice her ridiculous costume.

"OK...*clown*," I respond, "take the deck, shuffle it, make three piles, then pick one."

She does as I ask, and I lay out a spread. I look at the first four cards and start talking. I read what I see. I do what I always do.

After I'm done, I glance up at her. I'm met with a vacant stare.

She's looking at me like I'm an insect she wants to squash, like I'm a fraud.

Nothing I've said has connected with her. Nada, Zero. Zilch. "I'm sorry," I say, "Then, I can't read you."

Most people are disappointed under these circumstances, but they accept my response and leave; like a persistent fool, the clown insists that I continue. I explained to her that the remaining six cards in the spread foretell the future...and if the first four cards didn't mean anything to her, then really, what's the point?

I apologize to her again. "Sorry, I don't think I will be able to read you," I say, hoping this time she'll get the hint.

The clown is pissed.

I tried to give her the money back, but she refused to take it. She gets up and storms away from me...the big orange wig bouncing like fluffy cotton candy as she disappears into the crowd.

I've come to accept that whatever is working through me when I read is very fickle indeed. It is like a rare shy woodland creature, extremely elusive that will only show itself to those whom it trusts. Those rare souls who are gracious enough and willing to listen to the information offered.

The clown was obviously not worthy.

The night continues to unfold horribly. It's by far the worst experience I've ever had reading Tarot. Halfway through the night, I realize that everyone is hiding behind a mask. The Tarot usually doesn't have a problem slicing through a surface exterior to get to the real truth, but tonight, for some reason, it is not working. The magic is not here.

When I start to doubt the mystical power of the Tarot, the cards retaliate with swift precision.

A man and woman approach me. They want to be read together. I explain to them that I only read one person at a time but they don't back down.

This corporate event has certainly attracted an insistent group of pushy people.

They must be in sales, I think to myself.

I grow tired of resisting them. "OK," I reply, exasperated, "Why not?"

The couple squeezes into a chair together. They're extremely flirty with one another.

When I lay out the spread, something jumps out at me immediately. Not one, but two pairs of Kings and Queens pop up in the 10-card spread: The King and Queen of Wands and The King and Queen of Cups…but something is awry. The King of one suit is beside the Queen of the other and vice versa. They've swapped partners.

The two people in front of me are either cheating on their spouses or lying to each other.

They look at me eagerly, smiling from ear to ear. "What do you see?" the woman asks, "Tell us!"

I don't want to open my mouth. The swinging royal couples are the only thing I *can* see. I'm surprised they can't see it. It's obvious. I try to be as tactful as possible.

"I see...two couples..." I say cautiously, "But they're with different partners…"

I point to the cards. "See?"

Both of them look down. By the look on their faces, I can tell that the couples are now visible to them. They're not smiling anymore. It's like I've caught both of them in a lie. The Tarot has the ability to do this; slice through the bullshit and reveal the hidden truth if and when the recipient is ready to hear it. It cuts both ways...like a double-edged sword. It's an awkward situation. Everyone, myself included, wants this to be over.

At the end of the evening, I vow never to read on Halloween night again, and I realize that if I have a gift for anything, it's the ability to get myself into uncomfortable situations.

Miami
Nov 25, 1999

I wake up early, itching to consult the Tarot to see if it can prepare me for the day. The deck obviously made it into my carry-on. I pull a card: The Sun. I'm relieved. The Sun is one of the most favorable cards in the Tarot. It is the Destiny of The Supernatural East. I'm even more excited for the sun-filled day ahead.

I'm standing at the designated meeting spot at the top of Lennox Avenue and Lincoln Road. I've arrived a few minutes early and am waiting anxiously, periodically looking up at the clock tower. Crystal Ball is late. A part of me is worried that he may not even show up at all. This is Miami, after all. As I watch the cars drive by, I realize that I don't even know who or what I am looking for.

A black SUV with tinted windows pulls up beside me. The passenger side window lowers to reveal an animated man waving at me from the driver's seat. I climb into the vehicle and introduce myself. Cristobal is nothing like I'd imagined. He's more of a compact, bouncing rubber ball than a crystal one. He's very charismatic and talks with his hands as he drives. They're waving all over the place and, thankfully, make contact with the steering wheel every so often as we shoot across the Venetian Causeway. His cell phone is ringing off the hook. He tells me he has to take the calls. I cannot avoid eavesdropping on his conversations as I am sitting right beside him. They're intense and heated and in Spanish. He sounds like a busy professional. I suddenly feel incredibly inadequate.

Psychic Fair Not Fair
Toronto
1997

Eagle Eye organizes small psychic fairs in rural towns across Southern Ontario. A dozen psychics participated in this event. He asks me if I want to be a part of the team.

I am the newest member of this psychic task force and, by comparison, appear to be the weakest link. Many of these psychics are career professionals. They all have promotional material that documents their extensive experience. People flock to their stations to book a reading. These seers have wait lists stretching out into the end of the day, and because human beings, in general, want what other people want, even more people gather around them. I'm out of my league.

This is not a five-dollar question scenario. When I want to set my price at $20, the other psychics pounce on me, swinging their big psychic dicks around. They tell me that I cannot undercut them. They are charging $60 and I have to charge what they're charging.

I sit at my station, decorated with the Egyptian tapestry that would become my bed in a few short years. I am situated between a couple of winged horse sculptures I've set up on the table, shuffling and re-shuffling my Tarot deck all day. I don't have any takers. I'm bored. I'm wasting my time. I resent the other psychics. For something labeled as a Fair, this is anything but.

People don't even stop by my booth on the first day. They stand at a distance, afraid to approach me. I know they're judging me and my abilities. I am by far the youngest reader in this group. What's worse is my booth is beside La Contessa. I have to sit there all day and listen to her tell five different clients; it's literally the exact same thing.

"Oh yes, change is coming. You're going to travel. You're going to meet someone." she exclaims.

I don't want to judge her. I know she's clairaudient. It's possible she's just hearing the same thing over and over again?

I know I am.

Late in the day, a young woman approaches me, and I am assuming it is because I am the only person available. It's not a particularly earth-shattering reading. I read what I see and hope it means something to her because it means absolutely nothing to me.

The more I read in these settings, I realize that people who seek out spiritual guidance are generally troubled, and if the pain is great enough, they are willing to pay money for the possibility of any kind of a solution. I feel the heavy weight of this. This isn't a party trick anymore. It appears my gift of giving direction on a film set has transformed. Only now I'm offering direction to strangers on how to maneuver themselves out of life situations instead. I feel like a therapist...a sponge absorbing people's sadness, and a part of me wants to get hosed down. I remember La Contessa's words to me the first time I met her.

"Oh, yes. I have to wash my hands after each client. I just wash away their dreary lives with soap and water...and they're gone, down the drain."

I am sharing a room with La Contessa this weekend. We are getting ready for bed when she asks me if I would read her. Because I've hardly read anyone all day long, I am happy to do it. Part of me wants to sit across from her, look her in the eye, and say, "Change is coming. You're going to travel. You're going to meet someone," But I don't. I hand her the deck and tell her to shuffle.

La Contessa is sitting upright with perfect posture, her hair in a tight bun. I look up at her periodically as I'm moving through the spread and the great bird seems to shrink before me. By the end of the reading, her hair has unraveled and she's sunken into her chair with her legs curled up around her. She's pulled a blanket over her body, and this makes it look like she's wrapped in a cocoon. With the covering around her, all I can see are two frightened eyes peering out at me. She's become a shrouded owl. I ask if she's OK.

"Yes…oh yes," she whispers, but I don't even recognize her voice.

The next day is more of the same. More shuffling. More waiting. More nothing. At one point, a woman in a fur coat walks into the room. She's older, yet there's a wistful vulnerability about her. You can tell she was a real stunner in her earlier days.

She clutches her coat at her throat and heads directly for me.

"I was told to come see you," she says.

This makes me sit upright from the slouched position in my chair.

As she sits down across from me, I am assuming the woman from yesterday has told her who I am, for that's never happened before.

I am forever amazed at the power of word of mouth, and for some reason, this makes the whole trip worthwhile.

Miami
Nov 25, 1999

Crystal Ball drives us to a restaurant in Miami called Soyka. It's the latest venture from the man who created News Café on Ocean Drive and The Van Dyke on Lincoln Rd. I have never been to the Mainland. All I really know is what locals call 'The Beach', SoBe...my safe little square in the world, the area between Ocean and Alton, Lincoln and 12th.

The tables at Soyka are set with crisp white tablecloths. Elegant wine glasses sprout up from the top surfaces like crystal flowers. It's an airy space with huge windows and lots of light. It has been an eternity since I've eaten in a place like this, let alone for a business lunch. I am thrilled that Crystal Ball will be picking up the tab. I dare not even reach for my wallet to pretend to make a diplomatic gesture to pay for fear he will call my bluff.

None of my credit cards work anymore. I have $8 in my pocket, ten dollars less than any of the appetizers priced on the menu.

Crystal Ball is an art director who services a lot of commercial productions that shoot in Miami. I am hoping he has not invited me to lunch under the impression that I have a project for him. I feel like a fraud.

Perhaps that clown was right all along?

Our appetizers are served, but I've lost my appetite. I confess to Crystal Ball that I am looking for work and do not have any upcoming projects. I tell him I don't even have representation. I say I'm 'between agents' and that I'll do anything. I think of Ricardo as I say this and his self-imposed demotion from Chilean director to Miami grip.

I'm not quite sure I have it in me to make such a drastic change.

I have nothing against grips; they are an invaluable and integral element of any film shoot, but I don't think I would be a very good one.

Crystal Ball, it turns out, is a dreamer, and when our entrees arrive, we talk about the films we would make if we both had limitless resources.

To my surprise, both our ideas for our passion projects involve doppelgängers, look-a-likes who switch places, only to find out that life isn't that much different on the other side.

Crystal Ball glances to his left, "Oh My God!" he exclaims, "I don't believe it."

I glance over in the direction he is looking, half expecting to see our doppelgängers or at least a pair of twins.

Instead, I see two men in their mid-thirties being seated at a table ten feet away from us. They look normal enough and are smiling and talking with one another.

Crystal Ball leans forward.

"See those two guys?" He whispers.

"Yes," I answer back, intentionally not looking at the pair to avoid bringing unwanted attention our way.

"This is the third time I've seen them this week!" He confesses, "Each time, it's in a different part of the city, a different restaurant, and a different time of day! I'm minding my own business when the next thing I know, these two men are next to me. It's weird, huh?"

My eyes light up. I love synchronicity! I absolutely love it! Coincidences and synchronicity are two of my favorite things! It's possible I love them more than drugs and sex. These kinds of incidents are proof to me that something larger is at play. That there is a grander plan. Life is indeed a magical experience that cannot be explained.

"You should go talk to them," I say. Crystal Ball laughs nervously.

"They probably have a message for you," I stress. Crystal Ball laughs again.

For the next few minutes, the more I try to persuade Crystal Ball to go over and talk to the two men, the more he digs in his heels. You'd think I was asking him to walk over hot coals to pet a nest of rabid cobras. He's not budging.

I'm furious. Yesterday I imagined this man as an enlightened sage, but it appears Crystal Ball can't see a damn thing! I don't want to get too judgmental, though; he is buying me lunch, after all.

Why won't he go talk to them?

What message do they have for Crystal Ball? What is the Universe trying to tell him?

My curiosity is burning.

Then, right on cue, his phone rings. "I have to take this call," he says. And there it is...

A pause.

This gives me a moment to reflect on the situation at hand. I am looking at Crystal Ball while he's facing me, speaking directly into his phone, but I can't hear a thing he's saying. He's muted, for my thoughts are far too loud. It occurs to me that this man has a job, a phone, a car and enough money to take a stranger to lunch in an overpriced restaurant. He has a life. Crystal Ball is not going to get up and talk to the two men because he doesn't have to.

As I stare at him intently, deep in conversation with his arms flailing around, he reminds me of myself... a busier, shorter, more animated, Latin former version of myself. I look down at the ring on my finger. It's at that moment when I have an epiphany. It's like a heavy stick has been pounding on my brain from a variety of different angles and has finally burst it open like an overstuffed piñata.

I'm here! I'm a part of this equation, too!

My heart starts to race.

Could it be possible that Crystal Ball has been running into these guys all week long because they have a message for *me?*

I am the one at the end of my rope. I am the one with $8 in my pocket.

Maybe *I* need to talk to these strangers.

Then I see it all too clearly! The Crystal Ball *is* working its magic...but never how I imagined it would! These men are the key to my future. I'm sure of it. It's like I've been driving on an empty tank down a dark, deserted road for an eternity, and in the distance, a huge glowing sign surrounded by flickering bulbs, forming the shape of a directional arrow, reads 'THIS WAY'. I look at my lunch companion, this stranger called Crystal Ball, who I've only just met. He's just ended his phone conversation. It's crystal clear what I need to do next.

"Well, if you don't want to go over to speak with them…" I announce, patting each corner of my mouth with a white cloth napkin, "then I will."

Crystal Ball stares at me with a mixture of wonder and disbelief.

I stand up and walk towards the two men. I stride confidently between the negative space that separates our tables. I am sure I can hear the sound of invisible walls crashing at my feet.

The White Party Toronto
January 24, 1998

A thin white veil is all that separates me from the rest of the club. The venue is The Masonic Temple, a former place of worship built in 1917 that's been converted into an event space. Tonight, it's the site for a different kind of worship: The White Party, a drug-induced circuit event that doesn't have the most politically correct name. Under normal circumstances, I would be face-deep in white powder, in the thick of it all, but tonight, that's not the case. I am giving Tarot readings. This is another one of Eagle Eye's cast-off gigs.

I am situated in a hallway between two of the bars on the second floor. As I am setting up, one of the bartenders is stocking his bar with cases of alcohol and keeps passing back and forth through my sacred space. I'm a little irked, but he's handsome with short blonde hair, one of those incredibly attractive people blessed with otherworldly beauty. We nod at each other as he passes by, his muscled arms wrapped around another case.

The doors are not scheduled to open for another half hour. I decide to take a moment to center myself. I take out a silk cloth from my leather bag and lay it flat on the surface of the table. I shuffle the deck. The cards are familiar and worn, as I've been reading for a few years now. I close my eyes to collect my thoughts. I take deep breaths and mentally prepare myself for the evening to come. I am hoping my spirit guides will work through me. I pray that I do not attract any clowns.

When I open my eyes, the bartender is in the seat across from me. He's even more stunning up close. I'm a little intimidated.

"What's going on here?" He asks.

"I'm reading tonight," I reply.

"Go on then," He says, nodding his head.

This was very presumptuous of him. I didn't do readings for free anymore. A part of me resents him, along with all the other attractive people in the world, assuming they can get things for free because of their looks. I'm about to tell him 'No' or at least negotiate free drinks in return, but something tells me to just do it. It is the beginning of the night. I see it as a sacrificial act of goodwill, a loss leader, an offering to the Tarot gods.

I hand him the cards, tell him to shuffle them, and then I lay out a spread. The first card to appear is the Queen of Cups, crossed by the Three of Swords, then Justice in the reverse position, followed by the Five of Cups.

I attempt to decipher the spread. Court cards are people. The Queen of Cups is a woman with blonde hair and blue eyes… like him, and Cups represent Love.

The Queen is most likely his girlfriend, I think to myself.

This card is crossed by The Three of Swords. The image on the card is a heart impaled by three swords: kind of self-explanatory…his heart is broken…he's split up with his girlfriend. The third card: Justice in the reverse position: Basically, 'Injustice'… something happened, and it was not fair.

My mind tells me his girlfriend cheated on him.

The fourth card: The Five of Cups. The image on this card is of a man in a black cloak, consumed with grief, and five discarded gold cups on the ground at his feet. I know what this card means. It is pretty self-explanatory, too: Extreme sorrow and loss of Love…but I'm perplexed as to why the Five of Cups has appeared when the Three of Swords is basically the same thing. I'm confused, but I start to talk without really thinking.

"I see a woman with blonde hair and blue eyes...like you..." I say, "Something happened that wasn't fair...your heart is broken...Did your girlfriend cheat on you?" I ask.

He stares at me for a moment.

"No, but you described my mother. She had blonde hair and blue eyes like me," he says, devoid of any emotion, "She died in a car accident a month ago." I'm hit with a truck.

I don't know what to say…I can't even make eye contact with him anymore. All I am able to do is look down at the spread. It's all there. Why couldn't I see it before? That's why *both* cards pertaining to inconsolable loss have appeared.

It is all I can see now. Everything is clear. How could I have been so insensitive? I know better than to add my own bias to a reading. I feel shallow and inept...for only being able to see his surface beauty...and for assuming good-looking people didn't suffer heartache...tragedy and loss have no boundaries. No one is safe from the pain of life. I muster through the rest of the reading. Afterward, he stands up, gives me a hug and thanks me.

I look at the spread again. I'm in awe at how powerful the cards can be. It is a testament to the fact that there are strong unseen forces working in the Tarot...as in life itself.

Miami
Nov 25, 1999

I come to a dead stop in front of the two men at Soyka. They pause their conversation and glance at me as if I'm their waiter. "Hello," I blurt out. The two men nod.

I immediately feel incredibly stupid. In an instant, my confidence has evaporated like a drop of water in the Sun. I stumble through Crystal Ball's story, but I realize I don't even have any of the specific details. I point to Crystal Ball, still seated at the table ten feet away. He waves at them from a distance, on yet another call, with his phone pressed up to his ear.

"Oh yes!" They exclaim.

They recognize him. I'm relieved. They appear to appreciate the coincidence and we continue talking. The men seated at the table are two of the friendliest people one would ever want to meet. Their names are Frank and Mark. Frank's Italian and originally from Buffalo. He is a hair and make-up artist with a big, flashy smile and an even bigger personality. He reminds me of old-school Dean Martin Hollywood glamor. Frank's been living in Miami for years.

"From the beginning," he declares, "When Drag Queens ruled the place! They would travel around in packs in the daytime! Can you believe it?"

Mark is a designer. He's quieter, more reserved, Jewish from New York, with a dry sly sense of humor.

"Daylight's not the most flattering lighting for a Drag Queen," he says, and they both burst out laughing.

The two of them are comedy duo worthy, and their energy is infectious. I've only just met them, but I feel like I've known them forever. We're lifelong friends who've lost touch but have met by chance at the market and are catching up on years of missed stories. We've been talking for a while until I realize Crystal Ball is standing next to me. He's brought into the fold of our conversation, and the four of us continue to talk. As I am standing there, my mind is racing…there must be a deeper reason for this coincidence. There has to be more. I am sure of it. Will we all be working on some fabulous project together? Hopefully, it will be one in which I will be a director and not a grip.

Their food arrives. I realize I have crashed their lunch and apologize for the intrusion, but they don't seem to mind.

Mark asked if either of us had any plans for Thanksgiving the day after tomorrow. Crystal Ball has three engagements.

Of course, he does.

Mark shifts his gaze to me.

"I'm Canadian," I say flatly as if this somehow lessens the fact that I do not have an invitation anywhere. "I don't have any plans," I confess.

"A friend of ours is having a party. You're more than welcome to join us," Mark says, "No one should spend Thanksgiving alone."

"That would be great," I respond.

Secretly, I am relieved. I will be able to eat on Thursday!

CHAPTER 8
THE GIVING

Babbo
Toronto
1975

We call my father 'Babbo', it is the Italian equivalent of 'Daddy'. Babbo plays the piano…and he knows how to play people, too. He also sings. There are countless photographs of him at parties, red-faced and sweaty, belting out Italian folk songs and opera classics from his Pavarotti-esque vocal cords. He was the life of the party, surrounded by hordes of people, drinking homemade red wine out of little Italian glasses. Babbo leveraged his powerful voice whenever he was displeased in any situation, public or private, commanding his windpipe like an angry fog horn. This was a negotiation tactic, and it always worked. In any number of retail outlets, his cringe-worthy vocal performances would continue ad nauseam until an exasperated salesperson had to summon a nervous manager to deal with the crisis. Babbo inevitably demanded to speak with the top person in any organization. It was only then that he was certain that he was dealing with his equal. He relished watching people squirm. I could see it in his eyes. I was embarrassed for him…and for me.

Babbo is the equivalent of an Italian 'Karen'. I feared that one day, his antics would culminate with my entire family being escorted out of the mall by security, but that never happened. Babbo always got his way. I can still remember his face gloating. He knew an exasperated manager would give him whatever he wanted just to get him the hell out of their shop. I was surprised he treated sales staff in this manner, considering he was a salesman himself. Babbo was always selling something; it didn't matter what: English lessons to Italian immigrants fresh off the boat or silver and gold trinkets in a jewelry store.

Later, he set his sights on real estate because bigger ticket items suited his larger-than-life personality. Strange, though, for someone who sold houses, I don't really remember him being home that much. He was always out with clients, showing properties at all hours of the night.

Weekends too. Sometimes, he did come home. I would hear the familiar sound of his car: the steady hum of an Oldsmobile Cutlass Supreme driving up the driveway. The engine would turn off. The car door would open and close. Babbo was home. I was terrified.

American Thanksgiving
South Beach
November 25, 1999

Mark is already at the corner of Lincoln Rd. and Lennox Ave. when I arrive.

He reaches over from the driver's seat to swing open the passenger door. We breeze over the Venetian Causeway, up Biscayne, and then turn onto a side street. I'm on the Mainland again. My little eight-block surface area has really started to expand. We park and enter a sleek, modern building. The building is a lot higher than the Lopotomy Apartments, higher end, too. We pass a concierge and whisk up an elevator. The door swings open onto a large, beautifully furnished condo with artwork on every wall.

Floor-to-ceiling glass windows offer a stunning view of the bay. White boats are scattered across the blue water behind an enormous white dining room table overflowing with food. I almost want to cry. I have not been eating lately...then again, I haven't really eaten in years.

The room is packed with people. I usually feel a twinge of anxiety when entering a party, especially when there are a lot of strangers I don't know or a lot of screen doors, for that matter, but for some reason, that feeling is not there.

Frank is in drag as his alter-ego, Franka. Franka is even more entertaining than Frank is if that's possible. She's wearing a long blonde wig and silver sequenced gown with a white faux fur fox wrap draped around her bare shoulders. She's at the baby grand piano belting out a show tune. When she's done, Franka gets up and does an impeccable Cher impersonation by flipping her hair back and licking her lips. She turns around, looks over her shoulder, and winks at the crowd. Everybody cheers. Franka is the life of the party, and she knows it. She struts over to us.

"You made it!" she says while giving me two air kisses.

The three of us sit on the terrace, eating and drinking sparkling water, looking out onto the Bay. The conversation is as effortless as the sailboats gliding on the water. I try to be entertaining...a more interesting version of myself. I talk about my life as a director in advertising. I tell them The Ostrich story. I share a few anecdotes about reading Tarot cards and my life on the club circuit. When they ask a few probing questions, I tell them the truth about my living arrangement at the Lopotomy...that my credit cards are maxed out...and that I don't even have a cell phone anymore.

Franka motions to the seagulls flying over the bay, "The birds don't have checking accounts," she exclaims, "You're going to be just fine. The Universe takes care of everybody."

Franka launches off into a spirited monologue about a segment she did for a local news entertainment program on make-up trends.

"Marci Consuela at Channel Seven really is a piece of work..." Franka starts off, "Before we're about to shoot, she comes up to me and says, "Listen, Franka. This is about make-up trends. I'm looking for short sound bites about make-up. Capish? If you start talking about the Universe again, I'm turning the camera off." Franka drops her jaw with expert comic timing.

We all burst out laughing.

"I like your ring. Can I see it?" Franka asks.

I slip the ring off of my finger and hand it to her. I tell them the incredible story of how it came into my possession.

"That's amazing," Mark says.

Franka inspects the object and announces, "This is a David Yurman. He sells his jewelry at Neiman Marcus. Look here. It's engraved." she says as she hands the ring back to me, "This is an expensive ring."

I take the ring back and look at it. I never noticed the engraving. Mark tells me that after dinner, some of the people at the party will be going to a meeting. He asks me if I want to come. This sounds a little suspicious. I am a little apprehensive.

"A lot of us here don't drink," Mark says, "That's what the meeting is about. The meeting is about 'not drinking'."

I don't answer right away. Part of me thinks this is some kind of a scam, a pyramid scheme.

"I'm going," Franka chimes in.

"From what you've told us, it sounds like you're hitting rock bottom," Mark says, "The meeting will help. You're welcome to come if you want."

A gathering of people talking about not drinking is definitely not my kind of scene. I may have been partying a bit too much with coke, crystal, E, GHB, K, MDMA, and magic mushrooms the last few years, but drinking was the least of my problems. I'd have an occasional Bloody Caesar, Bloody Seizures, we'd call them, but that was it.

Mark and Franka look at me with anticipation, waiting for my response.

Later that night, I'm quiet as Mark drives me back across the causeway. The bay is as dark as night. The meeting was dreadful. I was bored. It was not as entertaining as Franka and Mark, or Frank and Mark either, for that matter. Once I walked into the room, part of me just checked out. Everyone in attendance looked like a retiree, retired from work and life, retired from caring too...and not one ounce of fashion sense between the lot of them. There was no way in hot Miami hell I belonged to this group.

Just before he drops me off, Mark tells me that there is another meeting tomorrow.

For the love of God. Please no. I think to myself.

"It'll be better," Mark says, "I promise...You'll like it. Tomorrow is Birthday Night. I'll pick you up at seven. We can grab a bite beforehand if you want."

Mark lives on the mainland. I am not sure why he is taking the time to drive all the way back and forth over the causeway to chauffeur me to these bland meetings, but I don't have anything else planned tomorrow night...or any other day for that matter, so I agree.

Hockey Night In Canada
Toronto
Saturday, December 6, 1975

Saturday night is Hockey Night in Canada. Babbo is perched on the edge of his chair watching the game, wearing a white wife-beater undershirt and holding a stubby beer bottle. He is devouring the game and what is inside the bottle, too. I sit on the floor beside him and just watch. His face is beet red, and a nervous tick works its way up and down an enormous thick vein pulsing in his neck. The thing almost has a life of its own. It causes Babbo to spontaneously cackle uncontrollably. He is sweating, too, and his eyes bulge out. They dart back and forth, anxiously following the puck. He is panting like a salivating dog mesmerized by a bird fluttering around in a tree.

Babbo's stocky body is twisting and contorting in direct correlation with what is happening on the screen.

I am amazed that even though he is right beside me, he is not in the room; he is on the television set... in the game, on the ice. I am riveted. It is far more interesting to watch him than what's happening on TV. That is when I noticed his big arm. It is fat and fleshy with an ugly, oblong, disfigured immunization scar that stretches across his bicep just below his shoulder. I have seen this mark before but had never really examined it close up. The skin looks like it has been chewed. I move in closer and tap it a couple of times. Babbo doesn't even know that I am there. It is like I am invisible. I hit the mark again, this time harder. I hear a nervous cackle, but it is not because of me. The puck narrowly misses the net and ricochets off of the boards. It is obvious that this intoxicated, overweight, armchair athlete doesn't even know I exist.

I am not sure what prompted me to do what I did next, but at the time, I thought it was a good idea. I take a deep breath and open my mouth as wide as I can. Like a pit bull going in for the kill, I aim for the scar, clamping down as hard as I can. At first, Babbo doesn't even flinch. I dig in deeper, and that is when it is like I have struck oil.

Babbo is not on the ice anymore. He is most definitely in the room, yelling with all the force of his Roman gladiatorial ancestors. I have heard this kind of screaming before, but this time, he is not getting 50% off a Harry Rosen suit. He struggles to get up out of his chair. As he rises to his feet, I am lifted with him like a fish on a hook, my jaw permanently attached to his arm.

He desperately tries to shake me off to no avail. I lock my grip. I am not going anywhere. I am sure I can feel my incisors sinking through his leathery, salty skin. I do not know why I am doing this, only that it feels good. I can hear the pain I am inflicting on him. His scathing screams are musical. They remind me of the pathos at the end of a tragic opera. It is as if I am playing him like an instrument, pushing the boundaries of his range as a tenor. His voice shoots up an octave.

My mother rushes in from the kitchen, holding a dish towel. She is screaming, too. We live in an Italian household, so screaming, especially on a Saturday night, was not out of the ordinary, but tonight's performance was particularly inspiring. I am swinging around the room, my body flailing like one of those blow-up inflatables in front of a car dealership. Babbo strikes me with his free hand, desperately trying to break the father-son bond between us, but that was broken years ago. I am pleased my clenched jaws have not failed me. My mother attempts to wedge herself between us.

The blows coming from Babbo are getting progressively harder. I invariably reach a tipping point where the pain I am receiving is greater than the pain I am inflicting. I have no other option. I have to let go.

Later in my life, I would learn that 'letting go' would be an admirable trait that I would practice to the best of my ability...but in this instance, it was not a good idea.

As I fall, I can see the imprint of my teeth on his skin, framing the scar like a priceless work of art. Babbo is in an insane state of rage. I have never seen him like this. Even though my mother partially protects me, she cannot provide adequate defense. I am a hockey puck between two opposing teams, inundated with slap shots. We slide down the hallway as a brawling group. I am maneuvered and handled. I ricochet off the wall and am hit through a doorway. The action is a blur of adrenaline and energy. It is far more exciting than any hockey game on TV. I don't know what is happening anymore; I only know that Babbo is scoring a lot of points.

The door slams shut. Mamma and I are on one side of it, and Babbo is on the other. He is beyond frantic and pounds on the barrier with his fist. Each strike causes the door to pulse like a beating heart. It looks like it may burst free from its hinges at any moment. I look at it in fear. Babbo warns me that if I know what is good for me, I will stay out of his sight for the rest of the night.

I have crossed a line. I am in a penalty box. I am numb. I am bleeding. My mother holds a red-soaked dishcloth up to my nose. She asks me what on earth compelled me to do this. I have no idea. Even though I am holding my head back and facing the ceiling, out of the corner of my eye, I can see the invitations.

They are for my birthday party. Earlier in the evening, the envelopes were neatly stacked on my bedroom side table, ready to be distributed Monday morning. Now, they are everywhere, ripped and scattered on the blood-spattered floor.

Later that night, I could hear my parents talking. I slip out of my bed and tip-toe to the door to listen through it. The voices are muffled, but I am sure I hear my mother say that I want attention, even though I am sure that is the last thing I want.

I avoid eye contact with Babbo for several weeks, and he does not allow me to sit beside him when he is watching hockey anymore.

**Birthday Night
South Beach
November 28, 1999**

Mark picks me up at the corner. He's right on time again. I admire his punctuality. He asks me if I want to grab a bite before the meeting. When I don't respond, Mark senses my hesitation and offers to pay. I nod my head sheepishly. I am embarrassed. Again, I'm grateful that I will be able to eat today.

We go to a vegetarian restaurant on the mainland, and a server approaches us.

"The specials are listed on the chalkboard," he announces. The soup of the day is lentil soup.

**Lentil soup
Toronto
1977**

Babbo sits at the head of the dining room table with my mother to his left. On his right, wrapped around the table counterclockwise, descending both in age and favor were my three sisters: Gabriella, Ida, Virginia, and finally, me. I'm beside my mother. The table was the gathering place for the family. The main venue for high Italian drama…and for me, trauma.

The sturdy piece of furniture looked innocent enough: solid brown wood with decorative legs and a thick top surface that was split in two so it could be pulled apart and elongated by a couple of leaflets tucked underneath. The table was surrounded by six high-back matching chairs upholstered in brown and beige plaid.

One night, just before we are about to eat, Babbo announces that he will be making some adjustments to the seating arrangements. We are told this impromptu change will be permanent. My three sisters get to stay where they are, but my mother and I are told to switch places. I really do not want to move from where I am seated. Babbo insists. This new arrangement has me positioned beside him, on his left-hand side. There is dead silence at the table. Nothing good can come of this. I am sure of it. We are all sure of it.

To make matters worse, my mother turns to face me. She glances at Babbo as she speaks. Her voice sounds defeated. She tells me she cannot prepare 'my meal' anymore.

"You will have to eat what the rest of the family is eating," she says.

I whip my head around the table.

What's going on? I can't possibly eat what the rest of the family is eating. I can only eat one thing: breaded veal cutlet with mashed potatoes. I've eaten this for as long as I can remember. It's what I eat. It's the only thing I can eat.

Babbo is grinning at me like a smiling wolf.

The evening continues to unfold in the most horrific way. I am sure lentils are perfectly harmless little seeds, but the sight of them clustered together in the bowl placed in front of me ushers in dread as dark as the broth they're soaking in. Lentil soup. I want to gag.

Everyone around the table starts to eat. I move my spoon around, shifting the slop back and forth. I can't eat this. I can barely stand the smell. Babbo is devouring the soup like a ravenous beast. I glance at him out of the corner of my eye. His head and face are practically in the bowl. He's fully engrossed in this endeavor, using both hands, a spoon in one maneuvered like a shovel and bread in the other, soaking up the broth like a sponge. Every last drop of the slopping mess is shoved into his mouth. It's a revolting sight. The slurping sounds only serve to disgust me further.

When Babbo has finished, he sits back and wipes his mouth. He looks at me. His gaze shifts to my bowl. A scowl appears on his face. I can tell he is as disgusted with me as I am with him. We glare at each other.

He commands me to eat. I dip the spoon in the bowl and shift it around. I gather up a couple of lentils in the curve of the spoon. I'm stalling. I lift the utensil up to my face as slowly as possible. For my life, I cannot stomach putting the spoon into my mouth. I just can't do it.

Babbo's voice gets more forceful. He orders me to eat a second time. I don't move. He looks at me with contempt. Then, out of nowhere, he strikes me in the face with the back of his left hand.

Hard.

The slap surprises me. He really wants me to eat these lentils. I look down at the bowl. The family is silent. No one is saying anything. Part of me hopes that if I just look down and ignore him, he will go away... but he doesn't. He strikes again, this time with the open palm of his right hand. I know he's trying to motivate me into action but it's not working. When I'm hit a third time, my face is in shock. I cannot move a muscle.

The rest of the family pleads with Babbo to stop, but we all know he is just getting started. He tells everyone to shut up. They do. The more he strikes me, the more I am frozen. I keep looking down. My eyes are fixed on the bowl. I notice a rustic Italian pattern on the dish. I've never noticed it before or looked at it this closely. Purple leaves twist around the circumference of the white bowl and frame the earthy lentils beautifully. Some of the seeds are dark brown, and some are light brown. They are all pretty much the same size.

Babbo hits me again. I'm transfixed by the lentils. My eyes start to fill up with tears. The bowl gets blurrier. The colors blend together. I am mesmerized by the sight of it. I am not sure why I am crying. It's not because of the pain. It is because I am overwhelmed by a profound sense of sadness. I do not know when the next blow is to come, but it doesn't even matter anymore. I am fascinated by how beautiful the blurry bowl looks. Nothing really hurts anymore. When Babbo strikes me on the side of my head, the blow muffles my hearing. Now, the screams from my mother and sisters are just a distant hum, far, far away.

When I am certain this will all be over soon, Babbo uses both of his hands to *make* me eat. I can feel one of his strong hands on the back of my head while the other one envelopes mine. The metal spoon pries through my lips, forcing my mouth to open. It feels like it is pushing its way down my throat. In an instant, I gag. I really can't control it. It's an involuntary physical reaction.

The lentils spew out of my mouth like an explosion and land all over the table. My mother stands up. It's finally over. I am exiled from the table. Babbo delivers a parting kick as I walk away and tells me I will not be eating anything tonight. I am banished to my room.

Later, when Babbo is out for the evening 'selling real estate', my mother appears with a peace offering. She lays a plate of mashed potatoes and breaded veal cutlet on my side table. I look at her cautiously. She looks at me cautiously, too. It is like we have formed an alliance against a common enemy and are doing something highly illegal. She cuts the meat into smaller portions and squeezes lemon over it.

This dinnertime fiasco continues for several more years until, one day, when I am older, I get the courage to switch places with my mother again. I just do it. No one says anything. My mother is situated in between Babbo and me, like a buffer. She is a mother-buffer. She always has been. I would not have been able to survive my childhood without her.

Miami Beach
November 28, 1999
6:45 p.m.

"You really should try the lentil soup," the server says cheerfully, "It's to die for."

"I'll pass," I answer back dryly.

Mark and I are back in the car. We drive a few blocks and stop at a red light. A group of Colombian kids are crossing the street in front of us. They toss a soccer ball back and forth. One of them shows off his athletic skills, bouncing the ball off of one knee, then the other, and finally butting it with his head.

The House Two Doors Down
Toronto
Summer 1976

The Sun has set, but it is still light outside. I am playing soccer with the boys who live across the street. They are a couple of years older than me, but for some reason, they have let me into their group. The back lot of their house leads down a hill into a ravine by the train tracks. That is where we usually hang out, throwing rocks and smoking cigarettes.

We play seasonal sports on the street between our homes. Road hockey in the winter, football in the fall, baseball in the spring, and soccer in the summer. We yell 'car' if an approaching vehicle interrupts our game.

Everette, the oldest boy, kicks the ball in my direction. I am not a very good player; it shoots past me and rolls toward the house two doors down. The place has been abandoned for a couple of months. Contractors have been renovating the property and fixing it up. An oversized rotary dial 'For Sale' sign with Babbo's name on it is staked into the front lawn. The ball rolls into a large mound of garbage piled on the sidewalk: large black bags, a half dozen paint cans, and cut-off tree branches. It is as if the ball has led me to a treasure trove, and I ignore it while I inspect the findings.

I wrestle a cut branch from the bundle. My heart is beating with excitement as I pry open the lid of a paint can. I call the other boys over. They gather around. We peer into the can. It is half full of thick gray paint.

It doesn't take a rocket scientist to look at the cut branches and realize they look like giant brushes. It appears the Universe has conveniently laid out everything for us on a silver platter. A smile curls across my face. I dip the leafy branch brush into the thick liquid. As the stick sinks into the gray ooze, an idea sinks into my mind. I pull the branch out and walk over to the house with the dripping stick. I flick it, and paint splatters over the veranda. The boys laugh. The other cans are furiously pried open.

Moments later, in a frenzied free-for-all, every last one of us is using our artistic abilities to their fullest potential. We run paint-soaked branches over the windows and doors.

I have never done anything like this before. For some reason, it is exhilarating...certainly more fun than playing soccer.

Something in my peripheral vision whisks by my ear. A can of paint sails by me like a comet in slow motion, a thick gray liquid tail trailing in the wind. Paint explodes over the exterior of the house. The empty can hit the ground with a heavy thud. We all turn to see Everett standing behind us, grinning from ear to ear. This act is single-handedly more effective than all of our branch work combined.

It is at that moment that we all know we've gone too far. The frenzied look in our eyes transforms into dread. We scatter in different directions like rats.

The rush of excitement stays with me all night. It is impossible to sleep. I keep thinking about how exhilarating it was to simultaneously create and destroy.

The next morning, everyone on the street is talking about what has happened to the house two doors down. In the daylight, the home looks defaced. People are out on their porches, coffee cups in hand.

They are shaking their heads. How can something like this happen on our safe little street? Who has done this? Why? Everyone is using a word that I've never heard before. I am hearing it repeatedly. There is something intriguing about this new word. There is a seductive ring to it. It is an interesting combination of consonants and vowels. I am so intrigued by this new word that I am compelled to look it up in the dictionary.

Alone in my room, I reach for a dictionary. I flip open the page to where words begin with the letter V.

Van Dal Ism.

Vandalism. When I discovered the word means to destroy property, my jaw hit the floor. I had no idea the carefree abandon we experienced the previous evening had been granted a designated word, but apparently, it had. At that moment, I became fully aware that this act was not the finest hour in my short life. In an attempt to re-frame the narrative, I tell myself that at least it expanded my vocabulary.

As I sit in my room filled with fear, guilt, and regret, a part of me is hoping this shameful moment will be over and forgotten. I was soon to learn that it would not be so. It would be one of the first events that would alter the trajectory of my life.

In the bathroom, I discover a glob of dried-up gray paint in my hair. I grab a pair of scissors and dispose of the evidence. I watch it whirl down the toilet. I am panicking. I check the rest of my clothing to make sure there isn't any other incriminating evidence. I find a large splotch of paint on the cuff of the sleeve of my jacket. I roll it up to hide the mark. Aside from that, there is nothing else that can link me to the house two doors down. I am sure of it.

That night at dinner, Babbo cannot stop talking about what happened. He is livid. He pounds the table with his fist. The tableware rattles. He announces that if he ever finds out who did this, he will beat the living daylights out of the delinquents. He tells us the police are working on finding the criminals. They will be caught and punished accordingly. I cut my breaded veal cutlet. I try to look normal as I chew.

The lie rolls

easily off my tongue,

sweet venom dew drops from a leaf.

A smooth pool of deception

Frees me from my reality

I bathe in it, I have no ground

My dagger slashes those nearby

like wicked arrows whistling through the wind.

They are all dead

My voice

My heart

My spirit

The next day, I am watching television when there is a knock on the door. I open it. Two uniformed giants stand in front of me. I have not seen men this tall in my entire life. They say hello, and I respond to them nervously. They want to ask me a few questions about the house two doors down. My heart starts to race.

They…want…to…talk…to…me! They want to come in.

"OK," I respond.

I turn and begin to walk towards the living room. The giants are behind me. My mind is racing, and with each step, I am frantically thinking about what I am going to say. When the giants sit across from me, my heart is beating so hard I am afraid that it will burst right out of my chest and onto the coffee table, splashing thick gray, guilt-ridden paint all over the room. As they talk, I glance back and forth between the two of them. I watch their lips move, and I start to think. I am thinking up a story. I have been caught off guard. I am unprepared. The back of my brain is telling me to play dumb. To tell them that I know nothing. My eyes shift back and forth between the two giants. I could open my mouth and tell them I have no idea what they are talking about. I could lie. It would be easy. They would go away, and I would get away with it. No one would ever have to know that it was I who vandalized the house two doors down.

There is something about the way the giants are looking at me. It is like they already know that I did it. They must have already questioned the boys across the street. What did they tell the giants? We didn't have time to corroborate our stories. The giants ask me if I know anything about what happened to the house two doors down. I am about to lie and tell them I know nothing. I am about to bend the truth like a metal fork, but as soon as I open my mouth, something incredible happens. I started to tell them exactly what happened! I tell them everything, and once I start, I can't stop. I am surprised at all of the words flying out of my mouth. It is like they have given me truth serum; full sentences are gushing out of me like a split pig.

As I confess, I start to cry… and again, something incredible happens. I have no control over it; it just happens…I am horrified at what I am doing, but once I start, I can't stop. I am off-script. I am improvising. I have no idea where this is going. As tears gush out of my eyes, my brain tells me to put a tiny little twist to the story. It is brilliant. It will absolve me of everything. And now, I do lie. Yes, I am going to do it. I can't stop.

"They…made…me…do…it," I gush between sobs.

That's it. They 'made me do it'.

I look at the giant policemen. I nod my head. I can't believe what I've just said. The tears have stopped.

There is an awkward silence.

Apparently, throwing all of my friends under the bus has put an abrupt end to the meeting. The giants just look at me, then at each other. They get up and leave. As the door closes behind them, dread rolls over me like a heavy fog.

Babbo will know! He will find out that it was me! I am the criminal who vandalized the house two doors down. The property he is trying to sell. I can see his fist hitting the dining room table and everything rattling on top of it. He will know that I was lying all along. I would surely be beaten beyond recognition. Part of me thinks he might even kill me. I want to run away. Yes, of course, that is the solution. I must run away as far from him as I can, but I know I have nowhere to go.

I have not known fear greater than this day when Babbo's Oldsmobile rolls up in the driveway. The sound of the engine turning off is like a death sentence. When Babbo walks in, he doesn't say anything. He walks past me, kisses my mother, and retreats into the bedroom. He ignores me. He's never done that before. I mean, he ignores me all the time, especially when he's watching the hockey game…but this…this is different.

Later that night, we are gathered around the dining room table, having dinner. I am seated in my designated seat when there is a knock on the door. Babbo rises to answer it. It is the boys from across the street. I can hear their voices. They want to know if I can come out to play.

Is it possible that everything is back to normal?

I hope so, but there is a trembling feeling in the pit of my stomach that does not go away. Babbo invites the boys into our home. I am not sure why he is doing this. He is behaving like Santa Claus on Christmas. Something isn't right. Babbo lines up the four boys in front of us and returns to his spot at the head of the table. I am confused. I am half expecting him to offer them dinner...but he does not do that. The entire family sits looking at the boys awkwardly, standing in front of the table.

Then, it happens.

Babbo explodes like an erupting volcano. He unleashes the beast onto this lineup of unsuspecting children. He shows them the monster that I thought only our family could see. He tells them to never speak to me again. He tells them that he will kill them if they even look in my direction. He pounds the table with his fist repeatedly. Everything on it shakes in fear. The boys do, too. They are beyond petrified. One of them has peed his pants. They bolt out of the house. I have never seen them run that fast.

The door slams behind them. I sit there, stunned. We eat dinner in silence.

From that moment on, those boys never speak to me again. And, by extension, I am an outcast by all the kids in the neighborhood. The boys across the street have now become my enemies. I am an immigrant Italian boy with a monster for a father.

Fortunately, we live in a corner house, and I can avoid running into them by hopping the back fence. That is the route I take when going to and from school. I know I am avoiding confrontation, but to be honest, it is easier for me. I have enough confrontations in my life, and I am only ten.

I watch from the window as they play street hockey in the winter, baseball in the spring, soccer in the summer, and football in the fall. I retreat into my room alone.

Solitary confinement is a pretty harsh punishment at any age, and for a young child, it can be unbearable. I lay on my bed, staring at the ceiling. As I sink into the mattress, my animosity toward my father sinks to new levels, deeper and colder than I ever thought possible. I am seething. The physical abuse was bad enough, but now he has added psychological warfare to his arsenal. I pledge my eternal detestation toward this man, this beast of a father.

As I ponder the whole situation regarding The House Two Doors Down, I realize that this event, coupled with my actions, has resulted in me amassing an array of enemies. Babbo and now the boys across the street.

Clearly, whatever I thought my plan was...it backfired.

As I sit in this prison cell of my own making, something extraordinary happens. Something floats to me like a gift parachuted from the heavens. I discover my imagination. It is a golden ticket, a magic key, a way to escape reality. I began to write stories and draw pictures because I didn't know what else to do. At school, the teacher tells me my stories are good. One of my stories is published in the local newspaper. My imagination becomes my lifeline, my survival tool. It was born from this traumatic event in my childhood, and I know it.

Just as I was about to enter high school, we moved out of the area to another house far away. My days spent jumping the back fence to avoid the boys across the street are behind me. This chapter is closed, but the experience, my stint in solitary, and the character inadequacies it created survive deep within my psyche. It rears its ugly head in social situations. I am different. I am an outsider. I am detached.

I look at the world as if separated by a thick sheet of glass, just like I watched the boys playing sports through the front window. I realize that this is why I am so comfortable looking through the lens of a camera. I am looking through glass. This clear barrier cures my vision impairment like a pair of glasses. It allows me to see...I am an observer. I am not a part of the action because this is what I am used to.

When I discover that the art of scrying, looking through glass, a crystal ball, or water, has been used for centuries to see into other dimensions, I am enchanted.

Was this connected to my ability to read the Tarot in some way?

The Toothless Tiger
Toronto
1985

Babbo comes home one day, and there is something different about him. His face has changed. So has his walk. He gathers everyone around the dining room table and tells us he is sick. We all pile into the Oldsmobile. The entire family is at the doctor's office. My father has prostate cancer. We are told that because they were too late in detecting it, the cancer has spread to his bones. There isn't much they can do for him now.

"The horse is out of the barn," the doctor announces.

There is a picture of Babbo taken when he was a younger man on the slopes of the Italian Alps. He stood in the center of the photograph, stripped naked to the waist, confidently taking a drag from a cigarette unfazed by the sub-zero temperature, surrounded by relatives bundled in layers of clothing who were clearly frozen to the core.

As I stare at Babbo, I realize the beast has finally met his match. Within a few months, he is reduced to a frail man. He tries to fight the cancer, but this opponent is far too strong. Babbo trembles. He cries as he struggles to make his way up a flight of stairs. He still glares at me, but he does not look like a rabid dog anymore. Now, he is an old, toothless tiger and spends most of his time in his armchair. It is the same chair that I bit him in years before, but now I don't have to open my mouth to inflict pain on him. All I have to do is turn my head and walk out the front door. I am 18 years old. Now, I am the one out at all hours of the night.

Babbo is in and out of the hospital. As the months pass by, he is in the hospital for longer periods of time. My mother stays with him overnight. The nurses have given her a small cot to sleep on so she can be there to help. The nurses are grateful for the extra assistance.

One day, my father goes into the hospital and never comes out. We are all home in the living room when we get the news. Friends and family drop by the house. It's packed. Everyone starts to reminisce about Babbo's larger-than-life personality, his powerful voice, and his spirit. They are turning him into a saint already, and he's only been gone a few hours. I watch the scene unfold in front of me...detached, through my pane of glass. Apparently, this pane of glass also shields me from pain because I feel nothing. To be honest, if anything, I am relieved. It is like the monster that terrorized me my entire life is finally gone.

All I can think of is the time my three sisters and I were trying to protect my mother from the beast. The four of us holding onto his limbs, using the weight of our bodies to try to stop him, was pointless. He was more powerful than all of us combined. He still managed to hit her. I couldn't share that story, so I didn't share anything at all.

At the funeral, I am a pallbearer. We carry the casket through the cemetery. It is a drizzling rainy day, and my shoes are trudging through the muck. I still feel nothing. The beast is dead. I am finally free.

Or so I thought.

As time moves on, the more I think I am free of Babbo, the more he has me in his grip. I have inherited 50 percent of his genes. I physically resemble him. His blood flows within me like thick gray paint.

Benevento, Italy
2002

I am on a whirlwind trip through Italy, visiting Rome, Venice, Florence, Milan, and Naples. I make a pit stop in Benevento to visit my father's family. I am immediately surrounded by an army of slow-moving relatives, elderly Italian zombies with their arms outstretched and tears in their eyes. Babbo's aging brothers and sisters circle me and touch my face…mesmerized.

"Vincenzo," they say.

It is as if my father has risen from the dead.

In a way, he had. He is still alive within me; I can feel him.

A young man stares out from photographs

He is my father, but I did not know him then

The resemblance is there, and I am here

I can see his youth disintegrate in pictures

Throughout the blanket of time

The image is aged, bent, and creased

His life complete

His face is hardened

but the anger in his hand is not yet there

My father

He is there, and he is here

He lives and breathes inside of me

My fear of him when I was young

Made me vow that he is not who I will become

The past is not the future

He is only where I'm from.

But as I age, my rage does fade

For I have learned

When I am dead

to him, I will return

Birthday Re-birth
Miami
November 28, 1999

Mark and I arrive a few minutes before the meeting is about to start. It's crowded because this is Birthday Night. There is only standing room at the back. We find a spot and stake our claim. I smile at Mark. I can't believe I am going to stand for an hour at one of these meetings. Mark was right; this meeting was entirely different than the night before.

It's only better due to the fact that it's comparatively fast-paced and there are more people involved, so my attention does not have time to wander. People march up to the front of the room and claim to have varying amounts of sobriety. Some have been sober for a year, three years, five years, sixteen years, and even twenty years.

I am certain all of these people are lying. How could this be possible? I stand in disbelief at the back of the room.

Liars!

The lights go out. A cake covered in candles is presented to the celebrants. Everyone starts to sing 'Happy Birthday', and I'm struck with a sense of nostalgia. I'm not sure why. I have memories of hearing this song at this time of the year. Why? I start to scan my memories. Then, out of the blue, I sense my father's presence.

Babbo.

He's here.

He is standing beside me. The hairs on the back of my neck stand on end.

This is not the first time I have experienced this phenomenon. I've felt his presence once before.

Everything Old Is New Again
Toronto
1997

I am up for a big directing job in the US through my American reps. The project is for the GM Pavilion at Epcot Center.

"Don't get too excited," my agent advises. "We're not going to get this job. Inside scoop says we are just a token fourth bid."

He dives into more detail. There are three people at the agency...a producer, an art director, and a copywriter. Each of them has a different favorite among the four directors bidding.

Again, he reiterates, "We are a distant fourth... but it would be good practice for you to meet with the creatives."

When I find out the GM brand is 'Oldsmobile' and the concept is about 'the limitless possibilities of the human imagination', a flood of memories washes over me.

Oldsmobile was my father's brand...The Cutlass Supreme. He owned two of them during his lifetime; the first one was dark forest green, the second tan brown.

I can still remember the sound of the vehicle as it drove up the driveway...and the feeling of fear that would engulf me when the ignition turned off. Memories of what happened with the house two doors down and how it led me to dive into the well of my imagination also bubble up to the surface from my subconscious.

This project appears to be connected to my childhood in some strange way.

I came up with a few ideas and had a conference call with the clients in Chicago. It isn't anything particularly special. I book another project in Toronto that falls on the exact same shoot dates. I couldn't do the GM job, even if I did get it. I get a call from my agent.

"You got the job!" he announces excitedly. "The clients love your ideas."

I am a little stunned.

"I thought we were a distant fourth?" I ask.

"We were. But for some reason, they couldn't all agree on anyone else. But...as it turned out, they could all agree on you," he says.

"Well, I've booked another job. I'm unavailable," I reply.

"The clients are willing to *move* the shoot dates... to accommodate your schedule," he says.

"Oh," is my only response.

As I hang up the phone, I am stunned. That's when I felt Babbo's presence beside me. He's gloating. He had a hand in orchestrating this imbroglio somehow. I am sure of it.

He is trying to help me...

Hands-On
Miami
November 28, 1999

I am certain I can feel Babbo's presence standing right beside me again, but I am not really sure why. I haven't thought of him since the Oldsmobile project. I am standing in this room full of strangers, listening to everyone singing 'Happy Birthday'. It is a spirited execution. The space is brimming with joy and emotion.

It is quite overwhelming. It is a strong, almost intoxicating sensation. Then, it hits me.

Today was Babbo's birthday.

Something starts to open up in my chest. I am feeling something. I am trying to decipher what it is. I take deep breaths. I am not sure what this feeling is, but then I can't deny it. It is love. I am feeling love. This is an emotion I have never felt in association with my father, so it is an overwhelming sensation. Babbo is here, trying to help me...again...to make amends for everything he had or hadn't done for me when he was alive. The song has stopped, and the celebrants have blown out the candles on the cake.

"Does anyone want to surrender?" a person at the front of the room announces, "Does anyone want to change their life?"

At that moment, I feel Babbo's hand on me…but this time, he is not hitting me with it. It is just a gentle touch on the small of my back…a little push. And because I am standing, I feel myself being propelled forward; my feet are moving…walking up towards the front of the room. Tears well up in my eyes. I don't know what I am doing. My body is moving of its own volition..

This was a course correction. It is another pivotal moment that altered the trajectory of my life.

I look down at my hands. I am holding a white poker chip. Apparently, I have been gambling with my life.

CHAPTER 9
MULCH ADO ABOUT SOMETHING

South Beach
December 12, 1999

For the next two weeks, Mark picks me up and takes me to meetings. He also drives me back home. I do not know why he is doing this. The meetings, as it turns out, are not that bad. They're entertaining. They make me laugh. They make me cry. They make me feel like a human being again. It's been fourteen days. Two weeks of going to meetings. Mark tells me it would help if I were to participate in my recovery, but I have no idea what that means.

I sit in the passenger seat and look out of the window as we drive across the Venetian Causeway. I call my family back home. It is good to hear their voices. They're pressuring me to come home for the holidays. They're worried. They will buy me a ticket. They tell me I can start again. They will help me. As they are speaking, I am looking at a palm tree swaying in the breeze.

The Ice Bath Cometh
Toronto
December 6, 1971

No one knows what is wrong with me. I've been sent to Sick Kids Hospital for an indefinite stay. Mamma has bought me a stuffed bunny because I am only five years old.

"This will protect you at night when I cannot be with you," she says as she hands me the toy.

The bunny is comforting at first, but unfortunately, it is of no use whatsoever when a nurse appears in the middle of the night, lifts me out of my warm bed, and plunges me into a tub of ice water.

Apparently, my temperature is off the charts, and this ice bath is the only way to bring it down. It is an unceremoniously rude awakening that happens nightly.

South Beach
December 12, 1999

"I am going to stick it out here a little bit longer," I say while continuing to look at the palm.

Toronto in December? I don't think so.

A Horror of Horrors
Toronto
December 12, 1971

I am still in the hospital for my birthday. My family brings a cake and balloons. I am told the little boy sharing the room with me can't eat anything sweet, or he will get sick, so the curtain between our beds is drawn.

This hospital is truly a horror of horrors. I think to myself.

I am not sure which of us has the greater cross to bear, but as I lick the chocolate frosting off my finger, I am sure it is him.

One day, the nurse wheels my bed into the hallway. I wave at the boy. My mother brings me a hotdog, and I am sent home. Apparently, my extended stint in this institution was because I am allergic to something called penicillin. They stopped giving it to me, and my temperature returned to normal. Problem solved. I am able to go home.

Miami Beach
December 18, 1999

I am sitting in a meeting when a woman says that she's allergic to alcohol; ingesting the liquid sets in motion a physical, mental, emotional, and psychological compulsion that eventually leads her to ruin.

I sit and listen to her. I am twenty-one days clean. Three full weeks without any substances, speedy and/or otherwise. My life has crawled to a pace so slow that it's unbearable. I want to run; I want to jump around. I want to have a million ideas coursing through my head and act on none of them. My financial situation is…how can I put this…bleak. Bleaker than bleak, if that is even possible.

I am surviving on cans of tuna and yogurt. I have an overdraft clause on my bank account and have been withdrawing money from it. My balance is well into the negative. This morning, when I inserted my bank card into the machine, it didn't come back out.

A notice appears on the screen indicating there are no funds available. The machine tells me to contact my bank immediately. I'm definitely not doing that. I stare blankly at the screen. I read and re-read the words over again.

They're on to me.

At the gym, I met a guy called Felix from Colombia. He starts a conversation with me while walking on a treadmill. I don't know why, but I like him immediately. He is a curious juxtaposition of extremes: a big hulking mass of a human being with the gentle nature of a flock of doves. It is quite the dichotomy, as if the audio and video do not match. He reminds me of my fair-skinned friend back home who speaks with a heavy Trinidadian accent. With this expressive Colombian, you think you're immersed in an over-the-top melodramatic Telenovela when you realize it's really a heartfelt French art film.

Even his name 'Felix' does not suit his physical appearance. I call him Pan instead because he reminds me of the mythological creature. Pan is an addiction nurse. For some reason beyond my comprehension, he insists on coming to meetings with me. As it turns out, there's a clubhouse on the beach just a few blocks away, so Mark doesn't have to drive back and forth from the mainland all of the time.

Pan comes with me instead. He is my new chaperone, and it's like an obedient watchdog is forever by my side. Pan is not an alcoholic or a drug addict, but he really likes the meetings...far more than I do. I start to call him an alcoholic-wannabe. We laugh because we know it's true, and I have discovered his dirty little secret. He claims that he's coming with me so he can better understand his clients, but I know he's lying.

I am slumped in a chair with my watchdog seated next to me. I'm beyond bored. The speaker is not very dynamic. He's talking in a dry, monotonous drone so softly that the air conditioning system easily overpowers him. I'm straining to listen, and when this proves to be too taxing, I give up. My mind starts to wander.

It's at that moment when Pan gently leans into me and whispers in my ear, "You're not listening."

I turn my head in disbelief. Was I that transparent? I muster up a polite smile and shift my focus to the front of the room. I try to look as though I am listening. I nod my head periodically to make it appear as if I am absorbing valuable information, but to be honest, I'm a million miles away.

A few weeks later, I interrogate Pan on his obsession with recovery and his incessant need to accompany me. I finally shake it out of him…

"Everyone should be required to attend those meetings," he admits, "to become better people."

At the time, I had no idea what he was talking about; however, years later, I would have the same revelation.

Pan has a long-time companion called Ron. Ron is a sharp, hard-core New Yorker, a razor blade right out of the Big Apple who hasn't lost his edge. The two of them have been together a long time and are a happily nagging couple, forever jabbing and sparring. It's another comedy duo, not as funny as Frank and Mark, but definitely a close second. They co-own a property on 15th Street just south of Euclid called 'The Elizabeth'. It's a beautiful two-story walk-up surrounded by a big black gate.

The exterior of the building is painted yellowish orange and is contrasted by the lush green vegetation on the grounds. They've restored the property and converted it into four apartments. They live on the top floor, in separate units across from each other, but both doors are always open, and they wander freely between both spaces like characters in a television sitcom.

I'm buzzed in through the gate the night they have invited me to dinner. Pan has folded napkins into adorable little tuxedo shirts and placed them in the center of the dinner plates. It is a wonderful meal because it's not yogurt or tuna. When we are having dessert, Pan looks at Ron and nods. Ron takes his cue. He tells me he and Felix have been talking. They think I seem like a pretty smart guy with a lot going for me, and they are not really sure why I am in the predicament that I'm in.

Join the club. I think to myself.

Ron asked me if I would be interested in doing some yard work for them. They know that I am in desperate need of money.

They will pay me fifty bucks. I stare at Ron and then glance over at Felix, who is smiling at me. On the one hand, I'm grateful. These days, I have managed to survive on almost nothing. Fifty dollars could last me a week or more. On the other hand, I am a little insulted...it is like a shovel has just impaled my pride.

Yard work! Really? Has my life come to this?

I am a film director, for heaven's sake. I did not come to Miami to do yard work.

The offer is far too beneath me to even remotely agree to it. Part of me considers negotiating a higher fee, but it's not even worth my breath. In my mind, I get up, make a scene, and storm out of the place. What I actually do is accept the offer graciously and ask them when they want me to start.

I wouldn't know it then, but what happened the following day would be a priceless experience that I would cherish for the rest of my life.

South Beach
Saturday, December 18, 1999

The following morning, I show up at the Elizabeth. It's 10 a.m. I'm not in the best mood. It is a hot day, but there are a lot of trees in the area, so it's cooler in the shade. I am about to do 'yard work for money'. I'm a lawn whore. Part of me wants to die.

Ron meets me at the gate and takes me around to the back of the house. We go into a shed. He hands me a rake. He grabs a few large industrial-size brown bags, and we make our way back to the front. Ron opens a bag. It's filled with chips of wood. He tells me to scatter the mulch along the property.

Mulch. I am beyond depressed.

To be honest, this is the first time in my life that I have even heard of mulch.

Ron points out where he wants the mulch, then hops in his black jeep and disappears. Pan is not around.

Probably at a meeting, I think to myself.

A grin spreads across my face.

I take a deep breath and decide to start. The mulch is not going to spread itself. I pick up a rake and walk to the edge of the property. I am standing on the cobblestone pathway, just in front of the black gate, when I look down. That's when I see it. Laying at my feet…another gift from the heavens…a little clear plastic bag of meth… right in front of me.

Is this for real? It can't be.

I reach down and pick up the bag hurriedly. Sure enough, it's a bag of crystal. I look around to make sure no one has seen me.

Thank God! is the first thought that pops into my mind.

I have been clean for three weeks…an eternity. Spending the last twenty-one days with myself has not been easy, let me tell you. A part of me thinks this is a reward for the accomplishment. Right on cue, like the pile of change and the ring, careless Floridians have given me something just when I need it most. I am holding the bag. It is cupped in my hands…

That is when I am hit with a lightning bolt. It's as though the clouds have parted, and a powerful ray of light has forced itself through the shade. I am illuminated with a magnificent spotlight, stronger than the Sun.

THIS IS A TEST!

Then, I hear a voice…something starts talking to me. This is what he, she, or it said…or what I heard, at any rate.

"The only reason you have been sober the last 21 days is NOT because you want to be; it's because you have no money.

It is not because you have the will to stop. We believe that once you can afford mind-altering substances again…you will be back to your old, pathetic self." The voice continues, "So…we are going to test you. We are going to give you this little bag of meth…for free. We will lay it at your feet. We will see what you will do. We want to be sure that once you have money in your life again, you do not use it to self-destruct. You can have a new life beyond your dreams, or…you can spread mulch. It's your choice, you decide. Oh, and by the way, we know you hate spreading mulch."

Then, as quickly as it appeared, the spotlight and the voice were gone.

Whoosh.

I find myself standing in front of Elizabeth with a rake in one hand and this small plastic bag in the other. My body is pulsing. My veins are pouring with energy.

What the fuck just happened? Who was talking to me? Where did this voice come from?

What was strange, too, was the use of the plural 'we', which I found to be disturbing. Was there a committee somewhere in another dimension watching me? Who is 'we'?

I find myself looking at my hands holding the bag. Part of me wants to drop it back onto the ground immediately to prove that I have the wherewithal to pass the test, but I don't do that. I put it in my back pocket for safekeeping instead. What I find peculiar about the whole situation is that I have never, ever, in my entire life, found drugs.

The Wheel of Fortune
Toronto 1997
Friday Night

The door opens. The Sphinx stands before me. This man is not my friend, but we see each other frequently, so there is a familiarity between us peppered with uncomfortable formality. I am a client. He is a tiny Asian man with nimble hands who packaged his product into tight, intricate rectangular origami wrappers made from glossy fashion magazines that were next to impossible to open. He was well-read and eerily cerebral in an unsettling way. The walls of his dark apartment were lined with bookshelves filled with books ranging from philosophy, mythology, and the occult.

The Sphinx turns and walks to his sitting area. I follow him. We sit facing one another. A large wagon wheel coffee table is situated between us. The circular table is functional. It rotates. As soon as I am across from him, The Sphinx gives the table a gentle spin, and a complementary white line appears before me. It is thin and elegant, like an after-dinner mint. The Sphinx studies me with a sly, odd grin on his face that I can't quite place, no matter how many times I look at him. It is a combination of a smiling Buddha, The Cheshire Cat, and a patient crocodile basking in the Sun. Most of the time, I just want to get what I came for and leave immediately, but I am forced to participate in this ceremonial ritual.

The actual 'transaction' is very civilized. There is no lewd act of money exchanging hands. This is not a dark back alley, even though I had to pass through one to get here. I place my cash onto the wagon wheel table, and with the delicate touch of his slender fingers, the wheel spins. It rotates 180 degrees, effectively replacing my thick wad of fresh, crisp cash with several tightly folded origami packets. The coffee table is like the Wheel of Fortune: The Tarot card, not the game show, although considering the situation at hand...both would apply. Instead of buying vowels to help me solve a simple puzzle, I am buying a mind-altering substance that helps me decipher the complicated labyrinth of my life.

The Wheel of Fortune spins round and round.

One day, you are up; the next, you are down.

When I am about to pick up the little glossy packets, The Sphinx stares at me with his eerie grin.

"It is poison, you know?" he says, smiling, "You do know that?"

The words slither out of his mouth, serpentine and seductive.

He utters this phrase every time, just as I am about to pick up the origami packages. At first, I was perplexed. I am not quite sure why he insists on reiterating this elemental fact to me. Then, after a while, it sinks in. The Sphinx wants to make it very clear to me that I know exactly what I am doing. He wants me to admit that I am taking poison by my own free will. He is not making me do it. He wants to be absolved of his part in this undertaking. Each and every time I look into the eyes of The Sphinx...I assure him that I know; I know that it is poison.

I have come to appreciate that this man carries the best poison in the city, and so I tolerate this exhausting ritual every time.

South Beach
Saturday, December 18, 1999

As I stand in the mulch, I can safely acknowledge that I am definitely riding a downturn as far as the Wheel of Fortune is concerned. Fifteenth-century mystics and Vanna White would unanimously agree. Also, I don't have to buy any more vowels. I can easily solve the puzzle.

"I'M F_CK_D," and I know it.

As I spread the mulch, I think about the clear plastic bag in my back pocket. It doesn't have the same allure as the glossy origami packets, but it's easier to open. There's faster access to the 'poison'.

Then everything becomes clear…crystal clear.

It's true! This is a test!

I'm charged with electricity. I feel as though I've just been jolted by a cattle prod. The blood is coursing through my veins. It's like I have just snorted a bump, maybe two. My brain is buzzing. I'm awake! Who knew spreading mulch could be so exciting? Is yard work always this illuminating? Is this why people garden? I must do this more often.

I start spreading mulch with a vengeance. I'm energized. I'm thinking. The voice that I heard…did I imagine it? I'm putting together the pieces of the puzzle…it's all starting to make sense. Was it possible that something was giving me the things I was finding in the streets? The mound of coins? The ring? Was this entity responsible for arranging the countless unexpected invitations to lunches and dinners when I could not afford to eat? Was it also responsible for assembling the odd army, the squad of support surrounding me? The unlikely combination of a Crystal Ball, a mythological watchdog, an art designer driver, and last but certainly not least…a big-hearted Drag Queen who ruled over her sun-kissed subjects with a benevolent scepter. Was something helping me?

For some strange reason, finding this packet does not make me want to devour its contents immediately; even though I was positive a few weeks earlier, I wouldn't have hesitated. But something is telling me that I should hold on to it in case of an emergency. I can keep this under glass like a fire extinguisher and 'crack' it open, if necessary, no pun intended. My mind is racing. I have not had this many thoughts running through my mind at once in a very long time. I can feel the meth in my back pocket. It's burning a hole in my shorts. I will not tell anyone about this. It will be my little secret.

Felix appears with some iced tea. He is as gracious as always and tells me the front of the house looks amazing. We go up to the rooftop and sit in the Sun. He gives me fifty dollars. He looks at me with a pleasant grin on his face. He thanks me for helping them out while he sips his iced tea.

"I found a bag of meth in the mulch," I blurt out.

The words come flying out of my mouth. I do not want to tell a soul, but for some reason, I cannot keep a secret from Felix. I know that if I do not confess immediately, he will lean over while we are sipping iced tea and whisper in my ear, "I know you have a bag of crystal in your pocket," The news doesn't faze Pan, but his eyebrows do hike up a notch.

He insists on chaperoning me for the rest of the day. As the hours press on, I know what he is doing. My watchdog is afraid to leave me alone. He thinks I will snort up the meth and spend the 50 bucks I just made on more. We run into Frank on Lincoln Rd, and when I tell him what happened, he decides to spend the rest of the day with us as well.

"If you have it, you're going to use it," Frank says. "It's just a matter of time."

I'm book-ended by these two individuals. They are bodyguards, literally protecting my body from myself. Again, I have conflicting emotions. On one hand, I am touched that they care enough to take the time to chaperone me. However, I am offended that they think my constitution is as thin as a plastic bag.

By the end of the day, I am sure I have convinced my entourage that temptation is safely at bay. It's possible they may have just been exhausted and finally surrendered to the fact that, at some point, they would have to let me go. The tapestry on the floor of the efficiency cannot accommodate the three of us. As I walk away from them, it's like I've dropped training wheels on either side of a bicycle. I am finally able to ride on my own. I will be OK; a part of me believes it, too. As the wind rustles the leaves on the trees, I am sure I can hear The Sphinx's eerie voice echo in the air.

"It is poison …you know."

A couple of days pass. I am still holding onto this toxic bag. The good news is I'm not using it...but I keep moving it from one hiding place to another. I enter the efficiency one afternoon to find my host sitting on a chair. I have been taking great strides to avoid this person, so I am a little surprised to see him, even though he lives here. The bag of meth rests on a table in front of him. He does not look impressed. I sit down across from him apprehensively. I confess. I tell him the truth. I tell him the whole unbelievable story about how this bag came into my possession...about the mulch and the lightning bolt and the conversation and the test. I tell him about Crystal Ball and Mark and Frank. I tell him about my father and his invisible hand pushing me to the front of the room. I spill it all out onto the table. I bare my soul. It rests beside the clear plastic bag of meth like an innocent dove.

Then, something unexpected happens. My host doesn't believe me. He doesn't believe any of it! Not...one...word. He informs me that I have an impressive imagination. He particularly doesn't believe that I am sober. I am gobsmacked. A big wad of gob smacks me. It hits me right in the face, and I almost fall backward. If ever there is an emotion so exasperating, especially for a chronic liar, it's having someone think you are lying when you are telling the truth.

"Give it to me then," he says, "Since you can't use it, give it to me. I have a party on the weekend."

The thought of this is unbearable. "No," I respond.

If I can't have it, no one can. I snatch the little bag of meth and dash to the washroom. I hold it over the toilet. My host looks at me from the threshold. My thumb and forefinger separate, and the little bag slowly flutters down to the water. It sits on the surface...floating. I stare at it. I don't really want to do this, but I have no choice.

I reach for the handle on the side of the tank. I press down. The little bag swirls around for what feels like an eternity and then disappears down the whirling vortex. It is a dramatic gesture. I have never, ever thrown any recreational substance away.

I look up at him. I am sure this validates my story somehow. My reluctant host looks at me like I am a dirty parasite. He smiles at me maliciously, then gives me two weeks to get the hell out of his apartment and the fuck out of his life. It is a few days before Christmas. I have nowhere to go. Part of me wants to dive in after the meth…swirl down the whirlpool of despair into oblivion.

That night. I walk along the streets of Miami, gripped with fear. I notice a young man. We smile at one another. I follow him down the block, over a fence, and into an abandoned building. We move along a dark corridor. I almost fall through a missing plank on the floor. This is dangerous, and I feel so delinquent. But I am in a dangerous, delinquent mood.

When we are gathering up our clothing, he tells me his name is Marcello and he can see dark spirits.

"A gargoyle-like creature perched up around us and watched for a while," he confesses matter-of-factly.

"This thing…it's attached itself to you. You've … befriended it somehow."

"Great," I think to myself, "that's all I need right now."

If someone were to tell me right then and there what was to transpire in the next couple of days, I would never have believed it.

CHAPTER 10
WHEN THINGS BEGIN
TO MUSHROOM

Miami Beach
December 28, 1999
8 a.m.

I wake up on my section of the floor. The end is near…I can feel it. It's not just the conclusion of the Millennium. Something deep inside of me senses the certitude of a deadline rapidly approaching. It is a beautiful day, but I don't go to the beach. I can't be spending my time laying on a towel soaking up the Sun with my head in the sand anymore.

I make my way to Lincoln Road instead, have a cheap three-dollar breakfast at the Cuban place, and then head to the bookstore just a few shops down. I navigate the aisles and locate a film directory for the City of Miami. I flip through the book and find the section that lists film production companies based here.

There are about ten on the page. I cannot afford to buy the book, so I inconspicuously jot down the names and numbers of each company on a piece of paper as if I am doing something illegal.

When I am sure my host has left for the day, I head back to the Lopotomy. I open the door a crack and listen. It is quiet. Still. My host is not there. Even though I have a key, I feel like I am breaking and entering, if only to make a few telephone calls from a landline. I dial each number and, without fail, am greeted by a recorded voice prompting me to leave a message. I gather up the courage and speak to the receiver.

I tell them who I am and why I am here. I make my way down the list. I parrot the spiel over and over and am reminded of my days operating the Wilde Beast, but now I'm running the wild animal that has become the rollercoaster of my life. My attempt to sound cheery and professional in my delivery is thin and surface-worthy. Deep down I know each message will just be deleted. I am not sure why I am even doing this. It feels like a shot in the dark…a last-ditch attempt. A vibrational ripple out into the emptiness of space.

Miami Beach
December 28, 1999
11:00 a.m.

I reach the last name on the list. Tribe Films. I call the number. I am surprised when a human being actually answers. I go through my spiel. They tell me to hold. A moment later, someone comes onto the line. The voice is upbeat and energetic.

"You're a director?" the voice asks.

"Yes, I'm from Toronto," I announce.

"You have a reel?" the voice questions.

"I do," I reply.

"Can you come in this afternoon?" the voice inquires.

"Yes, of course. I most certainly can," I respond.

"Let's say 2. Does that work for you?" The voice asks.

"Yes, yes, it does!" I shoot back.

I hung up the phone, astonished. I walk to my carry-on and unzip it. My director's reel also made it into the small rectangular suitcase. My heart starts to race a little bit. It feels like I'm about to take off.

The Blue Rocket
Toronto
June 30, 1996

The little blue pill is handed to me in a small, clear plastic bag. It's called a Blue Rocket. I am told this little tablet will rocket me into another dimension.

I'm cautioned to take it "when I'm in a good space", whatever that means.

It is the start of a holiday long weekend.... not that long weekends mean anything to me. I am still under retainer, so my entire life is like one big long weekend. Nevertheless, on these occasions, the rest of the city conspires with my stress-free frame of mind. Circuit parties are super-sized. There's usually a huge event on Sunday night where a big international DJ is flown in to headline an event.

I have adopted the practice of going to the clubs alone. I prefer the anonymity of it...even though everybody knows who I am. I see a lot of the same faces. It's like we're all trapped in a jar. I have friends...or acquaintances rather...people I know, but I have no intention of being a part of a group. I don't want an entourage weighing me down.

I am a lone wolf at heart…and to be honest, no one can really keep up with the Energizer Bunny on steroids.

Toronto
Monday
July 1, 1996

My plan is to hop into a cab and pop the Blue Rocket en route. It's about midnight when the countdown to lift off begins. I'm in the west end of the city and the event is way over in the east end. It will take about ten minutes to zip across Lakeshore Boulevard. I'll get there in no time flat, fully riding the missile and ready for the evening's festivities to commence.

I don't put on a seat belt in the back of the cab, but I strap myself in for the intergalactic journey. I pop the pill as the car heads for Lakeshore turns left, and swerves right into an impossible traffic jam. It's like we've just veered into a parking space. There are cars everywhere. I look around in a panic. Nothing is moving. We are inconveniently positioned at the end of an automotive conga line that's skidded to a halt.

This is not good. A metaphorical monkey wrench launched directly into my flight path. This will certainly throw me off course. I'm sitting on a time bomb… and it's ready to explode.

Then it happens… Blast off.

Reality shifts. I can feel it slipping out of my grasp. I am propelled into another dimension…flying in the back seat of the car even though we're dead stopped. It's an odd juxtaposition of speeds. It feels like I've been torn in two. My spirit is being wrestled from my body. Cars are floating by. I am mesmerized by them. They are like drifting metal orbs gliding through space. I can see inside of the bubble cars. They are filled with passengers …when I look into their eyes, I am sure I can see right inside of the people, too.

A child stares at me with big, round eyes. I see innocence…wonder…and then she rolls away. Another metal and glass bubble floats into view. An old woman with deep lines on her face. She is staring at me. It is like she can see inside of me, too...the void, the emptiness. I'm certain of it. The bubbles are trying to tell me something. They're showing me time…how a lifetime can disappear in the blink of an eye. How we are all just floating through time.

What is happening?

The Blue Rocket is veering off-course, taking me somewhere that I don't want to go, but I can't stop it. The gravitational pull is far too strong. I grip the seat in front of me. The spacecraft is out of control. It careens into a black hole… A deep well of sadness. It cracks open a part of my soul I never knew existed.

The cab pulls up to the entrance of the event. Tears are gushing out of my eyes. I am a sobbing mess. I can't go into this event. I am in no state to be in a public setting. This is not how I was expecting to spend my night. I tell the driver to take me back home. He's confused. I tell him to take me back home again, this time more forcefully. When I am in the safety of my apartment, alone, I weightlessly float down into this cracked well of sadness and into the darkness of the black hole...on further investigation, I'm certain it's closer to blue.

Many years later, I will be told that sobriety is about being rocketed into the fourth dimension...but I won't have to ingest a blue pill to get there.

Miami Beach
December 28, 1999
1:55 p.m.

There is a spring in my step as I walk, reel in hand to the address I've scribbled down on a piece of paper. The production company is located on Washington Avenue, just at the base of Lincoln Road and only a few minutes away. It's a bright, white, open-concept modern office... very Miami. I meet with the executive producer. His name is Craig. He's a blond-haired, blue-eyed, overly-energetic stereotypical agent. A 'let's have lunch', wink and finger pointing, 'catch ya later' kind of guy. It's not really my style, but he seems genuinely sincere…and the truth is…I don't have any other options. I pop in the 3/4" tape and show him my work.

"I think I may have a project for you," he says.

My ears perk up.

"Something landed in my lap a couple of days ago," Craig continues, "None of the directors on my roster are right for it."

I stare at Craig in disbelief and blink a couple of times.

Is this actually happening?

"You're perfect for it," He explains, "You're exactly what they're looking for."

When he asks me if he can submit my reel to them for consideration, I just nod my head in a dreamlike state.

Craig asks me for a contact number. I give him the Lopotomy landline number. I specify I can only receive calls between eleven and five.

He cocks his head to one side and looks at me suspiciously for a moment but doesn't ask any further questions.

I smile awkwardly, shake his hand, turn, and walk away.

The Phoenix
Toronto
1998

"Want to try it?" Stephan asks, holding the clear vial up to my face…

That's a stupid question, I think to myself.

I grab the little container that looks like a perfume sample and ingest the contents immediately. The clear liquid looks like water but burns with acidic intensity as I've just knocked back a shot of paint thinner.

Everyone is raving about this new drug. My expectations are high. I am preparing for an instant rush but don't feel a thing. I look at Stephan, disappointed.

"It'll kick in," Stephan says confidently.

Fifteen minutes later, I am hit with waves of euphoria. The undulations are strong and powerful. This is a new feeling. I am unaccustomed to the overall effect of this unfamiliar drug. It's like driving a new car where all the controls are in different places. I can feel the music pulsing through my veins. The base is synced up with my heartbeat… Stephan has disappeared and that's just fine by me. I'm dancing in the clouds, free to have my own adventurous trip on this peculiar high.

We are at a nightclub in Toronto called The Phoenix. It's a large, boxy structure with three levels. I make my way down a narrow staircase to a large bathroom. The music is distant and muffled by the labyrinth-like layout. The sound has been fuelling my energy, and because it is muted, so am I. I'm drained. I need to sit down.

I enter a cubicle. The euphoria vanishes just as quickly as it appeared. The waves are gone, and somehow, they've swept away my ability to breathe as well. I gasp for oxygen, but for some reason, the air is not able to make it into my lungs. I am not sure what is happening. I try to exit the cubicle but I don't know whether to push or to pull. I'm disoriented. I'm panicking, trying to do something as simple as opening a door. My throat is constricting. It feels like the weight of the world is compressing down on my chest. My lungs are going to implode.

A calm washes over me. I have accepted the fact that I will die in this narrow cubicle. I'm sure someone will find me at some point. They will have to call an ambulance.

Paramedics rushing through a dance club. I've seen it many times before. I can't believe this is happening…to me… I am going to die…here… beside a toilet.

How embarrassing. I had so much potential…it wasn't supposed to end this way…

The door swings open. Stephan is standing in front of me. His eyes are as wide as saucers. He grabs me without hesitation. We are out of the cubicle. We are running now… staggering up the steps… to where I do not know. I can feel my body shutting down.

We burst through the front doors of the club. I am hit with a blast of cold winter air. The crisp oxygen has the frigid power to pry open my mouth and force its way through the airway to my lungs. I gasp.

Once the freezing air is in me, I feel an equally powerful force emanating out of me. Green projectile vomit lunges out of my body. Linda Blair…Exorcist kind of vomit, like I am expelling a demon from my soul. The lime-coloured slime flies horizontally across the length of the walkway like a putrid fountain.

I collapse on the sidewalk, gasping for air. I am in shock. This is the closest I have ever come to dying. Yanked back from the jaws of death, risen from the ashes like the namesakes of this nightclub. I am a Phoenix, but in no way, shape, or form do I feel reborn. Stephan tells me that we took far too much all at once. Apparently, this drug comes with directions, and one is supposed to distill it with water and sip it gradually throughout the night.

Who knew?

The following weekend, we are at a different club, and a different DJ is spinning, but really it's all the same. Stephan holds up another clear vial.

"Want to try this again?" He asks.

I grab the tiny container from him and pour it into a bottle of water. I am not sure why, but I am committed to mastering this clear liquid that will become known as the date rape drug, GHB.

Only I am not quite sure...if I willingly ingest it on my own, am I raping myself?

Miami Beach
December 29, 1999

I down a bottle of water in the Miami mid-day heat. When I enter the efficiency, the answering machine is blinking. I press the button anxiously.

There is a message from Craig. The clients love my work. They want to meet me. Am I available tomorrow?

I replay the message several times because I can't believe what I am hearing. I'm overwhelmed. I have to sit down in the tiny bachelor apartment that I have broken into with my key. I grip onto the edge of the seat and look at the ring on my finger. I twist it around a couple of times.

Is it possible it's working its magic?

The Astro Plane
Toronto
1998

I am seeing a past-life therapist called Charlotte. This eccentric woman is in her 70s and looks like an aging art school teacher smack dab out of that decade. She wears chunky costume jewelry paired with loose-fitting frocks in loud, vivid prints. Her dyed-blond, curly, frizzy shoulder-length hair frames thick glasses that make her eyes look impossibly magnified as if they're swimming in a glassy fishbowl. Charlotte was recommended by La Contessa, who told me she is good but expensive, and both of those are true.

When I tell my mother I'm exploring past lives, she rolls her eyes and says, "I'd just worry about this one if I were you."

When I walk into Charlotte's apartment, she immediately tells me she sees gaping holes in my aura. She compares it to the Ozone layer and explains to me that my choices have been akin to a herd of cows expelling methane gas into the atmosphere of my life. She looks at me with compassion as if she knows my dirty little secret.

"The work I do can repair the gaps," she informs me. "It will take a few sessions."

Apparently, I've been ignoring my spiritual life as if it were a woolly sweater tucked away in the closet, and voracious agnostic moths have been chomping away at it. These aura holes are not good. Charlotte tells me undesirable spiritual entities can easily obtain access to my body through these vacuous pockets.

Charlotte uses hypnosis to guide me through several past life regressions. I lie down on the modest couch in her living room, and she sits behind me on a chair. Charlotte tells me to watch her finger as she moves her hand back and forth until my eyeballs roll into the back of my head. I am not sure if I am hypnotized, but there's a sinking sensation...like I have fallen back into my body...like I'm being pushed down into myself, like a spring-loaded snake back into a can. It's an uncomfortable feeling...inhabiting this body. I have not been here for a very long time.

I see Charlotte once a week for several weeks and I experience several past lifetimes. I am not sure if these lives are real or just a product of my over active imagination.

After each session, I extend my hand filled with cash to pay Charlotte for her services, but she waves her arm and tells me to put the money in a large bowl on her dining room table. As I chuck in the bills, it makes me think of The Sphinx's wagon wheel coffee table. I am not sure why all these people insist I pay them through their inanimate belongings, but I do as I am told.

Charlotte, it turns out, is also an experienced guide on astral projection. I am all too eager to be out of my body, and we have several sessions exploring this practice as well. It appears the universe is keenly aware of what I am doing on this spiritual plane. A project to direct a video for a dance track called 'Astroplane' falls effortlessly into my lap.

In an attempt to capture the essence of this free-flying otherworldly place, I came up with a concept that involves young gymnasts twirling in slow motion through state-of-the-art lighting effects. Something magical appears on the film. The images look even better than I imagined they would. The acrobatic innocents floating through the light transform into ethereal beings. They're mesmerizing.

"I smell a Music Video Award," the director of photography predicts.

Six months later, he's right. The video wins an award, and later that night Stephan and I are at an after-party at The Phoenix. During the course of the evening, we have a heated argument. I leave the event.

In the parking lot across from the venue, I jumped from behind. At first, I'm sure I'm being mugged, but when I turn around to confront my attacker, it's Stephan. He looks like a crazed lunatic with enormous eyes bulging out of his head. He's clearly intoxicated and in an insane state of rage. Later, he'll confess to me that he was abusing anabolic steroids, but this piece of information is of no use to me now. I'm in survival mode, fighting him, fending off this madman with every fiber of my being. I can't believe this is happening. My adrenaline is pumping into overdrive. As I am on the ground wrestling this maniac, a thought drifts into my head.

What the fuck? I won an award tonight! Is this what happens to Meryl Streep when she wins an Oscar?

I'm not sure if my weekly regressions with Charlotte have been effective. Apparently, the gaping holes in my aura are allowing undesirable entities access to my person in the physical world as well.

Miami Beach
December 30, 1999
2 p.m.

Craig picks me up at the top of Lincoln and Lennox. We shoot over the causeway to the Design District on the Mainland.

We pass by Soyka. I look at the restaurant as we drive by. It's incredible what's transpired since that day just over one month ago.

We enter a modern building and walk through the lobby dwarfed by a sculpture of a giant high-heeled shoe. We ride up the escalator and meet with the CEO and a couple of marketing people in a glass boardroom. They brief us on the project. They're looking for an image campaign to brand a new start-up called Eritmo.com., a Latin music website. The shoot has a celebrity attached to it, Enrique Iglesias.

The clients want me to create a campaign for this project. The owner likes my work and keeps referring to me as *'an artiste'*. I have not been in a creative business meeting in a very long time, and the entire situation feels surreal. I nod my head and listen. I try to play it cool. They list all of the marketing objectives and tell me what they want to accomplish with the launch. I am aware and attentive. It is Thursday afternoon, December 30, a day before the end of the millennium. They ask me when I can have something to show them.

"Monday," I reply hastily.

When the words come out of my mouth, I feel like an idiot. They stared at me from the other side of the table, deadpan and expressionless, and then all burst out laughing.

"Monday is a holiday," The CEO says.

In an attempt to imply that my answer was intended as a joke, I chuckle with the rest of the group.

When the laughter dies down, I open my mouth and offer, "Tuesday?"

I want to kick myself.

They have no idea how desperate I am...but if I keep talking, they're definitely going to find out. The CEO smiles. He tells us that he is going to Colombia for a week over the holidays. He's available the following Thursday.

"Next Thursday works," Craig responds.

Next Thursday?

That's one full week. To most people, a week is not a lot of time to schedule a follow-up meeting, especially at this time of the year...but for me, a week...is an eternity away.

The Mushroom Cap.
Toronto
May 6, 1999

The Bessies are an annual event in Toronto celebrating the best in Canadian advertising. They are like the Cannes Lions in France but not as prestigious or glamorous. It's a dreadful daylong affair held in a downtown hotel. It starts out with an opening reception, followed by a catered lunch and an award ceremony in the grand ballroom. A second reception kicks off after all of that, and by this time, industry participants are plastered beyond belief. It's a self-indulgent ceremony of shameless networking, brimming with arrogant ad execs and egos. The place is dripping with pomp, pride, and desperation.

Every year without fail, the moment I step into the venue, it's like I've stepped into a huge pile of steaming bullshit. The ambience kicks my social anxiety into overdrive. I'm awkward and inadequate. Insecurity is perched on my shoulder like a large looming vulture, gripping me with razor-sharp talons. I am aware of its presence. My attempt to self-medicate does not loosen its hold. Its claws penetrate deep into my skeletal infrastructure and easily steer my body through the crowd.

I avert my eyes to avoid any human contact with professional acquaintances. Conversations are centered around work. Projects you have done, are currently working on, and/or prospects on the horizon. As I haven't done anything in months and have nothing booked in the near future, it's an ego-deflating encounter. It's impossible to escape the embarrassing reality of my non-existent career, and much easier to avoid the situation entirely.

I spend most of the time maneuvering through the crowd with an air of caution as if walking through a land mine. I navigate my way to and from safe zones, bathrooms located on either end of the grand space. I'm most comfortable when I'm sitting in a cubicle alone.

The vulture loosens its grip ever so slightly, and I'm able to move my arms just enough to give myself a little bump before heading out for another distressing lap.

The very last time I attended this wretched gathering, I was sure the assortment of chemicals coursing through my body was not helping my professional networking abilities, so I decided to go organic instead. I had a bag of magic mushrooms that I was saving for a special occasion and figured that this was the event where they were most needed.

I dump the contents into some boiling water and sip the tea as I head to the event. The mushrooms are horrendous to the taste; they're vile, venomous things. If anything's poison…these fungi definitely are, but I force myself to consume every last drop of the yellowish brew. When the cup is empty, I chew the rubbery hallucinogens and swallow them whole.

I'm strategically late when I arrive, purposefully missing the first reception. People are entering the grand ballroom. I merge in with the crowd effortlessly. I find my seat.

There are ten of us wrapped around a circular table. I am situated beside an outspoken lesbian I have never met. She's loud and brash, monopolizing the conversation. I let her talk. The more she does, the less I have to.

I start to feel the effects of the drug when the first course is served. It suddenly dawned on me that the Bessies Awards Luncheon was not the most appropriate venue for a peyote adventure. I'm way out of my element. The room is far too bright. I'm as paranoid as a bloated drug mule passing through a Turkish security checkpoint. My strategy is to keep a low profile...to be invisible. I laugh when the table laughs and nod my head in agreement if the group is unanimous on the point of discussion. I try to blend in like a socially awkward chameleon.

As the meal progresses, I'm pretty sure my understated performance has gone unnoticed. In a few minutes, the room will go dark, and the award ceremony will begin. The show will provide a collective distraction. The commercial eye candy will become the center of attention. I will be able to hallucinate to my heart's content.

The woman next to me leans back in her chair. "That was delicious!" She boasts.

Everybody at the table nods in agreement. That's my cue. I nod, too.

"It was," I blurt out.

The woman shifts her gaze to meet mine.

"Oh really?" She says loudly, "You wouldn't know it by looking at your plate."

I freeze with fear. I am afraid to look down...but I have to. When I do, it is obvious that I haven't eaten a thing. I've just been shifting food around the entire time, pretending to eat. I scan the circumference of the table nervously. A swath of empty white plates all around. The table erupts with laughter. Now, I am the center of attention. Busted. I cannot think. I have no response.

There is no witty comeback. I just sit there looking like a liar. It's Sesame Street all over again; one of these things is not like the other...and it's me! The laughter continues.

Everyone is laughing except for the executive producer who is representing me. He and I make eye contact from across the table for a prolonged period of time.

The lights dim just as I'm exposed for the fraud that I am. The award ceremony begins. I sit in the dark...I'm facing the screen...but I can't see or hear a thing. I am not hallucinating, either. All I can keep thinking about is the way the man who is paying me large amounts of money each month is looking at me.

He knows.

Miami Beach
December 30, 1999
3:30 p.m.

Craig knows it was a great first meeting. He's in an amazing mood as we drive back to the Beach. He mimics the CEO as we glide across the Causeway, calling me *'an artiste'* repeatedly. He drops me off on the corner of Lennox and Lincoln and asks me if I need anything.

A part of me wants to say, 'Money, food, and a place to stay.' Instead, I say nothing. I smile at him. Craig has no idea what my predicament is, and I need to keep it that way. I need him to believe I am a hot director...a creative professional...*an artiste*...even if I don't believe it myself.

"Happy New Year!" He says before speeding off in his SUV.

I watch him drive away, left standing on the street with nothing in my pockets except a whole lot of hope.

I rush to the efficiency, break into the unit with my key, and begin to work on the project. I have to come up with something spectacular, and I know it. I make a point to steer clear of any concepts that may involve ostriches…or any large land mammal for that matter.

K-holes
Toronto
January 1999

K is one of the letters in my alphabet soup, short for Ketamine, which is a pet tranquilizer. It has become popular in the clubs because, apparently, we are all animals that need to be tranquilized. K-holes are a fresh, new kind of hell. Ever since I have rolled this letter into my curriculum, I find myself falling head-first into one of these K-holes every so often. They seemingly appear out of nowhere. The experience is not unlike tumbling into an uncovered manhole. Being in a K-hole is like being barely conscious at the bottom of a deep well that is impossible to escape. You are aware that a massive dance party is happening just out of reach, but as much as you try, you're unable to participate. It's a wet towel slopped over your face.

I do not like the feeling of K. While in this hole, I am definitely not K, K? However, as with all the other letters in my soup, my self-imposed dedication to master this consonant is required to earn my doctorate in self-medication 101.

Miami Beach
December 30, 1999
7 p.m.

A wealthy billionaire is having a New Year's Eve party. Mark tells me he's looking for someone to read Tarot at the event. It pays $500 cash for four hours of work.

"Are you interested?" He asks.

The Disaster
Toronto
1999

My trips to The Sphinx are multiplying logarithmically. I have other suppliers and backup options in case of an emergency.

Individuals who are able to supply me with any of the letters required to spell R-E-L-I-E-F, but The Sphinx is my go-to guy. The origami packet contents are a daily staple. Tina, otherwise known as crystal meth, is forever looming in the background. She's an aggressive companion, always trying to elbow out the competition.

It's 11 a.m. on Tuesday morning. I've been up all night and have depleted my resources. I make a quick stop to see The Sphinx, otherwise known as Carl. He opens the door reluctantly. We sit down for our usual faux friend repartee, but the tiny Asian man is unusually distant this morning.

Something's off; his attitude has altered ever so slightly, but it's noticeable. I drop my cash on the wagon wheel table and give it a whirl, but the money just spins around the circumference of the circle and comes back to rest in front of me like unwanted sushi.

The Sphinx tells me I've been seeing him too much…like we are in some kind of a relationship or something. I suppose we are, considering I see him more than anyone I know. He asks me why I am back so soon, given the fact that I was just here yesterday and the day before that, too. I scan his expressionless face and attempt to decipher something from his waxy visage.

He reiterates, "It's poison, you…"

"Yes, yes, I know," I reply, interrupting him, "I need more. I need more poison."

The Sphinx talks to me like he's diffusing a bomb, "I think you should…slow down.'

I glare at him from across the wagon wheel as if we are some kind of Western stand-off. I didn't even get a customary complimentary line.

"Anyway, I'm out," he confesses, "The city's dry. There was a huge bust a few days ago."

I know he's lying. A part of me wants to grab him by the ankles and shake the origami packets out of him…but I don't. I snatch up my cash and leave. I storm down the staircase.

Who does he think he is? Cutting me off like a frayed shoestring. I'll call Tina. She never turns me down.

As it turns out, Tina is there for me. Her presence over the next few days culminates in what I like to refer to as The Disaster of 1999. This destructive force is a combination of an earthquake, hurricane, tsunami, and tornado rolled into one. The tectonic plates of my reality are shifting.

The ordeal lasts three days without sleep. By the 40th hour, I have regressed to some Egyptian time, far before Christ.

I find a large tree branch in the park and decide to use it as a walking stick. It is thicker on one end and looks more like a prehistoric club, something a Neanderthal would drag around. I carry it with me wherever I go…clutching it like a protective blanket.

People look at me suspiciously as I enter and exit the lobby of the luxury building I am living in, but by this point, I'm used to people looking at me. I'm different. I am not like the others. This fact has clearly been established ever since my childhood.

Holy Communion
Toronto
1973

Babbo insists that the color be white. His suit is white. Mine will be, too. I am too small to remember all of the details, but I do remember this...when we enter the cathedral, there are endless pews of little boys, all wearing black suits, sitting on one side of the room. On the opposite side, endless rows of little girls in white. My heart sinks like a rock in a pond.

How could they do this to me?

I trudge down the aisle alone, head down, trying to be invisible, but I stick out like an albino in a tar pit.

When I take my seat beside the uniformed black-attired boys, they jeer and snicker, "You're on the wrong side."

I am singled out. It's the red raincoat all over again, but this time, I know that telling them I am Head Fireman won't work. I have no defense. I am positive my parents have known from the start that I am different than everybody else...and are dressing me accordingly. I desperately want to blend in with the masses, but this appears to be an impossible task.

The Disaster Part II
Toronto
1999

By the 50th hour, the tremors intensify. I look at everything I own with disgust. I cannot bear to be associated with any of it anymore. It all reeks of the past.

I am compelled to destroy my personal belongings. I rip through the space like a twisting Tasmanian Devil. I use a chisel and hammer to smash everything to bits. Clearly these possessions have been possessing me all along. I get rid of the debris down the garbage chute, a little at a time, stuffing as much as it is humanly possible through the narrow square opening. I watch it disappear into oblivion.

By the 65th hour, I am dreaming lucidly. Ghastly-looking creatures surround me. Miniature goblins, gnomes, fairies and trolls. Their faces are absolutely everywhere, watching me through the thin veil of camouflage that we call reality. I know I must photograph these creatures to prove their existence. I rush to the store, dragging my prehistoric club along with me, and purchase an army of disposable cameras. I must document this unseen world. I am not sure if I am on the brink of a major discovery or have dipped my toe into the waters of insanity either way...I'm compelled to photograph it. When the harsh Sun rises, my hallucinations do, too.

There's a knock on my door. I rush over and peer through the peephole. It's John, a work colleague. One of my only friends not on the party circuit. He's normal and as good as a human being can be. He's arrived unannounced.....or has he? We usually meet on Fridays to work on script ideas. I have no idea what day it is.

If it were anyone else, I would not answer, but John is different. He gets me. He understands the lengths a creative being must go to in search of inspiration. For him I will open the door, just a crack.

We have a sporadic conversation through the sliver of the opening between us. He knows I'm high. He wants to know what's going on.

"Give me a second," I respond.

I shut the door and reopened it a few minutes later. I hand him a torn portion of a Häagen-Dazs ice cream wrapper.

"There," I announce.

He looks at the disposable wrapper in his hand and then looks at me, confused.

"What am I looking at?" he asks.

"Can't you see it?" I question.

"See what?" he replies.

"The Face of God," I reply.

John looks at me out of the corner of his eye, then back down at the wrapper. It's clear he has no idea what I'm talking about.

"I've got to go," I blurt out.

I snatch the wrapper out of his hand and shut the door.

I watch him awkwardly standing in the hallway, confused for a moment, through the distorted fisheye hole in the door until he turns and walks away.

I look at the Divine Being in my hands.

Why can't he see it?

I take a picture of the wrapper.

The Aftermath

A week later, when the disaster is over and the dust has settled, I am rummaging through the aftermath. The creatures that lurked around me have retreated back behind the veil. They are not really visible in the photographs I've taken. The torn portion of the Häagen-Dazs ice cream wrapper looks like I've taken a picture of a torn portion of a Häagen-Dazs ice cream wrapper. When I show the pictures to John he looks at them intently.

"Carrie Fisher sends postcards from the edge," John says, "…you, my friend, take photographs."

A Million Reasons
Miami Beach
New Year's Eve
1999

I have imagined this night for over a decade. I longed for the moment when ecstasy and inevitability would collide, creating an explosive eruption of hedonistic debauchery that would catapult me into a new millennium. Yet here I am, the night has finally arrived, and none of the letters of the alphabet could tempt me to alter my state of mind. I am very aware that I am still in the thick of the great, grand test that the imaginary committee has assembled on my behalf. This was the final exam.

Apparently, the toxic concoction I had been secretly planning to ingest on this special occasion was, in fact, not a secret at all. The committee was well aware of my intention to P&P (code language in certain circles, which means 'party and play'), and they've countered with an alliteration of their own; 'potential and possibility'. They've upped the ante. There is so much dangling in front of my face, just out of reach…my mind keeps wanting to cycle into the future to find out how it's all going to turn out, but I know that's impossible. I just have to focus on what is right in front of me…the now.

Mark is picking me up in a few minutes. He will take me to a billionaire's oceanfront mansion, where I will read Tarot cards. If I make it over that hurdle, I will get a little chunk of money. If I can be trusted with that, I will have the opportunity to approach a bigger hurdle with a greater amount of money on the other side of it. This feels like an impossible task in a video game with varying levels of difficulty. If everything goes my way, I may truly be able to start a new life here. That's a lot of 'ifs', and I know it. Many things have to go in my favor in the next few days, and if they don't, I will have to call my family and ask them to buy me a ticket back home.

I'm painfully aware that nothing has really gone my way for a long time…I haven't worked in years…that is, if you don't count maneuvering mulch around a landscaped property. I fully understand the terms of this examination. Failing is not an option…neither is 'partying or playing'. It is the furthest thing from my mind. The stakes are that high, and I know it. I still cannot believe what's unfolded since my gardening venture at the Elizabeth. If I pause to reflect on it, the sequence of events is incredible. If this indeed is a test, and I pass…hopefully, spreading mulch is something I can put in my past once and for all.

Mark picks me up. We drive for about half an hour. I thank him for suggesting me for this gig, especially since he has no proof whatsoever that I can actually read. We approach an architecturally streamlined mansion on the edge of the water. I shake the billionaire's hand, and he leads me down a path to a small table and chairs surrounded by torches with a view of the water.

I am in awe of where I am. I take it all in. I retrieve my three decks from my black leather bag and set them on the table. This is where and how I will spend my gateway to a new millennium.

Miami Beach
Jan 1, 2000
2:30 a.m.

The car creeps along Washington Ave at a South Beach senior citizen's snail's pace. At this rate, I'll be getting home in 2008. The roads are still unbelievably packed. Mark's been so chivalrous, chauffeuring me around all night. I tell him I can walk the rest of the way. Taking me all the way home will add at least an hour to his trip, maybe more. Mark looks at me cautiously before I exit. I reassure him the Devil has no power to seduce me to the other side tonight. I thank him again, then jump out of the vehicle.

As I wade through the messy slop-fest that is Washington Avenue, it's like I am trudging through swamp water. I am surrounded by an unending bog littered with intoxicated souls. They're everywhere… zombies infected with a mind-numbing virus. I realize it is the first time that I am not among the inebriated undead. If anything, witnessing the drunken, drugged debauchery stone-cold sober has ripped off the rose-tinted goggles that created the illusion that I was actually missing something. It's given me the ability to see the truth with utmost clarity. It's unsettling. I am mindful to tip-toe through the madness. I am sure-footed. I do not want to slip into the swamp and become one of the zombies. I am glad my millennium plans have fallen through. I have $500 cash in my pocket, the most money I've had in months. I am able to breathe for the first time in weeks but I'm not in the clear yet.

I am excited for what's to come, but if other new beginnings to other New Years are any indication, I really have no idea what's going to happen as the months unfold…let alone tomorrow.

The Underwear Vigilante
Toronto
New Year's Day, 1993
2 p.m.

A faint scratching sound wakes me up. I look around and see the front door knob jiggling. I stare at it intently. It jiggles for a few seconds and then stops. After a moment, it starts up again.

I'm transfixed by the door knob, and then it dawns on me that someone is on the other side of the door, trying to break in. I am on the couch because I could not make it all the way to the bedroom. I tap my sleeping companion on the shoulder. When he wakes up, I point to the door. His eyes widen. We tip-toe to the door, both of us wearing matching gray boxer briefs. We are trying to communicate with each other without speaking, waving our arms around like we are playing an intense game of charades. The jiggling intensifies. Clearly, the person on the other side of the door is getting frustrated.

In retrospect, we should have just called 911 and let the police handle the situation, but we didn't do that. That would be the sober thing to do...but residue from the various substances we've ingested the previous evening is still coursing through our veins. We feel invincible. Our strategy is to open the door and startle the thief with the element of surprise. The two of us should be able to apprehend him easily...that *was* the plan.

We straddle the door on either side. We silently count to three. We swing the door open, but the thief bolts down the stairs immediately. I am compelled to chase him, bounding down the stairwell two steps at a time. The man is literally just inches away from my grasp. We're down one flight, then another, and finally a third. The thief bursts out the front door. A blast of frigid air hits me in the face, but in the heat of the moment, I am not phased by the drastic change in temperature. My bare feet plunge through the fresh snow.

It is only after we turn a corner that it dawns on me I am chasing a man down the middle of the freezing cold street in nothing but my underwear.

We live in an area of the city called Cabbagetown, a pocket of Victorian homes in the east end of the downtown core. It's a quiet, residential, affluent area…but on this slumbering New Year's afternoon, there is a streak of insanity tearing right through it.

"Stop that man!" I shout as I run. "THIEF!"

There are a few people on the sidewalk, but they just watch us race by. They're clearly not getting involved. We're down another block when, without warning, the criminal stops dead in his tracks. He turns to face me. I stop a few feet from him. It is the first time I saw his face. He's a thin, gaunt, wiry man with a dark beard and wild, sunken eyes.

He's holding a large screwdriver in his right hand. We are both out of breath, panting like dogs, looking at each other. Neither of us is sure what to do next until a glint appears in his eye. The man looks at me with a malicious grin. He's noticed I'm practically naked. He motions to the screwdriver.

"I'll use it on you." he threatens.

At that moment, standing in the middle of the road on this cold January afternoon, weaponless and in nothing but my briefs, it was crystal clear to me that I should abort this mission. My fellow vigilante is a slower runner and about twenty feet behind, steadily approaching us. He's coming in hot with reliable momentum and obviously hasn't had the chance to reflect on the situation at hand. When he shows no signs of stopping, the bandit turns and continues to run. My backup breezes past me. Intermission is over.

The chase has started up again. It's like a naked wintry relay race.

"Stop!" I shout.

But no one is listening to me today. I am a naked man screaming in my undergarments in broad daylight on the first day of January. The affluent people in this neighborhood must either think I am homeless and high or a member of the Polar Bear Club on my way to my annual dip in Lake Ontario. Exasperated, I reluctantly follow their footprints in the freshly fallen snow.

When I turn a corner, I see that my fellow vigilante has apprehended the thief. They're struggling in the narrow space between two homes. I catch up to help. The two of us together are easily able to overpower him. With the screwdriver safely on the ground, we stand in the middle of the street, holding him on either side. People emerge from their homes. They're clapping. They're cheering. Someone tells us that they've called the police. A woman shouts at us from her porch and asks if we need anything. With all of the excitement over, I start shivering like a frozen chipmunk. I look down and my bare feet.

"Something to stand on would be nice," I yell back.

The thief looks down, too. He's spotted an opportunity…a chilly Achilles heel, one might say. He stomps on my feet with his heavy boots, and this kicks my adrenaline into overdrive. I'm propelled into beast mode. I knock him to the ground and shove my elbow into his throat. The gaunt man pleads for me to let him up, but I ignore him.

All I can keep saying is, "Shut the fuck up!" with respect to anything the thief has to say. My vocabulary is reduced to these four simple words. He's dangerous. I'm angry. I don't trust him one bit.

When an elderly distinguished gentleman approaches us in his bathrobe and suggests I let the man up, the only way I can respond to him too is, "Shut the fuck up!" I glare up at him. He takes a step back. He looked at me as if I was a dangerous criminal. In hindsight, my reaction was probably not the best response, but I was in a blind rage, flopping around naked in the snow like a fish on ice. I'm sure this innocent bystander had good intentions, but he clearly didn't have the full context of the situation at hand.

The police arrive. They put the thief in cuffs and into the back of a squad car. We're in the back of a squad car, too, but only because the officers have offered to drive us home. Everyone in the street is clapping. We are heroes.

We are required to testify in court. The DA approaches us.

"Are you the Underwear Vigilantes?" He asks.

We sheepishly nod. The DA tells us the man we apprehended is a lifelong career criminal with a record as long as his leg. The list includes assault with a deadly weapon.

"You did a good thing," he says…"But next time, leave the heavy lifting to the qualified professionals."

South Beach
January 6, 2000

I meet up with Craig and brief him on the concept. He sits and listens, plugging numbers into a spreadsheet while I talk. When I'm done, he hits a few buttons and then one more. The color drains from his face, and even though he's tanned, he looks like a ghost.

"We're coming in at $250k per spot," He says, "That's a million dollars."

It's a high number. Craig stares at me. We make eye contact for an extended period of time. The clients never gave us a budget. We have no idea how much money they have. I can sense Craig's apprehension. He's hesitating. He doesn't want to price ourselves out of the project.

I understand his concern…and given the circumstances of my present financial situation, I'm baffled as to why I don't have any... but I don't.

"Let's go for it," I reply.

As we drive to the Design District, I'm already in the zone. I'm awake. I'm alive. I'm on. I have to be. I haven't given a presentation for a long time. I'm a little anxious, but I know once I start talking about something that I believe in, my energy becomes infectious...an incessant virus.

We glide up the escalator past the giant shoe. After some quick pleasantries, I launch into my pitch. I don't want to waste their time. I know they are curious to hear what I've come up with.

When I'm done, I can tell I've hit it out of the park. The CEO, in particular, loves everything. He's overjoyed, calling me *'an artiste'* again. From the corner of my eye, I can see Craig beaming like the Sun. I breathe a sigh of relief. I'm pretty sure we've landed the job from a creative perspective. Now, it's all down to the money.

The CEO shifts his attention to Craig.

"How much is all of this going to cost?" He asks.

Craig looks down. He opens a file folder. He's shuffling through the budget. He starts to talk, but he's stalling, humming and hawing. He's speaking…his lips are moving…but he's not answering the CEO's question.

Say it, I think. Say it!

I'm willing Craig to say the number…but my telepathic powers aren't working. They're not having any effect on him.

We're losing the room; I can feel it. I cannot let this happen. This is usually not in my nature but I can't help myself. I'm forced to take out my rifle and shoot the metaphorical million-dollar elephant in the room.

"We're coming in at $250k each," I blurt out. "A million for all four."

The CEO slowly turns his head to look at me, then shifts his focus back to Craig.

The bullet has brought Craig back down to earth. He's back in the room.

"Yes, a million for all four," Craig confirms. The CEO looks disappointed.

"I don't have a million in the budget for production," he confesses.

My heart drops. It's two floors down, a squashed wad of pink bubblegum under the giant shoe. I knew this was too good to be true. I'll have to go back to Toronto.

"But I do have half a million," he says,

My heart bounces back. It lands in my throat. It starts to beat faster.

Can this actually be happening?

"Can we produce two?" He asks.

"Of course we can!" Craig replies.

It's a deal! Everybody stands up from the table. We shake hands. We're told to begin production immediately.

We just landed a half-a-million-dollar project! The committee has been watching me! They have deemed me worthy to not self-destruct! They trust me with money! I trust me with money! I've been plucked from the brink of despair. I feel like I've just won the lottery. It truly is a miracle.

I've passed the test!

Frozen
Toronto
1996

I'm failing miserably in my attempt to live a normal life. My housekeeping skills get a low mark, too. My home has become a designated crack house. There's an endless stream of people in my living room, but they're not living...they're barely existing. They're not really friends either. They're acquaintances...and acquaintances of acquaintances...strangers, really. They will not leave for days on end.

I fall asleep with an assortment of people gathered in my living room, and when I wake up, a slightly different configuration will be assembled.

One day, I woke up, and the four people living on my couch told me an ice cream truck had passed by. They got me a cone.

"It's in the freezer," one of them says just before he bends over to snort a line.

When I open the ice box, there it stands… sandwiched between a frosted bottle of vodka, three empty ice cube trays, and a bright pink gel-filled eye mask. The cone looks like the Leaning Tower of Pisa, frozen at a forty-five-degree angle. It is the saddest thing I have ever seen. I just stare at the cone. I don't have the energy to eat it. I take a picture of it instead.

I thank the strangers for the cone. Then I ask them to leave. They're surprised at my request and a little offended. I am pretty sure they don't have anywhere else to go.

Miami Beach
January 7, 2000

My belongings are packed into my little black carry-on with wheels again. It is a few days before my eviction termination date. I am on the move, about to leave the Lopotomy for the final time, but on my way out, I knock into a side table, and a small decorative horse falls to the ground. A leg snaps off. I will have to fix this before I depart, or my host will think I did it on purpose.

I rush out to the drugstore and buy three different kinds of glue. I desperately try to repair the broken thing. The broken parts are so small that I need a giant magnifying glass to complete the task. My hands are shaking. I'm sweating, too.

Nothing is working. The severed appendage is refusing to bond. It's impossible to repair. I give up. I set the pieces down. I realize it's meant to be. I leave the tiny broken horse on the kitchen counter along with the different kinds of glue and a handwritten note.

'Sometimes, no matter how hard you try, once some things in life are broken, they just can't be repaired. Hope you have a good life.'

I glance around the tiny efficiency one last time. I close the door and lock it behind me. I slide the key back under the door through to the other side. I wheel my carry-on down the narrow hall. I am excited to finally be leaving the Lopotomy.

Was the mind-altering procedure successful?

Little did I know it was just getting started.

South Beach
January 7, 2000

Craig puts me up in a hotel. It's not a super fancy hotel; it's not the Delano…, but I am extra cautious with the diva-like demands right now. The ostriches have taught me a very valuable lesson on how far to push my agenda. I should just be happy that I am not sleeping on the floor. The Egyptian tapestry can stop having to work double duty as a mattress. It can just go back to being a decorative swatch of fabric. I have a bed. In fact, there are two double beds to choose from in the room.

I am relieved I have somehow maneuvered myself out of the most difficult situation in my life thus far. Soon,

I will be flushed with cash. I have negotiated a creative fee, a directorial fee, and a post-production fee. All of those fees add up amount to a big chunk of money. It's no wonder the committee had to test me to make sure I could be responsible with this small fortune…a big lump sum…all at once. Under these circumstances, the pre-Y2K me would have inhaled all of it faster than an industrial-strength vacuum cleaner.

Craig advances me some petty cash. He hooks me up with a real estate agent to help me find a place to live. He takes me to his bank to set up an account…I don't have any American ID, but he vouches for me…the same way Eagle Eye would vouch for me on psychic gigs. Craig hooks me up with an immigration lawyer so I can legit get an 'O' Visa, a Visa for … 'artistes'.

I feel like I have won the lottery.

I want to book Crystal Ball for this project, but he's unavailable. He's already booked.

Of course, he is.

I hired Frank for hair and make-up, and when he finds out that part of his job includes slathering a muscular male model with oil, his eyes bulge out of his head like those of an animated cartoon character. Frank is super attentive on set, a consummate professional armed with a slick tube of glistening grease. His attention to detail is unwavering, and his commitment is unmatched. He's always at the ready, prepared to glide to the talent quicker than a shimmering dolphin surfing a slip-and-slide whenever he's called on for a touch-up. Sometimes, calls for touch-ups come from Frank himself.

All in all, the project is a resounding success. I did it. I breathe a sigh of relief. Whatever just happened over the last 30 days has been a miracle.

"You're connected," Mark tells me one afternoon.

Franka nods, "Right?" then glances over to me and adds, "Do the work, honey…that's what it's all about."

I am excited for the future. I am excited about sobriety. If I'm this flush after just 30 days, a part of me thinks I'll be a billionaire myself in no time. Now I understand what all the fuss in recovery is about. However, my predictions regarding my financial future were not to be. I would come to discover that the imaginary committee was a far more clever lot than I had originally imagined. Not only were they monitoring my every move… and aware of my thought process, but this inner intel gave them the ability to manipulate me. They knew I was accustomed to immediate gratification, so that's what they gave me. They showed me what I wanted to see…and what I wanted to see at the time was the money.

Later, much later, I was to learn that this financial windfall was never about the money…even though I desperately needed a cash injection at the time. The money was about making me believe…that sobriety was real.

That it was worth it…that I was worth it…

But why? Why me?

I would be tested again. There would be many more tests along the path...and they would be even harder than the one I just passed.

CHAPTER 11
RESTORATION

My eyes seek happiness.

My legs move hard over mountains, searching,

My arms reach out, grasping,

My hands open the present

Only to find that it is empty

It is ironic, simply really,

As I shift my gaze, It is invisible

But it is surely there.

Joy.

At my fingertips.

South Beach
January 2000

Crimson red mixes with sky blue and becomes a vibrant, luscious purple. I am in awe of the chemical reaction. Transformation... happening right before my eyes. It's magic. I'm thirty-three, but I'm finger painting like I did in kindergarten. I've regressed to a simpler time. This child-like activity is like an extra-strength gummy, a chewable Valium. Mixing paint colors with my fingers does not require client approval. It does not need a pre-production meeting. I do not need a two-hundred-thousand-dollar budget. There are no trucks filled with equipment. No actors to stroke. No stylists, make-up artists, or production designers to brief. There is no AD telling me to hurry up.

There is not an obnoxious, opinionated gaggle of advertising pseudo-intellectuals standing behind me, looming over my shoulder, telling me what to do. I do not have to be a part of redundant, mind-numbing conversations with indecisive clients that challenge any semblance of rational thinking. Even the negative thoughts in my mind have gone on vacation.

I scoop a dab of bright yellow and a dollop of fire engine red. I can't wait to see what magnificent hue of orange this combination will create.

I want to stay here forever.

Toronto
1996

I'm sitting in a director's chair, looking at an empty set through a monitor. I am on a project, and not a particularly exciting one at that…but one that I am obligated to participate in to justify my retainer. I'm at the helm of this ship, trying to steer it through to completion, but the clients have proved to be a challenging lot, contributing an undercurrent of obstacles along the way. An actor has been in the wardrobe for over an hour. Production has ground to a complete stop like the gears of a machine jammed by an obtrusive object. In this case, the obtrusive object is an arrogant creative director.

"What's the hold-up?" I ask the AD.

"Go see for yourself," he replies, rolling his eyes.

My curiosity is peaked. I make my way to the fitting room. Upon arrival I find half a dozen clients surrounding the talent. The wardrobe stylist has withdrawn to a corner.

She's obviously given up.

"We've hit a snag," she whispers to me.

The CD looks at me with deep concern in his eyes. He is holding two belts. One in each hand.

"Do we go with the white belt? Or the black belt?" he asks, "We're not sure."

"It doesn't really matter…." I reply, "The shot's a close-up."

"Which one do you want?" He continues, ignoring my response.

"The black one," I answer back.

The CD exchanges concerned glances with the rest of his team.

"Are you sure?" He says cautiously, "We think the white belt looks better."

"White belt, then. Let's go," I retort.

As we are exiting the room, I hear a loud, desperate cry. "Stop!"

The general consensus has flipped. They've changed their collective minds yet again.

There are some projects which are like this at every turn. It is like dragging a dead horse around a race track.

Miami Beach
2000

I'm standing on my balcony, looking out over the vast blue ocean. It is a new millennium. I'm a new person. I have a new agent. I am living in a newly renovated, freshly furnished condo on 2nd and Collins, with an ocean view, just a block away from the beach. I have money in the bank. So much money in fact, I do not have to work for the rest of the year if I don't want to. I pay my entire year's rent upfront because I can't be bothered to write a check every month. I go to the gym. I go to meetings. I go to the beach. And I paint…I paint a lot.

The act of splashing color onto paper has become my new obsession. I am addicted to it. I am prolific. I am a gushing faucet. Paintings are pouring out of me; it is like somewhere, someone stepped off a hose. The tips of my fingers are so sore from finger painting that I started to use brushes. The paintings aren't very good, and some are downright ugly, but I don't care…it's the process that's important. I trust it because I feel something. The feeling is freedom. I can do whatever I want. I am an ostrich sprinting along a cotton-like cloud.

I am told to trust the process of recovery, too. I am told that this is the solution. I can't deny that the origami packets have led me to a dead end, so it's possible this is the road map that will guide me through the labyrinth...but I want proof...proof that it works...in this respect, I am no different than a skeptical person sitting across from me in a Tarot reading. I am told that because this program has worked for thousands and thousands of people before me…millions actually, it will work for me, too. I am not special. This sounds simple enough…but there's a catch. I must follow directions. They call them suggestions. I am to do what I am told…

Yeeeesh. This was going to be harder than I thought.

Snakes and Ladders
South Beach
January 2000

I am finally participating in my recovery. Mark gives me a big blue book and suggests I read it.

"It's about you," he says coyly.

I know Mark's banking that my chronic self-centeredness will tempt me to take the bait and dive into the literature. It doesn't. I am still somewhat speedy and partially blind. It is impossible for me to sit still or concentrate long enough to read a paragraph, let alone an entire book. What I can do...is go to meetings…and I go to lots of them.

Here, I am told to have an open mind. This is the least of my problems…because of what happened…because I have a bank account, and it's brimming with cash… because that stick burst my head open like a piñata when I stood up from the table at Soyka…my mind could not be more open than it is in this moment in time. It's gaping …ready to absorb whatever gets poured into it like a thirsty sponge.

I am told to take the cotton out of my ears and stuff it into my mouth. Apparently, I have been talking too much. I know nothing. I have two ears and one mouth, and I must use these features proportionally. I am told that while my mouth is moving, it is impossible for me to hear anything. The orifices in my head are like one-way streets with traffic signals. I must obey the rules of the road. Sobriety is an orderly and organized thoroughfare. Only one person speaks at any given time. This isn't a chaotic all-night party crowded with road-raging, motor-mouthed coke-heads spouting ego-driven monologues at each other. There aren't wordy verbal traffic jams gridlocked haphazardly in the air. No wrecked pileups of stacked sentences clogging an intersection. Meetings are far more civilized. I sit in my seat, a head trauma victim at the DMV, cheeks cotton-stretched to capacity, ears clear and ready to listen.

In this state, I hear many things.

I am told that my mind is like a dangerous neighborhood. It's not safe for me to wander there alone. Chances are, I will eventually be led down a dark alley, for this is where I am most comfortable. I am told I am a creature of habit with a built-in forgetting system. This convenient design flaw erases any memory of the pain my addictive behavior has caused, inevitably guaranteeing a never-ending loop of history repeating itself. I am a white rat in a laboratory experiment that knows how to navigate through an impossibly complicated maze to find that big hunk of cheese.

"Your thoughts are like a serial killer in a horror movie," Franka exclaims, "the call is always coming from inside the house."

"When that happens, call us instead," Mark offers.

I am told asking for help is the hardest thing for people like me to do. I must not be afraid to reach out for help. I am told to call at least three people a day. I must attempt to be inherently interested in other people's lives. This second part was going to be a little more challenging.

Me, Myself and I
Toronto
1998

Three subjects that excite me the most are me, myself, and I. Either of these topics can be discussed, analyzed, and celebrated with expert knowledge, at length, and with ample exuberance.

I am overly animated at brunch. My eyes are lit up. I'm glowing. I am holding court, disclosing the juicy details of my adventurous life to my captive audience of one, Cathy. I am aware that the surrounding tables in our vicinity are eavesdropping on my 'me, me, me' monologue…that fact is not lost on me. I'm speaking loud enough, and they are within earshot, so they don't have to try very hard. I'm back from a weekend-long circuit party in Montreal and on my way to shoot a project in LA.

My plane leaves in a few hours, but I have time to squeeze in a quick catch-up brunch with Cathy to loudly brag about how fabulous my life is in this room full of strangers. I use my hands and arms to express every detail of my existence. To reinforce the fact that I am packed and ready to go, I end my speech by flipping down an imaginary suitcase lid and zigzagging my hand sharply through the air in three distinct right angles as if zipping up invisible luggage. Cathy's eyes dart around as if she's watching a performance. I've inherited this exaggerated way of communicating from my oldest sister, Gabriella.

In the family, we refer to it as Gabisthenics. It's like calisthenics; only words have to be streaming out of your mouth at the same time. It's a fusion of talking with your hands, the art of mime, charades, and the fact that we are simply Italian. I'm sure, given wide-spread exposure,

Gabisthenics would rival sign language as an official standard of communication for the deaf, hands down, no pun intended. However, considering the paltry low numbers of current practicing members, it will have to suffice as a lesser-known underground art form. To the casual viewer, watching members of my family express themselves can be both exhilarating and exhausting. You'd think we were at a rave or attempting to land multiple aircraft at once.

When I'm done talking and have nothing left to say, I flop back in my seat like someone has just yanked out my batteries.

I will allow my brunch companion to contribute to the conversation, but if it isn't about me, my eyes glaze over, and all I can muster up is a half-hearted, deadpan, one-syllable, monotonous response.

"Really?" I reply, suppressing a yawn.

Cathy bursts into hysterics. She finds my comatose responsiveness to anything that doesn't revolve around my preferred topic amusing. She will tilt her head back, half close her eyes, and mimic my behavior. I snort with laughter because it's true. I haven't heard a thing she's said. Even when I am consciously trying to listen to her, the back of my mind is still thinking about me. I can't stop it.

South Beach
2000

Mark tells me this self-centered characteristic is not particularly unique to me. It's a standard feature for people in recovery, along with the built-in forgetting system. I am told that when sharing in a meeting, there is no reason whatsoever to be nervous.... No one is listening to a word

I'm saying. They're all thinking about themselves. They're carbon copies of me.

Recovery is like a tennis match at Wimbledon. Everyone here is a highly-ranked player with deeply ingrained, flawed survival techniques. The match will start out cordial at first…but it will evolve in intensity. Passionate volleys back and forth will drive the game into an unconscious battle of will and determination. Each participant will fiercely swing their racket in a shameless display of competitive dexterity. Chances are I will get struck by a speeding ball. I am told to let them hit me. The speedballs will speed up the process of my recovery.

We are in a fishbowl…or a shark tank, and I am sparring with the best of them. I am like a white-collar criminal with a minor felony who finds himself in prison learning from the masterminds of organized crime. I am told I can use these jousting showdowns as practice sessions while I ready myself for interactions with normal people in the real world.

I discovered a lot of people in recovery do not want to be there, and they certainly don't want to do what is suggested.

"This feels like I'm being fucking brainwashed," I overhear a young woman complaining.

"Maybe your brain needs washing," The wise woman sitting across from her quips back.

Some people dig in their heels and adamantly refuse to go up the steps in the twelve-step program. They're hoping that they can take an elevator without having to do anything. They latch on to other climbers. They want a free ride, but I am told there are no shortcuts. You have to do the work. This is like a game of Snakes and Ladders. A ladder can help you ascend to a new state of being, but your old behavior is looming just below the surface like a snake in the grass. If you get bitten by the snake of temptation, you slither back. You regress to your old pathetic self. When you slip off the slippery slope that is sobriety, you can't just take up where you left off…you have to start all over again…at the beginning. You're at the bottom of the board game…counting days. Sobriety must be continuous…it cannot be cumulative.

I am told meetings are like band-aids. They make you feel better, but it's a temporary solution. What we really need is major surgery. Stitches to mend our bleeding souls. The work is the only thing that will stop the hemorrhaging on a permanent basis.

I am told a lot of my problems stem from the fact that I have control issues…Pan pronounces this 'Eeesoos'. My behavior is comparable to that of an actor on a stage who wants to be in charge of the entire production, the other actors, the lighting, the props, and the direction of the plot. I avert my gaze when I hear this. I look at the floor. This sounds suspiciously close to what I've been doing to earn a living as a director for most of my life.

I am told I am not in control anymore. I am told to just follow the directions in the book…it's that simple. I am told people like me do not like following directions …we don't like reading manuals; we want to figure it out on our own. I am told I don't have to do that anymore. I am told I am not driving the bus any longer. I must let go of the steering wheel. I must go with the flow. My driving privileges have been suspended. I am just another passenger. It is advised that I will have a better chance of getting to where I am going if I am on the bus and not around the bus. Consequently, in the program and not around the program.

An older man from the Deep South says, "Gad is driving the bus."

Apparently, He always has been.

Recovery is filled with paradoxes. I am told that surrendering is the path to victory.

"Put the gun down…the war is over," Luna says to me over lunch one day.

She's a stunning, rail-thin model from Ethiopia who reminds me of a young Iman. She tells me this is a simple program for complicated people. I am told that I am a complicated person. It appears every step along this portion of the path will go against every grain in my being. I am told that God…or as my southern compatriot would pronounce it…Gad did not throw me a life-preserver, pull me onto a rowboat, and get me to the safety of shore just to beat me up with a baseball bat.

Again, I am told to trust the process.

I realize that people in recovery really like metaphors. I figure we have that in common, if nothing else.

Manifest Destiny
Miami Beach
February 2000

A strange thing starts to happen with this finger-painting business. I notice something, and it's a little unsettling at first. Part of me thinks it's my overactive imagination playing tricks on me. I am positive that I am meeting people who resemble my drawings. It's odd. I'm drawing colorful people, and colorful people are being drawn to me. My whimsical sketches appear to capture the essence of a person…and then they will appear.

When it happens more than a few times, I become fully aware of it. In my thoughts, I am sure this can't be possible. I don't tell anyone about it…but my senses are on high alert.

I See Horses
South Beach
February 2000

One day, out of the blue, I paint a seahorse. The creature appears out of nowhere and has a horse's head, a fish's tail, and a man's torso with arms, hands, and palms turned upwards as if in meditation. It's inspired by the mystical, mythical combination of humans and animals from one of my medieval Italian tarot decks. I am mesmerized by the creature, and I will paint two more in as many days. The first is black, the second green, and the final one red. My first triptych, even though I am not aware of the term yet.

Pan invited me to go swimming at a remote conservation area a few days later. The park is a bit of a trek out of Miami. It's lush and green, secluded and devoid of our mortal enemy at peak season…the tourists. Boulders line the lagoon-type atmosphere.

I dive into the water and float around, mindlessly looking at the sky. A small clump of seaweed drifts towards me. It's green and mossy and floats right in front of my face. I am dumbfounded when I see what's nestled inside.

This cannot be possible.

My vision is fooling me. It can't be real. I initially think it is a children's plastic toy that's been lost at sea but it's not that at all. It's a seahorse! The sea creature is five inches long, camouflaged in the greenish moss. To my astonishment…when I pick it up, it moves. I have never seen a real, live seahorse before, let alone come face to face with one in the wild. I am speechless. I am sure this mystical seahorse has appeared to tell me that my inkling is true…what I am creating in my paintings is manifesting in this dimension. I am co-creating with the divine in some awe-inspiring capacity! It's a message to me, clear as the sky.

A huge smile bursts across my face. There are tears in my eyes. It's like I have finally caught a little jumping fish, only this is so much better. This magical manifesting seahorse is proof of the divine…of something larger at play. I want to take the little creature home; I want to hold onto it forever, but I know I have to let him go. I put him back into the clump of seaweed and push it away.

I do not tell Pan…or anyone for that matter, about what happened.

It is my little secret.

This phenomenon has happened before…The ability to manifest something seemingly out of thin air…and it will happen again in the future, too.

Silent Secrets
Toronto
June 1998

Cinema advertising in theaters is a relatively new concept. The clients are looking for a director to create an ultra-modern image for a little-known Canadian brand of vodka called Silent Sam. It will be one of the first ads to hit the big screen, and they want to appeal to a young, affluent urban demographic. This is an opportunity to create something grand and cinematic.

I look over the creative while in a downtown coffee shop. The boards are moody, but the concept is missing something…an edge…a deeper thematic draw. It's there, just below the surface…I can feel it. Then, in the quiet of my thoughts, the subtext surfaces…it reveals itself as plain as the words on the page…*silence.*

How could I not see it before? It's been there all along… Silent Sam.

This becomes the key that unlocks the gateway to my imagination. Vivid pictures appear in my mind's eye connected to the theme of silence: muzzled Dobermans, padded walls, and as a central figure…an apocalyptic mime with a zippered mouth and haunting features…an Uncle Sam-inspired figure ominously pointing a finger, in search of urban denizens to join the underground elite. Uncle Sam, Silent Sam. The visions are so strong that I am compelled to write my thoughts on paper. It is like I can see the future.

Moments later, I am on the street, when a young man approaches me. His eyes are unbelievably bright. They're hauntingly alive and glow as if he knows me.

"Hi, my name is Leo," He says, "I'm a mime."

"You…did…not just say that…" I retort.

I shuffle through my belongings. I feel compelled to show this apparition my scribbled hand-written notes. It's bizarre. It's unexplainable. I will wind up winning the bid and shooting the project. Leo and I became friends for a short period of time…but he was taken from us quite suddenly, silenced at a very young age while still in his twenties.

The Bull Ring
Toronto
2006

I got a grant for a short film called Dances with Bulls. It's a tongue-in-cheek parody about the battle of wills in relationships. It is set in a bull ring with a sexy female matador pitted against a muscular gladiator wearing a horned helmet and nose ring.

We shoot the dancers on a green screen and create a miniature set of the bull ring for the background plates. I decide to build it. I've never done anything like this before, but there isn't any money for a production designer.

I constructed an 8 ft semi-circular model replica inspired by the Plaza Del Toro, arguably the most famous bull ring in Spain.

On the weekend, I meet a bullish-looking guy in the clubs, and later at his place, he tells me he's an art director. He pulls out his portfolio and when I open the book, the first thing I see is a huge photograph of the Plaza Del Toro.

It was one of those moments again.

I am initially cautious about pursuing this relationship but the attraction is just too strong. Little did I know it at the time, but after a couple of years of carefree dancing, this individual and I would lock horns in a bull ring of our own.

I know this manifestation stuff is powerful, and from this point, moving forward, I'm careful as to the thoughts that I think, not to mention the creative pursuits I pour my energy into.

"The universe is very particular about how it will respond to our intentions," a woman once told me. She told me that she wanted to be more loving and prayed to God to 'open her heart'. A month later, she had to be rushed to hospital for emergency open-heart surgery.

"I should have been more specific," she said with a smile.

Miami Beach
2000

As I float in the water, floating in the magical memory of the seahorse, a part of me thinks I should start drawing piles of money, but I know it doesn't work that way.

I draw people…and more will appear.

The Three Davids
South Beach
February 2000

This a story about three Davids. A Hallowed Trinity that appears along this portion of the path. A triplet of identical namesakes, each thoroughly unique: The first is young and mystical, the second…seasoned, wise, mature…and the third…well, he's immortal.

The First David

Heather's one of those whip-smart fire-cracker types who gets shit done. The kind of red-headed dynamo in red-rimmed glasses you want organizing your life or your closet...or both. She's a freelance Production Manager at

Tribal. When I ask her how to send a FAX, she nods her head and motions me to follow her.

"Welcome to the 90s," she quips back without missing a beat.

I like her immediately, even though she knows that I'm technology-challenged with no clerical office skills to speak of. She's adamant about introducing me to her best friend, David.

"You have a lot in common," She says, "You'll love him."

Heather's right. When we meet, I'm amazed at how similar our life paths have been. It's uncanny. It's like we've had parallel journeys in alternate dimensions. We're both free-spirited Sagittarians of the same age, born just a couple of days apart. He is blonde and has blue eyes, but his hair and eye color are real. David's an artist, too. He's an illustrator and co-owns the gym I work out at on Alton Road.

The other thing we have in common is the Tarot, but the thing that blows me away is that he's illustrated not one, not two, but three Tarot decks! The first one is on Angels, and the second and third are based on characters from Anne Rice's Vampire Chronicles and The Wizard of Oz, respectively. Angels, Vampires, and Wizards! I love all of these mythologies and have so for all of my life.

The two of us become fast friends. It's refreshing to have a conversation with someone and be able to say something like 'Oh yes, The Seven of Swords' and have them know exactly what I am talking about.

"Could I illustrate you… as one of the archetypes in the Major Arcana?" David asked me one day.

"I'd love that!" I exclaim, "Which one do you think I am?"

"I think you're The Magician," he replies.

I would have cast myself as more of The Fool, but I don't put up any resistance. The Magician is the first card of the Major Arcana, right after The Fool, which is zero. The Magician represents manifestation; magicians are able to make things appear out of thin air.

David gave me the illustration a few weeks later, and the drawing is in his signature style. He's drawn me as a powerful Magician with six arms sprouting out of my body like a Hindu god. Two arms are up above the head, summoning the heavens, while the other four master the elements of earth, air, water, and fire.

I cannot deny that there have been countless magical moments in my life...moments that have caused me to pause and wonder, but I am far from a magician. If I have any magical qualities at all, it is that I am able to see the magic if and when it is there.

I show David the ring on my finger, the one I found in the street, and share with him how it came to be, for that has been my greatest trick so far.

The illustration reminds me that when I was a child, in my walrus phase, no less...I wanted to be a magician.

The Magic Show
Toronto
1977

I'm given a magic kit for a birthday present. The back of the box assures me that it contains everything I need to know to become a master of illusion. There are fold-out instructions inside that offer a step-by-step guide on how to perform a few classic tricks.

A couple of years have passed since the fiasco with the House Two Doors Down. I have made a new friend called Costa, who shares my obsession with magic and has just moved into the neighborhood a few blocks away. We save our allowances, and purchase two white rabbits from the local pet store.

My parents won't let me keep any animals in the house, but Costa has a shed in his backyard. Both bunnies live there, even though one is mine.

Costa and I practice perfecting the tricks every day. When we're satisfied with our magical abilities, we decide to share our talent with the world and put on a magic show. We plaster the neighborhood with hand drawn posters promoting the event. Even at this age, I appear to have an inherent understanding of the fine art of advertising. I am aware of the subtle nuances of the written word and the power of suggestion a carefully crafted sentence can imply. On the poster, I listed 'live rabbits' as a featured bullet point, even though the rodents would not be part of any trick. They will not be materializing out of a hat or anything.

The rabbits will just be sitting in a cardboard box, chomping on carrots.

On the day of the event, we set up a small table and fold-out chairs in my backyard. The show goes as well as one might expect a show to go put on by a couple of children performing magic tricks from a flimsy store-bought kit in a cluttered backyard in front of a row of six children. At the end of our set, an older kid calls us out on the false advertising.

"What about the rabbits?" he yells like a dissatisfied customer, a heckler from the back of the row of six children.

All I can do is sheepishly point to a cardboard box beside a coiled-up garden hose a few feet from me.

"They're in there," I reply.

D Squared.
Miami Beach
March 2000

David is friends with another David and insists I meet this other man.

"You will love him," he says.

This second David is in his seventies, but a chronological number does not stop this force of nature from living an exuberant life.

When I meet him, the first thing he says to me is, "I'm David Leddick…rhymes with headache."

I love him immediately. He's quite the character, very much in his own league. David rides an old model bicycle with a large wicker basket strapped to the front of it while wearing an enormous wide-brimmed straw hat strapped to his head. He sits perfectly upright when he rides it and looks like Miss Gulch in the Wizard of Oz. When he speaks, it is like a grade two school teacher explaining math to you for the first time, slow and deliberate.

David is never short on words of wisdom and can drop random clever anecdotes casually into any conversation with effortless flare.

He will say things like, "Always moisturize your neck. You never know. One day, it may be your face."

This second, seasoned David has led a full life and had multiple careers. He worked in advertising during the Mad Men 60s, was a commercial director, and was the international creative director for Revlon and, later, L'Oréal. Today, he writes books and splits his time between his homes in Miami, New York, and Paris.

When explaining the rationale of his current quest for a property in Montevideo, David will say, "As one gets older…one must continually travel further south…and get blonder."

David is working on a book about gay men of his generation and the courage it took to come out.

"It's never too late to come out," he exclaims, pausing to reflect for a moment, then adds, "although that's not completely true."

David continues to tell us about one of his research subjects who realized he was gay at ninety-two.

David looks at us blankly, "I told him, 'It's too late'."

This David is also an avid art collector and has curated several large glossy coffee table art books, many on the male nude.

"I'm an expert on the male form," he would say, then wink discreetly.

Any Given Sunday
Toronto
1999

I'm coming down off of a high, wandering the streets of the city, looking for something to anchor me to this world. I'm drawn to a large bookstore in a high-end mall near Yonge and Bloor. I'm wandering the aisles aimlessly, searching for something…for what, I'm not quite sure. I can't possibly read anything in the state I'm in. I'm just looking at book covers.

I inevitably gravitate to the big glossy coffee table books on photography. Pictures are the only things that have the power to make me stop. My eyes need candy. I flip through page after page, photographs, still images, moments captured in time. Humanity is on display, and so is creativity in all of its diversity. A twinge of inspiration tingles in my soul. I yearn to dive into these alternate realities. I want to escape my present state of mind. The act of flipping pages appears to be the solution to livening up my dreary existence.

Then I see it. It's a small book with intriguing cover art. The image is artfully cropped to perfection. It's a photograph of a handsome face, to be sure, but there's no upper part of the visage…just a classic nose, full lips, and a chiseled cleft chin. It's perfectly anonymous. The book is fat and chunky, like a thick brick.

It's called The Male Nude by David Leddick.

Miami
April 2000

When David discovers I've been painting, he expresses interest in seeing my work. I invite him to my studio, and when he steps through the door, I can't believe the man who created the book I used to flip through at the bookstore in Toronto is now in my apartment. As David wanders through my studio and looks at my work, I can't stop thinking about whether I unknowingly manifested him somehow, too.

I've lined up my paintings around the room. It's like a gallery for dogs and toddlers because everything is on the floor, propped up against walls.

David looks around. He pauses for a moment and puts his hand up to his chin.

"I think there is something here," he declares. He walks to one of my drawings and picks it up.

"I am surprised you are able to convey so much emotion with so few lines."

I have never sold a painting before. That afternoon, David buys five of them.

Male Nude
South Beach
July 2002

I am meeting the Davids for lunch. Cowboy hats have become all the rage, and I've been wearing a black straw model for the last month.

When Tarot David shows up wearing a white cowboy hat, David Leddick looks at us deadpan and confesses, "Well, I'm embarrassed."

This makes me roar with laughter, and I'm compelled to take off my hat for the rest of the meal. I am showing the Davids my latest work...several new paintings and some photographs. David Leddick reaches for a picture of a painting and one of the photographs and lays them side by side on the table.

"I think this is a double-page spread in my new book," he announces.

My jaw drops.

When the book is published, I wonder if these images will one day help anchor a lost soul, as so many pages in other books have done for me before.

David to the Power of Three
Florence, Italy
June 2000

I turn the corner and see him in the distance, standing in his magnificence, naked and alabaster white…a God towering over mere mortals.

The divine scale of Michaelangelo's David is truly impressive. Photographs do not do the marble sculpture justice. The masterpiece is a testament to the fact that in art, size definitely demands attention.

It's ironic that this most famous sculpture in the world stands as a colossal giant, considering he's the David in the David and Goliath story. With a rock in one hand and buck-naked save for a slingshot draped over his shoulder, he's ready to stand in the face of adversity and conquer an impossible opponent.

He's going to take a shot...because, honestly, it's all any of us can do.

I am staring at this huge sculpture in this palatial art gallery, certain that Michaelangelo must have been divinely inspired to wake up every morning and summon the energy to chisel this masterpiece out of an enormous slab of marble.

I can't imagine ever having that kind of discipline to create something as great or as grand.

Fridge Magnets
Toronto
1994

My refrigerator door is plastered with a David Dress Me Up fridge magnet set, consisting of a naked David cut-out and an array of stylish clothing options. One can mix and match his wardrobe to reflect the current season or the current seasonal affective disorder you're suffering from.

I've been depressed for weeks. The depression amplifies my slothful frame of mind, so much so that my concept of cleaning the kitchen consists solely of rearranging the fridge magnets. I don't have the energy to do much else. Giving the flat two-dimensional statue a style makeover is the only outlet for my deadened creative spirit.

The Size Queen
Miami
August 2000

I am back in Miami as a legitimate resident with a three-year 'O' Visa for *artistes*.

Eduardo is an artsy Colombian with a mad flare for furniture design who creates ginormous couches. His clients include Versace and Sylvester Stallone. Eduardo's whimsical style is inspired by a Dali-esque aesthetic. He has a pronounced glint in his eye that makes him look just a little bit off-kilter.

When I flip through his portfolio, the furniture looks normal-sized, but like Michaelangelo's David, when a human being appears in the same frame…the scale immediately reveals itself. People are dwarfed by the 40-foot-long furniture by comparison. I'm certain my toddler self would have been unscathed from any pointed corners had these monstrosities been installed in our living room.

"I'm a Size Queen," Eduardo says, the glint in his eye sparkling ever so slightly.

Eduardo's multi-level home is painted in deep jewel tones and cluttered with eclectic artifacts. I am not quite sure what the deal is with Eduardo, but I suspect it's something. He reminds me of an unbalanced tight-rope walker, continually on the verge of tipping over but somehow able to regain his balance.

If I were to diagnose him by the juxtaposing nature of his pets, I would say he's manic-depressive. He owns a hyper-active Jack Russell terrier darting around like it's high on coke and an ancient wrinkled tortoise that moves as if it's heavily sedated.

"That's Salvador," Eduardo says as the reptile inches past us.

Upon entering my studio, Eduardo glances at my work, "Go bigger," he says immediately, "People have huge homes here."

Later that day, I'm inspired. I rip out pages from a watercolor pad and glue them together to create a large canvas. I take out some paint and begin to work furiously. It is fun to work at this scale, and it's freeing to a certain extent as I cannot really see what I am doing. When I'm done, it's as if I've been in a trance. I'm exhausted. I go for a swim.

Upon my return, I'm in awe of what's on my wall. The colors are a rich and luscious hue of purple. It's like someone broke into my apartment while I was away, painted something fabulous, and then left. It's by far my best work to date and like nothing I've ever done before.

I've turned a corner in my evolution as an artist. From this point on, all I want to create are big paintings.

As it turns out, I am a Size Queen too.

The act of ripping up paper to create a larger canvas is cathartic. It makes me realize I like destroying things as much as I love to create. I have developed a deeper understanding in regards to the free-for-all that was unleashed during the fiasco of The House Two Doors Down. This act of tearing things apart and putting them back together again becomes a symbolic gesture…and later a cornerstone of my artist's statement.

We're perpetually recreating ourselves. Our former identities are continually being destroyed. A new chapter is started, and a page is turned. The past is ripped away and discarded…and as time goes by, the texture is added to our faces, a small crease here and a wrinkle there… evidence of a life lived.

Thankfully, Botox has been discovered and will become wildly popular as the years progress…so some of these lines, on the surface at least, can be erased.

Miller Time
South Beach
August 2000

Frank wants to introduce me to an established art dealer by the name of Robert Miller.

"He's huge…" Frank exclaims enthusiastically, "he discovered Mapplethorpe."

We're gliding through the streets of Miami in Frank's bare-bones black jeep that is stripped of its rooftop and doors. Frank is pouring out Robert Miller stories like an over-zealous barmaid at Oktoberfest. During this steering-wheel monologue, even though he's not in drag, Franka pops through occasionally, making an appearance here and there in a subtle gesture or nuanced glance.

"Rumor has it he sold Georgia O'Keefe's collection to Calvin Klein for a small fortune," Frank boasts… "I heard the deal went down in the middle of the desert, like a Colombian drug deal. You know… private jets, briefcases full of cash, the whole shebang."

Frank smiles. Franka winks at me.

"Robert knows everyone who's anyone," Frank announces excitedly, "The last time I ran into him at a Wolfsonian fund-raising event, he was escorted by a Persian Princess. Royalty darling!"

We stop at a red light. Frank looks at me.

"Anyway, I told him you're an artist and that David just bought some of your work." He continues, "He wants to meet you. I'll set it up."

"Oh wow! Thanks." I reply.

A cool breeze rushes past us, and the air temperature drops significantly. Frank tilts his head to one side as if he's a Basset Hound sensing something. He swivels his head in my direction and looks at me, dead serious. Then, a calm comes over him.

"We're going to get wet," he exclaims.

"How do you know?" I ask.

"Honey, I've been driving this topless thing ever since I got to the beach. It's a sixth sense. I just know." he states as he looks straight ahead, "Oh yes…It's going to happen."

Without fail, a few minutes later, we're hit with a torrential tropical storm. Water is pelting us from every angle imaginable. I had no idea rain could fall vertically, horizontally, and diagonally all at once, but it's possible. I am being schooled in the hard and true facts of Mother Nature. The two of us are braving this extra-strength power-turbo carwash while strapped into our seats, defenseless save for our resilient spirits.

When It Rains, It Pours
South Beach
August 2000

The tropical rainstorms in Miami are positively spectacular, and I'm often mesmerized by their grandness. On a few occasions, I'm compelled to throw myself into the madness of the storm. I will run through the showering streets in nothing but my shorts and shoes. My actions are reminiscent of my brief stint as The Underwear Vigilante…except for the fact that I'm not chasing anyone, and it's not minus ten. The experience is both refreshing and exhilarating, and I feel connected with nature. It is as if I am being cleansed by raindrops from heaven…

I will watch palm trees withstand the most powerful winds. Their slender trunks seemingly defy gravity, bending and stretching as if made of elastic. Lush, leafy tops swaying like a mermaid's hair underwater.

Sometimes, the expansive ocean sky offers an unobstructed view of the most extravagant light show on Earth. It is a brilliant display of crackling energy. Streams of white-hot lightning will appear across the sky like a giant X-ray, exposing an invisible network of veins and arteries.

It is quite true that when it rains, it pours.

South Beach
August 2000

This pouring phenomenon is happening with regard to my life in sobriety as well. Someone has definitely stepped off the hose. Things are coming to me left, right, and center right out of the blue. I am like a magnet attracting positive things.

The world appears clearer and sharper. The colors are more vivid. I feel like I am on some perception-enhancing drug…but I am told this is just the way reality is supposed to be. I've been deadening the experience with drugs all along. I am holding onto my life with both hands….high on the adrenaline. I am on a surfboard, riding the wave of life on the sunlit beach that calls itself Miami. 'Ami' is the French word for friend, and this city has certainly befriended me. It is the gift that keeps on giving. I am showered with abundance.

One Drop

"You've most likely been teaching your whole life…" The woman from The Miami Ad School says, smiling, "You've just never been aware of it."

Even though I haven't taught a day in my life, I am offered to be part-time faculty at the school, instructing a class on commercial production. I teach a three-hour course once a week in the evening. I'm excited to inspire young creative minds.

Two Drops

The woman behind the counter of the Van Dyke News Cafe looks at me and asks, "Are you an artist?"

I am uncomfortable with the title, but I nod to her. I am wondering how she knows but then realize I am carrying a bag of art supplies from the little store called Creation across the street.

"May I see your work?" She asks.

I have a few photographs on me, and I show them to her.

"We display local artists here," she informs me, "we're looking for someone next month. Are you interested?"

Three Drops

I am bidding on a Coca-Cola Christmas commercial set in Santa's workshop. I think Eduardo would be good at set design and pick up his portfolio. It's late at night, but something tells me to glance through the book.

As I am flipping through the pages, a personal photo slips out of the back of the book and falls to the floor. When I reach down to pick it up, I can't help but smile.

The picture is something that one would get in a mall during the holidays. It's a photo of an infant bundled in a onesie sitting on Santa's lap. The caption under it reads 'Merry Christmas'.

...*Merry Christmas indeed.* It's one of those moments again.

Something just told me I just got this job.

Mr. Miller.

Robert Miller lives just a block away from me in one of the enormous modern monstrosities on the southernmost tip of the island. I bring five David-sized paintings with me, rolled up and secured with rope. Robert is a quiet, reserved man who uses metal forearm crutches to maneuver his way around his spacious modern condo.

"Big is good," he says as soon as I walk through the door, "Art is sold by the square foot."

Robert tells me he has started to paint again, too. The unit is filled with paintings of what look like primitive bowls.

He gives me a tour of his lavish condo and his personal assistant serves us lunch on the terrace.

After lunch, I unravel the tube to display the first painting.

Robert nods and motions to me with a metal crutch to flip to the next painting. We do this until I've shown him all five. He shakes his head and tells me he doesn't like any of them. But he gestures to the purple one.

"This one, though..." he says, "is good." Then he asked me if I would give it to him.

Give it to him?

I'm taken aback. I cannot part with this one...not yet. I love it too much.

I tell him, "I'll have to think about it."

He stares at me for a moment, nods, and then asks me if I like to snorkel.

I never see Robert again after that day. I don't give him the purple painting.

" I would have handed it over in a New York minute!" Frank exclaims.

"He might just have sold it to someone famous ...someone r-r-r- rich!" Frank rolls his R's on the word 'rich 'as if he's a Ferrari revving his engine." That's how *you* become famous...fame attracts fame...they all travel in the same pack, dah-ling...like wolves. One has to know how to infiltrate them."

The Wings of Victory
South Beach

I am told I have to go to meetings every day. I use substances every day, and so I must participate in this new activity to counter the balance. Apparently, the imaginary committee includes an accountant who keeps score with beads on an abacus. I am told I am an addict and will always be an addict. That will never change. I am told that once a cucumber becomes a pickle, it's a pickle. It can't go back to being a cucumber.

The meetings are not so bad. The stories are far more entertaining than I had imagined they would be. They're high on drama yet filled with moments of levity and sprinkled with wisdom. I find myself whisked through the gamut of emotions. I'm laughing and crying, then laughing again. It appears everyone here has had as colorful a life as I have, if not more so. That little old lady knitting quietly in the corner used to be a world-class dominatrix…that soft-spoken man to my right was a drug smuggler for a Colombian cartel.

The stories are not only fascinating… they ring of truth, the kind of raw, unforgiving honesty that pries your chest open with a crowbar whether you like it or not. The kind of unprocessed truth that's not flattering…we're talking Mouth of Truth honesty, the ugly Roman mask carved in stone that re-assures all of us that the truth is not pretty.

Astrid, a bull dyke lesbian with ample sober time under her belt and balls to match, claims that when she was new, she used to come to meetings with a tape recorder taped to one leg and a gun to the other.

"I wanted to prove that this whole thing was bullshit," she admits, "Once that was accomplished, I was going to kill myself."

This woman has become a certified guru in recovery, and people clamor to work with her because they 'want what she has'.

Her response to her wild popularity is both brutal and wildly hilarious.

"Only the sickest of the sick are attracted to me," she announces, "So come on down!"

Frank is working with her, and I am working with Frank, so part of me thinks that by association, I am one of the sick ones.

The curious thing about all of the stories in recovery is that even though the details are all different, the one thing that they all have in common is the ending...we all wind up here...the home for misfits and defective toys.

All of us are forced to stop for one reason or another. I am told the act of stopping does not come easily for a lot of us. We're runners like Bio-engineered Replicants in Blade Runner. Our time is up...only in this version, we're human, and a relentless God is the thing that's hunting us down. There really is nowhere to hide.

Most of us don't fly through the doors of recovery on the wings of victory. For many, this is the last house on the block. All of us have experienced some earth-shattering traumatic event that has landed us here...a near-death experience, a court order, bankruptcy, or an intervention of some kind.

I cannot deny that my ticket here was by Divine Intervention. An express invitation, delivered loud and clear that afternoon at Soyka. When I think back to before that day, I never would have had the desire, will, or self-realization to come here on my own. I have no ability whatsoever in the art of self-assessment. Denial runs deep...very deep. I am that blind...and ironically, I can see that now. I feel incredibly lucky that by any means and for whatever reason, I made it here at all.

As I get a little further up the ladder, I am told that the whole process of recovery has nothing to do with all the illicit substances ingested over the course of a lifetime and everything to do with my *thinking*. I'm reminded of the Lopotomy Apartments and the mind-altering surgical procedure this entire journey instigated. Apparently, I am the problem…it wasn't any of the letters of the alphabet after all.

I am told to put up a sticky note on my bathroom mirror that says, "You're looking at the problem." I need to be reminded every morning who the true enemy is.

"Really, we're on all of the steps, all of the time…" Frank says when he picks me up in his black Jeep.

I'm wearing white track pants and a black cut-off T-shirt. Frank is wearing the same thing.

"We're spending too much time together," he says dryly.

There's a lot of talk about God in recovery. I am told this God can be a white-bearded man in the sky, a squirrel, a doorknob, or anything I choose, but it cannot be me…God can definitely absolutely, positively not be me. I am not God…that is made painfully clear. God is something else.

Because of my Catholic upbringing, my experiences with the Tarot, and the fact that I am positive an invisible committee is continuously monitoring my every move, I have no problem whatsoever with the idea that someone else is running the show. Some people have a major dilemma with the concept of God…Gad…like it's a dirty word or something. They are happy to complain about it ad nauseam, too.

"Jesus Christ…" I'll mumble under my breath, slouched in my seat, "What's their problem?"

I am told I need to work a program of recovery even though I don't really know what that means…but if this means making endless lists and going to lots of meetings and doing what I am told, then I am doing it…because I can look out at the view of the ocean from my new stylish apartment…I believe.

On some level, I am acutely aware of the fact that this process is confronting the unholy union of speedy blindness forged into the very fabric of my being since childhood.

In recovery, I find myself stuck between a rock and a hard place with nowhere to go. I am forced to work with the rock as the hard place is not going to budge. It's difficult to do…it's uncomfortable. When the rock finally moves, I unearth a plethora of my inadequacies. It's like picking a beautiful stone up off the beach and then turning it over to discover it's covered in maggots.

There are things I never saw before…and it's not pretty. It's Mouth of Truth ugly. That's recovery.

I am told this process will take time…It took me years to become who I am, and it will take years to recover. I am not going to change overnight.

CHAPTER 12
THE SLIPPERY SLOPE OF SOBRIETY

The Wedding
Toronto
April 12, 1980

The cuff links are impossible to fasten. I set them aside and move on to the suspenders, tie, vest, jacket, and this thing called a cummerbund. There are so many parts to this tuxedo, I need instructions on how it all fits together. I can't ask Babbo...he's just not that kind of a dad. I am not sure what's the point of all of these accouterments, but it's all here, so I do my best to figure it out. I'm surprised this outfit doesn't include gloves and a top hat. I'm sweating like a hog in August when I finally have everything on. When I look at myself in the mirror, all I see is a perspiring fourteen-year-old with acne who looks slightly out of place in an ill-fitting suit.

My father's favorite, Gabriella, is getting married today. I am an usher. The affair is a big Italian thing with as many parts as this rented tuxedo. I wouldn't know it at the time, but today will also be a wedding of my own.

My sister will be walking down the aisle to marry her high school sweetheart, but I will be walking down the aisle, too. While still a virgin in the cathedral of alcoholic bliss, I will be introduced to the sweet allure of liqueur lingering beneath the veil of temptation at the open bar. I will come to love the absolute intoxication my soulmate will provide as we navigate through the dreary monotony of this dreaded existence hand in hand.

The next morning, I wake up in a haze to find most of my family hovering over me. It is well into the middle of the afternoon. I am not really sure what happened the night before. It's time to return the tuxedo.

"Where is it?" They ask.

I scan the room in a panic. The only things that are left crumpled in a pile on the floor are the shirt, pants, socks, and shoes, and half of those items belonged to me. Everything's gone. Vanished into thin air. I have no idea where any of it is. The members of my family look at me with a thin veneer of disgust. They turn and walk away. They shut the door.

I knew then and there that there would be consequences to being wed to such a selfish, fun-loving kleptomaniac. As the years progress, the union would be tumultuous at best. This companion would provide carefree abandon, and while I was distracted, things would disappear, insignificant things like cuff links and cummerbunds.

Years later…when there was nothing left to take, and all I had was a carry-on with wheels, I realized what it really wanted all along was my soul.

Sobriety was the divorce, but temptation is always just an arm's length away, a snake slithering around The Garden of Eden.

The Rising Falling Star
Miami Beach
September 2, 2000

I am standing in the middle of Van Dyke News Cafe. My first art show, and I've only been painting for six months. I am surrounded by my artwork and a network of new friends and acquaintances. There are over fifty people here. People from recovery, work, school, the gym, and the beach. Craig approaches me. He's beaming. He tells me we landed the Coca-Cola job. It's a rush. It is like doing a big fat line of coke. More money will be coming my way! I am a star. I am glittering with potential. The Star in the Tarot's Major Arcana represents interior light and the celebration of the 'Gifts of the Spirit'.

Towards the end of the evening, when most of the people have left, a waiter appears with a bottle of champagne. Some production people from work have purchased this as a token of their appreciation and to celebrate the night and the upcoming project. The waiter pops the cork and pours six glasses. He hands one to each of us. We're standing in a circle. I am with six people I hardly know. I don't know what to do. I'm holding the glass. It feels strange in my hands. They're toasting me, holding up their glasses. I can't deny I feel like my lucky self again. I am overwhelmed by a double dose of dopamine, blinded by the rush of validation. These people like me…they really like me…like how Sally Field felt when she accepted her second Oscar.

I bring the glass up to my lips. I don't want to be doing this, but I am not sure what to do. The only reason any of this is happening is because I am sober. I passed the test. There is nothing I am more certain of…so drinking champagne to celebrate just doesn't make sense. I am a socially inept, polite Canadian who can't say 'no'. I look around the circle of people. We are all making eye contact, and then…it happens. The snake slithers out of nowhere. It wraps itself around me like a boa constrictor, tightening its grip at my core. There is no escape. It faces me, eyes gleaming, jaws stretched to reveal dagger-like fangs, and like a jilted lover, the angry reptile goes in for the kill.

The bubbly concoction fizzles down my throat. I feel myself sliding, too. I'm a falling star. In an instant, I'm at the bottom of the board game.

What happened?

I know deep in my heart that I failed the test…the test that was given to me by that imaginary committee months ago in front of Elizabeth. I got a big fat F. I know it…the committee knows it, too. Everybody knows it.

And even though I've not lost anything…I've lost everything.

What have I done?

The next day, I'm compelled to tell Mark and Frank what happened. They're non-judgemental. I had a slip, that's all. People slip. It's a slippery slope.

They remind me again about my built-in forgetting system. It's a part of my design. I am somewhat comforted, but I don't tell them that the slithering snake of success has nested inside of me. It makes me question everything that happened.

Was it really that bad?… It wasn't really that bad, was it?

Although deep down inside, I know that it was. I was one step away from homelessness. I was sleeping on the floor. I could not afford to eat. I was hopeless.

Then it dawns on me, like the harsh morning Sun after an all-night bender...*I am my own worst enemy.*

The call *was* coming from inside the house...Franka was right.

Snakes in native teachings represent transmutation. It is only through multiple snake bites that one becomes immune to poison and is able to transcend the toxic concoction. This process allows one to shed their skin like a serpent and transform into a new person.

I think about all the poisonous bites I have survived in my lifetime...the ones I have received and the ones that I have given too.

In Chinese astrology, I am a double snake. My penicillin allergy medic alert bracelet is branded with intertwined serpents.

It turns out the snakes have been there all along.

Skipper
Toronto
1977

I want to join the scouts. I am not sure why. Perhaps I am looking for a father figure. Babbo is never home. Perhaps I am looking for more male companionship. At home with my mother and three sisters, I am surrounded by enough estrogen I can grow breasts. Perhaps I am looking for friends, as I have spent enough time in solitary confinement. Maybe I'm just influenced by popular culture because, on television, it appears to be what American boys do.

My parents do not want to invest in the green shirt until they are sure that I am committed to this new enterprise. Yet again, I am singled out by my wardrobe. Like the red raincoat and white suit, my appearance is a dead giveaway, and I'm not like the others. I am the kid at the end of the line, not in uniform. I don't have any badges, either.

I desperately want to conform. I want to blend in.

The headmaster is an overweight man with glasses called Skipper. He is kind, thoughtful, and attentive to all the boys. I like Skipper. I am not used to this kind of behavior from older male figures. We are separated into five groups that consist of five boys each. We meet in the basement of a church down the street at 7 p.m. once a week. Skipper announces there is a scout jamboree on the weekend. My parents have signed the consent form. I plead with them to buy me the green shirt for this event, and they do.

It's a Saturday morning, and all the scouts have assembled in front of the church. We are lined up in front of the big yellow bus. I am wearing my new green shirt, but before I am able to climb aboard, Skipper asks me to help him get some boxes from the church basement. One of the older boys says he can get the boxes, but Skipper declines the offer.

"We got it," he says and motions me to follow him.

Skipper and I enter the church and head down the stairs towards the basement. It's dark in the stairwell, but Skipper does not turn on the lights. We are at the bottom of the steps when Skipper puts his hand on my shoulder. He maneuvers me under the stairwell and corners me into a wall. He presses his body up against mine, puts his arms around me, and holds me tight. I can feel the fat from his belly pressing into my chest and face. I am scared. I don't know what is happening.

I don't know what to do. I want to run away, but I cannot wrestle myself out from the weight of his large body.

I always liked Skipper. He had a kind face, but now, as I look up at him from this angle, there is something unsettling about it. Skipper tells me to be quiet and continues to press up against me. He starts humming and begins to rock back and forth. I want this to stop. I want to run away.

We hear a noise. The older boy calls out Skipper's name. He is halfway down the steps. Skipper quickly moves away from me and picks up a box beside us. The older boy shouts down that everyone is on the bus. Skipper tells me to pick up a box. I obey him. We carry them up the steps and to the bus, but I cannot get on the vehicle. I tell Skipper and the older boy that I can't go to the jamboree. I tell them that I have to go home. I run all the way back.

I tell my mother the jamboree was cancelled. I shut the door to my room. It's safe now. I never go back to scouts again, and I don't tell anyone what happened. Babbo tells me he knew I would quit. They should have never bought me the green shirt in the first place.

A Line of Coke
Miami
October 2000

It's a sweltering day in Miami, but you wouldn't know it from the studio shoot blanketed in fake snow. The set is bursting with all things Christmas. Workshop elves, a mixture of little people and children donning pointed prosthetic ears, are milling around the studio. Santa is smoking a cigarette in the parking lot. Eduardo is fiddling with a giant candy cane. Fake frosted camera-ready Coca-Cola bottles are lined up on the prop table. This is the only line of coke I have seen in any way, shape, or form in a very long time.

One of the elves is standing on an apple box adjacent to the craft table, surrounded by the crew. Even with the added booster, everyone still manages to tower over her, hanging onto her every word. She's sharing lurid anecdotes about her job as a waitress in an event stretch limo and then continues to enlighten her entourage with the unfiltered untold truth about little people orgies that are apparently all the rage at little people conventions.

I'm appalled. I am certain these are not the kinds of conversations that elves would be having in Santa's workshop.

She's ruining the Christmas-y mood, but the crew appears to be absolutely enthralled by her stories, so I don't intervene. A slutty elf has infiltrated my set, but I am far from a Yuletide saint.

The Bathroom Stall
Toronto
1999

An anonymous encounter in a bathroom stall can be a thrilling experience. The venue certainly has enticing advantages, but there's no question that it's dimensionally challenging to work within. On one such occasion, my co-conspirator and I navigate the landscape, exploring the spatial inadequacies. We grip onto the cubicle door for support. It clatters back and forth violently during our passionate exchange. Unbeknownst to us, the intense, frenetic activity, causes the lock mechanism to disengage. What were the chances? We did not see that coming.

Without notice, we are suddenly catapulted out of the chamber, exploding through the door like human projectiles launched from a cannon. As we stagger across the room, limbs flailing, pants around our ankles, zipping along the floor like out-of-control Geisha girls. Our attempt to regain our composure is unsuccessful. We narrowly escape being concussed by a row of porcelain urinals on the far side of the room, and our landing is far from graceful. We wind up a discombobulated mass of flesh and clothing on the cold tile floor. The situation is beyond embarrassing. Certainly not the thrilling experience I was hoping for.

The Divorce
Miami
September 3, 2000

Frank tells me I can get back on the horse, the bus, the ladder, the lifeboat, or whichever metaphorical object of my choosing. I've slid to the bottom of the board game.

I can pick up the dice and start over. I am ashamed and crestfallen, but I decide to begin the process all over again.

I am more cautious this second time around. I am wary of the snakes in the grass, the mulch, or wherever they may be lurking. Now, I know that what they say is true. My addiction is cunning, baffling, and powerful.

I am told while I am getting sober, my disease is like a prison inmate, locked up but definitely not idle. It is doing push-ups, squats, and deadlifts. The damn thing is mirroring my workout routine! It is getting stronger, poised to break out the instant it sees a crack in the wall or my vulnerable constitution.

I must be vigilant to keep it at bay. My life is at stake. I am convinced I need to be one step ahead of this invisible opponent. I beef up my workout regimen. Mark tells me I've most likely transferred my addiction…the heavy lifting I should be putting my energy into is step work. He's probably right, but I can't deny that I'm looking more buff. I slide a 45-pound plate onto the bar and then another 25. I straddle the bench press. I'm sure I can pump out one more set.

Grease
Toronto
June 1978

The movie Grease has just been released. I'm obsessed with the film and the soundtrack. I have a crush on Olivia Newton-John, and I think John Travolta too.

Costa and I have added another member to our group, an Asian boy called Ken. We call ourselves The Three Musketeers. At lunchtime, we go to Costa's house because both his parents work and the house is empty. We put the Grease soundtrack cassette tape into a boombox and play it over and over again. We belt out 'Summer Lovin', 'Sandy', and 'You're the One That I Want'.

Ken has a higher voice, so he sings the girl parts.

Sandy
South Beach
September 14, 2000

Sandy is a six-foot-three former New York model with dirty blonde hair and classic chiseled American features. He's not Olivia Newton-John, but he definitely acts like her. He's a big, giddy schoolgirl wrapped in a man's muscular body. Sandy shows me his portfolio from his days in the fashion world. We flip through his photographic past, and he points out career highlights as well as the lineage of his multitude of noses, tracking them with accompanying bracketing timelines like they've had lives of their own.

"This was the original," Sandy says when he opens the book and looks at the first picture, "I had it until 1984. A little too much of a hook for my liking."

He stares at the photograph like he's looking at a long-lost family member, then turns the page and says, "Sayonara."

He flips through the portfolio, pausing occasionally to give me juicy sidebar fashion-runway anecdotes.

"This shoot was an absolute nightmare. The photographer kept pestering me for sex," Sandy confesses, "I let him blow me at lunch just so we could get the damn shot."

Sandy turns a few more pages and stops on another picture.

"Nose Number 2," he looks at the image with disgust, "1984 to 1987. That thing practically killed my career…couldn't wait to get it off of my face."

Sandy quickly turns the page and continues to flip through the portfolio, finally stopping on an image of him in a Tommy Hilfiger print ad, "Nose Number 3." he announces, smiling triumphantly. "Finally got it right."

Sandy has had quite a life in the Big Apple. He's bitten a large chuck out of it, but it's bitten back too. A high-end clothing brand once commissioned a replica of his body for a mass-produced mannequin. After a binge weekend, he found himself wandering the streets alone in sketchy desperation. When he came face to face with a team of his better-dressed mannequin selves staring back at him from a storefront window on 5th Avenue, he knew it is a sign.

"That was a wake-up call if I ever had one," he says.

Sandy tells me he quit modelling shortly after that because of the ludicrous demands at a casting call.

"They kept telling me to smile with my eyes," he scoffs while rolling his eyes to the back of his head, "After the fifth try, I was over it."

Sandy left the room, New York and his modelling career behind.

He found a new life in Miami Beach, working as a real estate agent. This is his first attempt at recovery, and I am starting over, so we bond like glue. Sandy is as vain as I am and shares my narcissistic obsession for physical perfection. We become 'work-out partners', and I am soon to discover this relationship is sacrosanct, even more so than any kind of significant other.

We grip onto dumbbells, barbells, and kettlebells like we are striving to be the belle of some imaginary gay ball. If we are not at a meeting or the beach, we are working out at David's gym on Alton Road, as if we are training for an extreme makeover.

Sandy and I never miss a training session, and we're always on time. We're supportive of each other and spot one another until failure without fail. Each of us helps push the other beyond our capabilities and into our potential future better-looking selves.

Our workouts are not only physically intense, they're emotionally cathartic, too. They're like full-service therapy sessions with energy drinks, protein shakes, and laughter. We tell each other everything, from our deepest, darkest secrets to our frivolous wants and dreams. We spare no details when confessing our over-indulgent sexual escapades either.

Nothing is edited. There is no filter. Everything is over-shared in the strictest of confidence, mostly while we're treading on adjacent elliptical trainers that sit atop a raised platform in the gym. We call this space 'The Cone of Silence,' but the acoustics allow everyone in the facility to hear absolutely everything we are saying to each other between breathless pants. I am not fazed by the attention.

It makes me feel vaguely nostalgic and reminds me of my brunch performances with Cathy in Toronto a lifetime ago.

Most of the people in the gym are dedicated bodybuilders. Laughing, chuckling, giggling, or any outward display of levity is frowned upon. To some degree, so is excessive talking. It appears grunts and groans are the only socially acceptable sounds, and they are exclusively used if one is attempting to lift a weight that is far beyond one's capability. This is serious business, and our antics are not making us any friends anytime soon.

Sandy and I are usually howling with laughter before, after, and in between sets. We are definitely giving our solar plexuses a workout if nothing else. Joy is bursting at the seams, like the bulging veins in our forearms. While mirroring each other on the cable machine, we are certain we have created a new Olympic sport, a discipline we like to call 'synchronized weightlifting'.

Before one of our training sessions, Sandy offers me a testosterone shot.

"In Miami, giving someone a shot of testosterone is like offering them a shot of espresso," Frank says dryly.

When in Rome… the shot becomes a part of our workout ritual. This involves each of us alternately bending over with our shorts around our ankles, so one of us can inject a shot of testosterone into the other's ass cheek.

The two of us are wholeheartedly dedicated to our holistic approach to mind/body/spirit recovery. We're not sure if we are growing spiritually, but our bodies are easily getting enormous. At one point, after an intense tricep/bicep super set, our arms are positively gargantuan. I stare at both of us in the mirror in disbelief. It's as if our arms have been ripped off and replaced with ginormous ones from male action figure dolls.

We christen this exercise 'Armageddon' and are compelled to put our Cirque de So Gay signature stamp on every exercise in our workout regimen. We are sure members in our vicinity think our code names 'Bring the Bowl to the Diva', 'Ass'n Abs'n Ass', and 'Milk The Cow' are euphemisms for salacious sexual shenanigans, but they should know from our Cone of Silence confessionals that we have nothing to hide.

Frank will occasionally join us for a workout if he is feeling fat. Sandy and I won't let anyone else infiltrate our tightly guarded bubble, but Frank is the exception. He is granted an unlimited exclusive guest star pass in our two-man show whenever he wants. With Frank in the mix, the laugh factor multiplies tenfold.

Upon entering the facility, Frank will glance around, take a deep breath, and boldly announce in his best impression of Faye Dunaway as Joan Crawford, "There's a lot of talent in this room, fellas."

At one point, he will walk around the weight room as if he were carrying an imaginary clipboard and judging some sort of contest. Then he'll saunter back to us with a big grin on his face, nod to some juice monkey doing squats, and declare, "Best in Show…definitely Best in Show."

Porn Stars
Miami
2001

The Dog and Pony Show that is South Beach definitely has a lot of candidates qualified to be 'Best in Show'. Many well-known Porn Stars make the beach their home, and many workout at our gym. Most are young, fit, and attractive with marketable appendages, but there are a few exceptions. The industry caters to an array of niche predilections, and some of the men don't fit the stereotypical mold.

I meet one of the latter who looks like an overweight accountant from Albuquerque. I would never have pegged him as someone who dabbled in this line of work, but he is notably proud of his vocation.

He offers unsolicited information about his calling unprompted and, in the span of our short conversation, refers to himself as a 'porn star' on more than one occasion. He tells me he's in demand because he has 'a special skill set'.

"Not many people can do what I do," he boasts.

I take the bait. I ask him what he's been in.

"Fist Pigs 4," he replies.

It's the 4 that throws me off. I'm surprised the first three instalments were such a resounding success they required a sequel. I had no idea fists or pigs were that popular, but apparently, they were! This was like the Fast and Furious fisting franchise!

A week later, I was in the hospital for a colonoscopy. Franka picks me up after the procedure. She shows up with a pink piglet puppet in her hand and entertains me with an impromptu ventriloquist routine.

"I'm a fist pig, too!" The piglet squeals, "I really spring to life when a fist is shoved up inside of me."

Street Vendors
South Beach
2002

Artists, craftspeople, and street performers have organically started to blossom along Lincoln Road like a tropical flowering shrub. There are little splashes of color and life alongside the fountains and planters that grace the center of the bustling street. It is a testament that something special is happening here. One can feel it. The ground is fertile for imagination. A shirtless male model sells T-shirts too. He's surrounded by hordes of people and sells a lot of shirts by not wearing one himself. An artist called Anna, who creates small whimsical paintings, tells me that I should sell on the street.

"It's good," she says.

When I am back home, I shift my gaze to the stack of paintings that have accumulated on the floor.

Can I possibly do this?

I am a little petrified at the thought of dragging all this stuff out onto the street, but my bank account is rapidly dwindling again, so I decide to give it a try.

The next morning, I feel a twinge of anxiety in the pit of my stomach, but I gather up my courage along with the stack of paintings. I roll them into a tube and secure it with a piece of rope. I put on my cowboy hat, climb onto my bicycle, and balance the cumbersome roll of paintings under one arm. I ride along the pathway on Ocean Drive and find a little spot to set up shop. I never would have imagined I would be doing something like this when I first arrived at the beach a couple of years ago, but this journey has been nothing I could have imagined.

Now, by all outward appearances…I'm a street artist. This is by far one of my greatest fears, so the fact that I am able to do this at all is a miracle. It feels as though I am baring my soul to the world for all to see and required to stand beside it as well.

Usually, when I am setting up, a stranger will pass by and say something positive. It will give me the little jolt of validation I need to continue. Then, I sit and wait. This is retail…and most of my day is spent baking in the Sun and watching people walk by.

I find it fascinating that some people will just walk by like I don't even exist, absorbed in their own thoughts, while others will stop, react, and be affected in some way. I know when someone is interested when they look at something, walk away, and then return a couple of hours later. The first time I sell a painting to a stranger, it's a rush. My work is unframed and on paper, and I discover that this is an asset. Most people are here on vacation, so they are able to roll up the paintings, even the David-sized ones, and bring them onto an airplane.

The amazing thing about being right on the street is that you never know who is walking around South Beach. I meet interior designers, actors, and interesting people from all over the world. I sell four paintings to a French couple, and a few months later, they return and buy five more. Most days, I sell at least one painting. Anna was right. This is good.

I have become used to the routine. I am the guy in the cowboy hat selling seahorses by the seashore. I show up, set up shop, and tear down all in one day. I am the factory, the marketing department, the accounting department, and sales and promotions. What started out as a fun hobby has now become my main source of income.

I learn a lot about the art of bartering. My willingness to engage in this activity has a lot to do with whether I like the person or not, as well as how desperate I am for money.

And as the months pass, I become more desperate.

One Year
Miami Beach
September 3, 2001

I did it. One year clean and sober. I can't believe it, and even though I thought I would feel incredible, the truth is… I'm miserable. I am struggling financially again, struggling to be in my own skin. I feel as flat as an autumn leaf pressed between the pages of a book, that is…if there were seasons here. Inside, I am lost, and I know it.…

I have moved into a more moderately priced apartment that's not as nice and with no view of the ocean. I'm starting to doubt this whole entire recovery process. It is the first time in my life that I do not trust the inside of my head. I do not trust my thoughts.

Something needs to change…and little did I know, something was about to. Something was going to happen in 8 days that would not only affect me but it would change the entire world.

The Towers
Miami Beach
September 11, 2001

There is a Tarot card called The Tower. The image on the card is a medieval stone tower being struck by a bolt of lightning. The structure is crumbling while two people are falling to their deaths below. The card is a testament that nothing…absolutely nothing is permanent.

The world forever changed on this day… and my life did, too. The shock of what happened in New York appears to have reverberated all the way down the coastline and all over the Earth.

I feel as though I am standing in the ruins that have crumbled around me.

I would not know it then, but this would be the beginning. It would be the start of true sobriety. I would be able to rebuild my life.

They say when the student is ready, the teacher will appear...and when the dust settles, I see a silhouetted figure in the distance.

CHAPTER 13
THE LEPRECHAUN TEACHINGS

**The Leprechaun Teachings: A Life Beyond Your
Wildest Dreams
South Beach
September 20, 2001**

Patrick O'Flanagan is an eloquent, well-mannered, compact Irish man with sparkling green eyes who reminds me of a magical Leprechaun. There's a lightness around him as if he's coasting on a pink cloud. When we first meet, he tells me he will teach me everything he knows, and if I do what he says, I will have a life beyond my wildest dreams…on one condition…

I feel as though making a sacred pact with an otherworldly entity will have dire consequences down the line, but I have no other option but to ask him what that is.

"You must agree to give it away," he says.

"Is that it?" I respond, relieved.

The Leprechaun smiles, leans in, and whispers something as if it's the greatest secret in the universe.

"It's not your job to manage your life," he says.

My head explodes.

What is that supposed to mean?

If I don't manage things? Who will?

Modus Operandi
Toronto
1987

In film school, most of my classmates have famous parents who are well-established in the industry. Others are from wealthy, privileged families. I don't have either. All I have to cling to is my imagination, which is a consequence of my traumatic childhood.

There is no denying an unquestionable force that motivates me to excel exists deep inside of me. This drive compels me to show the world how damaged I am by working ten times harder than anyone else. A Modus Operandi that works like a charm. I am recognized. I am at the top of my class. I win awards, although I am not sure exactly what is being awarded. The awards are feeding the beast.

Evidently, I can make things happen. This truth ingrains itself in my being. It finds a comfortable spot beside The Unholy Union…and ultimately, they join forces. This thing manifests into a deadly multi-headed hydra that would put Medusa to shame.

This obsessive drive and sheer force of will is directly responsible for my premature launch into a director's chair… and also directly responsible for my rapid ejection out of it.

Free Will
Miami Beach
November 2001

I am kept on a short leash for this second attempt at recovery. The committee has not deemed me worthy of a financial buffer, so I am buffer-less. I spend most of my time intellectually jousting with The Leprechaun, sitting across from this pint-sized spiritual guru, battling grand philosophical concepts at length.

"Ultimately God gave us free will…so indirectly my will is God's will…was it not?" I ask him.

"You are most certainly correct," The Leprechaun says with a glint in his eye, "but all of those choices have led you to this moment. You're sitting in front of me, hopeless, desperate…looking for another way."

Bang.

My argument is shot dead. It's floating…lifeless in the water like a discarded plastic bag. The thing sinks below the surface and disappears. The Leprechaun has the ability to do that. He can root out any clever justification I may have and obliterate it with uncanny marksman-like precision. It's his magical superpower. Apparently, I am not the only one with a rifle.

He tells me he can do this because he used to be me.

I used to be me too…I think to myself. I have no idea who I am now.

"I know how you think," Patty O'Flanagan will say, "I know what you want…and I'm sorry to say …that's not going to work anymore."

The Leprechaun continues, "Maybe God's will for you is that you continue working the steps in recovery."

I just stare at him.

"You keep digging. I'll hold the lantern," he concludes.

I'm kind of confused. I don't know if I am going up a ladder or digging a hole, but I am grateful that this little wise leprechaun with glowing eyes is willing to stand by and help.

The Leprechaun O'Flanagan tells me that my will must be aligned with something bigger than myself. Not my own. The program will help me do that.

"This is about saving people's lives," he will say, "is that not more important than any frivolous plans you may have?"

Bang.

He's done it again. I nod my head like a baby chick in a nest.

I vow to do whatever this little Leprechaun tells me to do without question.

Cuba Libra
Miami
December 2001

My identity crisis in recovery is mirrored by the multitude of job titles I hold at this time in order to make ends meet. When the Towers collapsed, the economy did, too. I am forced to take an array of menial jobs just to survive. An eerie quiet has fallen over the beach. There aren't any tourists wandering around, and I am not selling any paintings. I am still teaching part-time at the ad school, but the income I make from that is nominal. Teaching at the school has not been as rewarding as I had imagined it would be. Most of my students remind me of the privileged kids I went to school with...on steroids. It turns out privilege has evolved. The breed of Millennials in my class exudes an unquestionable air of arrogance. They really don't want anyone to teach them anything…they know it all already. They want my job. Part of me wants to tell them to back off…I want my job, too. I haven't directed anything in months.

I am reduced to working as an assistant window dresser in high-end shops like Louis Vuitton, and I also cater waiter at events held at the Versace mansion, Vizcaya, and The Wolfsonion.

These jobs provide me with a window into the lives of the impossibly rich people in Miami while allowing me to take leftover bags of food home.

When an artist, Pascal, a wealthy descendant from the royal family in Monaco, comes to Miami for a pop-up art exhibition, I am hired to help in the gallery.

If only I could have this kind of space to show my work, I would be thrilled beyond belief, but here, too, I am only to be of service. I do what I am told.

I get a job in another gallery, if you can call it that. This one is a tourist trap on Lincoln Rd that sells paintings from mediocre commercial artists and pre-fabricated prints. It's a horrible place to work, and the owner is a tyrant with bad breath. Part of my job requires me to stand in the doorway and offer people shots of alcohol when they enter. This, I assume, is meant to lubricate their better judgment in an attempt to make their money free flow out of their wallets.

"Cuba Libra?" I will say, stone-cold sober while holding a tray of tiny plastic rum-filled shot glasses.

Cuba Libra?

I am anything but free…How did I get here?

The Leprechaun tells me the sober thing to do is to support myself, but a part of me wants to die. I am positive I do not need a special artist's Visa to stand here with this tray. I am worried a student of mine will wander into the space and unveil me as a fraud.

The Iron Imprint
Toronto
1997

I am apartment hunting in Cabbagetown and scoping a unit right next door to where I lived when I made my infamous appearance as the Underwear Vigilante a few years back. I am fully clothed and pretty sure I'm incognito. The suite stretches out over the entire top floor of a large Victorian mansion that sits on the North West corner of Winchester and Metcalfe, across from the Toronto Dance Theatre. The unit features a claw foot tub, an attic loft bedroom, interesting angular walls, and walks out onto a wooden deck that's as big as the place.

It's just what I am looking for, except for the fact that there is the imprint of an iron seared in the center of the carpet in the middle of the floor. It's the strangest thing I think I have ever seen. It makes me laugh out loud when I first notice it and then makes me ponder on how this scorched mark came to be.

Honestly, really, who irons anymore anyway?…and on the floor to boot?

I am perplexed as I attempt to decipher the sequence of events that led to this oddity of an art installation. It looks like the singed needle on a compass perpetually pointing South.

We are standing with the imprint between us when the landlord introduces himself as "Mr. Patience".

"I'm Mr. Impatience," I reply without skipping a beat.

"I'll take it," I exclaim, "that is…on the condition that the carpet can be replaced."

I look down at the mark.

My intention for the quick-witted response is to charm Mr. Patience to hand over the keys immediately and without reservation.

Inadvertently, I've also given him a window into one of my itchy personality characteristics. As it turns out, he is true to his even-tempered namesakes and insists on checking my references before handing anything over.

When I move into the space a few weeks later, there is no trace of the iron stamp. It's gone. The unit is a blank canvas, and I am free to leave my mark on it. Ironically, I purchase an iron shortly thereafter, but assuredly, its purpose is not to press clothes. I am working on an art project and require a piece of equipment that is hot enough to melt wax. I set up a station on the floor in the middle of the room. I am beyond careful with the heated device. I do not want history to repeat itself. The ghostly memory of the iron imprint resurfaces in my mind and makes me smile.

It's permanently singed there as well. As I work, I wonder if this is, in fact, how it came to be.

Deep in thought, I absentmindedly hit the standing appliance. The iron flops over. I reach out to retrieve it immediately, but it's too late. In an instant, the hot apparatus has left a burnt impression on the carpet. I stare at it in disbelief, mesmerized by the charred stamp. It's in the exact same spot as the previous mark, ominously pointing South. I am positive the house is haunted. I scan the room for a trickster spirit. Something… an entity with an affinity for housework, perhaps, adamantly wants this signature impression to exist on this floor. I am, in fact, destined to travel South in a few short years, and it is possible that this is some kind of a sign. A prophetic pointer foreshadowing the direction I am ultimately to take.

I am beyond embarrassed when I have to explain to Mr. Patience what happened. We are facing each other as we did months earlier with the imprint between us. He stares at me with an awkward smile, and a part of me thinks he thinks I did it on purpose.

I am thoroughly convinced that sometimes things are just meant to be…no matter how hard one tries to change them.

The Leprechaun Teachings: A Menu of Choices
Miami
January 2002

The Leprechaun O'Flanagan and I are sitting on a patio just off Lincoln Road. He often says things that make me laugh out loud because they are so true.

"If you want to drive an alcoholic crazy," he announces while momentarily glancing up from a menu, "don't call them back."

I break into a smile. I can relate. I hate it when that happens.

The server arrives, and Patrick orders a pesto prosciutto panini.

"Sobriety is just a menu of choices," he says.

It appears that the world is an all-you-can-eat buffet, and it's up to the consumer to make appropriate nutritional selections.

"Active addiction robs us of the power of choice…" Patrick adds a little later while biting into his sandwich. "The definition of insanity is doing the same thing over and over again, expecting different results."

As he is explaining this to me, I wonder if my mother was, in fact, my first dealer, cementing the foundation of my addictive tendencies with breaded veal cutlets. I am certain her intentions were good, but like dropping bread crumbs onto a path, she may have unintentionally mashed up my psyche along with those yellow flesh potatoes and set up the foundation for a plethora of misguided developmental patterns.

Mamma also used sugar as a motivational tool. She would bribe me with the thinly veiled promise of chocolate and say… "If you do this or that…I will give you 'something good'".

One was never quite sure what the 'something good' was. There was always a sense of mystery surrounding the thing hidden inside of her handbag…like in 'Let's Make a Deal', you never knew exactly what was behind door number three: a brand-new car or a box of Rice-A-Roni.

In my negotiations with Mamma, more often than not, I took the bait.

The 'something good' was usually chocolate, but sometimes, after all was said and done, all she would do was drop a Tic Tac into my hand.

A Tic Tac?

I was hornswoggled.

Not that there's anything inherently wrong with a Tic Tac, but when you're expecting chocolate, a breath mint just isn't the same.

The more I think about it, the more I am beginning to believe that Mamma really was the master engineer who laid down the gastronomical groundwork for my express train to crack town. I cannot deny the fact that I have expectations, and if I like something, I want more of it day after day, week after week, year after year. Apparently, today, I can choose how I want to live my life…it's a menu of choices, after all. Even though deep down inside I know I have no choice but to do whatever my Leprechaun instructor tells me to do.

I am instructed to reach out to The Leprechaun every morning to get my day off to the right start. During these conversations, the disembodied voice on the other end of the line appears to know exactly what I'm thinking. I do not tell him that I am depressed, lost, and directionless. He just knows. He's aware that my random thoughts are like rogue ping-pong balls bouncing around in my head and that I have several going at once. He knows that this cacophony of sound builds in intensity to the point where I want to throw my red paddle up in despair. He tells me to harness the balls one by one like a Bingo machine and make a list of what needed to be done. Then…just go through the list.

Bingo!

It sounds surprisingly simple, but it works. People in recovery really like lists, charts, and columns, but I can't deny that I feel better after I have accomplished some of the tasks.

The Leprechaun tells me if I follow his teachings, I will establish something called 'sober reference'. When I have built up enough 'sober reference', I will be able to refer back to my actions in sobriety and see what has transpired. This will become my experience, and I will come to trust in this new set of principles with which to live my life.

I hand over my mind to the Leprechaun like a brain on a platter. I don't trust the serial killer inside of me. It's like I am stripped to the core, naked and raw, baring my soul to the light of the Sun.

Nudes
South Beach
March 2002

I am stripped to the core, naked and raw, baring my soul to the light of the sun…and climbing onto the ledge of a house. In my mind's eye, this will be a great shot, but I am not behind the camera. I am in front of it. A couple of photographers have come into town, and David Leddick has asked a few of us if we would be willing to pose for them.

Sandy and I agree because we are both self-admitted narcissists and believe a photo shoot will inspire us to get into better shape.

I am initially self-conscious when I first drop my drawers, but surprisingly, after a few minutes, walking around naked feels like the most natural thing in the world. While up on the ledge, I can see over the tall bushes that surround the house, into the street and oncoming traffic. A part of me wants to wave.

"Sobriety is to be worn like a loose-fitting garment," The Leprechaun will say...but as I lounge on the ledge stripped to the core, I realize I much prefer to wear nothing at all.

The location we are shooting at is a beautiful home owned by an older gay couple who have been together forever since the 60s. One of them is called David, but he is not a part of the Trifecta of Davids... he's a part of a couple known as David and Lee. One seldom sees them apart. Their respective hairstyles have been frozen in time and have stopped evolving since the 1970s. Lee has dark shoulder-length Robert Plant classic rock star curls. David has a Shaun Cassidy/Farrah Fawcett blond feathered do, parted in the middle.

These men are two of the kindest people one would ever want to meet. Their spacious home is like an art gallery and historical gay museum rolled into one. Every square foot of the place is full of homoerotic art…from black and white photographs, paintings, sculptures, and even tiny Fabergé eggs covered with erect Grecian Gods.

They tell me their claim to fame was inventing the edible underwear but had to give up the patent to the mob who apparently gave them 'an offer they couldn't refuse'.

Lee is an artist, too. His work is an amalgamation of different mediums from different decades. He shoots models with a video camera, then takes a Polaroid of a frame off of a television set, scans the image into a computer, prints it out onto canvas, and adds some paint. The overall effect is voyeuristically hypnotic.

Lee and I are members of a group of artists who live in Miami. One day, Lee is having a conversation with some of the artists. I approach them, assuming they are in the midst of an enlightened conversation about art, but to my dismay, they *are* discussing art…the high cost of shipping it.

The Leprechaun Teachings: Action
South Beach
May 2002

Leprechaun O'Flanagan explains that recovery, whether one is clothed or naked, replaces unconscious repetitive behavior with mindful, self-esteem-able actions. I am told my default setting is to be selfish, self-centered, and live in fear. I am told in order to be able to be a useful participant in this world, useful to others, and to myself, I must separate feelings from facts. Feelings have absolutely no value to me. What I *do* is what is important.

"This is an action-oriented program," The Leprechaun will say.

I am reminded of all the times I have shouted out 'Action!' on set and now wonder if it was really an order directed at myself.

To get further clarity on what is going on in the complicated annals of my mind, The Leprechaun instructs me to take an inventory of my life. He tells me to pretend

I am a store manager, and it's my job to take an inventory of the goods for sale. I must scour over every aisle. I *am* the store, and apparently, I have stored unwanted merchandise on some of the shelves. I must isolate and identify things that are of no use to me anymore…things like rotten bananas. I'm not to judge or criticize the rotten bananas…I just have to identify them and separate them from the other unspoiled fruit. Here is where it gets tricky. I do not have the power to throw the bananas away…I just can't.

Apparently, I can't throw anything away. The only one who can remove anything from the store…is a power greater than myself, God…Gad. He is able to discard the rotting fruit from the store, which is me. I can't.

A part of me wants to argue, 'If I'm the store manager, can't I just hire someone to do this inventory for me?'

…but I can't do that either.

Horses in the Window
South Beach
June 2002

I am able to throw away things in my apartment. I'm downsizing. I am moving again…out of my studio and into a smaller, less attractive space. I decide to get rid of a painting of three horse heads on a piece of wood. I don't really like it, and it's just too heavy to move. I set the piece outside, along with the rest of the garbage.

My neighbor sees the painting and exclaims, "What's this? I love it!"

I'm a little surprised by his comment, and when I tell him I am throwing it out, he asks me if he can have it.

"Sure," I say, "Take it."

The Last Straw
Toronto
September 1971

I have a crush on my Grade One teacher. Miss Moore. She is kind and thoughtful. At the start of the year, the class is told to create a picture on black craft paper using toothpicks. I create a toothpick boy on a toothpick bicycle. The tires are the most challenging part of this project. I had to break a lot of toothpicks in order to create a circular shape, and at the end of it all, they still looked kind of square. The boy is a fragile stick figure, but he is happy and free, waving his skinny toothpick arms up in the air. I love the picture, and Miss Moore loves it too.

She put the picture up on the board, front and center, with other pictures around it. It stayed there all year.

Toronto
June 1972

It is the last day of school before summer vacation. Miss Moore has cleared off the board and is handing everyone back their artwork.

She calls out my name and I walk to the front of the class. Miss Moore is holding the picture of the toothpick boy and asks me if I want it back.

I love the picture, but I love Miss Moore more. I am happy to give it to her as a token of my love for her. I am moving into grade 2 next year, and I will miss her dearly. I am sure she will miss me too. The picture will be something that she can remember me by.

"You can have it," I say.

Miss Moore smiles, "Thank you," she replies.

Everyone waves goodbye to Miss Moore. We all leave the classroom excited for summer vacation and for what's to come.

I am halfway down the hallway when I remember I left my pencil case on my desk. I hurry back to retrieve it. When I entered the classroom, it's empty. Miss Moore is gone. My pencil case is right where I left it. I walk down the row of little wooden desks to pick it up. I'm about to exit the room when something makes me look down. That's when I see it...in the garbage can. The toothpick boy on the toothpick bicycle, his arms in the air, waving for help. I am devastated. I quickly scoop him up. I save the boy from oblivion...but I cannot save myself from the painful realization that Miss Moore did not love me back.

She threw me away.

South Beach
June 2002

Sandy and I are about to start our workout at the gym.

"I saw a painting of yours in the window of a framing store," he says, "The one on Alton Road."

I have no idea what he's talking about.

"It's definitely yours…" he says, "has your name on it, unless someone's copying you." Sandy continues, "Three horse heads. Has a for sale sign on it."

After our workout, I head to the store. It's closed, but as I approach the window, there they are. The horse heads I wanted to throw away… the painting my neighbor took….it's now for sale in a storefront window on Alton Rd… saved from oblivion just like the toothpick boy.

Sometimes, human beings are not granted the same fate. Sometimes, they disappear into oblivion. Sometimes, they throw themselves away.

Toronto
January, 1999

Stephan hangs up the phone. His voice is flat. His face is expressionless. They found his cousin. She was a homeless drug addict and missing for days. Her lifeless body was in a dumpster.

She just threw herself away.

The Leprechaun Teachings: Tools
South Beach
August 2002

I use a scalpel to

carve jewels in my eyelids

So I may see the world

in its distorted beauty crumble

Give me a shovel

and I will not dig my grave

I will use it as a spoon

to feed the giants poison

The Leprechaun tells me that recovery can be used like a tool belt wrapped around my core. This new accessory can be accessed at my disposal and replaces my antiquated, archaic tools.

Apparently, I can use The Leprechaun O'Flanagan as a tool too. He invites me to call him whenever I'm angry. This is the strangest invitation I think I have ever received. I'm not sure why he wants me to do this, but he tells me he can take it.

"Don't hesitate to reach out, especially when there is something that's really pissing you off," he says, smiling. Then he adds, "I don't extend this invitation to everyone, you know," as if I am a part of an exclusive club.

I'm not sure if this man is some kind of sadomasochist seeking unsolicited abuse, but I take him up on his offer.

This is another one of the Leprechaun's superpowers. He has the ability to diffuse my anger like he's hosing down an angry protester.

He unveils what's really going on, what's lying below the surface, beneath all the rage. He can talk me down off of a ledge…even when I am not naked and lounging on top of it.

Who Will Stop The Wind?
South Beach
December 2002

I'm running out of money again. This keeps happening to me. I'm exhausted from this repeating ritual. Whatever I do, it seems I cannot escape the circumstances of my financial predicament. It's like the iron flopping over onto the carpet...like it's meant to be. I'm a starving artist, literally. I desperately need to sell a painting.

Today I would let even my most cherished work go for little to next to nothing, just so I can eat. It's Sunday, which is usually the best day to sell.

When I arrive at my spot by the steps, I'm greeted by a gentle gust of wind. It hits me square in the face, blows past me, and dissipates just as quickly. This little blast of air was to be an ominous foreshadowing of what was to transpire in the not-too-distant future, but I did not know it then. I stand still for a moment to assess the situation. Part of me wants to lick my finger and hold it in the air but I don't. I decide the conditions are not that bad and continued to set up.

I rest several of my larger paintings on the steps and attach them to a line with clothespins to make sure they're secure. Once I have them down, a second gust of wind materializes, seemingly out of nowhere. It's a short, powerful blast. It catches one of my paintings, and the artwork flies into the sky like an airborne kite. It lands several feet away, and I rush to pick it up. A few minutes later, there's another gust. This one is stronger. Two more paintings break away. They soar into the air and land even further down the street.

The blasts of air start to manifest more frequently ...they're persuasive and more robust, too. They're like contractions on a pregnant woman, and the sky is definitely dilating.

Paintings are flying away at inconsistent intervals. I have to chase them down the street, and before I'm back, even more take flight. I swear out loud. I feel like a plate spinner at a sideshow circus, and not a very good one at that. I'm running from one painting to the next, attempting to retrieve them as they soar down the street.

The wind is relentless, and the artwork is getting damaged. I know I look ridiculous, but I still can't bring myself to leave. I need to sell something. I need the money.

I am sure if I stay just a little bit longer, the wind will die down, someone will show up, and I'll sell a painting.

It's happened before. But the gusts just keep coming, stronger, thicker, and faster than ever.

It reaches a point where none of the paintings are on the line anymore. I am kneeling on all of them to keep them secure. My wish to make a sale today has vanished like the opaque petals of a dandelion disappearing in the breeze. Nothing is going how I had hoped. I'm fuming and because The Leprechaun tells me to call him when I'm angry, that's what I do.

"You're trying to stop the wind," The Leprechaun says. I want to burst into tears.

"I need to sell a painting…I'm broke," I reply.

"Go home," The Leprechaun calmly advises, "Surrender."

I am literally on my knees…in the middle of this street that has transformed into a virtual wind tunnel. I feel like I am in the middle of a hurricane.

"I told you…it's not your job to manage your life," he says, "You're not trusting that you'll be taken care of."

There it is again.

Bang.

The Leprechaun's words penetrate my soul…

I have no choice but to surrender. If I were to raise a white flag then and there, it wouldn't have any problem flapping gloriously in the windstorm above me.

I cannot stop the wind.

I pick myself up from the ground like a wounded animal.

Defeated, I roll my work into a tube and secure it with rope. I bike home. I drop the rolled-up tube on the floor and just stare at it. I'm not sure what to do…

Maybe I should find another spot?

I know this is an insane thought. I have to get out of my apartment immediately. I grab a towel and head towards the beach.

The waterfront is like another world entirely. It's hot and sunny.

I find a spot, put a towel down, and gaze out at the ocean. My acrimonious cardio session in the wind tunnel has done a number on me. Adrenaline is still coursing through my veins. I take deep breaths. I attempt not to think about my financial situation… I am trying to do as The Leprechaun has suggested… I'm trying to believe that I will be taken care of. I look at the blue waves, and I take another deep breath. Just then, a soft wind caresses my face.

What a beautiful breeze… I think to myself.

The irony hits me like a ton of bricks.

It's a beautiful breeze!

A smile cracks my face open. I noticeably laugh out loud. Not less than twenty minutes ago, the wind was driving me to the brink of despair...now it's a gentle offering of peace.

I become conscious that, left to my own devices, I am an insane person trying to stop the wind… but with the help of my very own Leprechaun, it's possible for me to bask in the Sun. Recovery is making it painfully clear to me that everything...absolutely everything around me hinges on how I choose to relate to it. Wind can either drive me crazy or bring me joy.

The next day, I'm blown away, and not by the weather conditions. I get a call from someone who has wanted to purchase some of my work for a while but has been out of the country. He asks me if he can come over to buy a painting and if he can bring a friend who wants to purchase something too.

"Sure, I'm around all day," I reply.

I hang up, and even though I'm inside, feel as though I am being bathed by a ray of light sent from heaven.

The Leprechaun Teachings: Service
Miami
March 2003

My tough Leprechaun teacher doesn't tolerate any of my bullshit. He refuses to co-sign any resentments. He's definitely not Tina. If I complain about anything, absolutely anything, he will offer a new point of view. When I complain that a meeting is boring, he does not empathize with me.

"Did *you* contribute?" He will inquire as if he's prying me open with a stick.

When I answer 'no', Patty O'Flanagan tells me it's my job to be of service at meetings. I can't just sit there. It's my job to 'carry the message'. It's like he told me way back at our very first encounter: I have to give it away.

The Leprechaun teaches me to approach every meeting like it is one giant brain...and every person in the room is like a single cell in that brain. The cells speak to each other...they contribute to the whole. Each person's contribution is either one of faith...or fear...it cannot be both.

Alcoholic cells reek with fear. Recovered cells emanate faith. The net outcome of each meeting is based on the fear/ faith ratio. If fear wins, the alcoholic brain is left swimming in an ocean of vodka.

I am told I can not be a passive bystander. I cannot let fear win. I must share my experience. I must share my light.

The Leprechaun reminds me that when we come into a program of recovery, we are like black holes; drinking, sucking, snorting, fucking everything possible into the vortex without ever obtaining satisfaction. Recovery stops all of that...and, in time, transforms us into a light source, helping to illuminate the way for others. Again, he reminds me… "You do the digging, I'll hold the lantern."

I am told to share the message in meetings, not the mess. The mess is to be dealt with privately by a stern Leprechaun teacher.

The Village
Miami
May 2003

Sandy and I are asked to speak at a double speaker meeting at a treatment center called 'The Village'. We are told it's hard-core. Most of the people in the facility are low-bottom crack addicts and homeless street kids trying to get clean. Meetings at The Village can get rather bleak. In an attempt to solve this dilemma, two speakers are brought in to double dose the message of hope and recovery.

I arrive a few minutes before the scheduled start time to find Sandy standing in front of the facility. He's wearing lime green short shorts and an incredibly tight cut-off top that exposes his mid-drift. It looks like he fell out of an aerobics class in a 1981 Olivia Newton-John music video.

I'm mortified.

Did he not get the memo regarding the venue?

I am about to say something about his choice of wardrobe, but he's beaming at me, grinning from ear to ear. He embraces me with his testosterone-infused arms. I don't have the heart to burst his big, red, shiny gay balloon.

A man called Rod emerges from the complex, greets us, and asks us if we're ready to go in. The entrance to The Village is intimidating. Two large security guards sign us in. We are buzzed through double-locked security doors with a chamber between them. This vestibule is like purgatory, the holding place between two distinct worlds…the free and the imprisoned, although to which group you belong does not necessarily pertain to which side of the door you are standing. The chamber and the harsh sound of the locking mechanism transport me back to the many times I've been buzzed through similar doorways.

Mental Institution Make-over
Toronto
1997

The three of us stand motionless in limbo, locked in the center chamber. When the door behind us is securely latched, the door in front of us buzzes open.

A nurse approaches and says, "She's in Room 15…" then motions down the hallway, "that way."

We walk down the dingy hall of the facility. Gabe has a large bag slung over her shoulder. Her daughter, Danielle, carries a hefty black industrial case with stainless steel clasps. I am carrying a parcel too.

We turn the corner, enter an open door, and come face to face with Virginia. She glares at us through one dominant eye. Her head cocked to one side with a mischievous grin smeared across her face. Her black hair is impossibly enormous. It's a massive, matted Amy Winehouse-inspired rats-nest of tangles and knots. We are all struck silent by the state of her appearance, the unkempt vision of our mad-hatted family member. We try to keep the mood light and positive.

"Hi!" we say in unison, "How are you today?"

Virginia doesn't respond. She's razor-focused, her radar locked on Gabe.

"Still fat," Virginia blurts out.

We're not sure if this is a question or a comment. It's such a harsh, unexpected salutation, loaded with years of sister-sister backstory. It causes everyone to spontaneously burst into laughter. It's the kind of remark that only Virginia can get away with...definitely an ice breaker. In an instant, we're transported to childhood memories of slinging insults at each other. Gabe laughs it off. She doesn't throw a counter-punch. What would be the point? Her target is far too easy.

The wisecrack is so amusing, from that day onward we adopt it as a standard family greeting for holidays and special occasions.

"Still fat," we will say to one another while delivering double-cheeked air kisses on Easter Sunday.

As I look around Virginia's stark hospital room, I am surprised that such simple joy can be found in familiar family dynamics even though we are in such a desolate place as this locked ward.

The three of us have come to give Virginia a make-over. Danielle is a talented hairdresser, ready for the task at hand, although I'm sure she didn't expect the monstrous mane that is in front of her. She begins the laborious process of tackling the knots. Virginia sits in an upright chair. A cape wrapped around her body, secured tightly at the neck, creates the illusion of a severed, talking head.

"What the fuck are you looking at?" The severed head barks when an overweight black woman in pink pajamas peeks around the doorframe and curiously watches the action.

The comment causes the woman to scurry away like a frightened animal, and the severed head gloats with satisfaction.

It takes two hours, but by the end of it, Danielle has worked a miracle. Virginia looks like she could swing her head around in slow motion for a shampoo commercial. We're amazed at the transformation, but it's only just begun.

Gabe reaches into the large bag and pulls out a variety of stylish clothes. Gabriella is the inventor of Gabisthenics, and it is still her default form of communication. She provides animated visual gestures when describing each article of clothing like she's trying to sell merchandise on the Home Shopping Network. Virginia rejects most of the items. She's picky. She'll squash up her face and shake her head. She reminds me of a homeless man in LA I wanted to give a bagel to one day.

"Is it gluten-free?" He asked, ultimately rejecting my offer.

I sit back and watch my sisters interact. I am amazed at Gabe's propensity for inventing new Gabisthenics gestures on the fly. When she pulls out a strapless purse from the bottom of the bag, she asks Virginia if she needs a clutch. Then, even though she's holding the item, Gabe takes one hand and shoves it under her opposing armpit while repeating the word several times.

"It's a clutch..." she'll repeat while performing the accompanying action, smiling. "You know...a clutch."

When all the bags are empty, Virginia looks good. Almost too good, that is, as long as she doesn't open her mouth to reveal toothless gums.

"You won't make a dime if you wear any of this while you're panhandling," I say just before we leave. "but at least you can put your money in your clutch."

I can't help myself. I look at Gabe when I say 'clutch' and perform the certified gesture for the word.

"Am I doing it right?" I ask.

We all laugh. This has been a good visit, one of the better ones...with Virginia, you never know what you're going to get, and some are definitely better than others. Virginia walks us to the limbo chamber and waves at us through the wire glass as we stand in the locked vestibule. We take a good, long look at her. We know that the next time we see her, the stylish clothing we just gave her will have disappeared, clutch included, and her hair will be back to its usual matted state.

But at this moment, we're happy to have helped her. I guess this is what the Leprechaun means when he talks about the joy of being of service. It makes you feel good...like you're doing some good in the world. We feel light as air; we could almost float away, but we can't...one of us is 'still fat' and is obviously weighing us down.

Miami
May 2003

Ron, Sandy, and I stand motionless, locked in the vestibule...the threshold between two worlds. When the door behind us is securely closed, the door in front buzzes open.

We walk down the hall of the facility. The walls are a dingy yellow, and the air is heavy and stale. We enter the meeting space and make our way to the front of the room.

"The faggots are here," A tattooed skinhead says, loud enough for us and most of the room to hear.

A few people laugh.

Sandy's short shorts are a dead giveaway. Of course, we're faggots.

This is going to be a nightmare. I am dreading this already. I gaze out into the room. Clearly, most of the people do not want to be here. They are slouched in their chairs, and some have their feet up. They look bored. They look angry. Their faces are hardened from life on the street. I am judging them, and I know it, but I can't help myself. I'm positive any one of them wouldn't think twice about slitting my throat for a hit, given a chance.

Sandy leans into me, "Can you go first?" he whispers.

I want to respond, 'No, you go first.' …but a part of me just wants to get this over with. I feel like I'm about to be thrown to the lions.

Rod begins to introduce me. I start to panic. I can't possibly tell these people what really happened. They will never believe any of it. I want to lie. I want to fabricate a sordid story to cater to this hard-core crowd. I want to tell them I was living on the streets and huffing crack cocaine in alleys, but I know I can't do that. I've learned my lesson with The House Two Doors Down: lying doesn't really work out for anybody, especially me. Chances are my lies will inspire them to lynch the lying faggots. I can see Sandy's green short shorts flapping in the wind on the flagpole out front. My only recourse is to tell the truth. It's my story. I'm sticking to it. I feel like a village idiot, but there's no turning back. I open my mouth and start speaking.

Before I know it, it's over. When I am done, the mood in the room has changed. I've connected with them on some level. After Sandy finishes speaking, everyone claps. When it's their turn to respond, a toothless black woman at the back of the room raises her hand.

"Sandy, you and I, we cut from the same cloth." She says, shaking her head in disbelief, "We are the same. Cut from the same cloth."

She makes me crack a smile. She and Sandy may be cut from the same cloth, but the particular shade of his lime green shorts is most certainly in a league of its own. The rest of the feedback from the people in the room is heartfelt.

It turns out that we are from different worlds but exactly the same. At the end of the meeting, a line forms, and most of the people in the room are standing in it. At first, I am not sure why they are lining up, and then I am told it is because they want to hug us.

They want to hug us.

The skinhead is in the line-up, too.

The Leprechaun Teachings: FEAR
Miami
July 2003

I wake up startled, gripped with FEAR…the Fuck Everything And Run acronym and not the Face Everything And Recover one. I'm not sure where this intense feeling is coming from, but it's definitely rearing its ugly head and wrapping its sticky tentacles around me. I'm debilitated. I was planning to sell on the street today…but at this moment, I'd rather stick needles in my eye. Exposing my paintings and soul to the world feels like the most impossible task. I am not sure why I am feeling this level of anxiety. It's not like I haven't done this before. But right now, at this moment, I just cannot do it.

I want to stay in bed. I want to disappear. I sit up and hold onto the side of the bed. The more I grip onto it, the harder it is for me to let go. My hand anchors me to the mattress.

The Girl in the Green Bathing Suit
Toronto
August 2, 1980

It's a blistering, hot summer day. The temperature is expected to hit 80 degrees. The swimming pool at The Beaches is an hour away, but it's worth the trip. The facility houses a regulation-sized Olympic swimming pool and diving area with two diving boards and two platforms, each higher than the next. The entire pool is surrounded by cement block-style stadium seating. Occasionally, an accomplished diver will climb to the highest platform and execute a spectacular dive. Everyone will cheer.

Today, the pool is crowded. People are roasting towel to towel around the circumference of the shimmering blue rectangle.

It was turning out to be a pretty uneventful, lazy summer afternoon, that is until a heavy-set young girl in a green one-piece bathing suit made her way up the 12-foot diving board. She slowly inches herself along the length of the platform and stops at the edge of it. She stands there for an eternity, trying to muster up the courage to jump. It's obvious this is her first time on the higher board. She looks like she's about to drop but then hesitates. She just can't do it. She's petrified. You can see her thought process reflected in her body language as she teeters on the edge.

Fear is holding her back. The girl in the green bathing suit is taking so much time gathering up the courage to jump that a line-up of boys has formed at the bottom of the ladder. They're getting restless. She's clogging the system. They shout up at her, coaxing her to take the plunge. The commotion draws the attention of everyone around the pool. All of a sudden, everybody is transfixed by the drama. All eyes are on the heavy-set girl in the one-piece green bathing suit, teetering at the top of the twelve-foot board. She's center stage.

The crowd starts screaming in unison, "Jump! Jump!"

There's a dark undertone to the chanting. I am not quite sure if the sentiment behind the rallying cry is meant to be encouraging. Something doesn't seem right. The crowd appears to have unconsciously crossed a line and transformed into an ugly mob. A vicious monster, projecting its collective fears and inadequacies onto this unsuspecting little girl. It's eating her up.

The girl decides she cannot do it. She retreats to the back of the diving board, but the younger boys have made their way up the ladder and will not let her pass. I am not sure if she knows these boys or not, but they are quite adamant that the only way down for her is off the edge of the board.

"Jump! Jump! Jump!" The chants grow darker and louder, reaching a feverish pitch as the girl in the green bathing suit teeters on the edge.

A part of me wants to save her…a part of me wants to stand up and tell everyone to shut up. I want to run to the board and tell the girl she can come back down the ladder if she wants to…but I don't. I just sit there and watch.

Then, as if filmed in slow motion…the little girl's body goes listless. It is quite uninspired. Her legs buckle under her. She just drops off the board. Her arms are slightly outstretched, Christ-like, a sacrificial offering to the God of Fear. An insignificant splash breaks the still water. The little girl disappears below the surface. Everyone erupts in cheers. The drama is over.

One after the other, the pent-up boys leap off the diving board. My attention is drawn to the heavyset girl as she struggles to lift herself up out of the pool. I am not sure what she is going to do next. Then, I see her run towards the ladder. She feverishly climbs up the steps. She rushes along the length of the board and flings herself into the air without hesitation. As she plummets, one can feel her exhilaration. The expression on her face is pure, unadulterated joy…but the crowd ignores this second jump. It's not even registered. They don't care anymore. They're on to the next thing.

My life is lived in shallows.

I skirt around the edges, skim the surface, ride a wave

An evil current lurks below

It will surely drown me

If I venture too far down

My bloodstream is my ocean Red water

Vast and pure

I do not hold my breath, for it is of my body

I dive...

South Beach
July 2003

I let go of the side of the mattress and fall to the floor. I lie motionless for what feels like an eternity. My head feels like it is being squeezed in a vice. I stare at the stack of paintings. I am out of money again. I have no choice. I have to do this. I crawl towards the artwork.

The bike ride is exhausting. The pedals are as heavy as bricks. It feels like I'm biking up Mount Everest. I'm balancing my rolled-up work on one knee and resting the other end on the handlebars. When I get to the steps, my fear magnifies tenfold. I don't want to do this. I want to abandon my work. I want to run. Fuck Everything And Run.

I slowly unroll my work and start to set up. Almost at once, I am approached by a young woman from Seattle who is interested in one of my paintings. She tells me she does not have any money with her, but she'll go to a bank machine and come back. As the woman walks away from me, a large black man stops his convertible on the opposite side of the street and runs to greet me.

"I love your work!" he exclaims, "I had to stop because I knew if I came back later, you would be gone."

I am a little overwhelmed by his exuberance, and just like that, my fear disappears. It evaporates into thin air; it's gone. The man tells me he is an actor from New York. He's interested in a painting. One that is closest to my heart...one of my cherished favorites….but I let him have it. I let it go. Once I do, it's like a dam has burst. The woman from Seattle returns, hands over some money, and walks away with a painting. Not less than thirty minutes later, a German family stops in front of me. A young girl points to the sea horses. She loves them. Her father buys three of them! Before the hour is up, I am selling two more paintings to an Argentinean couple. This is the best day I have ever had. I've been here for less than three hours, and I've sold seven paintings to people from all over the world! This has never happened before. It's unbelievable. It's an avalanche.

"The gifts of sobriety are on the other side of fear," the Leprechaun tells me, "the catch is, we have to gather up the courage to walk through it…and that, my friend, is easier said than done."

All I can keep thinking of is that at the beginning of the day, I was destitute and gripped with debilitating fear…now I am soaring above the clouds with a thick wad of bills in my pocket that amount to almost three thousand dollars! Like the girl in the green bathing suit, I gathered up the courage to jump, and I'm brimming with pure, unadulterated joy. Had I stayed in bed…and succumbed to the despair, I would still be there, gripping the edge of the bed…

Had I made *that* choice…none of this would have happened.

The Leprechaun Teachings: The Pot of Gold
Miami
September 2003

Friday

The woman on the other end of the phone tells me if they do not receive $200 by Monday, my power will be cut off. I can't believe this is happening…again. I cannot pay my bills again. When I hang up the phone, my mind starts racing.

I must do everything in my power to prevent this loss of power.

My mind reverts to Jay like a default setting. Jay is a career flight attendant who has been flying for decades. He's become my biggest art collector. He's purchased a total of fourteen paintings from me, five large ones and several smaller pieces. A part of me thinks he just feels sorry for me and is giving me money in exchange for my doodles on paper. He'll lend me what I need if I ask him. It's a given, a lock. When I'm in a financial jam, he's my go-to guy. He's lent me cash before. He lives in a sprawling two-bedroom condo on the Venetian Causeway. Money does not seem to be an issue for him. Jay appears to be the best option for my current financial dilemma…that is, until I consult The Leprechaun.

The Leprechaun O'Flanagan just stares at me. "Don't ask him for any money," he says.

I think this is the most preposterous thing I have ever heard.

Why not?

I am certain the Leprechaun has not heard me correctly, and so I reiterate my predicament.

"My power is going to be cut off on Monday. I don't have the money," I repeat.

"I heard you the first time." The Leprechaun replies.

I stare at him in desperation.

What else am I supposed to do?

The Leprechaun takes a deep breath, "When you ask people for money…it is like you're shouting up at God…" The Leprechaun looks to the sky and cups his hands around his mouth in an attempt to make his voice carry further, "I don't need your help! I've got it covered!"

The Leprechaun looks me dead in the eye, "God says, 'Fine, you're handling the situation, you don't need me.' "

Bang.

There it is again.

I never quite looked at it this way.

Saturday

I am sitting across from Jay at the Mexican taco place on Alton Road. The dinner is one of awkward pauses and stilted conversation. The main course is desperation, and the appetizers and dessert are angst and anxiety. It's the most uncomfortable meal of my life, an agonizing experience of epic proportions because Jay is not the most talkative person on the planet, and I am afraid to open my mouth. I have to force myself to keep it shut. I am sure if my lips separate, the words, "Can you lend me $200?" will come flying out.

Jay knows something is up. He knows I am withholding information. It is one of those dinners where no one is present, and all parties are ultra-aware that everyone is thinking about something else. It's a relief when it's over.

As Jay rides away on his bicycle, a sense of dread engulfs me. I see my powerless self in my powerless home...sitting in the dark, fuming with anger. It will cost even more money to have the power restored. Jay was my last chance. A part of me wants to call out after him, but I don't. The Leprechaun teaching is at the forefront of my mind. I don't like it, but I don't want to shout up at God and tell him that I don't need help. I most definitely do!

Sunday

I am out on the street with my paintings. It's a hot day, and no one even acknowledges me. It is like I'm invisible. It's one of those "What am I doing with my life?" days. I'm questioning how I got to this point. I used to be a successful commercial director, and now I am sitting on the street corner, desperate to sell a painting for a few hundred dollars.

I start to pack up. It's not going to happen today.

As I am gathering up the paintings, I hear a man's voice behind me, "I'll give you two hundred dollars for that one," he says.

The hairs on the back of my neck stand on end. I turn around.

"What did you say?" I ask him.

He points to one of my paintings. "I'll give you two hundred bucks for that one," he repeats.

"Sold," I announce.

He reaches into his pocket, pulls out $200, and hands it to me…and then he is gone.

I am standing there stunned yet again by The Leprechaun's teaching.

The Leprechaun…he was right yet again!

Was this a "co-incidence"? Or was something proving to me that my actions did have consequences? On some level, I knew this had nothing to do with the money. The Leprechaun showed me there wasn't gold to be found in the pot at the end of the rainbow. It was something far better…

It was God.

The Leprechaun Teachings: The Spiritual Bank Account
South Beach
January 2004

The Leprechaun tells me that the job in my life is simple. It's to help others. It's to carry the message.

He tells me I must do this...I have no choice. This will save me from myself.

Apparently, a large portion of this work requires that I listen.....but giving my attention to another human being is one of the hardest things in the world for me to do...just ask Cathy. I don't know if I'm ready to do this, but The Leprechaun says that I am.

"Each day of being of service in recovery is like making a deposit into a spiritual bank account." The Leprechaun will say casually, as if he's talking about the weather, "One day, you will be able to withdraw from it when you need it the most."

I like the idea of a spiritual bank account. I think of a spiritual branch and spiritual tellers with spiritual wait lines and hidden spiritual bank fees...but to be honest, I have no idea what the Leprechaun is talking about...then I meet Rafael.

South Beach
February, 2004

Rafael is a little older, heavyset with salt and pepper hair, a gray goatee and overly big gray eyes. He reminds me of an animated woodland cartoon character: an earnest woodchuck or an anxious groundhog. There is something different about him. He is not like the other people I have attempted to help. Rafael is seriously making an honest attempt to change. I am surprised at his willingness. He is desperately trying to embrace a new way of life. He's kind and thoughtful and takes my suggestions. I am his Leprechaun and I develop a soft spot in my heart for him. Rafael calls me every day. We meet for about an hour every week. I finally feel like I am making a difference in someone's life. We're making progress.

73 days later…

Rafael doesn't call me on day 73. He's MIA the next day, too. I don't see him at meetings. He's disappeared, vanished into thin air.

I'm worried.

Over the course of my sobriety, I discovered that this happens a lot. People just vanish…and I'm not quite sure if they've moved away, passed away, or just don't want to do this anymore. A lot of times, it's the latter, but sometimes it's not.

Someone will lean over to me and say, "Remember that woman who was sitting in the back row last week? The one with red hair who was talking about her daughter?"

They will pause momentarily, then shake their head and continue, "She OD'd. Paramedics tried to save her…but it just wasn't in the cards."

Molly
Toronto
August 2014

Molly is a petite millennial with short, cropped, bleached blonde hair. She's covered in tattoos with piercings on her face and piercing eyes to match. A lot of her body art features text from recovery…. 'Let Go' is visible on one of her wrists, and 'Let God' on the other. 'By the Grace of God' is etched across the top of her slender shoulders, spanning the width of her back, and compliments her perfect posture. I am not sure if these markings serve as visual reminders or if she's trying to absorb the principles of the program by any means possible as if the deeper connotation of the words will sink into her skin and somehow penetrate her soul.

Molly asks me to help her work the steps. "If you're willing…of course I'll help you," I respond.

I use the word *willing* a lot these days…I find it ironic that at the beginning of my journey in recovery, I never really quite knew this word's true meaning. I was not aware of the deeper implications of its intentions and the faith required to motivate me into action.

Molly is willing. She calls me every day, and we meet once a week. We usually meet on the lower level of a high-end mall at Yonge and Bloor, the same mall where I would wander through the bookstore aisles years earlier, looking for something to anchor me to this world.

I suppose I have found one.

Molly and I sit at a table under the escalators. I prefer this spot because I like to think that, symbolically, we're building a foundation.

Upon our first encounter, there is no denying that this young woman is a troubled soul…beyond her struggles with addiction, she has a lot of other issues. It is said that recovery can work in these instances, too…and it does.

Molly is able to stay sober for one year. I present her with a medallion. She looks happy. She appears to be getting better, on the exterior at least.

A few months after that day, I am waiting for her under the escalators. Molly is twenty minutes late. She shows up with a cast on her wrist. "Let God" is not visible anymore. God has vanished. He's covered in plaster. I asked her what had happened.

"I had an accident," Molly says while glancing away.

Then she looks directly at me, piercing me with her icy eyes. A sly grin appears on her face.

"I'm lying…" she confesses, "I pushed my TV…onto my hand…on purpose."

I am a little concerned. I am not a qualified mental health professional. I'm out of my league.

"Why would you do that to yourself?" I ask. Molly doesn't answer me. She looks away again.

"I'm not sure this is working anymore." She says, "I'm sorry."

I watch her get up and walk away from me.

'By the Grace of God' is visible on her shoulders, partially obliterated by the white spaghetti straps of her white summer blouse. A part of me wants to call out after her, but by this time, I've learned to let people go. I know I can't save anyone if they are not willing to save themselves.

I didn't see Molly for a few years, and then one day, I ran into her on the street by chance. She looks happy and smiles, but I know she's an expert at hiding her true emotions. Like all of us in recovery, she knows how to put up a good front.

We talk for a little bit and catch up on superficial details.

Before we part ways, Molly says, "You know, when I was working with you, that was the best my recovery has ever been."

"You can always call me." I respond, "Even if it's just to talk."

She smiles at me and walks away.

A short time after that day, someone told me that Molly had taken her own life.

South Beach
March 2004

When I don't hear from Rafael for a week, I begin to worry. I'm discouraged. I really thought he was getting it.

I am told people have to want this. People have to reach out to me, not the other way around. The Leprechaun tells me not to call Rafael but after two weeks pass without any contact, my curiosity is killing me. I am positive something must have happened to him.

I dial his number. The phone rings and rings and rings, then finally picks up, but all I get is an automated voice telling me the number has been disconnected.

What happened to him?

It's as if an animated eagle has flown by and snatched him up in its talons.

He's disappeared.

Miami Beach
April 2004

I'm doing everything the Leprechaun tells me to do, but things are not going my way. I'm struggling again. I'm starting to get that sinking feeling in the pit of my stomach, like I'm in a rowboat, and it's slowly filling with water, and there's nothing I can do to stop it. The money I've made is dwindling away. I feel like I did when I just got here, but this time, I'm not finding magical things on the street.

Nothing.

I'm starting to think I was fooled. That this whole adventure into sobriety was a trick of some kind. Patrick *tricked* me. The word was right there in plain sight in his name all along.

There's an endless stream of people who show up in recovery, and most will disappear. They embody the transient nature of South Florida.

Trying to help them feels like a waste of time. They're like commuters rushing through a revolving door at Grand Central Station. I'm the door, spinning in circles.

It's exhausting.

Faces washed away at sea. Rafael is a distant memory. I am holding on, but part of me wants to join them.

I am told that every last person is helping me more than I am helping them but I do not for the life of me know how this can be so.

South Beach
Friday night, 7 p.m.

Maria invites me to a dinner party. She is a vivacious Cuban Lesbian, a copywriter in advertising who creates her own artwork on the side. She tells me to come around seven. I usually go to a meeting on Friday nights at that time but I decide to skip it. I'll take Maria up on her dinner offer instead.

When I get to her flat, the space is brimming with energy. Upbeat Latin American music is blaring and a collection of interesting, creative-looking types are here. We are an urban mixture of gay, straight, male, female, younger and older artists, writers and musicians. It feels like I'm transported back in time to a Paris salon in the 20s.

We're all squashed into Maria's tiny galley kitchen, collectively preparing the meal. It's a communal effort.

Maria is stirring something in a big pot. I am chopping a carrot. With each slice, I remember pulverizing these crunchy vegetables through the spinning blades of my juicer. That seems like a lifetime ago. Everyone is drinking either beer or wine. We're laughing and talking and chopping like we're actors in a fabulous lifestyle commercial. I could not have cast it better myself. I am offered alcohol several times, but I'm fine with sparkling water.

When dinner is ready, we move to the dining room. Maria has whipped up a wonderful pasta/paella fusion creation. I am offered wine again at dinner, but I clutch onto my sparkling water with steely conviction. After that fiasco with the champagne bottle, I have learned my lesson. I have learned how to say 'no' in social situations. I am not afraid to use my sobriety like a protective shield.

I look around the dinner table. I like these people. They're definitely more dynamic than addicts in recovery. I feel like I am cheating on my lover, but I cannot deny I am having a good time.

Is it possible these witty, fashionable artists, writers, and musicians are my real tribe?

During the course of the meal, my dinner companions became more intoxicated. Maria is laughing just a little too loudly and slurring her words.

We move into the living room for dessert and sit on a collection of chairs, couches, and sofas arranged into a makeshift circle.

It starts to dawn on me that I'm watching everyone through a pane of glass.

Something starts to turn.

The glass is getting thicker.

I'm feeling detached. I was laughing with these people just half an hour ago...now I am just pretending to laugh. I can hardly hear them through my own thoughts. I'm drifting away. I try to suppress the voices in my head. I try to immerse myself in the conversation. I try to listen. I try to be interested but nothing is working. I'm disconnected, and I know it.

Fernando, a Puerto Rican musician sitting to my left, takes out a bag of weed. He rolls a joint, sparks it up, takes a long drag, then passes it clockwise. Each person in the circle takes a deep puff. It's good shit, apparently.

Everyone comments on how 'smooth' the pot is. My eyes are riveted on the joint, following it as it makes its way around the smoky circle. It's passed from person to person, slowly but surely getting closer.

I'm not doing that. I am not going to throw away two years of sobriety. I think to myself.

It's a snake slithering about. I can feel it....and I'm not going to slide to the bottom of the ladder again.

The rolled-up coiled cigarette is passed to the person sitting to my right. The viper is beside me, poised to strike. The diamondback gazes at me with its hypnotic stare, forked tongue flickering out of its serpentine mouth.

In a heartbeat, my thinking flips like a banana pancake on a hot, greasy grill.

Just one puff, one little puff…that won't hurt, will it?

My hand is poised to reach for it. My cell phone rings.

I instinctively reach for it instead. The display says 'Rafael calling'.

Rafael.

I'm immediately more interested in what happened to Rafael than what is happening in the room right now. It's been months since I've spoken to him. Instinctively, without thinking, I burst out of my chair and stepped onto the balcony.

'Rafael?' I say as I answer the call.

Recovery promises conscious contact with God. It's a comforting thought to think there's an all-mighty entity that is aware of our existence and loves us unconditionally. However, it can also be an incredibly frightening experience…that there is a God…aware of everything we are…or are not doing.

As a warm breeze caresses my face, Rafael tells me he checked himself into a treatment center and has been there for the past three months. They took his phone away. He wasn't permitted any contact with the outside world.

I keep listening.

He continues to speak as I look out over the dark sky.

"I smoked a joint," he confesses, "that's how it started…"

I'm struck by a thunderbolt.

What did he just say?

Was there a hidden camera somewhere pointed directly at me?

A prying telescope from the building across the street? Some surveillance apparatus?

"That led to crack..." Rafael continues, "My life became a nightmare all over again."

Then he says, clear as a bell... "Don't do it. It's not worth it."

I pull the phone away from my ear and look at it in disbelief.

Did he actually say, 'I smoked a joint' and 'Don't do it'?

It's like Rafael is a powerful psychic mind reader and isn't even aware of it. We talk for a few more minutes and Rafael tells me he cannot wait to start working together again. He hangs up, and I stand on the moonlit balcony for a moment.

Rafael's call just saved me.

I go back into Maria's living room and tell everyone that I have to leave immediately. I hug Maria quickly and walk out the door just as fast. In the hallway, with the door safely shut behind me, I breathe a sigh of relief.

That was close.

11 p.m.

When I get back to my apartment, I still can't quite believe that what happened on the balcony actually happened.

What was that?

I sit in the dark for a while. The streets are packed with energy. I can hear the pandemonium of a bustling Friday night on South Beach seeping in through my windows. The sound seeps into my head as well. I don't know what to do with myself. I am on edge. I can't stay here alone. I need to get out. I need to go for a walk.

I am moving through crowds of people on Ocean Drive, then Collins….I'm looking at them through my thick pane of glass. It's incredible how one can be immersed among hundreds of people and still feel alone. My loneliness is crippling. I am surprised I can walk… I am floating again….like I was when I first got to Miami Beach…but this is different…it's an emptier feeling if that's even possible.

I have lost faith in recovery. It's not working for me anymore…and now I truly don't know what to do. It is clear to me that I do not fit anywhere in this world…and the more people I see, the more alone I feel. I walk through the twisting corridors of Twist, a popular club on

Washington Avenue. My insides are twisted in knots. I have to get out of this bar...off of this street.

I walk down 11th. I start to move away from the noise. The sound fades away into the background, and with each step, I am engulfed by the soothing darkness of silence. When I am far enough away, the seed of a thought emerges from the blackness of my soul.

It materializes ...out of nowhere...a teeny...tiny... harmless... thought...and blossoms into an orchid bursting to life on a crisp spring morning.

You don't want a joint. What you really want is...COCAINE.

As soon as that thought manifests itself, I hear my name being called from a distance. It's barely audible...that at first, I almost don't hear it. Then, it cuts through the air a second time, this time louder. I turn around...and there, running towards me...is none other than...

Rafael.

I cannot believe my eyes. He materializes out of the darkness...like a mystical seahorse from the vastness of the ocean. Rafael's out of breath but his eyes are beaming. They are big and gray and radiating. I stare at him in disbelief. I am certain that this cannot be possible. This cannot be real. This is most assuredly surreal. It is as if his phone call earlier in the evening was not enough...not powerful enough to convince me of the truth. So now here he stands...manifested in front of me...in the flesh. An angel...an apparition sent from heaven...

The Angel Rafael.

"I thought that was you!" Rafael says between pants, "I am so happy to see you."

I continue to stare at the apparition. "I am so happy to be back," Rafael says.

Then, as if something is speaking right through him again, he says, "Don't do it. It's not worth it."

I know Rafael is talking about his own experience…but he is speaking to me as if he has just read my mind. I know this is not possible. He has no idea what I was thinking. But I am certain that something has heard my thoughts and is using Rafael as a vessel….a channel…a messenger to save me from myself…my thoughts, the snakes, the serial killer that lives inside of me.

Rafael approaches me. He gives me an enormous, heartfelt bear hug. He tells me he will be in touch. As he turns to walk away from me, I cannot contain my tears. They are streaming down my face despite my attempt to stop them. I feel like I have been hit with a spiritual sledgehammer…much stronger than the thunderbolt that struck me earlier in the evening.

It's invisible, but its impact cannot be denied. It has knocked any inkling to use any kind of mind-altering substance clear out of my head. It has vanquished that thought…obliterated it out of existence.

The Leprechaun told me working with others was like making a deposit into a spiritual bank account. It feels like I've just cashed out my life savings…and it's saved my life.

The message was delivered, this time loud and clear. My faith was back…and in a big way. This experience cemented it…something really does not want me to poison myself anymore….well…because it's poison.

I go home. I go to sleep, certain that I am being cradled in the arms of God.

The Parking Lot
Miami Beach
NYE 2004

Franka and I are late for David's New Year's Eve party. It's 11:45, and we're still looking for a parking spot. The beach is insane. Parked cars are shoehorned into spaces so closely together it looks like they've somehow been slotted in sideways. We circle the streets like a hawk searching for prey. The time is 11:52. After our fifth lap, we decide to look for an alternative solution. When we come across a multi-level parking garage, it's a gift sent from the gods.

We wind our way up the first two levels. The garage is jam-packed, too. It isn't much different than the street. We continue to circle up the structure like a desperate corkscrew winding its way through the dry cork of an empty bottle. Two more levels and still no luck. As we move up the tower, my anxiety levels are rising as well. It's 11:57. We're definitely not going to make the 'Eve' part of the party. We're going to celebrate the New Year in this gray whirlwind of despair. I am hoping this will not be an indication of the year to come.

Then, out of nowhere, one final turn and the winding path spits us up onto the rooftop of the garage without notice. We are in the open air under a magnificent starlit sky with a spectacular 360-degree view of the city. A giant clock tower directly in front of us displays the time. It's 11:59. A moment later, the clock strikes twelve. The black sky explodes into a cavalcade of color.

We are engulfed in an incredible display of dazzling fireworks both near and far and are serenaded by the gleeful cheers of intoxicated people hoping for a brand-new start.

It is the best place to be…and we never could have planned it.

People tell me this is what recovery is like. With each passing day, as we struggle through the grind of our daily existence, we are winding our way up toward some kind of spiritual awakening. Instead of finding a space to park our car, we will discover a space where we can park our fears and marvel at the magnificence of it all. One day, we will serendipitously stumble upon a miracle.

They tell us it would be wise not to leave before that occurs.

CHAPTER 14
A COLD HOMECOMING

Toronto
January 2005

It's like being dropped into an ice bath all over again. I'm back home, enduring a Canadian winter after being in Sun-drenched Miami for five years. It's January. I desperately need to wear a coat. I am reduced to traveling on public transportation as my days of using taxi cabs as a free-wheeling wardrobe accessory are a luxury of the past I cannot afford anymore. On a bus, I see a notice that reads, 'Stand back from the white line'. As I gaze at the warning, a part of me wishes I had taken that advice years earlier.

The professional reception is also a cold, hard slap in the face. I'm a far better director with several international projects under my belt… but no one will hire me. Looking for work in the ad industry is as ego-deflating as ever…it's as if I'm attending The Bessies all over again. Things have drastically changed in my absence. Budgets have gotten smaller, and it's super competitive. Most of my contacts have either retired or moved on. Younger creatives have replaced them. I call former colleagues to see if they can secure me a meeting anywhere with anyone. One of them tells me she could probably get me an interview with a restaurant manager for a server position.

When I finally land a meeting with a production company, things don't go well. The Executive Producer pressures me into revealing exactly where I am living. She's like a relentless ferret digging for dirt. I want to lie, but I can't. The program of recovery has taught me to be rigorously honest... but clearly, this is not a virtue that is honored in the cutthroat world of advertising.

"You're living with your mother?" she spits out in disgust. Her parting words seep with arrogance, "I'm sorry, I can't help you."

It's true....she can't help me.

Living with my octogenarian mother in an assisted living senior's residence is devastating. I clearly do not fit the demographic of the rest of the occupants. I am sleeping on a wafer-thin mattress that lives coiled inside of a compact loveseat. The thing unfurls itself like a cranky metal tongue, and love is certainly not the emotion I feel as the bony skeleton frame digs into my back through the flimsy mattress. Honestly, this is worse than the tapestry. I am staring at the ceiling. It's bleak. I am five years sober…yet pretty much dead inside. I've held on to my sobriety since that night Rafael saved me, but I am skirting with another low point, depressed beyond despair.

Recovery has led me down a garden path…and this time, the winding passage has led me to a senior citizen's housing complex. I want to jump off the roof.

It's the iron flopped over all over again, but this time, I am under it…a two-dimensional version of myself…squashed by life.

I have countless phone conversations with the Leprechaun. He tells me to accept whatever is happening in my life without question.

"God is like a jealous lover…" he will explain, "A gay Puerto Rican possessive top that doesn't like to be ignored…and the bastard will clear everything away in order to be acknowledged."

I hold the receiver bleakly while I listen.

"He's not punishing you…it's out of love," he says.

I feel like I've been hornswoggled again as I sit on the little love seat…like I performed all of the necessary actions but didn't get the 'something good'. I got the package of Rice-A-Roni.

The Leprechaun tells me not to have any expectations… "Expectations are resentments waiting to happen." he will say cheerfully, "Take action and turn over the results."

I listen to my little Leprechaun teacher…I never quite looked at it that way, but all I want is a job and an apartment of my own.

Is that too much to ask?

"Who cares what you want?" The disembodied voice will say to me from thousands of miles away. "What you want is usually not the best thing for you," he continues, "Can't you trust that what is materializing in your life is exactly what is supposed to be happening?"

I'm silent while I listen to him speak. I have no response…

I cannot accept what is happening.

And then he says these words to me… "Can you have the grace to let your life unfold?"

I realize I do not have the grace to do that. I am graceless. I'm demanding. My entire life has been wanting what I want… when I want it and that was almost always yesterday.

"You do not know better than God," he concludes.

Bang.

I hang up the phone. As he has done on so many previous occasions, The Leprechaun O'Flanagan has obliterated my defenses.

I cannot deny the fact that he is right again. I do not know better than God.

The Bridge
Toronto
February 2005

I am crossing the Bloor Viaduct bridge when I notice something is different. Since I've been away, a wire monstrosity has sprouted up vertically and out diagonally around the original railing. The supplemental fencing stretches up at least twelve feet and resembles the bars of a prison cell. This barricade has been erected to deter people from jumping off the structure.

It's a suicide barrier.

Hotline help telephone numbers are clearly visible on large signs on either side of the bridge. I am a little shocked by the architectural addition. I was not aware this was a problem that progressed to the point where necessity warranted the erection of a barrier. Even though I am at the lowest point of my life, I cannot fathom ending it. I know that I would be jumping to a conclusion from which there would be no return.

A Recipe Of Sorts
Toronto
June 10, 1996

Devin works in a trendy clothing store on Church Street. He flirts with me while I try on T-shirts that are three sizes too tight for me.

"If you want to go any tighter…shop in the kid's section of Sears," he suggests with a sly smile.

His comment makes me laugh. He's a good salesman. He has the gift of gab. A few days later, it dawned on me that the children's department was not that bad of an idea. I take his advice and find a couple of wearable tanks.

We are sitting on his bed when Devin tells me his boyfriend committed suicide a month ago.

Our conversations up until now have been flirty and surface-worthy, so this comment is a bit of a surprise. It sounds like he wants to talk about it, so I let him. I listen. A month ago, his boyfriend found out he had HIV. He couldn't deal with it. He made himself a salad and laced it with poison. Devin found his lifeless body crumpled on the kitchen floor.

"His ashes are under the bed," he says, "Do you want to see them?"

Well, this encounter has certainly taken a dark turn.

Devin gets down on his hands and knees and reaches under the bed. He pulls out a cardboard box and opens it to reveal a clear plastic bag full of gray ashes.

"This is all that's left of him," Devin says flatly. "I have the note, too. The police let me keep it…the suicide note. They weren't supposed to…but they let me. I'll show it to you if you want?"

I'm not sure I really want to see the last words of a young man before he decided to kill himself…but something makes me say yes.

Devin pulls out a folded-up piece of paper in the box and hands it to me. The note is short, and it looks like it's been scribbled quickly. It's just a few sentences…with no real explanation as to why he's choosing to do this.

His words haunt me for weeks. I wonder if someday I will suffer the same fate. I'm inspired to write a poem for this young man whom I never met and, sadly, never will…

A Recipe of Sorts

The last words of a man scribbled in haste

The last thoughts of life are never a waste

Is there something to learn from his final meal?

Coward or hero, his ashes are real

Relief from this world in a light, lethal bite

A salad to die for

A healthy way out

Lettuce and anger, three parts despair

Shredded carrots and dreams have taken him there,

Green onions to cry for, peppered to taste,

Slated tears on a wound, thrown on in haste

There is

One final touch

One bittersweet dose

A light vinaigrette dressing…laced with poison, of course

I'll leave a fit corpse on this beautiful day.

I'll forever be young

It will be better this way

The meal is now finished; the deed has been done

The table is dirty, wasn't it fun,

Let's pick up the dishes shattered beyond repair.

Sweep up the mess and remember his hair,

Blowing like water in the cool summer air

On this beautiful day, I really must say

I'm sorry to leave you

But trust me to say...

It will be better this way.

The Grill
Toronto
March 2005

The Grill is a high-end seafood restaurant off the beaten path. It's the perfect location to wait tables because I'm positive I will not run into anyone I know. The eatery is true to its name, and during the course of a shift, I am regularly skewered, roasted, and flambéed by the chef, who is also the owner. He's a first-class bully and relishes abusing most of the wait staff. I am the new guy, and my punishment is harsher than that of the rest. He's breaking me in, and I'm already broken, so it's that much easier for him to snap me in two. The tyrant abuses me verbally. He fishes for weak spots. I take the bait willingly, even though I am seething inside, holding dead fish in my hands: grilled salmon on one plate and seared black cod on another. I let him do it because I am unhappy with where my life has wound up. It's clear I deserve the abuse. It's Babbo all over again.

A young waitress who has just graduated from university with an architecture degree works part-time at The Grill on weekends. One evening, two architects are discussing blueprints for a pricey downtown condo development at one of the tables. The men strike up a conversation with her and are so impressed with her comments they hire her on the spot. I watch it happen, standing on the sidelines while cleaning oil and vinegar containers. It's the kind of incredible, lucky thing that used to happen to me. Now, it appears I am obligated to witness it happen to other people. It's hard to swallow. I am happy for her, but deep down inside, I'm heartbroken. It's like I've been forgotten.

One day, I opened the restaurant, set up the dining room, and put cutlery onto all of the tables. A fork here, a fork there, a fork here, a fork there. As I am placing down forks circling the tables, I decide to let go of my dreams, too. I drop every last dream like a fork on a table. It's as simple as that. I resign myself to the fact that this is what my life has become…and this is what it will forever be.

South Beach and everything that happened to me there is a distant memory. My dreams have washed away at sea. There are no magical fish jumping through the air here. They're all dead, motionless on trendy square plates. All I am left with are empty shells and the stench of fish on my hands.

Swept Away
South Beach
November 2004

I get a call from Craig. The company is closing the South Beach office. Craig will be working out of his home in Fort Lauderdale instead.

The apartment I am living in has been sold. I have to downsize even further and get rid of most of my belongings. A person I know called Marco wants the seahorse triptych. When I meet him, he tells me he doesn't have the money with him. Something is off…I can feel it but I give him the painting anyway. I have to. When Marco gets in his car, he glances at me as he drives away. I know by the look in his eyes he's just stolen my work. I never see him again.

I move into a small room in a house on Pine Tree Drive.

Everything is changing, shifting, moving. The tide is retreating...and taking everything with it.

Even my paintings have stalled. I am drawing the same face over and over again. Even though I try to create something new, it appears my hand has a mind of its own. It appears the well is dry.

Thunderbolt
South Beach
November 2004

I am hit with a thunderbolt again, but this one has not come from the heavens; it's floating in the Bay.

The white yacht stretches before me. It's at least 100 feet in length, with the word Thunderbolt etched along the back of it.

The boat belongs to a banker from Michigan who has a second home here in Miami. When I step onto the vessel, I realize I should have charged him more for the painting, but it's too late now. A deal is a deal. It was nice enough for him to invite me onto this luxury liner to show me where the artwork would live. I cannot believe one of my paintings wound up on a yacht. I struggle to accept the fact that while I am forced to downsize into smaller and more modest living arrangements…most of the artwork I've sold hangs on the walls of really beautiful homes. They are in mansions and stylish new condos with ocean views. This one is getting a permanent ocean view.

The Fork in the Road
Toronto
May 2006

It's been a dreamless year of circling tables, setting down forks, and walking in circles. I am dead inside, delivering lifeless fish and seafood on square white china. I have been sending out resumes, but it feels like I am just shooting them out into the stratosphere. There's never a response.

Then, like a well-worn memory, it occurs to me that my imagination is my survival tool. I cannot let it go. I applied for a grant and made a short film about a man who gets trapped in a revolving door…the monotony of everyday existence. This unbearable dilemma is my current experience of reality, as most of my time is spent revolving around tables. Ever since childhood, I have known that the only way to escape any prison in the physical world is up and out into my imagination…for that is where true freedom lives.

A few weeks later, the chef at The Grill hurls an insult at me, but it shoots right through me like a transparent brick. I am amazed when it happens. He is, too. We are both aware of what has just transpired. The jig is up. Whatever unconscious game we've been playing with each other…it's over.

The following week, I got a job at a television network in Promotions.

CHAPTER 15
A TIMELINE

A Whale of a Summer
South Beach
2001

Whitaker's mother is a sprightly woman in her seventies who looks like a wise, wrinkled elf. Her skin is brown and leathery, an attestation of a life spent in the sun. Her hair is a short white bob, and her eyes shine bright blue.

When Craig tells her that I paint, she wants to meet me. She's an artist, too.

"I started to paint when I was in prison," she says, taking a drag from a cigarette while looking at me coolly.

I'm a little taken aback by her honesty. "Tell me more," I reply.

Turns out Whitaker's mother was dating a man who was smuggling drugs into the country. When he's busted on his boat, they charge her, too, even though she didn't know anything about his shady business dealings.

"Prison was the best thing that ever happened to me," she says.

Every time this woman opens her mouth, she throws a wicked curveball. I like her immediately.

She confesses that with four kids and eight grandchildren she never had any time to herself. Prison, it turns out, was a luxury.

"God works in mysterious ways…" she says, "that's where I picked up a paintbrush. Never would have done so otherwise."

I look at her as she speaks. Her story reminds me of my childhood stint in solitary.

When Whitaker's mother discovers I read Tarot, she's all too eager to find out what's in the cards. We spend the rest of the afternoon on the balcony, drinking sparkling water and talking in the Sun.

A week later, Whitaker's mother showed up at my studio with her daughter, Candace, who was visiting from Key West.

They are here under the pretext to see my paintings but I know that she's really brought Candace here for a Tarot reading. I am happy to do it.

One of the things that I've discovered is that when there is not a financial transaction at the end of a reading, the universe will pay me in some other way…and it's usually far better than money.

On this occasion, I got a whale. A baby whale, but a whale nonetheless.

Candace leans back on my white sofa after we're done. She looks at me and then proceeds to tell me a story.

"A baby pygmy sperm whale washed up the shores of Key West on the first day of summer; everyone named her 'Summer'," Candace says, "Marine biologists turned down attempting to save it. They said calves rarely survived without their mother. They were just going to let it die."

"That's despicable," chimes in Whitaker's mother.

Candace glances at her, "Yeah, I know…" she says, then continues, "A grassroots movement has started to help to save Summer."

"They need volunteers to look after the whale. It's just a calf, and so someone must be with it 24/7," She says, "I was thinking maybe this is something you might be interested in."

"It sounds amazing," I reply.

"They're looking for individuals who understand what's at stake," she continues.

Candace stresses that word was getting out to the wrong people. This was not a 'come play with the whale' sideshow attraction. This was life and death. They were looking for a certain kind of individual. They wanted enlightened whale enthusiasts. She gave me the number and told me to call.

The next morning, I spoke to someone over the phone.

"Summer is booked solid all weekend," The voice says on the other end of the line as if the whale is an in-demand hairdresser. "But you're welcome to come down, and if there are any cancellations, we can squeeze you in."

"I'd be coming from South Beach," I reply.

"Oh," the woman responds, "That's quite a drive."

I asked Tarot David if he was interested in joining me for this incredible once-in-a-lifetime opportunity, and he readily agreed. We rent a car and head to the Keys. Even if we don't get squeezed in with the whale, it's a few days away from the Beach…even though it's another beach.

The drive from Miami to Key West is an amazing one. There are sections where the road stretches out between the keys, and there's a vast expanse of water on either side. David is an extremely careful driver and holds the steering wheel with his hands at ten and two o'clock. The cloud formations are spectacular. It is one of the most beautiful skies I have ever seen, and I insist David look at it. We are both in awe of the magnificence stretched across the expansive sky, so transfixed by its beauty that David forgets he is driving. The car swerves. We almost fly off the road and into the water. It's a frightening moment, but after it's over, we laugh it off. It's a combination of relief and adrenaline. We almost died.

A few minutes later, when we've regained our composure, I say, "It wouldn't be such a bad way to go.….dying while looking at a gorgeous sky… I could live with that."

"It would be quick to be sure," David replies.

"Think of it: the last thing you'd be looking at was a masterpiece touched by The Hand of God. One moment, you would be looking at the clouds, and the next, you'd be floating up among them," I say, "It would make the perfect ending to a short story or a film."

"You'd be the only person to think of something like that," David answers back.

He quickly glances at me and smiles, keeping his focus on the road.

Key West
July 2001

We follow the directions to the site, drive up a dirt road, and stop at a trailer. Inside, we meet Callie, a responsible-looking woman in a wet suit. She confirms that Summer is, in fact, booked the entire weekend. Callie tells us that word has spread quickly, and there has been an outpouring of support from the community. They have more than enough volunteers who have signed up to help save Summer. However, there is a less glamorous service position available, and that is to sit on the sidelines and log Summer's actions in a log book. There is still space to do this. She tells us that right now, in fact, there is a volunteer with Summer and space available to record the whale's actions in the log book.

"Are you interested?" She asks.

David and I look at each other and nod. We drove all this way; let's at least see the whale.

Callie takes us to the side of the ocean. I am surprised that Summer is in the open sea. I thought they would have her in a tank or in a pool or something…but no, the whale is in a large cove that has been netted off to keep her safe while allowing her to be in her natural environment. We sit down on a rock. Another woman is chest-deep in water with the whale. Summer is about 10 feet long and has a grayish-whitish color. I flip through the logbook and stop at the next available blank page. Callie tells us to make a note of anything we see or anything the woman in the water tells us. We both nod our heads. We are obedient. We want to show this woman that we are responsible, trustworthy individuals and that we understand the subtle nuances of whale watching. We want to prove to her that we have not driven 168 miles just to cavort with a whale. We observe the scene intently. Summer swims in a circle around the woman in the water.

I jot down:

9:02: Summer swims in a circle.

It seems pointless, but I do it anyway.

I glance back at the notes from previous volunteers. I feel like I am cheating on an exam but I just want to make sure my hour of logging is on par with the rest of the volunteers. I can't imagine what else I am going to log except for '…Summer swims around.'

What else could the whale possibly do?

The woman in the water yells up at me, "Summer's crunching," We ask her what that means but she doesn't tell us.

"Never mind. Just write that down in the book," She hollers up in the same sharp tone.

I jot down:

9:54: Summer's crunching.

David and I look at each other and mutter under our breaths. 'What's her problem?'

I figured she was one of the fatigued volunteers and had been working round the clock without any sleep, so I let her attitude slide. For some reason, even though we are just sitting on the sidelines and not in the water with Summer, we're having fun. I am surprised that whale watching was such an enjoyable way to spend a Friday night. The hour has flown by.

We make our way back to the trailer and return the logbook. Callie thanks us.

"There's been a cancelation," she says, "we have an opening tomorrow morning at 6 a.m."

6 a.m.?   That is so uncivilized, I think to myself.

I figure this will be a once-in-a-lifetime experience, I look at David, and we both say, 'Yes'. There is only one spot, though. Callie tells us that only one of us can go into the water. We didn't want to overwhelm the whale. Only one of us can have the once-in-a-lifetime experience. The other one will have to sit on the sidelines and watch. David tells me to take the spot.

Part of me wants to say, 'No, you take the spot,' but I don't do that; I blurt out "OK, Thanks." instead.

6 a.m.

A male volunteer greets us, and he takes me around the trailer. He fits me in a wet suit, and before I know it, I am in the water. A woman is in with Summer, and I wade over to them.

"Hi, I'm Jennifer," she says.

Jennifer tells me to just let Summer "Do what Summer wants to do."

Yes, of course, I'm not going to try to make the whale jump through a flaming hoop or anything, I think to myself.

And with that, Jennifer is gone. She is up out of the water, and I am alone with Summer, the whale, in a sectioned-off part of the ocean.

The Sun is rising. A flock of tropical birds fly overhead. It is a magical moment. It is surreal. I am a city boy, and most of my life, at 6 a.m. on a Saturday morning, I would have just been getting back home from the clubs, strung out and sketchy. Yet here I am, awake, alive, wearing a wet suit in the ocean, helping to save a whale…

"Summer's crunching!" I yell up to David and we both burst out laughing.

Baby pygmy sperm whales resemble sharks, they're the same shade of gray with similar features from the snout to the dorsal fin. At one point, Summer swims away from me and disappears beneath the surface of the water. When I look up, I see a fin poking up out of the water, swimming towards me in a steady gate. It has been an image I have feared ever since my childhood, ever since Jaws. *Please be Summer the whale and not a man-eating shark,* I think, as the fin gets closer.

There is something about this marine mammal that is extra special. I am only with her for a short period but I bond with her. I wave to David, who is on the sidelines, taking notes. My hour with Summer is priceless. She spends most of her time with me. Her breathing is paced, but every once in a while, she seems to breathe a little more erratic. I can feel her heartbeat. The heartbeat of a whale. I am in awe. I am only nine months sober at this time, and so I am told that I am a baby, too. We are two creatures on this planet just trying to survive.

The hour flies by. The next volunteer has come into the water, and I am on the sidelines taking off my wetsuit.

David is a little disappointed that he has not been able to get in with Summer, but a woman comes up to us and tells him there is an availability at four this afternoon. A smile bursts across his face.

4 p.m.

David is putting on a wetsuit when a volunteer tells me that I can go into the water, too, to clean up some of the algae and seaweed that has collected in the cove.

There is a moment when David and I are in the water with Summer between us. Both of us can feel her heartbeat. David's eyes are shining as bright as the Sun.

Later when we are getting out of our wet suits, David lifts up his watch from out of his shoe.

"My watch…it's stopped!" he exclaims. He shows me the dead watch face.

"You want time to stop," I say.

Tears well up in his eyes because he knows that it is true. I kind of do, too.

A Timeline
Toronto
2022

I am a producer at a television network and have been for years now. I work in the promotions department, creating on-air promos for entertainment properties.

"Next Week on Blah, Blah, Blah."

As a producer, my job is to spin things. I am a professional liar. I make something look more attractive than it actually is. I know how to do this. I have been doing this my whole life. I can zhuzh something up…twist the truth, and make someone want more. It's the modern equivalent of creating a poster for a magic show that may or may not feature live rabbits.

Most of my day is spent sitting in front of editing software. Promos are cut into time increments of thirty seconds, but because the world is moving at a faster pace and the modern viewer has developed a shorter attention span, promos are now fifteen, ten, and even five seconds long. The sequence of audio and visual clips that make up a promo live on something called 'A Timeline'. I have to be creative within this time frame. There is a frame around the work…like a border around a piece of art, but in this case, the boundary is time…a dip to black at the beginning and the end that signifies a finite construct. I have 30 seconds. That's it. No more. No less. I cannot color outside of the lines.

A lot of the time within these precious seconds goes towards marketing objectives. Everything is always 'ALL NEW' because, honestly, no one wants old. Once you're over 55, most advertisers don't even want to know you exist. You're a ghost. Another portion of time goes towards titles, sponsors, and network branding. Once that is taken care of, there's only about 18 seconds left for creativity.

It's always a battle of Art vs.Time. I know this battle well.

Along with running and zhuzhing…I've been fighting this battle for most of my life.

Art vs. Time
Toronto
November 3, 1977

When I am 11 years old, I'm mesmerized by a commercial on television. It's a camera called a Polaroid that magically spits out pictures instantly. Well, this is quite possibly the most incredible thing I have witnessed in my short life. I never really ever wanted anything as a kid…but the moment I see it, I must have this instant camera…instantly. It is the first time I have experienced the phenomenon of craving. I am positive once this thing is in my hands, it will make me happy, just like the smiling people on the television set. Even at this age, I crave instant gratification. If I take a picture, I want to see it immediately. I don't want to take it somewhere and get it one week later.

I have no concept of money at this age, but I assume this device is far more expensive than anything I've ever received as a birthday present. I decide to tackle the situation strategically. I was born in December…on the 12th day of the 12th month, and this year, I will be 12. I am assuming this synchronistic alignment of numbers will yield me a substantial windfall, much like sevens lining up on a slot machine. I figure if I'm able to negotiate the camera to qualify as both a birthday and Christmas gift, my chances of receiving it will double. I target my mother.…and my oldest sister, Gabriella, who is like a second mother and works at a bank downtown.

Banks are filled with money, aren't they? Couldn't she just get some extra cash there?

I know that these two family members are my best options, and I start dropping subtle hints in early November, but as the month progresses, the hints become far more direct. I have never really asked for anything before, but I flat out just ask them for the Polaroid camera.

I know it is a long shot, but it's worth a try.

Toronto
December 12, 1977

On the morning of my twelfth birthday, my mother and sister walked into my bedroom. They are hovering above me, smiling. They're holding something behind their backs. I am certain they are grinning in anticipation of witnessing an eruption of glee that would rival Mount Vesuvius once I open the gift.

They hand me a wrapped parcel. The box is tiny. I have seen the television commercials. I understand scale. There is no way they could shoehorn a Polaroid camera into this miniature container. I am sure of it. My heart drops. I can feel it continue to sink. It just keeps falling and falling and falling. I hold onto the gift, but my hands are not moving. I can't even find the energy to open it. I just keep looking down at the small package, wishing it were bigger.

"Open it!" I hear the voices above me say.

I begin to tear off the paper, but I am dreading where this is heading. It's possible that a smaller camera is hidden inside, but that is not what I wanted. I wanted a Polaroid.

As I unwrap the gift, I'm a little confused.

Was I not clear? Did they not hear me correctly for the past month? Was there something wrong with my communication skills?

When I tear off the wrapping paper, it reveals a hinged container. I lift the lid, and there it is... the bland face of a watch staring up at me, dead in the face... expressionless. I gaze at the miserable, lifeless thing...the little ticking hand moving around the numbers. The watch is secured with a thin brown leather wristband that yearns to handcuff me.

Time. I don't care about time.

I am a kid. Time represents structure, order, and discipline. I don't want that. I wanted a camera. I wanted to escape through the lens of a Polaroid. I am happy when I'm looking through glass. Did they not understand? I wanted to be one of the happy people in the commercials.

My disappointment is genuine. Despite myself, tears roll down my face to express it. I cannot bear to look at this revolting thing that is not a camera. I certainly cannot look up at my mothers. I don't know where to look. I snap the box shut. This is the worst birthday of my short life thus far.

The box is yanked out of my hands. When I look up, through my blurry eyes, I can see they are holding another wrapped package. This box is bigger. I have never ever gotten more than one gift on any occasion. This is an unexpected twist. My heart has stopped falling. My tears have stopped, too. They are holding onto this bigger box, but they do not hand it over. They informed me that there was a Polaroid camera inside this second parcel, but after my response to their first gift, they decided not to give me *any* gifts this year. They turn, walk out of the room, and close the door behind them.

I'm not quite sure what just happened.

I am perched on the edge of my bed alone. This has been a rollercoaster morning of emotions. Later that day, they gave me the bigger box, but they take the watch back to the store. I'm overjoyed with the Polaroid camera, but after using up two cartridges of film almost instantly, there are no more pictures to take. I put the camera back in its box. I put the box in my closet.

Believe It or Not
Vancouver 1998

I am standing in the offices of one of the richest men in the country. We are shooting Jim Pattison, the wealthy business magnate, as part of a commercial for the Financial Post that features well-known personalities. I scan his spacious office. There are clocks absolutely everywhere. An opulent grandfather clock graces one corner of the room, and a free-standing Day/Night World clock is dead center with an army of smaller timekeepers in every shape, size, and form scattered throughout the space.

When Mr. Pattison, an older man in his seventies, enters the room, he is humble and gracious. I ask him about the clocks.

"Time…" the billionaire says, "it's the most valuable commodity in the world."

The Line of Time
Toronto
2022

I'm staring at the timeline on the screen in front of me. Editing is like sculpting sound and pictures…as if I am performing visual surgery on a body of work.

I can't help to be reminded of the timeline of my life. All of the experiences I've had, the beginning, the middle, and the end,…pieces of a puzzle that I can move around just like visual bits on a timeline. The different chapters of my existence…who I was, who I used to be, from my toddler self to my evolution to who I am now, as a full-grown man.

They're all me…but completely different people…just moving through time. Life isn't linear; it's a cyclical pattern.…coming back to where one started as a completely different person.

The symbol for the Tarot is a snake ingesting its own tail to form a circle. Know Thyself. My life has been a continuous Ring of Transformation…I've been continually reinventing myself. This ring is not something material that I can slip onto my finger. It is something much greater.

The Table
Blue Mountain
August 2019

Gabe and I are sitting at a large white-washed country table at Danielle's summer cottage. We have been talking late into the night, so the Gabisthenics gestures are subdued and uninspired but still faintly present. We're sharing stories of time gone by…of things that only she and I can truly understand.

As the conversation unfolds, I am astonished that she has no recollection of the extent of the abuse I received at the hands of my father. She is oblivious to any of it. She was Babbo's favorite and had an entirely different relationship with him. Because of this, her memories of the past are polar opposite to mine. So much so that today, she has a family of her own and stands proudly as its matriarchal figure, while I am still incapable of forming any kind of lasting human connection.

When I dig a little deeper, I cannot believe she has no memory of what transpired at the dining room table, the venue for so much of my childhood trauma.

I recount some of my darkest memories...of the lentil soup and of the day Babbo verbally assaulted the boys from across the street. Gabe doesn't remember any of them.

I am dumbfounded.

Then she says the most incredible thing, "This is the table," she says.

I look down in disbelief...

It's true!

The table looks completely different in this open-concept setting. It's been whitewashed and painted, so it's lighter and more modern. The leaflets are permanently installed, so the table stretches out much longer than it did in my childhood memories. The cream Parson chairs surrounding it are far better-suited companions than the originals, as is the stylish decorative bowl of lemons and limes that sits on top of it. The table looks grand as if it could be photographed for a spread on country homes in Architectural Digest.

I'm stunned to discover that I am sitting in exactly the same spot as I did when I was a child when Babbo made the impromptu adjustments to the seating arrangements...

I'm just to the left of the head of the table.

For a moment, I am ten years old again, powerless and afraid, sitting in the shadow of the beast, but then I am back. The table survived. It evolved and found a much better home.

It dawns on me that I did too.

Later that night when I'm in bed, I cannot sleep. I toss and turn.

I am the same age that my father was when he first got sick. I know this is a sign. I am running out of time. Most of my life is behind me. I am aware of my mortality. I ponder the moment of my childhood when I chose the camera over the watch. Dare I say that, today, I would choose the latter. I've been looking outward through glass…through a lens, for as long as I can remember. It's time to look inward and find a greater purpose. I want to be present for every moment.

Today, I want to know what time it is.

Mr. Pattison was right, "Time is the most valuable commodity in the world."

Summer's End
South Beach
July 2001

Candace called to let me know that Summer didn't make it.

The baby whale got caught in the net when she tried to swim out into the ocean. She drowned. I am hit with grief at the loss of this beautiful creature. The marine biologists were right all along. Statistically, calves don't survive without their mothers. I know I would not have survived without mine. I think of the heartbeat that I held that is no more. If time had stopped, Summer would still be alive, swimming freely like the magical being she is in the great blue sea. I am relieved that Summer did not die on my shift. I would have never been able to live with myself.

The volunteers organized a memorial service. A Whale Channeller showed up, claiming to have contacted the mammal from the spirit world. David and I make prolonged eye contact as Candace tells us what the woman said.

"Summer didn't want people to mourn for her," the medium explained, "It wasn't important that they save her body. Her presence here on earth was meant for a greater purpose…to bring human beings together to learn to work as one."

Everyone but the marine biologists…I think to myself.

I have a pretty open mind, but a medium who could channel dead whales seemed like a bit of a stretch. Then again, there are many things that have happened in my life, spiritual experiences, and things that I do not understand or can't explain… so I know that anything is possible.

And honestly, I sometimes feel like a channel myself…of what I have no idea…and sometimes I want to change that channel, but I can't because I'm me.

The experience with Summer got me thinking: do we have a greater purpose? Or is this just it?

The Séance
Toronto
Saturday, August 19, 2006

I am house-sitting for Eagle Eye. This gives me a little break from the cranky mattress that lives inside the loveseat at Mamma's. The apartment is on the first floor of an old Victorian house in Riverdale. Cathy lives a few blocks away and comes over one night. Our conversations are far more balanced. Recovery has taught me how to listen, even though Cathy still swears she catches me suppressing a yawn every now and then.

When I see her, something is up. I know her too well, and when I dig a little, she spills the tea.

"My mother and I had a fight before she died..." Cathy says while picking at a thread on her sleeve, "I hope she doesn't blame me for her death…I want to know if she's OK…if she's happy."

Cathy looks at me, "I'd love a reading if you have your cards with you," she asks.

"I don't have them with me, but you don't need a reading," I reply, "What you really need is a medium."

I am sure there is a book on how to conduct a séance somewhere in Eagle Eye's collection of occult literature. I scour the bookshelves, and when I finally find something, the title almost wants to make me laugh... The book is called 'How to Perform a Séance'.

The little paperback manual explains in detail how to establish genuine contact with the spirit realm.

Incredibly, the first paragraph says the best time to perform a séance is 8 o'clock on a Saturday evening, and as luck would have it…it's 6:45. I am by no means a medium, but we decide to give it a shot.

We do everything the manual tells us to do. We position the table and chairs to align with the North and South coordinates of the earth. The book suggests having fresh-cut flowers. We venture outside and pick a few from the front of the house. We light a candle. The manual instructs me to read through a protection prayer that will keep unwanted spirits away. The book tells us to be careful. We don't want to invite any unfriendly entities into our space. That's the last thing that I wanted to do. I had enough problems.

Cathy's mother was an eccentric woman, a mom-ager far before the term was coined, and single-handedly responsible for wrangling her children into a singing group called The Craddock Kids, who received a modicum of success for the 1967 Centennial song 'Canada'.

I ask Cathy precisely what it is that she wants to know by contacting the departed.

"I want to know if she's happy," Cathy responds.

We're ready to begin.

I reach across the table with my palms up. Cathy holds my hands.

We close our eyes.

"Will Doreen Craddock please join us?" I ask in a low, calm voice.

Silence.

Nothing.

I can hear Cathy breathing as we face one another with our eyes closed.

I repeat the request again. Still nothing.

I ask a third time, "Will Doreen Craddock please join us?"

The front door of the old Victorian house creaks open and slams shut. Heavy elephantine footsteps stomp up the staircase. We hear the rattling of keys. Another door opens and closes. Whoever this person is, he or she really likes slamming doors. It appears our attempt to connect with the spirit world has coincided with the arrival of Eagle Eye's thundering neighbor. The substantial footsteps clomp in the apartment on the second floor and come to rest directly above us…then silence.

I am not sure what exactly we have summoned, but it's certainly not Doreen Craddock. Cathy and I burst into spontaneous laughter. We are in hysterics, laughing until our faces hurt...until we can hardly breathe. It's a deep guttural roar that lasts for minutes, and when it dies down, Cathy and I make eye contact, but this only results in an eruption of more laughter that perpetuates the hilarity even longer. This is the longest, hardest, most I've laughed in a very long time. The intense joy transforms into euphoria.

I am elevated to a higher plane of consciousness. As I am in this exalted state of intense exhilaration, a thought creeps its way into my mind. It is subtle at first but then dominates my thinking with a quiet intensity. It is only after we have calmed down that I am able to share my thoughts with Cathy.

Without a doubt in my mind, there is only one reason we experienced such otherworldly bliss...her question, in fact...was answered.

CHAPTER 16
PIANO, PIANO

I'm the youngest of four and considered the baby of the family.

"The youngest child..." Charlotte once told me, "is the oldest soul."

By all accounts, babies do have it relatively easy right out of the gate, but what people don't tell you is that once the natural order of life takes its course, the youngest child in any family does have to endure a lot as they age into adulthood. They inevitably must witness the passing of their family...parents and siblings alike.

One by one, their family of origin disappears.

Piano, Piano
Toronto
2016

I am holding my mother's hand. She is lying motionless in a hospital bed. She is 92 years old and has outlived my father by more than thirty years.

My mother takes a shallow breath and, in her exhale, whispers, 'Piano, piano'.

The slow and steady progression of Alzheimer's has robbed her of most of her vocabulary until all that was left was two words, really just one word repeated… piano, piano. Those words were all that were left from an old Italian proverb, 'Qui va piano va sano et va lontano', which basically means, 'One who travels slowly will be healthy and go far'. This was her favorite saying. When she sensed my impatience in some situation or another, she would often convey their philosophical value to me. She knew who I was. She knew I was Mr. Impatience well before I did.

She was my mother, after all.

In the last few years of her life, these two words emerged as her personal mantra 'piano, piano'. She would walk slower, talk slower, and live slower…all while the world around her was accelerating at an unimaginable pace. These two words were her last, and she would utter them in barely a whisper like a peaceful echo, eyes closed, tucked under her covers…a baby once more.

As I sit here holding her hand, I can't help but wonder if these words are her parting message to me.

'Piano, piano.'

A nurse walks into the room to check my mother's IV. "Did your mother play the piano?" she asks.

I smile and shake my head.

Ooohfa!
Toronto
1975

Mamma is overshadowed by Babbo's larger-than-lasagna persona. She doesn't escape the wrath of his thinly veiled abuse either. He jokingly blames her on a genetic level for ruining the family because none of us can carry a tune.

He also draws an immense amount of pleasure in taunting her on family outings. He inches the green Oldsmobile away from her ever so slightly just as she is reaching for the handle. He giggles with glee, and the four of us squashed in the back seat are laughing, too. He tricks her ad nauseum and pushes her to the brink until she has a colossal fit on the sidewalk. Mamma throws her arms up in the air and shouts, 'Ooohfa!' in exasperation, then threatens to walk home alone. It is only at that point that Babbo apologizes profusely and promises to stop. When Mamma calms down and is ready to attempt another try, he does it yet again. We all find this hilarious. It is only afterward, when she is seated securely in the passenger seat, that Mamma laughs too.

None of us laugh when we have to go to an event as a collective family unit, though. Just before we are about to leave, Babbo lines all of us up from the tallest to the shortest and proceeds to scrutinize each and every one of us like a sergeant in a military inspection. Starting with Mamma and working his way through the line, he is particularly appalled at the state of everyone's hair. Babbo fashions himself a stylist, an arbiter of good taste, and he takes it as his responsibility to restyle the hair on our heads to his liking.

He places his left hand firmly on the back of one's neck…then, once he is sure he has a firm grip and you can't move, it is time to get started. He spits into his free hand and then, like a mad artist, sculpts the hair into some ridiculous coif. By the time he is halfway down the line, he is invariably out of spit and must resort to dragging three fingers across the entire length of his tongue to accumulate the desired amount. It is an appalling sight. I am at the end of the line and thereby forced to witness the horror succumbed to those before me.

The sight of everyone enduring this kind of indignity would have been hilarious, except for the fact that I was soon to suffer the same fate. I'm not sure if the fear of the anticipation of what was to come was worse than the reality of what was to follow. My only consolation was that by the time he got to me, his mouth was bone dry.

One thing's for sure: there is no mistaking to anyone who sees us; we definitely look like a family…But I am not sure if it is because we all have the same ridiculous hairstyle or because of the disgust on our faces.

902
Toronto
1985

Babbo's passing gives Mamma the space to come into her own… or at least have her own hairstyle. She sells the house and downsizes it into a one-bedroom apartment in a senior's residence a few blocks up the street. She's in apt. 902, it's small and simple and has everything she needs. I tell her that she's moved to 90210 but she doesn't know what that means. The cash from the sale of the house has made Mamma flush with cash and fiercely independent. She travels back and forth to Italy quite often.

When she's in her 70s, she tells us she still feels like a young woman. When I ask her why she doesn't re-marry, her comeback is quick and to the point.

"I've ironed enough shirts in my life," she says dryly.

I find this response amusing and yet incredibly revealing of her concept of what a woman's role in a relationship is to be. She remains single for the rest of her life.

Mamma is a Gemini, the twin of the Zodiac, and she embodies this extreme character dichotomy in her persona as well.

It's like there are two of her. One is the sweetest little old Italian lady you would ever want to meet. She clutches her purse with both hands as it rests on her lap and sits with her ankles crossed like a proper lady. She's cute and clever, too, and can feign ignorance at the drop of a hat by playing up her lack of understanding of the English language if she wants to avoid an unpleasant situation.

"No, speak EEEnglish," She will say to a telemarketer as she gently sets down the receiver.

The other Mamma, when she emerges, is a wild-eyed woman wielding a wooden spoon serving pasta arrabbiata. She's extremely angry at absolutely everything and doesn't have a problem expressing her emotions.

When an unpleasant memory, some resentment from the past, bubbles up, it can work her into an incomprehensible frenzy. She's like a scratched record stuck in a groove. She can't escape. Her frustration intensifies until her only option is to blow up like a projectile hitting a motherload. When this mamma comes out to play, one must steer clear of her immediately. I've heard the most ungodly string of unimaginable Italian swear words emanate from her mouth, vile phrases that would make a pit-stop trucker blush and run for cover.

On one such occasion, I bolt out of 902, struggling to put my jacket on to avoid being hit by the inevitable shrapnel. I run into an elderly man at the elevators.

"902?" he asks, "Giovanna's son?"

His eyes have lit up, and I can tell he's clearly interested in my mother in more ways than one. I nod my head. I'm a little embarrassed, somewhat thinking that he's heard my mother's jaw-dropping, foul-mouthed monologue…but he hasn't.

Instead, he adds. "She's such a classy lady."

Oh yeah? I think to myself.

A part of me wants to take this man by the arm and escort him down the hall to witness the classy Chernobyl-sized nuclear meltdown that's happening just a few feet away.

Hello Giovanna
South Beach
2002

When it's clear I am not planning to come home anytime soon, Mamma gets on a plane and comes to Miami for a week. Frank invites us over for dinner. And like the good Italian boy from Buffalo that he is, he's made classic spaghetti and meatballs.

Afterward, Frank sits at the piano and sings show tunes. Mamma is in heaven. I'm sure it reminds her of days gone by with Babbo.

Frank is a charmer and asks my mother to sit beside him while he belts out a personalized version of Hello Dolly, replacing 'Dolly' with 'Giovanna' for the entirety of the chorus. Mamma is perched beside him, smiling and swaying to the music. Frank is really getting into it, becoming more animated with every verse. He holds the last note for a few extra bars for dramatic effect and ends the performance by sliding down the piano keys. Everybody claps.

When the applause dies down, my mother turns to him and asks, "Do you know…Hello Dolly?"

Frank's face drops.

A few days later, I am hit with a vicious case of Hepatitis B. All I can do is lie on my paint-splattered white couch with a wet towel over my face, hoping to die.

It's at that moment that Giovanna sees right through me. Her words cut through my face shield like an axe.

"You're just like him," she says, "You do it to yourself."

I stare up into the dark, wet towel, exposed. I'm not quite sure how to respond. She's not telling me this to push my buttons; her tone is far too compassionate. I'm acutely aware that she knows exactly who I am. As I lay beside her helpless as I did in the hospital as a feverish six-year-old child, she's finally figured out that a stuffed toy bunny can't protect me anymore.

She was my mother, after all.

Touché
Toronto
1998

Mamma has not answered her phone all day. The phone just rings and rings in an eerie way, the way a phone rings when it's supposed to be answered, but it's not. When I call Gabe, she tells me she's been trying to reach her as well. It's close to 11:30 p.m. on a Friday, and we're worried. We decided we must go to 902 to investigate.

When we arrive, neither of us have keys. We buzz the intercom. Still no answer. My sister and I stare at each other but don't say a word. We are dreading what we may discover tonight.

We buzz the superintendent, who shows up in a bathrobe. He's very cantankerous and not pleased that we have woken him up past midnight. He returns with a key, and when we are in the elevator watching the floors ascend to 9, he becomes a little more sympathetic. The elevator is moving like a sloth on sleeping pills.

The doors open and close even slower, the way elevator doors do in a senior's home, with no risk of crushing an unsuspecting, slow-moving senior. We walk down the hall of the brightly lit floor. We stand in front of the door to unit 902. My sister and I glance at each other. The super slips the key into the door and unlocks it. My sister and I look at each other again. She makes me go in first.

When I enter the unit, I dread each step towards my mother's bedroom. I am not ready for this. I brace myself for what I may see…

When I swing open the door to her bedroom, she's not there. The apartment is empty. There is no sign of her anywhere. We're are not sure what to do next. We look at each other again. We are looking at each other a lot tonight.

Do we call the police? Is she a missing person? What do we do?

We're back in the hallway. The super locks the door. We descend to the lobby in silence. My sister and I are standing in front of the building, bewildered. It's way past 2 a.m.

That's when the cab pulls up. The car door swings open. Mamma emerges from the vehicle. She's dressed up and clearly in a good mood. She thanks the driver and hands him a fifty.

We're incredibly relieved that she is alive and well. We approach her. She's surprised to see us, and a guilty look sweeps across her face as if she's hiding some dirty little secret. We ask her where she's been all day. She's reluctant to answer us. We keep pressing her. We are standing in front of her, blocking her path to the entrance of the building like bouncers of a nightclub. She's put us through the emotional wringer tonight; we want answers… it's the least she can do. After a few more minutes of intense interrogation, we finally shake it out of her.

"The casino…" Mamma blurts out, "OK?"

She's getting pissed off. You can tell we're killing her buzz. Angry Mamma is starting to emerge.

"Can you let me know where you're going when you go out at night?" my sister asks.

My mother looks at her with disgust "Do you tell me where you are going when you go out at night?" she quips back.

Touché

…and with that closing line, Mamma pushes her way past us and makes her way into the complex. The glass doors open and close behind her as she disappears around the corner.

My sister and I look at each other again.

She does have a point.

A few years after that night, Mamma's gambling escalates and becomes a major problem. We are forced to step in and take control of her finances. She's livid with this arrangement and behaves like a strung-out junkie who's been cut off from their stash. We know things have progressed when we get a call from the bank. Mamma wants her money. She's refusing to leave the institution until she gets it. Apparently, she's becoming aggressive and frightening the staff. They are threatening to have security escort our eighty-year-old belligerent mother out of the building.

I'm well into my recovery by this point, and I know how slippery the slope to any addiction can be. All this time, I thought Babbo was the wild card, but it looks like Mamma can hold her own. I'm not surprised the extra cash created this little vice.

She was my mother, after all.

Fresh Tomato Sauce
Toronto
2006

I am sitting at the kitchen table watching Mamma while she makes fresh tomato sauce. I've been staying here at 902 since I've returned back from Miami. During this time, Mamma and I have many heart to heart honest conversations. We talk about the past. I ask her why she didn't leave him, why she put up with the abuse.

"He wasn't that bad," she responds in Italian while placing a plate in front of me. "It could have been worse.

He provided for the family. We stayed together for the children."

Then my mother adds, "He had a mistress for many years, you know. When he told us he was working, he was really spending time with this other woman and her children," Mamma continues, "She would call the house and ask to speak to her husband."

I'm a little dumbfounded at her cavalier attitude.

"At the end, when he was sick…she called the hospital. But when I handed him the phone, he didn't want to take her call."

I can sense that in that moment, my mother felt vindicated. My father did love her and was trying to make amends to her for his unspeakable conduct.

I am in awe of my mother's capacity for love and forgiveness. I wonder if I have inherited these qualities too…but at the time, I know that I have not.

The Moment
Toronto
2014

I visit my mother periodically to buy her groceries, pay her bills and check in on her. When it's time to leave, she insists on walking me to the elevator. The last thing I see as the sloth doors close is Mamma waving and smiling at me.

One day, as we approached the elevator, I turned to look at her, and she lost her balance ever so slightly. She stumbles and bumps her shoulder into the wall. She's a little disoriented, but she regains her composure and continues to walk.

That is the moment…that is the moment when my heart breaks.

It is the moment when I become acutely aware of her fragility, the fragility of life. It's the first time I am worried to leave her alone. I want to put my arms around her and ask her if she is OK. I want to go back and sit with her on her tiny loveseat, hold her hand, and ask her to tell me stories about when she was a child in Italy.

But I don't. I'm standing in the elevator. She waves at me. She smiles. The elevator doors close.

Once things start to decline, they do so rapidly. My oldest sister and I are the only children left who are able to care for her. It is a daunting task. We know it's dangerous to leave her unattended in 902. She is like a toddler and one with a surly attitude to boot. The slightest ripple or most trivial matter will make the spicy, angry pasta arribiata Mamma materialize instantly. The classy one is seldom around.

She begins to hoard her garbage and won't allow us to throw anything out. I am forced to invite a friend with me to distract her while I clean like a housekeeping mime. I can see Mamma through an opening in between the rooms, and if I make a sound too loud, she will falter in her conversation. There will be a subtle change of expression on her face and a side glance in my direction, but her social graces and the need to keep up appearances keep the angry mamma at bay.

Mamma is obsessed with paper towels and uses the white square sheets for everything imaginable. We disconnected her stove and arranged to have her meals delivered. It reaches a point where we know she cannot live alone anymore. My sister is willing to take her in, but

Mamma's fierce independence rears its ugly head. It's only after she has a fall that she's willing to go.

At my sister's home, Mamma is extremely cautious in the new environment, particularly when traveling from room to room. She's extra 'piano, piano'. She recites her mantra as she moves. If the flooring changes from hardwood to carpeting, she stops dead in her tracks and will stand motionless as if on the edge of a precipice. She will bring one foot out in front of her and tap her toe on the ground to make sure there is not a change in level that would cause her to tumble. It is only after she's positive she's on solid ground that she'll move forward.

One day… she does fall. We're devastated. I cringe when I see her face, bruised black and green and blue. I try not to imagine her falling, but when I close my eyes, it's all I can see. The doctor tells us the fall has caused a severe brain injury. She is bleeding internally. We are told she only has two weeks to live. My guts are ripped out of me. My sister and I take turns being with her. She is not really talking very much. When prompted, she still knows her name and, of course, whispers her mantra. Occasionally, she will count randomly. She will blurt out a number like 73 or 16.

My sister and I look at each other and wonder if she is trying to give us lottery numbers. My sister takes out a pad and paper and jots the digits down.

I am alone with her one afternoon in the hospital, holding her hand and asking her if she wants anything. She hasn't been speaking very much, so I'm not expecting a response.

That's when she says, "I want to live." Her words strike me to the core.

And surprisingly, she does live…she survives the two weeks and then some.

After 3 months, the hospital discharges her to a long-term care facility. And she's there for another year and a half after that.

I'm holding her hand. Piano, piano.

In the last year of her life Mamma is like a baby. She sleeps all day. The nurses feed her. I feed her, too. I will take a spoon and dip it into a small container of applesauce. I carefully bring it up to her mouth. I watch her chew and swallow.

I ask her if she is ready for more, and she will nod. I am not bothered to take the time to do this. I cherish every moment.

Her decline is slow and steady. There are many close calls where we feel she is at the end, but she always bounces back. Every day, she fades away a little bit more…ever so slowly…piano, piano. I think I have prepared myself, and I am ready to let her go, but when she finally does, I have not.

Toronto
Dec 6, 2006

The scene is reminiscent of an oil painting from one of the Masters. The lighting is soft and casts a celestial glow over the scene. She is lying peacefully on her back in the narrow bed. Her eyes are open, lifeless, and glossy, and she is looking up to the heavens as if in awe of the divine. Her jaw is open, frozen in a silent scream. Her arms rest gently by her side, hands palm up. A daughter on either side, heads bowed in sorrow, golden locks cascading over the gentle folds of a blanket as if carved from marble. They are grasping onto their deathly-still mother for one last time, holding onto a moment that will last an eternity.

I am awe-struck by the image. When I enter the stillness of the room, it is like I have stepped into a different dimension. The chaos of the emergency room slips away like an echo in a chamber. There is no turmoil here. There is only love and sorrow and loss and peace. Grief has come to hang its heavy head.

When one of my sisters, the second oldest, Ida, passes away, it is another blow to the family. It's like history repeating itself. She was named after my mother's sister, who was also the second oldest and also died young.

The Change Room
Toronto
Nov 12, 2016

I need to buy a black suit for Mamma's funeral.

I'm in the changing room of a shop when the grief hits me like a motherload of sorrow. A pick axe has struck me square in the heart. It has cracked me open. I am gushing tears, reduced to a heaving, sobbing mess. I can hardly breathe. I can't stop it.

As I hold onto the wall, I wonder if this is why they call it a change room. My life has changed forever. I'm unable to exit for almost an hour. I have to assure the salesperson through the door that I'm fine…but I know that I am not.

Hindsight
Toronto
February 2022

I am finally OK with slow. I am content to be moving at a snail's pace or not moving at all. I often think back to when I came back home from Miami years ago and had to live with Mamma in apartment 902. I realize that those moments were priceless. It was God giving me time with her…but I was unable to see it at the time. I was blinded by my own self-centered self-pity. It is only now that I am able to look back and truly see what was really going on. The Leprechaun was right all along.

Half of my family of origin have passed and are on the other side…there are only three of us left. Gabriella and I stare at each other like bookends from across an empty shelf. We wonder who will go next.

My bet is that Virginia will outlive us all.

More often than not, I will glance at a clock, and the time reads 9:02… When this happens, I know Mamma is with me…forever reminding me to travel 'piano, piano'.

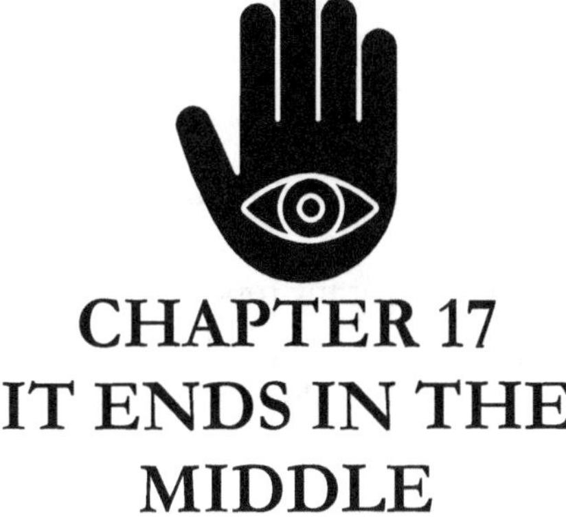

CHAPTER 17
IT ENDS IN THE MIDDLE

String Theory

String theory is a concept in theoretical physics that suggests reality is made up of infinitesimal vibrating strings. In my view, the theoretical strings that connect the universe are the emotional ones that bind us together as one.

The Middle Finger
Toronto
September 12, 1999

My contract is terminated shortly after my peyote performance at The Bessies, and I negotiate an acceptable severance package. It is clear my commercial directing days are over. I'm looking for a fresh new start. I have organized an impromptu gathering with my family to announce my plans to leave the country indefinitely.

"You can't do that," Ida objects.

Of my three sisters, the middle one, Ida, is as tough as press-on nails. Her temperament as the middle sister has always been comparable to holding up her middle finger to the rest of the family.

"Why not?" I respond.

She's cock blocking me. I can feel her trying to stop my escape. She has no idea how bad things are. She doesn't know I am at the end of my rope, yet she's trying to lasso me with what's left of the slack. I can feel the sticky invisible strings of family guilt desperately trying to pull me in like a straggling calf.

"What about Mom?" she says.

"You're all here," I reply.

Ida's husband touches her forearm. I can see by the look in his eyes he's letting her know she's way out of bounds.

"I thought you would be happy for me," I continue, "I need to do this. I'm sorry. I'm going. I've already bought my ticket."

Ida looks at me with contempt…her icy stare, a metaphorical middle finger thrust sharply in my face.

We do not know this at the time, but she is battling breast cancer for the second time. Cancer will soon move into her ovaries, and she will fight with every fiber of her being to live. Even though she will suffer tremendously, the pain will only want to make her live more. She will scoff at medical professionals when they give her an end-of-life prognosis…but ultimately…as with my father, she will lose the battle to this persistent foe.

Vertigo...Time to Go
South Beach
December 2004

The floor tilts and shifts. I am not sure what is happening. It makes me drop to my knees. Then, it is like I am crawling up a steep slope. It is taking every ounce of energy to scale this mountain. I make it to my bed. I flop onto it.

The world is spinning. I am breathing deeply, trying to restore my equilibrium. Vertigo...the combination of fear plus time multiplied by anxiety. My head is being squashed in a vice.

I have to leave Miami. All of the signs are there. I am renting a room in the mansion on Pine Tree Drive but when the house sells, I have to move immediately. I have a couple of weeks to find something else, but I don't have enough money. Certainly not enough for the first and last month's rent plus security deposit.

I have nowhere to go.

The Leprechaun says, "If you have a roof over your head tonight, you are OK."

I am not to jump too far ahead into the future. I have to stay in the now. The future is out of my control. It's a comforting thought but I can't help myself from blindly speeding ahead and imagining a catastrophic ending.

I am doing everything in my power to stay in Miami, but it feels like my dream of living here is slipping through my fingers, like fine grains of sand on the beach...or in an hourglass.

I wait until the 11th hour but God does not give me an apartment like he did with the 200 dollars. This time, I have no other option but to rely on my backup option, Jay. My safety net. He takes me in. I pay him a nominal fee…a few hundred dollars a month, to rent a room in his condo. I am back to being a parasite again, living off of the charity of a gracious host.

My calls back home are becoming dire. Things are progressing…and not in a good way. My mother's Alzheimer's is progressing. My sister's cancer is progressing. My sister's mental illness is progressing. I do not know if I will be able to handle it…everyone's pain. My struggles seem pale in comparison. I feel guilty for living in such a beautiful place, a virtual paradise, while everyone back home is going through such hardship.

The Leprechaun tells me God does not give us more than we can handle, but honestly, this feels like too much.

I am sitting in a chair, and I put my head in my hands in despair. When I shift my gaze, I am face to face with the lock mechanism on the lip of the door. A tiny word is visible on the lock…a brand name. I squint to read it…stamped out in silver block letters...

DEFIANT

The word slaps me in the face.

It's a message from the committee, I am sure of it. They want me to go home, and they are sending me messages. But I am resisting. It's true. I am defiant...I am afraid to go back, and the more I resist, the worse things are getting.

Then, the unthinkable happens. I am at the beach, and even though I know I have a hole in the front pocket of my shorts, I take off the Ring of Transformation and absentmindedly slip it in.

It is only later, while walking home, when I realize it's not on my finger anymore. I frantically check my pockets, run back to the beach, retrace my steps, and sift through the endless grains of sand. It's pointless. The ring is gone for good.

This is a clear message. The ring has served its purpose. It must be returned to the universe to help someone else in the alchemy of transformation.

Part of me is in need of a rush from the force of nature that is The Tree of Life but as I approach the intersection of Lincoln and Alton, I am struck by an eerie silence. The Tree of Life is gone.

It has disappeared, too. Vanished.

I am told the city cut the tree down. It was dead, rotting, and at risk of toppling over. It was a liability.

The skies are empty. The birds are nowhere to be found. I assume they've discovered another place to gather and celebrate the force of nature…sadly, I'll never know where that is.

Rumi and Simona
Toronto
1998

Rumi bobs his head up and down, pledging everlasting love and devotion to Simona. He's worshipping her. There's an unparalleled focus and undivided attention to his repetitive ritual. An impressive Mohawk crests on the crown of his head, and feathers puff up on his chest as he coos. He looks quite regal in his majestic quest. Then again, maybe he just wants to get laid.

I need doves for a shoot. They're certainly easier to acquire than a trio of ostriches. The animal wrangler supplies us with two gorgeous specimens from a local pet store. The project, a CD release for Deepak Chopra's A Gift of Love, features celebrities like Madonna and Demi Moore reciting poetry from the Sufi mystic Rumi over a seductive soundtrack. This was to be one of the best experiences I ever had with commercial work. It's one of those times when everything in the universe aligns. I'm exactly in the right place at the right time. I don't even have to bid on the project…it's just given to me. I'm in the thick of my addiction at the time…at the top of the spiral, about to have a wicked plunge.

A project about love is just what I needed.

New York
1998

The client at the record label is lovely. She's graceful and elegant with a posh British accent and impeccable taste. We don't even talk about the project. We talk about meditation, art, and poetry. It's a wonderful afternoon. She trusts me.

I'm astonished. This has never happened before…or since. Her attitude makes me want to create something extra special.

Toronto
1998

At the casting, a woman called Simona shows up in an oversized black and white hound's tooth coat, her hair pulled back into a tight wound bun. When she walks into the room, she reminds me of a stiff Russian doll and looks oddly out of place. I'm not sure she's appropriate for the role, and I wonder why her agency even sent her. When I explain to the actors what I'm looking for, Simona nods her head apprehensively.

Just before the audition is about to begin, she drops her coat to unveil an exquisite body that would put Aphrodite to shame and loosens her hair until it unravels into a gorgeous mane of thick black curls. In an instant, she's transformed. She's not only beautiful on the outside…her beauty is transcendent. It radiates from her core. She exudes and embodies the physical essence of the fragility of love.

She's as delicate as a dove…an inspiring muse. I'm mesmerized. I cast her without question.

On the shoot day, we capture breathtaking images. Simona is a dream. The camera loves her. The light caresses her face and sculpts her features into a photogenic masterpiece. The shoot is one of those rare moments where everyone on set is transported to a magical place where love and beauty reside.

The experience of working on this project is so powerful that when it's over, I cannot bring myself to return the doves to the store. I decide to keep them and name them Rumi and Simona. Rumi is male, slightly larger, and pure white. Simona is smaller, sleek, and elegant, her feathers an iridescent beige.

The doves, it turns out, are afraid of me. When I put my hand into their cage to give them food and water, they frantically flutter around to avoid the foreign intrusion. Their survival instinct has made them quick and nimble. I try to bond with them, but they want no part of it.

When it is clear I will be leaving for Miami, at first, I'm not sure what to do with the birds. Then, it dawns on me to set them free. I make my way to the rooftop, put the cage on a table, and open the door. I'm assuming the birds will rush out of their tiny prison immediately and fly away at once... but they do not. They're petrified. The doves have been raised in captivity. The safety and security of the cage is all they've ever known. They're overwhelmed by the sky, the wind, and the trees. They don't even move. They're frozen in fear. I sit and watch them for an hour. I am fascinated that they are not embracing their freedom. I wonder if I should just bring them back to the store.

Fear is a powerful, debilitating force…and much, much later in my life, when I am sitting across from people who are in the process of recovering from drug and alcohol abuse, I see this same quality. The cage door is open; they're free from the prison of their own making, but they're paralyzed, frozen with fear, and refuse to fly.

I decide to leave the birds on the rooftop to see if they will gather the courage to take flight if I am not around.

I look at them one final time and then head back downstairs.

When I returned to the rooftop a few hours later, the cage was empty.

They did it.

Then, in the distance, something catches my eye. I see Simona. She is on a tree branch very far away. I looked for Rumi, but he was nowhere to be found. He has left her behind. I am sad that after all of the love and worship, once given the opportunity, he just abandoned her.

From far away, Simona sees me. I can tell that even from this distance, she is petrified. Then, something incredible happens. She starts to fly…but she is not flying away. She is flying in a straight line, directly towards me. I hold out my hands. She flies right into them. Tears are streaming down my face. In this vast unknown world, I am all that she knows. I am what is familiar. And what's more…I understand the depth of her fear.

I let this trembling bird rest in the palm of my hand. She has come to show me love. I caress the little dove and reassure this delicate creature she will enjoy her newfound freedom. When we both know the moment is over, I give my hands a gentle tap. She rises from my fingertips like an ethereal angel, and this time flies away forever.

The Simonas
Miami Beach
2002

I'm blading along Collins, approaching 5th Street at my usual speedy stride, but something makes me stop dead in my tracks. I can't believe it. There is no mistaking it.

I approach the store window in a daze. A forgotten moment…a lost reflection…an image frozen in time…I want to put my hand up to the glass to revel in the memory. There before me is an enormous image of Simona, the model holding Simona the dove, released for all the world to see. I just stare at the picture from a lifetime ago. I am in awe.

How is this possible? Why is this here?

It is like a message again… sent directly to me. When the bewilderment fades, and I'm firmly back in reality, I realize it's a promotional poster for the release of 'A Gift Of Love 2: Oceans of Ecstasy'.

They've used an image from our shoot from years ago for the cover artwork: Simona holding the fragile bird in her hands.

The Simonas…I don't know where either of them are…both delicate creatures in their own right. I hope with all of my heart that they have found love and are free and soaring in the skies on God's great earth.

MIA
Miami
January 2005

I make my way through the narrow white tunnel as it twists and turns. This enclosed hallway will lead to the entrance of a plane. The aircraft that will take me back home. I am petrified that the trip will not only transport me to Toronto but also drag me back to the past, back to a time when I relied on my old ways of coping with life. I am afraid of the future...of what's to come.

I am boarding this flight because I have no choice. It's time to go back. The abbreviation for Miami International Airport is MIA. I've been Missing In Action for five years. In a lot of ways, my life feels like it is over. But I have learned to walk through the fear. Experience has taught me that there are incredible gifts on the other side.

The World
2016-2020

The World is a Tarot card in the Major Arcana that represents a lifelong journey coming to an end.

I am walking through the Hall Of Mirrors in Versailles. I am riding a camel in the Moroccan desert. I am in LA, driving a convertible along Sunset Boulevard. I am dwarfed by giant roots wrapped around the crumbling ruins in Cambodia. I am standing and the base of the Tower of London. I am walking across the Charles Bridge in Prague. I am on a glacier in the Rocky Mountains. I am in the South Of France, soaking in the Mediterranean Sun, lounging on a deck chair in Nice. I am wandering the tangled maze of streets of Venice. I am at the Dali Museum, just outside of Barcelona. I marvel at the ruins of Chichen Itza, the ancient archeological site in Mexico. I am in Zurich feeding swans in the Limmat River. I am at The Mall in Washington, DC. I am sitting in the stands of The Spanish Riding School in Vienna, watching white horses galloping majestically in circles. I am trudging up the hill to Edinburgh Castle. I am dancing at a nightclub in Berlin. I am on top of the Singapore Boat Building. I am at a concert at the Elbe Philharmonic Hall in Hamburg. I am at the Coliseum in Rome. I am at a train station in Glasgow. I am climbing the monumental staircase that leads to The Winged Victory of Samothrace at The Louvre in Paris. I am in Chicago, looking at my distorted reflection in the giant jelly bean. The chrome sculpture makes me think of Virginia.

Five Dollars
Toronto
September 15, 2019

Virginia lives in a small room at a government-run facility. Her psychiatric team has decided that she is not capable of making decisions regarding her well-being. I have been designated her power of attorney and drop by to check in on her from time to time.

Virginia has lost most of her teeth as a result of smoking crack. Her hair is cropped short because there has been a lice infestation in the building. She's rail thin and, as always, dressed inappropriately in her thrift shop aesthetic. She holds onto a tattered stuffed animal, and her actions are still extremely childlike, but the deep lines on her face are indications of a life that has been rough around the edges. There is a strong family resemblance. It's hard to look at her and not see myself. She is a living, breathing reminder of how my life may have unfolded had I continued down my path of addiction.

I give her a hug, and when I do, it's obvious she hasn't showered in days. She asks me for money but I cannot give her any. I pass her a coffee shop gift card instead, even though I know she is capable of selling this, too, if she really wants to.

I look deep into my sister's eyes and thank her for everything she did for me when we were children. I thank her for being there. Virginia cocks her head to one side, and for a moment, just a millisecond, I notice a shift in her gaze. I know that she's heard me. Then she blinks and asks for 5 dollars.

Strength, The Hanged Man, and The Hermit
Toronto
May 2021

I am hanging upside down in my penthouse loft in Toronto. For some reason, I find peace in this inverted position. I am The Hanged Man, suspended in time. There is not much else to do when in this situation but breathe like a bat in a cave or a baby in a womb that's about to be born. When I am upright and watching a documentary on

Diane von Fürstenberg, I discover she hangs upside down, too.

Has this been the secret to life all along?

Oddly, the world has been turned upside down and is in the midst of a pandemic. I am strangely comfortable in lockdown...my childhood stint in solitary confinement has prepared me for an isolated existence. I don't have the desire to travel anywhere anyway. I am happy to be with myself. The world grinding to a halt is a gift. I am The Hermit and have entered into a phase of introspection. I've finally found the courage to dive into the unknown waters of self. My fear of being alone, it appears, has been an illusion all along. The Hermit and The Hanged Man have joined forces to grant me Strength. These Three Major Arcana cards...like The Three Davids, My Three Sisters, and the Three-Headed Hydra create a powerful Trifecta all their own...A Holy Trinity of Solitude.

I hear the fluid calm of the water

Drink the fire to give passion to my thirst

I feel the Earth and swallow the air

So I can feel the sky within me

I give myself over to gravity...I surrender to the gravitational pull. I am stretching...stretching every muscle of my body as I hang upside down...expanding into my potential. I gravitate even further into my imagination...for that has been my strength all along.

I'm inspired to create photo collages from photographs of cities I've traveled to around the world. I cut up my memories and create something new out of the glossy architectural bits. I am dissecting the past...re-framing the narrative...seeing it in a brand-new way. I am creating a

Winged Unicorn out of classic Italian columns and structures. I have become acutely aware that I see everything through a filter… my lens… the pane of glass I've been looking through my entire life. I am perpetually shifting things around until it pleases my sense of aesthetics, be it color on a canvas, photographs in a collage, film in an edit, or words on a page. Even the furniture in my home is moved and then moved again within a three-dimensional context.

I wonder if any of it matters.

Am I just playing with fridge magnets all over again?

Is all of this as futile as rearranging deck chairs on the Titanic?

Lovers and Hostages
Toronto
May 2021

It appears my propensity for perpetually shifting things around manifests itself in people, too. In recovery, I am told that people like me do not have relationships. We take hostages.

As I survey the wreckage of my past, my speedy blindness, it turns out, has been in fine form in abducting blindfolded partners as well. Apparently, the serial killer that lurks inside of me has skills that are transferrable. He's an adept serial monogamist as well. It's messy and ungraceful. A string of dead relationships lie in my wake. I bounce from one relationship to the next, like a beach ball at an outdoor summer dance party. Things always start with so much promise.

There's always so much promise.

There's an immediate attraction. Lust, laughs, and sex.

There's always lots of sex.

Invariably, we move in with each other and spend every waking moment together. There are vacations and holidays.

Then, I'm not quite sure when it happens…but it always happens.

The turning point…things pivot…and not for the better, let me tell you. Love transforms into a venomous, hateful snake, slithering with animosity. I am left yearning to run, not walk, as fast as possible in the opposite direction from the thing I was running to with such conviction just a short while ago.

Inevitably, moving trucks filled with my belongings follow me like a row of obedient ducklings, zigzagging through the city streets.

I'm left shaking my head like a wet dog in a desperate attempt to get the water droplets of delusion off of me. One after the other, each relationship…shattered into a million pieces. I retrace my steps, pick up the sharp, pointy shards, and investigate the forensic damage. I see glimpses of myself in the reflective surfaces, subtle clues of who I used to be. Like a detective in search of an elusive serial killer at the scene of another crime, I notice something that intrigues me and yet also makes me want to gouge out my eyes…

A pattern emerges.

I can't be mistaken. I'm sure it is there. All of the hostages. They're the same person…manifested in different bodies, lined up… one after another, waiting to teach me a lesson that I refuse to learn. A pattern that I am destined to keep repeating over and over until it sinks in.

The Oyster

Scrape the inside of my mouth

And take my heart

Precious iridescent words

Stolen from a vanquished girl

Her worldly throat strangled

By a string of tangled pearls,

Treasured jeweled memories

Lie dormant in their cemeteries

For they are buried as I drown

Marinated in salt tears

There's been too much pain

throughout the years

to cry or die

Brittle little gem.

Perfect masterpiece

Mark my word

Take my world, steal the pearl,

For I will make another.

My ability to recreate myself has always been my greatest gift. I finally find the courage to release all of the hostages...every last one of them. I let them go...and in freeing them, I free myself. Turns out, these relationships have been distractions all along.

Now, I don't have the will or the desire to hunt anymore. I just can't do it. I know too much. The serial killer and monogamist have left the building.

A dog comes into my life instead, abandoned by one of the hostages. A white fluffy canine full of unconditional love and joy. He becomes my faithful companion. When I feed him, I have to put his ears up into a bun so they don't get soiled, and this makes him look like a smiling furry Buddha. A spiritual teacher. Today, the only relationships I am interested in pursuing are with this dog and God. A reversible anagram of partners.

Roots
Toronto
June 2021

I haven't spoken Italian in years. My mother tongue has been silenced, forgotten, packed away in a shoe box in my closet, gathering dust beside old Polaroids, painting supplies, a leather satchel of Tarot decks, and a manual on the convoluted intricacies of Gabisthenics...but a curious thing is about to happen...like curious things often do.

I am still in touch with The Leprechaun O'Flannagan. He lives in New York, and we communicate regularly. I call him every Sunday, and dare I say, what he told me on our very first encounter has turned out to be true.

Over the years, this magical Leprechaun has shared his wealth of wisdom, knowledge, and experience. He's also shared a multitude of incredible anecdotes that are a window into an incredible life of his own. Patrick O'Flannagan had a career in the arts and worked under the woman who discovered Tennessee Williams. He had the honor of introducing a young Meryl Streep to an older Orson Welles and traveled in the same circles as Andy Warhol. Luciano Pavarotti once told him his secret to transitioning to operatic high notes, and Franco Zeffirelli gave him a stage production drawing that hung on his wall. The day John Lennon was shot, Patrick O'Flannagan heard the gunfire from Leonard Bernstein's home in the Dakotas.

"There's an Italian-speaking Zoom meeting online," he mentions to me one day, "You're Italian, aren't you? You should check it out."

Experience has taught me that Leprechaun's suggestions often lead to incredible events, so I fully embrace his recommendation.

One of the things that recovery promises is that we will be restored to a former state of grace. When the mother tongue of my ancestors and the language of recovery intersect, it's like two worlds colliding. Two distinct parts of myself, distant cousins… meeting for the very first time. It turns out, I can still understand Italian and speak it too. I learned that recovery in Italy is faltering, so as the Leprechaun has taught me, I do my best to be of service. I help carry the message to my brothers on the other side of the world. In time, I will be a Leprechaun to a handful of Italians, who in turn will help others who will help others, and so on and so on. It's a miraculous experience, like witnessing a vine growing endlessly into eternity.

It is as if my roots have been restored. My Italian-speaking counterpart is a shade different from my English-speaking self. He's far more relaxed and lives life more fully, too.

This man listens to opera while he cooks, classics that Babbo used to sing, and takes long walks in the summer while enjoying a gelato. He own an Italian motorcycle, a Ducati, and respects the power of this vehicle as it zooms through the city streets. He speaks Italian to his dog, too...and when the canine's ears perk up, he's sure the animal understands him.

The Prickly Pear of Sicily

Fate is a curious thing. Many believe our destiny is predetermined the day we are born, and the events in our lives are stretched out before us like a red carpet. If our lives are not shaped by the choices we make, all we have to do is follow the path and smile for the paparazzi.

In the intricate world of the Divine, I believe the magnitude of it all is far greater and more unfathomable than anyone of us can imagine. It is quite true the trajectory of my life was forever altered by my childhood and the consequences I experienced from my involvement with The House Two Doors Down, but in many ways, my destiny was cemented years earlier, before I was even born, by a man I never met...and a prickly pear of Sicily.

Trani, Italy
1952

My mother's older half-sister, Mena, is marrying a Sicilian doctor. She did it! Bagging an accomplished physician and a handsome one at that is no small feat...it's like landing a prize pig at a local fair. Mena is brimming with joy, but that's soon to change. In a typical Italian tragedy befit for our family, two weeks into their marriage, the doctor eats a prickly pear from Sicily, gets food poisoning, and dies.

Everyone is shocked by the dramatic turn of events. Mena is distraught beyond reproach. In a desperate attempt to start over, she becomes a mail-order bride and marries a Polish man halfway around the world. My parents soon followed her to this unfamiliar land called Canada. Babbo is an opportunist, and he's intrigued by the opportunities this new world will provide.

Toronto, Canada
1980

Mena is a tiny woman and appears to shrink the older she gets. She's a dead ringer for Queen Elizabeth II. The resemblance is uncanny, and as children, we often wonder why our Aunt is pictured on one-dollar bills. We're disappointed when we discover we're not descendants of the Royal Family. Instead, it turns out our family is just royally screwed.

When Mena's second husband dies, the black widow is true to form. She buries the dead man and boomerangs back across the ocean, returning to her homeland to start over. Once there, she will marry yet again and eventually outlive this third man as well.

But my parents have settled in this new land. They have four children, and soon their children will have children as well. They've established roots. We stay...all because of a spoiled Italian pear that set in motion a chain of events that affected a multitude of lives. The prickly pears are called Bastardinos or Big Bastards, and they've lived up to their namesakes.

Fireworks and Waterworks
Toronto
July 4th, 2021

It starts like any other ordinary day. Then, I get an Instagram message from David and everything changes.

Frank passed away.

I stare at the phone in disbelief. He had a heart transplant. It didn't take. I'm gutted. I can't believe it. Somehow, I am sure the world is a less happy place. Miami certainly is. I spoke with Frank a few months ago. I was planning to go back to the beach for a visit. Now, I don't know if there's any reason to return. One thing is for certain: the annual fireworks on the Fourth Of July will not only commemorate the independence of a nation, but to me and many others, they will forever be a spectacular tribute, an explosive celebration for one of the most incredible human beings to have ever lit up this Earth.

"Life is about loss," The Leprechaun says when I share the news, "it's not about acquiring things. It's about letting go."

He tells me we have to have the grace to do this…and as time presses on, I discover that The Leprechaun, as always… is right in this instance, too.

It Ends In The Middle
Miami Beach
January 2005

When the plane takes off, I'm heartbroken to be leaving South Beach.

As I sit in my seat, all I can do is think about the adventure that unfolded before me while I was there. I will not know it then, but the miracle that everyone in recovery was talking about would eventually happen for me, too. It would take more than twenty years and not be the earth-shattering event I had imagined. It would be subtle yet sublime...but a miracle nonetheless.

For the first time in my life, I will be alone but not lonely and able to find immense joy in listening to the silence. I will take the time to remember and cherish all of the people that have come and gone. For since that day when Frank left this earth, many more would follow....

Whitaker's mother, David Leddick, John, Cathy, The Leprechaun, and my beautiful dog too. God's great squeegee may have cleared them away to a better place, but they will live forever in my heart and mind...and on the page as well.

On the flight, I notice Gustavo is working. We nod hello to each other. Later, when he motions me to the back galley, I just smile and look away. I turn my head, gaze out the window, and stare at the white puffy clouds. If I look long enough, I'm sure I can see the ostriches racing in slow motion, their majestic feathers billowing across the backdrop of a magnificent sky.

EPILOGUE
TIME TO SLAY

Toronto
February 2024

In 2020, I had an idea for a limited television anthology series called MADHOUSE. A literary agent by the name of Charles Northcote loved the concept and began to shop it around. He asked me if I had written anything else. I had 100 pages of a book that I'd been working on for twenty years. Charles read the unfinished novel and inspired me to complete it. However, he told me I would need at least 100 more pages for the work to constitute a book. Yeeesh. It took me 20 years to write what I had written. I didn't have another 20 years to write 100 pages more.

I began to work on the book whenever I had a chance, and to my surprise...it began to write itself. All I had to do was show up at my computer ready to take dictation like a courtroom stenographer.

At the end of the year, I had a finished draft of my manuscript. Charles loved the novel and told me he would forward it to literary agents he knew in the publishing world. The process of writing the book transformed me on a profound level, and I became comfortable trusting the universe. I just let go.

When I didn't hear back from Charles for a couple of months, I sent him an email. He didn't reply. The following week, I called him but all I got was a voice mailbox that was full, so I couldn't even leave a message.

I was worried about Charlie. The experience was not unlike that time when Rafael disappeared. In March of 2023, I decided to Google Charles and discovered that he had passed away suddenly in February. I was in shock. It felt like the universe had thrown me a curve ball, another blow. I was devastated, more for the loss of this human being, for had it not been for him, I would have never finished the novel. I really didn't know what to do.

In the summer, I decided to find another literary agent. The process was exhausting. I sent queries to 60 agents in Canada, the United States, and as far away as England. I received a few letters of rejection, but most people didn't even reply. The more I explored this industry I discovered that the publishing world was dying...no one read anymore... they scrolled.

Additionally, literary agents and publishers wanted modern authors to do more than write; they had to have a platform, too. A vegan chef with a million followers on Instagram who wrote a vegan cookbook would have a greater chance of getting his book published than someone like me. I was an unknown entity.

The experience was disheartening. I didn't know how to move forward. I decided to put the book in a drawer. It was mine, for me, and about me. There was no reason to share it with the world. I had changed as a result of writing the book. Maybe that was what this was really about. Friends and family encouraged me to self-publish and promote it myself, but I just didn't have the will to do that.

Then, one morning in August of 2023, I woke up, and 'the universe' told me what to do. It was a calling.

I had to *be* the book.

I was petrified and gripped with fear, but my experience has taught me that tremendous joy was on the other side of that fear. The novel inspired a one-man theatrical show called Sheer Blind Velocity. I had no idea how I was going to find the courage to share my truth with the world...but a part of me did; the part who's fearless.

His name is SLAYBOY.